THE RANCHER RETURNS

NEW YORK TIMES BESTSELLING AUTHOR

BRENDA JACKSON

HARLEQUIN SELECTS

HARLEQUIN® SELECTS™

Recycling programs for this product may not exist in your area.

ISBN-13: 978-1-335-40663-7

The Rancher Returns
First published in 2016. This edition published in 2022.

Playing with Temptation
First published in 2017. This edition published in 2022.

For questions and comments about the quality of this book, please contact us at CustomerService@Harlequin.com.

Harlequin Enterprises ULC
22 Adelaide St. West, 41st Floor
Toronto, Ontario M5H 4E3, Canada
www.Harlequin.com

Printed in U.S.A.

Praise for *New York Times* bestselling author Brenda Jackson

"Brenda Jackson writes romance that sizzles and characters you fall in love with."

—*New York Times* and *USA TODAY* bestselling author Lori Foster

"Jackson's trademark ability to weave multiple characters and side stories together makes shocking truths all the more exciting."

—*Publishers Weekly*

"There is no getting away from the sex appeal and charm of Jackson's Westmoreland family."

—*RT Book Reviews* on *Feeling the Heat*

Praise for author Reese Ryan

"Familial obligations and years of emotional baggage provide realistic obstacles to their romance.... This well-executed romance is sure to please."

—*Publishers Weekly* on *A Reunion of Rivals*

"I really enjoyed this story!... I'm a big fan of this series and look forward to what's coming next!"

—*Harlequin Junkie* on *A Reunion of Rivals*

"The author has a fun and fresh writing style and intertwines the lives of her main and secondary character with vivid detail."

—*Contemporary Romance Reviews* on *Making the First Move*

CONTENTS

Brenda Jackson is a *New York Times* bestselling author of more than one hundred romance titles. Brenda lives in Jacksonville, Florida, and divides her time between family, writing and traveling. Email Brenda at authorbrendajackson@gmail.com or visit her on her website at brendajackson.net.

Books by Brenda Jackson

Harlequin Desire

The Westmoreland Legacy

The Rancher Returns
His Secret Son
An Honorable Seduction
His to Claim
Duty or Desire

Forged of Steele

Seduced by a Steele
Claimed by a Steele

Visit the Author Profile page at Harlequin.com for more titles.

THE RANCHER RETURNS

Brenda Jackson

To the love of my life, Gerald Jackson, Sr.
My first. My last. My everything.

To everyone who loves the Westmorelands,
this book is for you!

To the 1971 class of William M. Raines High School,
Jacksonville, Florida. Best wishes on our
45th class reunion. Ichiban!

Plans fail for lack of counsel,
but with many advisers they succeed.

—*Proverbs* 15:22

Prologue

"Hey, Viper, your cell phone was going off upstairs."

Gavin Blake, known to his SEAL teammates as Viper, nodded as he set his coffee mug on a side table in the barracks' common area. Standing, he stretched the kinks out of his body and felt his aches all the way to the bone. Their last covert operation had been risky as hell, but they'd succeeded in destroying yet another ISIS stronghold.

In two days they would officially be off duty and most of his teammates would be heading for home. However he had other plans. Getting laid was at the top of his agenda. It had been too long since he'd shared a woman's bed and he'd already made plans with a beautiful bartender he'd met in Mississippi while helping his teammate Bane out of a fairly dangerous situation several months ago.

Gavin raced up the stairs toward his berthing unit and retrieved his cell phone from the gear in his bunk. He'd missed a call from Sherman Lott, the man who'd lived on the neighboring ranch for years. Panic floated through Gavin's belly. Had something happened to his grandmother?

Since his grandmother lived alone when he was away, Gavin had given their closest neighbors his contact information in case of emergencies. Of course the foreman was there, running the ranch in Gavin's absence. Surely if something was going on with his grandmother, Caldwell would have contacted Gavin. But what if this was one of those times when Caldwell had gone to Saint Louis to meet with one of their beef distributors?

Gavin quickly pressed the redial button and Mr. Lott picked up on the second ring. "Hello?"

"Mr. Lott, this is Gavin. Has something happened to Gramma Mel?"

"No, Gavin, your grandmother is fine physically. Not sure what's happening to her mind, though."

Gavin frowned, wondering what the man meant. Although she was nearing her seventy-fifth birthday, Gavin had never known a day in all his thirty-two years when Melody Blake hadn't been sharp as a tack. He'd spoken with his grandmother two weeks ago and she had sounded just fine to him. "What makes you think something is wrong with her mind?"

"She's allowed some fast-talking college professor to convince her that the outlaw Jesse James buried some of his loot on the Silver Spurs, and they plan to start digging up parts of her land next week."

Gavin refrained from correcting the man. The land was *their* property since Gavin legally owned all eight hundred acres jointly with his grandmother. Instead he concentrated on what Lott had said. His grandmother had given someone permission to dig on the Silver Spurs?

"There must be some mistake, Mr. Lott. You know my grandmother as well as I do. There's no way she would allow some man to—"

"It's a woman. A professor by the name of Dr. Harris."

Gavin drew in a deep breath. Who the hell was Dr. Harris and how had she talked his grandmother into agreeing to a dig on Blake land?

Rubbing a hand down his face, Gavin knew he would be flying home and not making that pit stop in Mississippi, after all. *Damn!*

"Gavin?"

"Yes, Mr. Lott, I'm here."

"I hated to call you knowing you're probably somewhere doing important work for our country, but I felt you needed to know what's going on."

"And I appreciate you doing so. Don't worry about a thing. I'll be home in a couple of days."

Gavin hung up the phone and cursed in anger. He then placed a call to his ranch foreman, Caldwell Andrews. The phone was answered on the third ring.

"Caldwell? What's going on at the Silver Spurs? Sherman Lott just called and he thinks Gramma Melody has gone loco. He said something about her allowing some professor to dig on the ranch?"

He heard Caldwell curse under his breath before saying, "I wish Lott hadn't called you, Gavin. Your grandmother is fine. She likes the professor. They talked and according to Ms. Mel she read the professor's report and it's legit."

Viper rolled his eyes. "Caldwell, you know as well as I do that there's no buried treasure on the Silver Spurs. If you recall, when I was in my teens, Dad allowed this outfit to come in and dig up parts of the land when they convinced him there was oil somewhere on it. Not a drop of oil was found."

"I remember. But I guess Ms. Mel figured a little digging wouldn't hurt anything since it's a small area, away from the main house and far away from where the cows are kept. It's the south pasture."

"The south pasture?"

"Yes. Nobody ever goes over there."

Nobody but me, Gavin thought. He knew everyone thought of the south pasture as wasted land since it had compacted soil, little or no vegetation and unsuitable irrigation. However, that part of the ranch was where he could escape and find solace whenever he needed to be alone. For some reason, going there always renewed his spirits. It was where he'd gone as a kid whenever he would miss his mother, where he'd gone after getting word about his father being killed in the Middle East. And last year he had camped out there a couple of days after returning from his mission and believing his teammate Coop was dead. It was there in the south pasture where Gavin had dealt with the thought of his good friend dying.

"Like I said, Gavin. Your grandmother has everything under control."

He wasn't so sure of that. "I'll find that out for myself since I'll be home in a few days. Don't mention my visit to Gramma Mel. I want to surprise her." When he hung up the phone, he rubbed a frustrated hand down his face.

"Viper? Hey, man, you okay?"

Viper turned to see four sets of eyes staring at him with concern. His SEAL teammates. They were Brisbane Westmoreland, team name Bane; Thurston McRoy, team name Mac; Laramie Cooper, team name Coop; and David Holloway, team name Flipper. The five of them had survived all phases of SEAL training together and were not only teammates, but like brothers. More than once they'd risked their lives for each other and would continue to have each other's backs, on duty or off.

"Viper?"

He heard the impatience in Mac's voice and spoke up before Mac's edginess got the best of them. "It's my grandmother."

"What about Gramma Mel?" Flipper asked, moving closer. Each of them had at one time or another gone home with Viper and met his grandmother.

"Is she sick?" Bane asked.

Viper shook his head. "No, it's nothing like that. My neighbor called to let me know that Gramma Mel gave some college professor permission to dig on our property. This professor has convinced my grandmother that Jesse James buried some of his stolen loot on the Silver Spurs."

The worried expressions on his friends' faces switched to relief and then amusement. "Is that all?" Coop asked, grinning, resting his broad shoulder against a wall.

"That's enough. Nobody has permission to dig on the Silver Spurs."

"Evidently your grandmother gave it," Bane pointed out.

"Well, that permission is being rescinded, and I'm going to make sure Gramma Mel and this professor know it."

"Did you talk to Caldwell?" Flipper asked.

"Yes, but he'll go along with anything my grandmother says. Now I have to head straight home instead of making that pit stop in Mississippi like I'd planned. Hell, that means I'm giving up a chance to get laid for this foolishness."

Mac grinned. "But what if Jesse James did hide some of his loot on your land? If I recall, he and his gang robbed a number of banks in and around the Missouri area."

Gavin frowned as he zipped up his gear and faced his friends. "There's not any loot on the Silver Spurs and nobody can convince me otherwise."

Chapter 1

Layla Harris smiled as she accepted the plate of cookies. "Ms. Melody, I wished you wouldn't have gone to the trouble."

She said the words out of politeness, knowing they weren't true. Nobody could bake like Melody Blake and she was glad the older woman not only liked doing so but also enjoyed sharing her baked goods with Layla. Especially when the snack included a delicious tall glass of milk that had been produced right here on this ranch.

"No trouble at all," Melody Blake said, smiling. "Besides, I enjoy your company. It can get lonely in these parts."

Layla knew the Silver Spurs was a good half-hour car ride from town. At least Ms. Melody had neighbors living fairly close who checked in on her regularly. Layla had discovered the land owned by the majority of the people in this area had been in their families for generations and most of it was used for ranching cattle.

There was something special about the eighteen hundred acres encompassing the Silver Spurs and the spacious Blake family ranch home. Layla had felt welcomed the moment she had driven into the yard. The sprawling ranch house was massive and Layla figured it had to be over fifty-five hundred square feet. What she liked most was the wraparound porch with a swing that faced a beautiful pond.

Ms. Melody, a retired librarian, had said she didn't mind living in the huge house alone because she was used to it, and reading and baking kept her busy. The kitchen alone was massive and it was where the older woman spent a lot of her days, creating mouthwatering treats. In addition to the huge main house, there was a spacious guest cottage located within walking distance.

When Ms. Melody had agreed to let Layla conduct her archaeological dig on the property, she'd also kindly invited Layla to stay in the main house, but Layla preferred the guesthouse. She could come and go without disturbing the older woman.

According to Ms. Melody, the Silver Spurs had been a prosperous cattle ranch for years. It had even survived when the majority of the men, including Ms. Melody's husband, left to fight in the Vietnam War. When her husband and son became full-time military men, they'd hired a foreman to keep things running smoothly. Ms. Melody also explained that although her grandson was active in the military as a navy SEAL, whenever he returned home he reclaimed his role as a rancher.

Layla met Caldwell Andrews, the ranch foreman, and found the man pleasant and capable. The same held true for the men who worked for him. They appeared to be hard workers who were dedicated and loyal to the Blake family.

There was so much about Melody Blake that reminded Layla of her own grandmother. Both were independent, in the best of health for women their ages and were active in their churches and communities. Only thing, Gramma Candace wasn't a baker. She preferred spending her time with a knitting needle instead of a baking pan.

"I thought I'd bake chocolate chip cookies this time. They're Gavin's favorite," Ms. Melody said, breaking into Layla's musings.

At the mention of Ms. Melody's grandson, Layla couldn't dismiss the shiver that went through her body. Gavin Blake was a hunk. Although she'd never met him in person, she had seen enough of the man to judge his looks thanks to the numerous framed photographs that hung on several walls in this house. Layla knew it wasn't the man's ego that was responsible, but the grandmother who loved her grandson and was proud of the fact that, like the father and grandfather before him, he was a navy SEAL.

From all the photographs she'd seen, Layla could tell just how well built Gavin Blake was, how drop-dead gorgeous. He was definitely eye candy of the most delectable kind. Any woman would be hard-pressed not to feel some kind of sensual pull whenever she feasted her gaze on his image.

Layla had studied one of the close-up photos, which showed dimples when he smiled, a blunt nose, stubborn jaw and full lips. His angular face made him look so much like the warrior she'd heard him to be. She'd also heard he was quite the ladies' man. That bit of information had been shared by some of the locals she'd met at the café where she occasionally ate lunch. Once they'd heard she was about to dig on Blake property, they didn't hesitate to give her an earful.

According to a very talkative waitress whose eyes lit up whenever she spoke of Gavin, Layla had learned he had been a local football hero who had put Cornerstone, Missouri, on the map after leading his high school team to the state championship. No one had been surprised when he'd gone to the naval academy since he'd come from a military family. His father had been killed in the Gulf War and very little was known about his mother. Rumor had it that she'd been pretty, a few years younger than her husband and the two had married within a week of meeting in New York. Apparently, she'd never adjusted to being a military wife or living out on a ranch and had packed up and left. To this day she had never returned.

"Your grandson and I have something in common," Layla said, returning her thoughts to the conversation, "since chocolate chip cookies are my favorite, as well."

As she bit into a cookie, she thought that chocolate chip being their favorite was *all* she and Gavin had in common. Unlike him, she hadn't spent much time enjoying the opposite sex. She'd spent most of her life in school, getting her advanced degrees and working toward tenure with little time for male companionship. She had doctorates in History and Archaeology, and at twenty-six she was the youngest professor at Flintwood University in Seattle. That position had come with sacrifices such as limiting her social life, especially when it came to dating. The only people bothered by her decisions were her parents. They were hoping a man would come along and put a ring on her finger and a baby in her belly. She was their only child and they didn't hide the fact they wanted grandchildren.

Nor had they ever hidden the fact they weren't happy with her career choice. They were both gifted neurosurgeons and they'd expected her to follow in their footsteps by entering the medical field. They hadn't been pleased when she'd chosen not to do so. The thought of someone digging a hole in the ground instead of saving lives didn't make sense to them. But she'd never felt the calling to be a doctor, and she knew history was important, too. Understanding the past kept people from repeating their mistakes.

"So, Layla, what's the game plan for today?"

Layla smiled. She liked Ms. Melody's attitude. When Layla had shown up on the Blakes' doorstep over a week ago she hadn't known what to expect. She definitely hadn't been prepared for the older woman to believe her story about hidden treasure. She'd faced so much cynicism from colleagues regarding her research she'd come prepared to argue her points. Ms. Melody had listened and asked intelligent questions. Plenty of them. The older woman had also taken two days to review Layla's research, which had resulted in more questions. It was only then that Ms. Melody had agreed, with a request for periodic updates.

Ms. Melody had told Layla that her grandson would most likely not support her decision, but she'd also promised she would deal with him when the time came. Besides, she didn't expect him to return home for a few months, and it was highly likely the treasure would be found by then. Layla hoped that was true. Her creditability with the university was on the line. The possibility of tenure was riding on the success of this dig and publication of her findings and techniques.

She'd participated in several excavations, but this would be the first one she'd spearheaded. Funds from the university hadn't been as much as she'd requested, due to budget cuts, but she was determined to make good use of what she'd been given and show results. The head of her department, Dr. Clayburn, hadn't offered much support. He'd even tried shifting the funds to another project. Lucky for her, he'd been out of the country when the vote had been taken.

She'd worked all her life for this chance to prove she was an archaeologist of note. If her research was correct—and she knew it was—she'd be the first one to find any of Jesse James's treasure, and she'd be the first to use some of the latest technology on a successful dig.

"Since all the permits are in order, I contacted the members of my team," she said, smiling. "They will be arriving in a week." Her excavation team consisted of students from the university, some from her classes and some from Dr. Clayburn's. She had spoken with every one, and they were as anxious as she was to get started.

"You have to be excited about that."

"Yes," she answered, though she knew that's when the pressure would begin. "The equipment will start arriving on Monday." Layla took another bite into her cookie before adding, "Again, I really appreciate you letting us dig on your property, Ms. Melody." It showed Layla that Ms. Melody believed in her work.

"There's no need to thank me. Anyone who took the time to read your research with an open mind would reach the same conclusion. It's historically documented that James and his gang robbed a bank in Tinsel and then headed to east Missouri before a sheriff'S posse drove them south. I think you're right. Given how fast a horse can travel loaded down with a cache of gold bars, it makes perfect sense that the gang holed up somewhere in this area before taking a chance to continue east. And it makes even more sense that they got rid of some of their loot before heading toward the state line. Like I said, your research was thorough."

An inner glow filled Layla. Although others had read the same documentation they couldn't forget her age or inexperience. Because of that, they assumed Layla was on a wild-goose chase, wasting university funds that were needed to finance more important archaeological projects.

At that moment they heard the sound of a vehicle pulling up in the yard.

Ms. Melody glanced over at the clock on the wall. "It's not even noon yet. I wonder who that could be."

Getting up from the table, Ms. Melody went over to the window and glanced out. When she turned back around, a huge smile covered her entire face. Layla heard the love in the older woman's voice when she said, "It's Gavin. He's home. The rancher returns."

Gavin grabbed his duffel bag from the truck before closing the door. He tilted his Stetson back on his head and looked at the car parked in front of what his grandmother called the guest cottage and what he called the party house. It was where he and his teammates would hang out whenever they visited.

Gavin hoped that his grandmother hadn't extended an invitation for the woman to stay on their property as well as dig on their land. If that was the case, he intended to send her packing quickly. He didn't want anyone taking advantage of his family.

He thought about what he was missing in Mississippi. He'd looked forward to being in bed with that bartender about now. Calling to cancel had been hard. Promising to head her way as soon as he'd taken care of this unexpected family emergency had satisfied her somewhat.

Walking around his truck, he took a deep breath of the Missouri air. This was home and he'd always enjoyed returning after every covert operation. Silver Spurs meant a lot to him. To his family. It was his legacy. It was land that had been in his family for generations. Land that he loved. He enjoyed being a rancher almost as much as he enjoyed being a SEAL. *Almost.* He would admit that being a SEAL was his passion.

Gavin appreciated having a good man like Caldwell to keep things running in his absence. The older man had done the same thing during Gavin's father's time. And Caldwell's father had been foreman to Gavin's grandfather, so Caldwell and his family also had deep history with the ranch.

While he was home, Gavin intended to return to ranching. He couldn't wait to get back in the saddle and ride Acer as well as help Caldwell and the men with the herd. And he needed to go over the books with Phil Vinson, the ranch's accountant.

However, the first thing on his agenda was a discussion with his grandmother about her giving someone permission to dig on their land. Hopefully he'd have everything settled by next week and he would hightail it to Mississippi. All he needed was one night with a woman and then he'd be good for a while.

He had taken one step onto the porch when the front door swung open and his grandmother walked out. She was smiling, and when she opened her arms, he dropped his duffel bag and walked straight into the hug awaiting him. She was petite, but her grip was almost stronger than that of a man. He loved and admired her so damn much. This was the woman who'd been there for him when his own mother had left. The woman who'd been there for him when he'd laid his father to rest sixteen years ago. She had, and always would be, his rock. That's why he refused to tolerate anyone trying to take advantage of her kindness.

"Welcome home, Gavin," she said, finally releasing him so she could lean back and look at him from head to toe as she always did when he returned from one of his assignments. "I didn't expect you for a few months yet. Did everything go okay?"

He smiled. She always asked him that knowing full well that because of the classified nature of his job, he couldn't tell her anything. "Yes, Gramma Mel, everything went okay. I'm back because I understand you and I need to—"

He glanced over his grandmother's shoulder and he blinked, not sure he was seeing straight. A woman stood in the doorway, but she wasn't just *some* woman. She had to be the most gorgeous woman he'd ever seen. Hell, she looked like everything he'd fantasized a woman to be, even while fully clothed in jeans and a pullover sweater. He didn't want to consider what his reaction would be if she was naked.

His grandmother sensed his attention had shifted. She turned around and smiled at the woman. "Layla, come out here. I want you to meet my grandson."

Layla? Where had she come from? Was she the granddaughter of one of his grandmother's fellow church members or something? He recalled Mrs. Cotton had a granddaughter who visited on occasion from Florida and her name was Layla…or was it Liza? Hell, he couldn't remember. He wasn't thinking straight. When this Layla began walking toward him, he ceased thinking at all. She was wearing stretch jeans and a long sweater and had an eye-catching figure with curves in all the right places.

Gavin fought for air as she neared. He studied her features, trying to figure out what about them had him spellbound. Was it the caramel-colored skin, dark chocolate eyes, dimpled cheeks, button nose or well-defined kissable lips? Maybe every single thing.

Wow! Was he that hard up for a woman or did this Layla actually look *that* good? When she stopped beside him, a smile on her lips, he knew she actually looked that good. He kept his gaze trained on her face—even when he really wanted his eyes to roam all over her.

Not waiting for his grandmother to make introductions, his mouth eased into a smile. He reached out his hand and said, "Hello, I'm Gavin."

The moment their hands touched, a jolt of desire shot through his body. It's a wonder he hadn't lost his balance. Nothing like this had ever happened to him before and he touched women all the time. From the expression that had flashed in her eyes, he knew she had felt it, as well. Yes, there was definitely strong sexual chemistry between them.

"It's nice meeting you, Gavin," she said softly. He even liked the sound of her voice. "And I'm Layla. Layla Harris."

Harris? His horny senses suddenly screeched to a stop. Did she say Harris? Was Layla related to this Professor Harris? The woman's daughter perhaps? Was she part of the excavation team? She looked young, around twenty or twenty-one. Now he had even more questions and he was determined to get some answers when he had that little talk with his grandmother. "It's nice meeting you, too, Layla."

It was only when she eased her hand from his that he realized he still held it. She turned to his grandmother. "Thanks for the cookies and milk, Ms. Melody. I enjoyed them. I need to run into town to pick up a few items. Anything I can get for you while I'm there?"

"No. I've got everything I need."

Layla nodded. "Okay. I should be back in a couple of hours."

"Take your time."

Giving Gavin one last smile, she quickly walked down the steps toward the parked car. He stood and watched her every move until she was inside the car with the door closed. It was then that he turned his attention back to his grandmother. Not surprisingly, she was staring at him.

"For a minute I thought you'd forgotten I was standing here, Gavin Timothy Blake III," his grandmother said in an amused tone.

So he'd been caught ogling a woman. It hadn't been the first time and he doubted it would be the last. "What can I say, Gramma Mel?" He grinned sheepishly. "She's awfully pretty."

He decided not to mention how he appreciated that sway to her hips when she walked, or how nice her breasts looked beneath her sweater.

"Yes, she is pretty. Come inside. Just so happens I baked some chocolate chip cookies this morning."

That made Gavin smile even wider as he picked up his duffel bag. His mouth watered just thinking about the cookies. Now if he could only get that image of Layla Harris's backside out of his mind…

"How are the rest of your teammates?" his grandmother asked, leading him through the front door. "You guys were together for over two months on this mission."

He glanced around as he entered. Everything looked the same. However, instead of smelling like vanilla, his grandmother's favorite scent, the house smelled of woman. Namely Layla Harris.

"Everyone is fine, just anxious to get home. Bane and his wife are renewing their vows in a few weeks and I plan to attend the ceremony," he said, placing his duffel bag on the sofa for now. "This was Coop's first covert operation after being rescued and he's good as ever."

The only reason Gavin shared that much info with his grandmother was because when he'd come home last year before the holidays everyone had believed Coop had been killed on assignment. The entire team had taken Coop's death hard. Then right before Christmas, they'd found Coop was alive and being held hostage in the Syrian mountains. Gavin and his team had been sent in to get Coop, as well as other hostages, out alive.

"This was Bane's first time back, too, right?" his grandmother asked.

Did his grandmother not forget anything? Bane, being master sniper, had been recruited to work in DC for six months teaching SEAL recruits. "Yes, we were glad to have him back, as well. And before I forget, I plan to head for Mississippi next week. I've got important business to take care of there." His grandmother didn't need to know that the important business was getting laid.

As soon as he entered the kitchen, he went straight to the sink to wash his hands and then quickly headed for the coffeepot. After pouring a cup, he turned and watched Gramma Mel arrange a half-dozen cookies on a plate for him. He smiled. Anyone else would eat just one or two, but his grandmother knew him well. He needed at least a half dozen to get things started. "You need a fresh cup of coffee?" he asked her.

"Thanks. That would be nice, Gavin."

After pouring another cup, he moved away from the counter to sit down and she sat across from him. He placed her coffee in front of her and grabbed for a cookie. She slapped away his hand. "Say grace first."

He chuckled, recalling the protocol she expected of him. After quickly bowing his head in silence, he grabbed a cookie and almost swallowed it whole. He loved his grandmother's chocolate chip cookies.

She shook her head as she took a sip of her coffee. Now was as good a time as any to bring up what had brought him rushing back to the Silver Spurs. "What's this I hear about you giving some professor permission to dig on our land?"

Gramma Mel raised a brow over her cup of coffee. "And you know this how?"

He held his grandmother's gaze. "Sherman Lott called. He thought I had a right to know."

She frowned. "As far as I'm concerned, Sherman needs to mind his own business."

Gavin stared at this grandmother as he bit into another cookie. "The way I figure it, Caldwell is the one who should have called me. He's paid to keep me informed about what's going on around here. But he wouldn't call because he'd think doing so would be disloyal to you. And we both know what you mean to him."

His grandmother didn't say anything. She just stared into her cup of coffee. There really wasn't anything to say. Gavin had known for years that his grandmother and Caldwell had a thing going on. He wasn't stupid. Nor was he insensitive. He wanted the two people who meant the most to him to be happy. He figured that one day they would stop trying to be so damn discreet. In the meantime, what they did was their business. He'd only brought it up now to make a point.

"Caldwell would have told you had he thought it was important," his grandmother finally said.

"Whatever." He took a sip of his coffee. "So what about it? Did you give permission for a dig to take place on our property?"

She leaned back in her chair. "Yes, I gave my permission and I see nothing wrong with it."

Gavin kept his cool. "Well, I do. Honestly, Gramma Mel. You actually bought into this professor's tale about Jesse James's buried treasure?"

"Yes, I read her research and found it thorough and convincing. I have a copy, if you want to read it for yourself."

"I don't need to read anything to know the research is false. There's no buried treasure on our land, and I'm against the idea of anyone digging around for nothing."

His grandmother leaned forward in her chair. "And I happen to disagree. But what you believe is a moot point since I've given Layla permission and from what she told me this morning, her equipment will arrive in a few days—"

"Hold up," he said, giving the time-out sign with his hands. "Why did you give Layla Harris permission? It's her mother who's running things, right?"

His grandmother look confused. "Her mother? I never met the woman. Layla is in charge or should I say Dr. Layla Harris is in charge."

Surprise made Gavin raise his eyebrows. "Layla is the professor?"

"Yes, and a very competent one."

Gavin shook his head, not believing such a thing was possible. "She's young."

"She's twenty-six. However, I admit she does look younger."

Twenty-six? That was still young and yes, she definitely looked younger. He drew in a deep breath, trying to force back the memories of just how she'd looked…in her jeans and sweater. And then the thought that she'd deliberately oozed her way onto his grandmother's good side made him mad.

"You might have given your permission, but I have not given mine. Something that major means we need to be in full agreement."

"No, it doesn't. If you recall, we agreed that anytime you were away on military business, I could make decisions in the best interest of the Silver Spurs."

"I don't consider digging up our land to be in the best interest of anything."

"I disagree. I'm excited about what Layla might find. And I also gave her permission to stay in the guesthouse."

The line of Gavin's jaw tightened. He'd figured as

much. Melody Blake was stubborn, but then so was he. He ate the last of his cookies, drained his coffee and stood. "I'm tired and need a full day of sleep. But we will talk about this again, Gramma Mel. In the meantime, I suggest you tell Dr. Layla Harris to hold up on bringing any type of equipment to the Silver Spurs."

And without saying anything else Gavin walked out of the kitchen.

Chapter 2

Layla pulled her car off on the shoulder of the road, unable to drive any farther. Once she killed her vehicle's ignition, she forced herself to breathe deeply a few times. Never in all her twenty-six years had any man wreaked havoc on her senses like Gavin Blake. Never had any man left her in such a mind-blowing sensuous state. Who would have thought a man could have her nerves dancing, her mind racing, her stomach swirling and her nipples actually feeling like they'd been stroked? She had been tempted to glide her hands over every inch of his sexy, sculpted body.

She had known he was the epitome of male perfection from all those photographs she'd seen. To be honest, that's where her troubles had started…with those photographs. In one, his lips had curved a little at the corners as he stared at her as if to say he knew exactly what she was thinking. She knew it was her wild imagination, but every time she glanced at that particular photo it was as if he was checking her out with those intense dark eyes of his. As if he knew her fantasies included him. Even in his photo, his muscular power had nearly overtaken her senses.

Pretty much like he'd done today. She hadn't counted on the real thing being even more explosive than his pictures. Before he'd realized she was in his grandmother's doorway, she had stood there spellbound as a rush of emotion made her body ache with desire. Then, when he'd noticed her, those eyes had made her yearn for something she didn't need. Something she had never needed. A man.

Gavin Blake had stood on his grandmother's porch wearing a pair of faded jeans and a T-shirt with his military tag hanging around his neck. Even wearing her sweater, she found the air cool, but the temperature hadn't seemed to faze him. Was he as hot-blooded as he looked?

The one thing she did know was that he was a big guy. Tall. Muscular. Built. She could imagine him as the football hero she'd heard he used to be, tackling players with little or no trouble. And she could definitely imagine him as a SEAL, taking on the bad guys to protect his country.

And she couldn't help but imagine him naked in bed…with her. Unfamiliar sensations raced through her just thinking about it. When he had touched her hand while staring into her eyes, she'd forgotten all about Ms. Melody standing there and had all but purred out loud. Blood had pounded through her entire body. She doubted she would ever use her hand again without remembering the feel of him. If her body reacted from a single touch to her hand, she didn't want to imagine him touching her anywhere else…her breasts, her stomach, between her legs. And when he smiled at her, she'd been a goner. She could still feel the impact in the pit of her stomach.

She had never experienced this kind of need in her life. She didn't even have a battery-operated boyfriend like some of her single female colleagues joked about owning. Sex was something that had never been on her must-do list. She'd put her energy into her academic career. But there was something about Gavin that made her think of heat and desire. Something that made the area at the juncture of her thighs quiver. Made her hormones sizzle.

Drawing in another deep breath, Layla admitted she needed to get a grip. She wasn't in Cornerstone, Missouri, to lust after the man who jointly owned the land she needed as an excavation site. All she wanted to do was stay on schedule and have a successful dig. Besides, Gavin Blake probably looked at other women the same way he'd looked at her. Hadn't that waitress in town enlightened Layla as to just what a ladies' man he was? Now seeing was believing.

Seeing was also a warning to keep her common sense intact and be on guard. An involvement with Gavin Blake was the last thing she needed, even though her body was trying to convince her otherwise.

There was something else she should be concerned about, something she just remembered. Ms. Melody had said that her grandson might be against the idea of a dig on the Silver Spurs. Although Ms. Melody had given the okay, would Gavin's return change anything?

The thought of losing the permission she'd gained sent nervous jitters through her.

Maybe she should talk to Gavin Blake herself. She would present her research to him the same way she'd presented it to Ms. Melody. Layla wanted to believe he was reasonable. It wasn't as if she would be digging all over his property. She had narrowed it to one location.

Yes, she would talk to him herself, but only after she talked to Ms. Melody—and after Layla convinced herself she could talk to him without every part of her turning to mush.

Gavin's eyes flew open and his entire body went on full alert. His ears picked up the sounds around him and it was then he recalled he was back in the United States and not in some godforsaken country where he had to be on guard 24/7.

It was always this way for the first few days after he returned home. He had to regroup and get his mind back in sync with normal life, deprogram from battle mode and ease back into the life of a rancher.

Glancing at the clock on his bedroom wall, he saw it was ten at night. He wasn't surprised that he'd slept nearly nine hours straight. His ears perked up at the sound that had woken him. Was that a harmonica? Granted it was far off, but he could still hear it. His teammates teased him about having sonic ears, because of his ability to hear a sound over a hundred feet away.

He wasn't sure if that was a blessing or a curse when he involuntarily eavesdropped on conversations he wished he hadn't. Like the time Mac was outside the barracks and downstairs in the yard talking to his wife on the phone, telling her in explicit sexual terms what he planned to do to her when he returned home from their mission. Gavin had heard every single word and the details had nearly burned his ears. They had definitely made him horny as hell. For a fleeting moment it had made him wish he had a wife or an exclusive woman he could return home to instead of a little black book filled with names of willing women.

Gavin pushed the whimsical thought from his mind as he lay in bed and listened to the music. It sounded pretty damn good. He sat up and rubbed his hands across his face as if to wipe away the sleep. Pushing the bedcovers aside, he eased out of bed. Not bothering to cover his naked body, he strolled over to the window, pushed aside the curtain and looked out. The October air produced a chill that would send shivers through a normal person's body. But because of his SEAL training, Gavin could withstand temperatures of the highest and lowest extremes.

The way the moonlight crested the rocky bluffs, dissecting the valleys and rolling plains, was simply breathtaking. There was nothing more beautiful than Silver Spurs at night. For as long as he could remember, he'd always been moved by the grandeur of the land he was born on.

The harmonica stopped and he knew the sound had come from the party house where Layla was staying. Since the woman was still in residence, he could only assume his grandmother had not delivered his message. Had she done so he was certain Professor Layla Harris would have left by now.

Maybe he should talk to Layla Harris himself. Make it clear where he stood. He moved back toward the bed. Instead of getting into it, Gavin ignored the voice of reason saying he should wait and talk to Layla in the morning and grabbed his clothes off the chair. After sliding into his jeans he tugged his T-shirt over his head. He put on his socks and boots and headed for the door.

The music from the harmonica started up again.

Layla placed her harmonica aside. Playing it relaxed her and she would always appreciate her grandfather for teaching her. She could vividly recall those summers when she would sit on the front porch of her grandparents' New Orleans home and listen to her grandfather play his harmonica, then beg him to teach her how. When Grampa Chip passed away ten years ago, his request had been that she play the harmonica at his funeral and she had.

Thoughts of losing the grandfather she adored always made her sad and that was the last emotion she wanted to feel right now. Even when she had no idea what would happen with this dig, she wanted happy thoughts. Earlier, Ms. Melody assured Layla that all was well. Her grandson was too exhausted to think straight and he needed a full day of sleep.

Layla hoped that was good news considering she had all that machinery on the way. She figured Ms. Melody knew her grandson better than Layla did. She would wait for Gavin Blake to get his full day of sleep. Hopefully, after another discussion with Ms. Melody, he would see things the way his grandmother did.

Layla glanced around the guest cottage, thinking how much she liked it here. The place was larger than her apartment in Seattle. She definitely didn't have a huge living room with a fireplace or a spacious master bedroom with a large en suite bath with a walk-in shower and Jacuzzi tub. The cottage also had a loft that could be used as additional sleeping space, and an eat-in kitchen. She loved the wood floors throughout and the high ceilings. And because it sat a distance away from the main house, she could play her harmonica without worrying about disturbing anyone. That was something she couldn't do at her own apartment.

She stood to stretch and was about to head toward the bedroom when she heard a knock on the door. Glancing at the clock on the wall she saw it was after ten. Usually Ms. Melody was in bed every night by eight since she was such an early riser. Had something happened? Had the older woman decided not to butt heads with her grandson and didn't want Layla and her team to dig on the Silver Spurs after all?

Layla moved toward the door. It didn't have a peephole so she leaned against the wooden frame and asked, "Who is it?"

"Gavin. Gavin Blake."

Her gaze widened and heat swirled around in her lower belly. She tried forcing the sensations aside. Why would Gavin seek her out at this time of night? Had something happened to Ms. Melody? From their talks, she knew the older woman suffered occasionally with migraines.

She opened the door and the man stood there, almost bigger than life, and looking as yummy as a chocolate sundae. He was dressed as he had been that morning. Jeans. T-shirt. Western boots. But her brain wasn't computing *what* he was wearing as much as *how well* he was wearing it.

Although it was cold, he wasn't even wearing a jacket. He leaned in the doorway looking exactly like any woman's dream. Hot. Sexy. And then some. He was one of those can't-get-to-sleep nighttime fantasies that left you hot and bothered with no relief in sight. It was those thoughts that had her unable to speak, so she just stood there and stared at the penetrating dark gaze holding hers as her heart beat violently in her chest.

She knew SEALs stayed in shape, but the body of the man standing before her was simply ridiculous. She knew of no other man whose body was so well built. So magnificently toned. His jeans appeared plastered to him in the most decadent way. He made her think of wicked temptation and sinful delights.

Doubting she could stand there much longer without going up in flames, even with the blast of cold air, she swallowed deeply and then forced her voice to ask, "Is something wrong with Ms. Melody?"

From the look that quickly flashed across his features, she could tell he was surprised by her question. "What makes you think something is wrong with my grandmother?"

Layla sighed deeply. "What other reason would bring you here?"

That, Gavin thought, was a good question. Why *was* he here? He had heard the harmonica. And had quickly figured out the source was Layla in the party house. So what had driven him out into the night? He definitely could have waited until morning to talk to her about the dig. Had he come here just to stand in the doorway to try to get his fill of looking at her?

"Gavin?"

And why did the sound of his name from her lips send desire throbbing through him? In his horny state, it wouldn't take much to push him over the edge. "Yes?"

“If nothing is wrong with Ms. Melody, why are you here?”

He crossed his arms over his chest. “I heard you playing a harmonica.”

Layla’s jaw dropped in surprise. She must have been shocked that he heard her. The guest cottage was far away from the main house and on the opposite side of the bedrooms. Gramma Mel had probably told her he would be sleeping hard for a full day.

But he wasn’t sleeping. He was here. He rubbed his hand down his face in frustration. He needed to get to Mississippi fast or else…

Or else what? He would begin thinking of Layla Harris in his bed? Too late. His mind had already gone there. More than once. Those thoughts had pretty much settled in the moment he’d laid eyes on her. Having her at the party house wasn’t helping matters. Typically, all he had to do was snap his fingers to get any woman he wanted. Why were his fingers itching to be snapped? With Layla Harris, would it be that easy? Why didn’t he think so?

“I am so sorry,” she said now. “I didn’t mean to wake you. I know you need to get all that rest and—”

“You didn’t wake me.”

“But you said that you heard me playing.”

“I did, but that’s not what awakened me.” Gavin figured there was no reason to tell her how disrupted his sleep patterns tended to be during his first few days back home. Which still left her question unanswered. Why was he here? Why had he sought her out? In the middle of the night? “You play very well,” he said.

Gavin thought she was even more beautiful than she

had looked this morning. He blamed the easy smile that touched her lips.

"Thanks, but I'm sure you didn't come all this way just to give me that compliment."

No, he hadn't. He'd actually come to give her hell for feeding his grandmother a bunch of crock about buried treasure on their land. So he needed to say what he had come to say. "We should talk. May I come in?"

It was funny he would ask. After all, she was the visitor on his land. This was his house. Ms. Melody had told her that Gavin and some of his SEAL teammates had built it a few years ago as a place to hang out whenever they visited.

Gavin and his friends could get loud and rowdy here at the cottage without disturbing his grandmother. That accounted for why the place was so spacious with the cupboards bare—except for a refrigerator stocked with beer and wine coolers. Not to mention that a deck of cards seemed to be in every room.

"Yes, of course you can come in. You own the place."

"But you're my grandmother's guest."

Had he said that to remind her she wasn't *his* guest? To remind her that her presence on the Silver Spurs was something he didn't support? Layla would find out soon enough.

She moved from the door and he followed, closing it behind him. "Would you like something to drink?" Grinning brightly, she said, "There's plenty of beer and wine coolers in the fridge."

Gavin chuckled. "I'll take a beer."

She nodded. "One beer coming up." She felt his gaze on her backside.

"Here you are. I feel funny doing this," Layla said, coming back into the room carrying a cold bottle of beer.

He lifted a brow. "Doing what?"

"Serving you your own beer."

"No reason that you should. You're my grandmother's guest."

That was the second time he'd said that, Layla thought. Not one to beat around the bush, she crossed the room to hand him the beer, and then wished she hadn't. Their hands had only briefly touched so why was heat filling her? And why was he looking at her as if that same heat filled him?

She quickly took a step back and wiped her hands down the sides of her jeans.

"You think that will get rid of it?"

She met his eyes. She knew what he'd insinuated, but she wanted to be sure. "Get rid of what?"

"Nothing."

He then opened the bottle and took a huge gulp. Afterward, he licked his lips while she watched. Her chest tightened. He lowered the bottle from his mouth and held her gaze. "Want a sip?"

She drew in a deep breath to clamp down on her emotions. Was he offering to share his beer? For them to drink from the same bottle? Doing something like that was way too intimate for her. Evidently not for him. A distinct warmth coiled around her midsection. The way his eyes darkened wasn't helping matters.

She should call his bluff and take a sip. But that might lead to other things. It might give him ideas. The same ideas floating crazily through her head. The last thing she needed was an involvement with a man. Any man. Especially him. Her work was too important to her. The idea of an October fling was not. "No thanks. I had one earlier and one was enough for me."

Instead of saying anything, he nodded and raised the bottle to his lips to drain the rest. She watched his throat work. When had seeing a man drink anything been a turn-on?

When he finished the bottle and lowered it, she asked, "Want another one?"

He smiled at her. "No, one was enough for me."

She couldn't help but smile back at his use of her words. "I don't know, Gavin Blake. You seem like the sort of guy that could handle a couple of those."

"You're right, but that's not why I'm here."

His words were a reminder that he hadn't shown up tonight for chitchat and drinking beer. "Yes, you said you wanted to talk. Is there a problem?" Layla knew there was and figured he was about to spell it out for her.

"Who taught you to play the harmonica?"

She'd expected him to just dive in. His question threw her. "My grandfather," she said, angling her head to look up at him. "He was the best. At least most people thought so."

"And who was your grandfather?"

"Chip Harris."

Surprise made Gavin's jaw drop. "Chip Harris? *The* Chip Harris?"

Layla nodded. "Yes," she said, intentionally keeping her voice light. Very few people knew that. It wasn't something she boasted about, although she was proud of her grandfather's success and accomplishments. He'd been a good man, a great humanitarian and a gifted musician. But most of all he had been a wonderful grandfather. Her grandparents had helped to keep her world sane during the times her parents had made it insane.

Layla saw Gavin's dark, penetrating eyes suddenly go cold. "Is anything wrong?"

"So that's how you did it."

She raised a brow. "That's how I did what?"

"How you were able to talk my grandmother into going along with your crazy scheme of Jesse James's treasure being buried on my property. You probably heard she's a big fan of Chip Harris, and used the fact that you're his granddaughter to get in good with her. Get Gramma Mel to trust you and—"

"You jerk." Anger flared through her. His accusations filled her with rage. "How dare you accuse me of doing something so underhanded, so unethical and low? You might not know me but you know your grandmother. How can you think so little of her to imagine she has such a weak mind she could be taken in by anyone? How can you not trust her judgment?"

Layla drew in a disgusted breath and then added furiously, "For your information, I never once mentioned anything about my relationship to Chip Harris to her. Ms. Melody's decision was based on my research, which she took the time to read. And she asked questions and found some of her own answers. So regardless of what you believe, her decision was based on facts, Gavin Blake. Facts and nothing more."

Gavin was stunned by Layla's rage. When her words sank in, he regretted accusing her of manipulating Gramma Mel. He'd crossed the line and he knew it. He owed her an apology. "I'm sorry. I should not have accused you of that."

"But you did. Save your apology for your grandmother.

She's one of the most intelligent women I know. But tonight you made her out to be a woman who can be influenced easily by anything, especially name-dropping. Like I said, you should know your grandmother better than that."

Gavin didn't say anything. Probably because he knew she was right. His grandmother was as sharp as a tack. She'd told Layla so many stories of how he'd tried to pull one over on her…unsuccessfully. Maybe he should do what his grandmother had done and read Layla's report for himself.

"I should not have come here tonight," he finally said.

"No, you should not have, especially if you came to talk that kind of BS. I don't have time for it."

Layla's words seemed to irritate him. "You don't think I have a right to question why you're here?"

She didn't back down. In fact she took a step closer. "You have every right. But you already know why I'm here. If you don't agree with your grandmother or you want to question why I feel a dig on the Silver Spurs is warranted, I can understand that. But what you did, Gavin, is question my integrity. I take that personally."

"You have to admit the idea of buried treasure on my land is pretty far-fetched."

"Maybe to you but not to me. You're a SEAL. I'm sure there are times when you engage in covert operations where the facts lead you to believe your assignment will be successful…although logically it doesn't seem possible."

He frowned. "It's not the same."

"I think it is. I did my research on the life of Jesse James. Five years' worth. I studied his life, specifically that bank robbery in Tinsel. That's what led me here. If you took the time to read my research, you would see it's all there. All I'm asking is for you to give me the same courtesy Ms. Melody did and take the time to read my work."

"I don't have to read a report to know what you're claiming isn't true."

In frustration, Layla blew out a breath and threw up her hands. "Why are you so stubborn?"

Instead of answering he gave her a careless shrug of his broad shoulders. "I'm not being stubborn. Just realistic."

He wasn't even trying to be reasonable. "So what do you want, Gavin? Since you believe that I've hoodwinked your grandmother and I'm a lunatic on the hunt for buried treasure, did you come here tonight to ask me to leave? To tell me to get off your property because you won't allow me and my team to dig?"

When he didn't say anything but continued to stare down at her with those dark, penetrating eyes of his, she knew what she'd just said was true. "Fine. I'll leave in the morning."

She moved with the intention of walking around him to show him the door. He surprised her when he reached out and grabbed her arm. The moment he touched her it seemed every hormone in her body sizzled. She couldn't move away from him. His hand skimmed down her arm in a sensual caress.

"What do you think you're doing?" She heard the tension in her voice and felt her heart rate quicken. Their gazes held and something hot in the depths of his eyes held her hostage. She wanted to break eye contact and couldn't. How could any one man have so much sex appeal? Create such primal attraction?

Layla became angry with herself because of her reaction to him. The man standing in front of her had destroyed her plans. He'd placed her in a difficult position with the administration at the university and with her team. She'd have to cancel excavation and lose her funding. She might never get another chance to prove her theories. Yet at that moment all she could think about was how fully aware of him she was.

"What I'm doing is touching you," he answered moments later, as if he'd needed time to give her question some thought.

Well, she had news for him. He should keep his hands to himself. So why wasn't she telling him that? And why was there a throb inside her? One that had started in her stomach but was now going lower to the juncture of her thighs? And why, when she saw his head lowering, did she just stand there? When his lips touched hers and he wrapped her in his arms, she sank into him. The same way he was sinking into her mouth.

The kiss was making her forget everything, even the fact that he wanted to throw her off his ranch. The only thing she could concentrate on was how his tongue was moving around in her mouth, sending shivers up her spine until she heard herself moan.

But he was moaning as well, and then he deepened the kiss. She recognized this for what it was. Lust. And that usually led to sex. If that was his plan, he could take it elsewhere. She had no intention of getting involved, no matter how fleetingly, with a man who refused to take her work seriously.

She pulled her mouth free and took a step back.

"Like I said. I'll be off your property in the morning." She then walked around him to the door.

Before opening it, she glanced back at him. He stood in the same spot, staring at her as if she was a puzzle he was trying to figure out. Seriously? Did he think she was that complicated? As far as she was concerned, he was the problematic one.

He was the man who, with very little effort, it seemed, could tempt her to lower her guard, to surrender to this need he created inside of her. A need she hadn't realized even existed. And it appeared he was dealing with his own need if the huge bulge pressing against the zipper of his jeans was anything to go by. There were just some things an aroused man couldn't hide.

"We need to keep sex out of this, Gavin." She'd had to say it, considering the strong sexual chemistry flowing between them. Chemistry both of them were fully aware of.

He stared at her for a long moment, saying nothing, but she saw the tightening of his jaw. Had her words hit a nerve? Had they made him realize that she wasn't as gullible as he thought?

When he began walking toward her, her heartbeat quickened with every step he took. Never had she felt such a strong primal attraction to any man. Even his walk, his muscled thighs flexing erotically with every step, tripped her pulse. It had her drowning in the sexual vibes pouring off him.

When he came to a stop in front of her, he grabbed her hand to keep her from opening the door. Immediately, like before, they became attuned to each other. Why was there such a strong physical attraction between them? No man had ever made her forget about work. But she struggled to remember that work was the reason she was here. That and nothing else.

"Don't know about you, but I can't keep sex out of it, Layla. I think you know why. Whether we like it or not, there's a strong sensual pull between us. I felt it the moment I set eyes on you this morning, and if you say you didn't feel it as well, then you would be lying. You might pretend otherwise, but you want me as much as I want you."

No matter what he said, she would deny it. She hadn't come to the ranch for this. She had come to Cornerstone, Missouri, to do a job—to prove her theory and move up in her career—*not* to have an affair with a navy SEAL who could overtake her senses. A man who was proving, whether she wanted him to or not, that she had sexual needs she'd ignored for too long. But regardless of that proof, under no circumstances would she sleep with him. Doing so would be a very bad idea. It would be a mistake that could cost her all she'd worked for up to this point. Besides, hadn't he all but told her to get off his land?

Instead of a straight-out denial, she said, "What I want is to be allowed to do my job. I need to do that dig, Gavin."

His gaze hardened. "Why? To prove me wrong?"

"More than proving you wrong, I need to prove to myself and my peers that I am right. There's a difference, but I don't expect you to understand."

Yes, he understood the difference. Hadn't he felt the need to prove that he was his own man? To prove that being a SEAL hadn't been about his grandfather's and father's legacies but about establishing a legacy of his own? The first Gavin Blake had been handpicked to be part of the first special operations unit that became known as the SEALs. And Gavin's father, Gavin Blake Jr, had died a war hero after rescuing his team members and others who'd been held hostage during Desert Storm.

For years, he'd thought being Gavin Blake III was a curse more than a blessing. You couldn't share the name of bigger-than-life SEAL predecessors without some people believing you should be invincible. It had taken years to prove to others, as well as to himself, that he was his own man. Free to make his own mistakes. Now he cherished the memories of the heroes his grandfather and father had been and he was proud to carry their names and to continue the family legacy of being a SEAL. In the end, he'd realized becoming his own man hadn't been about proving anything to others but proving it to himself.

A part of him wanted to believe that Layla's issues were hers alone. They were her business to deal with and not his. But for some reason he couldn't let her go. His curiosity pushed him to say, "Don't leave the Silver Spurs just yet, Layla."

He saw that his words surprised her. Gave her pause. "Why? You ridiculed my years of research, accused me of manipulating your family and told me not to dig on your land. Why should I stay?"

"To convince me that you're right."

He could tell from her expression she thought what he'd said didn't make sense. "I can't do that unless you give me permission to excavate, Gavin. That's the only way I can prove anything."

Gavin was totally captivated by Layla Harris—by her passion for her work, and this passion between them. Why? He wasn't sure. She was beautiful, but he'd been around beautiful women before. She was built—with lush curves, a nice backside and very attractive features—but all those were just physical attributes. Deep down, he believed there was more to Layla Harris than just her beauty, more than her intelligence. There was something inside of her she refused to let surface. And it was something he wanted to uncover.

One thing for certain, he honestly wasn't ready for her to leave the Silver Spurs. But she was right. Why should she stay if he wouldn't allow her to dig on his property? He gritted his teeth at the thought of any woman making him feel so needy that he'd allow her to dig up the south pasture, his special place. But he quickly remembered he'd gone six months without sex, which had a way of crippling a man's senses.

"It's late," he heard himself say. "Let's talk more tomorrow."

"Will talking tomorrow change anything, Gavin?"

All he knew for certain was that he couldn't think straight being this close to her. But the last thing he wanted was to wake up tomorrow and find her gone. "It might," he said. "I'm not making any promises, Layla. All I can say is that right now I'm exhausted and can't think straight." He would let her think his muddled mind was due to exhaustion and not the degree of desire he had for her.

"Will you read my research?"

He wouldn't lie about that. "No. You can go over the important aspects of your work when we meet tomorrow."

She stared at him for a long moment as if weighing his words. Finally, she said, "Alright. I'll stay until we can talk."

Relief poured through his body, quickly followed by frustration and annoyance. No woman could tie him in knots like Layla seemed capable of doing. "I'll see you tomorrow."

When he'd first arrived, her hair had been neatly pulled back. Had he mussed up her hair when he'd kissed her? Maybe that was why the loose curls now teasing her forehead were a total turn-on.

"Good night, Gavin."

That was his cue to go. "Good night." He opened the door and stepped out into the cold Missouri night.

Chapter 3

Layla awakened the next morning wondering what she'd gotten herself into. Would remaining an additional day to meet with Gavin really change his mind?

There was always the possibility that it could, which was the reason her bags were not already packed. Besides, she was a fighter, a person who didn't give up easily. It had taken over a year to convince the university to give her funding for the dig, and another six months to get them to ease off some of their restrictions and ridiculous conditions. Even now, she wasn't sure the heads of the department believed in her 100 percent, but at least they were giving her a chance.

Now all of that forward momentum—the work that could change the history books and earn her a tenured position—could end because of Gavin. She drew in a deep breath. What was she going to do? Short of sleeping with him, she would do just about anything to convince him to reconsider.

She shifted in bed to look out the window. She'd thought she had a beautiful view in her high-rise apartment overlooking downtown Seattle—until now. The rolling plains, majestic hills and valleys of the Silver Spurs were awesome. The concrete jungle she saw each morning from her bedroom window couldn't compare.

She loved it here. She wouldn't mind returning to visit. But this time, she wasn't here for a vacation. She had a job to do and she hoped Gavin wouldn't stand in the way of her doing it.

Gavin.

He thought she'd been manipulative enough to use her musician grandfather's name to get in good with his grandmother. Although he had apologized, those accusations still bothered her. Yet in spite of them, she had allowed him to kiss her. And it was a kiss she couldn't stop thinking about. A kiss so deeply entrenched in her mind that she'd thought about it even while she'd slept. She was thinking about it now while wide-awake.

Layla realized that kissing, something she'd never enjoyed doing before, wasn't so bad, after all. At least with Gavin it wasn't bad. Evidently other guys had lacked his expertise. Not only did he have a skillful tongue, but he knew how to use it. The feel of being in his strong arms had sent pleasure throughout her entire body.

She drew in a sharp breath as memories flooded her, filling her with a longing for them to kiss again. Yet how could she even contemplate repeating that kiss when she wasn't sure she even liked him? The one thing she did know was that she definitely desired him and he'd been arrogant enough to call her out on that.

In frustration, she rubbed a hand down her face. She needed to rid her mind of thoughts of Gavin. She'd never mixed business with pleasure and she had no intention of doing so now. The most important thing in her life had always been her work, and she deliberately avoided relationships to keep her focus where it should be. She wouldn't let her attraction to Gavin interfere with what she needed to do.

And the first thing she needed to do was get out of bed and start her day. Gavin said they would talk today and she could only hope for the best.

It was early evening when Gavin finally opened his eyes and he immediately thought about the woman staying in the party house. The woman he'd kissed last night.

Layla had mated her tongue to his with an intensity that made every muscle in his body throb. It was as if she had just as much passion bottled up inside as he did. And he'd unleashed it all with that kiss.

He would love to pick up where they'd left off last night. Take the passion to a whole new level. That made him think of other things…like making love to Layla. How it would feel to run his hands through her hair, lock his mouth and his body to hers. Become immersed in all that sexual energy they seemed to generate. He got hard just thinking about the possibilities.

Gavin glanced over at the clock. He had slept the day away, but he had needed the sleep. Images of Layla had sneaked into the deep recesses of his mind, whether he had wanted them to or not. She'd been in his dreams.

He wanted her.

There. He'd confirmed it in his mind without an

ounce of regret. He was a man with needs and that kiss last night had totally obliterated any desire for the Mississippi vixen. He'd lost interest in heading south as planned. Nor did he want Layla to leave the ranch. But like she'd reminded him last night, unless he agreed to let her dig on the property, she had no reason to stay.

That meant he had to come up with a plan.

He rubbed sleep from his eyes, remembering that he had detected a few insecurities lurking within Layla last night. Something about her need to prove herself. What was that about? Did he really want to know? Did he even care?

Yes, he cared. He would go so far as to say that he even admired her spunk. Layla was tough and he had a feeling he hadn't even seen half the strength she possessed. She had to be resilient to have become a college professor at such a young age. He could see her holding her own when it mattered. He couldn't help but smile when he recalled her saying that he needed to keep sex out of this situation. Little did she know he had no intention of doing that. Their attraction was too strong and he intended to use it to his advantage.

As he stood to head for the bathroom, he halted upon hearing voices. They were his grandmother's and Layla's. His body immediately reacted to the sound of Layla's voice. They were in the kitchen. And he could tell his grandmother was enjoying the conversation.

He could understand why Gramma Mel was so taken with Layla. Although he never thought about it much, his grandmother probably got lonely around here whenever he was away. Even though she had Caldwell, there hadn't been another woman staying on the Silver Spurs since Gavin's mother had left.

He tried pushing thoughts of Jamie Blake from his mind like he'd always done. Why should he think about the woman who hadn't thought of him? One day she'd packed up and left, drove away leaving only a letter claiming she needed time away and would return. She never did. That's what had bothered Gavin the most, knowing a woman could just walk away from her husband and eight-year-old son without looking back.

Refusing to think about his mother anymore, Gavin entered his bathroom to shower. He hoped Layla stayed in the kitchen with his grandmother for a while because he definitely needed to talk to her.

Layla's hand tightened on her glass of iced tea the moment Gavin entered the kitchen. She didn't have to glance behind her to know he was there. His presence filled the room and sent all kinds of sensations vibrating through her. She was a little irritated that she was so aware of him. The sexual chemistry she'd hoped was a fluke was back in full force.

"Gavin, I figured the smell of food would wake you sooner or later," Melody Blake said, smiling at her grandson.

When he moved into Layla's line of vision she had no choice but to glance over at him. "Yes, it definitely did," he said, answering his grandmother but staring straight at Layla.

Then he spoke to her. "Layla. How are you today?"

She wanted to tell him she'd been fine until he'd made an appearance. She couldn't stop her gaze from roaming all over him. He stood near the window and the fading afternoon light highlighted his features, his clothing, everything about him. Not for the first time, Layla thought he had to be the sexiest man alive.

When he lifted a brow, she realized she had yet to answer his question. "I'm fine, Gavin. Thanks for asking."

She quickly switched her gaze away from him and back to her plate. Why had she waited so long to answer? Doing so had made it obvious she'd been checking him out. Thoroughly.

"I left your food warming in the oven, Gavin," Ms. Melody said, breaking the tension.

"Thanks, Gramma Mel. All I've been able to think about these last few days was getting back to your home-cooked meals." Gavin opened the oven to peek inside.

After getting his plate out of the oven, he smiled at Layla and crossed the kitchen to sit in the chair beside her, brushing his thigh against hers. He said grace and then lifted his head and looked over at Layla. He caught her staring at him again. She knew his touch had been no accident. Totally deliberate.

He pasted an innocent smile on his face and asked, "So, Layla, how was your day?"

Layla gritted her teeth. The nerve of him asking how her day had gone when she'd been waiting to meet with him. She hadn't mentioned anything about Gavin's visit last night to Ms. Melody. There was no way Layla could have mentioned it with a straight face, especially when she couldn't help thinking of the kiss they'd shared.

Knowing he was waiting for her response, she said, "My day has been going great."

"Gavin, I'm glad I got to say hello before I leave," his grandmother said, standing to her feet.

Gavin looked at his grandmother. "Where are you going?"

"The civic center. It's bingo night and Viola is picking me up. She should be here any minute."

It suddenly occurred to Layla that she would be left alone with Gavin. That shouldn't be a big deal since they still needed to talk, but it was. Already nerves stirred in the pit of her stomach.

"We'll take care of the kitchen," she heard Gavin say. "Layla and I need to talk anyway."

Ms. Melody looked back and forth at the two of them before directing her gaze to her grandson. "I think that's a good idea." At the sound of the car horn, a smile touched her lips. "That's Viola."

Before Layla and Gavin could tell her goodbye, Melody Blake had grabbed her purse and was out the door.

That's when Gavin turned his attention back to Layla.

When Gavin saw Layla loading her dishes into the sink, he said, "You don't have to help me with the dishes."

She shrugged her shoulders. "I don't mind."

Her back was to him and he couldn't stop his gaze from covering every inch of her backside, wrapped tight in her skirt. And before she'd left the table, more than once he'd checked out her pink blouse, noticing the deep V neck. There was nothing like seeing a little of a woman's cleavage every now and then. Made him wonder what her breasts looked like. How they would feel in his hands. Taste in his mouth.

"Your grandmother forgot to mention she made a

dessert," Layla said, breaking into his thoughts and turning around to meet his gaze.

"What is it?"

"Peach cobbler. Do you want some?"

That question was not one she should be asking him. Not when he had an erection nearly hard enough to burst out of his jeans. Yes, he wanted some, but his thoughts weren't on the peach cobbler.

Why did the picture of her standing at his grandmother's sink make a pang of desire shoot through him? The hair she'd worn down and around her shoulders yesterday was now confined in a ponytail. It wouldn't take much to walk across the room and set it free. After doing that, he would proceed to do all kinds of naughty things to her. Gavin shifted in his seat to relieve the pressure against his zipper.

"Yeah, I'd love to have some," he said in a deep, husky voice. And he knew Layla had figured out they weren't talking about peach cobbler.

She didn't say anything, just stared at him. He wished she didn't look so damn sexy while she sized him up, trying to figure him out. There wasn't much to find out on that score. He was a horny bastard and would remain so until he'd taken care of his sexual needs. That meant they needed to talk, and the sooner the better.

"We can talk while eating peach cobbler," he said.

Layla seemed relieved to finally begin their discussion and returned to the table with two plates of peach cobbler. "Where do we start?" she asked, sliding one of the plates in front of him before sitting down.

He picked up his fork and looked over at her. "We can start by talking about us."

Her expression clearly said that wasn't what she

thought they should be talking about. "We agreed to discuss the dig and not this thing between us."

Gavin wondered if Layla knew that "this thing" actually had a name. It was called physical desire. "I think we should talk about us before discussing the dig."

She gave him an annoyed look. "Why? I told you last night we needed to keep sex out of it."

Yes, she had said that, but did she actually think they could keep sex out of it when there was so much chemistry between them? So much that even now he would have no problem taking her right here on this damn table? "You're an intelligent woman, Layla. I'm sure you're well aware of how the human body operates. All of us have needs."

"Speak for yourself, Gavin."

He watched her nervously gnaw on her lower lip and heated lust danced up his spine. He was trying like hell to figure her out. Was she denying she had needs, as well? He knew from last night's kiss that that was a lie. Her denial made Gavin wonder about her experience level.

"Are you saying you don't want to have sex with me?"

As if the question shot her to full awareness, she leaned over the table and glared at him. "I don't want to have sex with you, Gavin. I don't want to have sex with anybody. All I want is to do my job. A job you refuse to let me do."

They weren't getting anywhere. For some reason he didn't want to talk to her about the dig until he found out why she kept certain emotions in check. So he tried another approach.

"Tell me about yourself, Layla."

Layla lifted a brow. That was clearly not what she'd expected. "I graduated from high school at sixteen and immediately went to college. Graduated with my bachelor's degree in history, then went on to get a master's in archaeology. My doctorate is in both history and archaeology."

"And you're just twenty-six?"

"Yes. I went to college year-round. I've worked on dig sites as an undergrad and while working toward my PhD so this won't be my first excavation."

"But it will be the first one you've been in charge of, right?"

"Yes, that's true."

He leaned back in his chair, deciding to keep her talking about the dig for a while, after all. He doubted she realized that whenever she talked about her work she lowered her guard. "So you admit you're inexperienced."

Layla frowned. He could tell she wasn't sure if they were still talking about the dig. "I don't think of myself as inexperienced, Gavin, so you shouldn't think that, either."

"Then tell me what I should think."

After several moments, she said, "You should focus on the fact that my being here is the result of several years of research. I didn't just wake up one morning and decide to do this. I've tracked each and every one of James's bank robberies in this area. Mapped out every possible trail he could have taken, every single place he and the gang could have hidden out. Then I obtained records of this land and the surrounding properties. I had my team digitally re-create how this area would have looked back then.

"The Silver Spurs would have been the ideal place to stop over because of the low-hanging trees. And the lake between here and the Lotts' spread would have allowed the gang time to wash away their scent and stay hidden from the sheriff's posse. I could even see James's gang being smart enough to use a decoy to send the posse racing in another direction. One away from here to give them time to bury their loot and lighten their load."

Gavin was trying not to get caught up in the sound of her voice. He wanted to hear the words she was saying. She was excited about her work and discussing it energized her. He couldn't help noticing the glow in her eyes, the confidence in her voice, the smile on her lips. The same lips he had tasted last night.

She was trying like hell to convince him that she was onto something, that she had researched her findings and believed in everything she was telling him. He knew there had to be a number of doubters…like himself.

When she stopped talking, he shifted his gaze from her lips to her eyes. "I take it you've already surveyed the area, used ground penetrating radar on the location already."

She nodded. If she was surprised by his knowledge of her preliminary assessment, she didn't show it. "I've gone further. I was able to get an infrared spectrum."

He lifted a brow. "How?"

"One of my students is big into digital technology and created it for me. That's the advantage I have over others working on this subject, I'm bringing this excavation into the digital age."

The technological aspect was an area Gavin was somewhat familiar with. The military already used all sorts of futuristic developments. It was important whenever they were sent into enemy territory that they didn't step on booby traps or buried explosives.

She looked at him expectantly, as if he would question what she said. He merely nodded. "I'm familiar with the use of high-tech digital to detect buried items."

She smiled, obviously glad that he was following her. "All the equipment my team and I use is state-of-the-art, some have never before been used in an archaeological context and they were developed exclusively for this dig by students in my department," she said proudly.

Because she was young he couldn't imagine her getting others to rally behind her for the cause. Whether she knew it or not, that spoke volumes about her character as a leader. It would take a strong individual to coax others on board. He knew how that could be.

"It's too late today but tomorrow I want to check out the area you've targeted." What she would discover was that he also had a high-tech camera, one designed by Flipper for marine purposes. However, it had proven effective at detecting objects underground, as well.

"Alright."

He heard the hope in her voice and figured that was because he'd shown interest in the dig site. She probably thought he was almost on board. That wasn't the case. But he wouldn't tell her that yet.

When he didn't say anything else for a while, she lifted a brow and looked over at him. She even had a little smile on her face. That glow brightening her eyes almost undid him. "Any more questions, Gavin?"

There was something else; something he had to know. "Yes, but not about the dig. It's something about you that I want to know."

"What?" she asked, lifting an arched brow.

He held her gaze steadily. "When was the last time you made love with a man?"

Chapter 4

Layla gaped, certain Gavin hadn't asked her what she thought he'd asked her. What man would inquire that of a woman…especially one he'd known barely twenty-four hours? However, from the look on his face, he evidently saw nothing wrong with the question. He was sitting there waiting on an answer.

She lifted her chin and crossed her arms over her chest. When she saw his gaze shift from her eyes to her upraised breasts, she dropped her hands. "Do you actually expect me to answer that?" Somehow she managed to get the words past a constricted throat. The way he stared at her was making her head spin.

He shrugged massive broad shoulders. "Don't know why not. We're sexually attracted to each other. Just want to know what I'm dealing with when we decide to go for it and take the edge off."

Go for it? Take the edge off? Layla shook her head, clearly missing something. She knew they were attracted to each other; she got that. What she didn't get was him thinking that attraction meant they would eventually decide to "go for it." She had no intention of going anywhere. She was here to do a job and not indulge his fantasies…or her own, for that matter.

"I think you need to explain what exactly you're getting at. We agreed to keep sex out of this, Gavin."

"I didn't agree to any such thing. You suggested it but I didn't agree to it. Why would I?"

"Why wouldn't you?" she countered, not understanding his way of thinking.

He leaned back in his chair and her gaze watched his every movement. Restrained and controlled. She wondered if his actions were intentional, to put her off-kilter. When he picked up his glass of tea, her gaze automatically shifted to his hands. They were large and calloused. They were the same hands that had sent shivers up her spine last night.

Memories of their kiss suddenly bombarded her and then her gaze shifted to his mouth as he took a swallow of iced tea. She was drawn to the way his mouth covered the rim of the glass and the way the liquid flowed down his throat. But what really got to her was the way he licked his lips afterward. When he caught her staring, those penetrating eyes darkened as they held hers.

"Want some?"

She snatched her gaze away. The lump in her throat thickened. She was glad to be sitting down; otherwise it would have been impossible to stand on both feet. The look he was giving her had her weak in the knees.

Somehow she managed to clear the lump in her throat and hold up her glass. "No thanks, I have my own."

His eyes blazed as they continued to hold hers. "I wasn't offering you any of my tea, Layla."

She sucked in a deep breath. He couldn't have set her straight any plainer than that. There was no need to ask what he was offering. That was the moment she knew Gavin Blake intended to be a problem. One she needed to deal with here and now.

"You never did answer my earlier question. When was the last time you were with a man?"

She set her glass of tea back down on the table. "And you never answered mine about why you wouldn't agree to keep sex out of it." Feeling flustered, she added, "We need to talk."

A smile touched the corners of his lips. "I thought that's what we were doing."

There was no way he could have thought that. What he was doing was deliberately getting her all unglued. If he thought for one minute his arrogant behavior would make her run, then he didn't know her very well. "There seems to be some sort of misunderstanding here."

"Is there?"

"Undoubtedly. I'm here to do a job…that is, if you let me stay to do it. But under no circumstances am I here for your pleasure, Gavin. I don't play those kinds of games. Evidently just because we shared a kiss last night, you've gotten the wrong idea about me. I need to set the record straight now. So hear me and hear me good." She leaned part of the way over the table toward him. Although his face was void of any expression, she was certain she had his undivided attention.

"I am *not* here to engage in an affair with you, if

that's why you want to know about my sex life." *Or lack thereof.* But that was something he didn't need to know.

Gavin didn't say anything. He knew she assumed his attention was on her words. In truth his attention was on the mouth delivering those words. Her lips were perfectly shaped with a little cute dip in the center. He liked the play of that mutinous tip whenever she frowned and how those same lips folded pensively when she appeared in deep thought. But more than anything, he couldn't forget how those lips felt beneath his. Their lushness. How delicious they'd tasted. How sweet.

When she got quiet after delivering her spiel, he figured she thought she had set him straight. Far from it and it was time to let her know where he stood. "Are you finished?"

She seemed surprised by his question, but nodded nonetheless and said, "Yes, I'm finished." She then straightened in her chair, her posture a lot more relaxed than it had been moments ago.

"Evidently, there's a lot you don't understand about sex, Layla."

Her body tensed again. And somehow those gorgeous lips looked even more sensual. "What's there to understand?" she asked.

Gavin continued to study her. He saw her nonchalant expression and noted her features had taken on a blasé look. Her apparent indifference to this discussion of sex could mean only one thing. She'd been cheated of something he considered as vital as breathing. Reaching her level of success in such a short period of time meant something had been sacrificed. An active sex life, perhaps?

"I want you and you want me," he said, deciding to point out the obvious.

"And?"

He forced himself not to smile, thinking she was pretending not to have a clue. Then it occurred to him that maybe she wasn't pretending. Maybe it was time to explain to her what it meant whenever a woman became the object of his personal fantasies.

"And..." he said, "we *will* sleep together."

She sat up in her chair, straightening her spine. Her lips went from sensual to tense but turned him on even more just the same. "No, we will not," she said adamantly.

He smiled. "Yes, we will. It's inevitable."

She frowned. "No, it's not. Just who do you think you are?"

He figured it was time she knew the answer to that. "A man who wants you. A man who intends to have you. A man who will show you, Layla Harris, just what you've been missing."

Layla tried to keep her heart from pounding deep in her chest, while at the same time fighting off the heat stroking through her body. She knew she shouldn't ask but she couldn't hold back.

"And just what do you think I've missed?"

"Hot, raunchy, mind-blowing sex. Evidently over the years you've been too preoccupied with other things to indulge. Don't you know it's not good to deprive your body of meeting certain needs?"

Her frown deepened. "I haven't deprived my body of anything."

"Haven't you? Why do you think you're so attracted to me?"

Layla actually rolled her eyes. Really? Honestly? Had he looked in the mirror lately? When was the last time he'd studied all those photos Ms. Melody had plastered on the walls. Any woman would be attracted to him. Even now he sat there not doing anything and still looked sexy as hell with that well-toned body of his. And here she was sitting across the table from him. Right within kissing distance.

As far as she was concerned, Gavin Blake was eye candy of the richest kind. Passion personified. But she definitely wouldn't tell him that. She would deny everything he'd said with her last breath if she had to.

"I am not all that attracted to you." At least she hadn't completely lied and said she wasn't attracted to him at all.

"You want me to prove otherwise?"

What was it with men always wanting to prove things when it came to sex? "No, thanks. That's not necessary."

"I think that it is."

He'd said the words in a low, vibrating tone with a sexy rumble she wished she could ignore. But there was no way, what with all the shivers oozing down her spine. "Are you trying to scare me off, Gavin?"

He lifted a brow. "Scare you off?"

"Yes. Say all these things so I get angry enough to leave the ranch, sparing you the trouble of making a decision one way or the other about whether I can dig on your land or not."

"Is that what you think?"

To be honest, she didn't know what to think. She

needed his land and all he had on his mind was sex. That made her wonder…

"Then are you trying to box me into a corner? Implying that I will have to sleep with you before you'll give me permission to dig?"

Gavin shook his head. "I would never put pressure on you to sleep with me. But be forewarned, Layla. If you hang around here doing that dig, we *will* sleep together. There's no way we won't. Your own body will betray you. When it does, I will be ready for the opportunity."

Seriously? If he thought her body would eventually weaken, he didn't know her. And that was the point, one she couldn't lose sight of. He *didn't* know her. He didn't know about her dedication when it came to her work. Nor did he know of her ability to be single-minded when it came to her career goals. She could put everything out of her mind except what was most important. She was driven to be successful in her field, and she wouldn't let Gavin—or any other man—stand in her way.

He was pretty sure of himself where women were concerned. A man couldn't look like him, be built like him, and not be in demand and get any woman he wanted. All Gavin had to do was snap his fingers and she figured the women came running. Being denied anything from a woman would be foreign to him.

"Think whatever you want, Gavin, but I'm not the kind of woman you're used to. I won't break."

He rubbed his hand over his chin as he studied her. "Would you want to bet on that?"

Layla frowned. She had no intention of betting on anything and she proceeded to tell him that. He only smiled, and it was one of those smiles she was getting to know too well. The one that made her body sizzle when it should make her angry. His smile all but said he had her where he wanted her.

"Would you be willing to bet on it to guarantee your dig on the Silver Spurs?"

That piqued her interest. "Depending on what you have in mind." She hoped she was not setting herself up for something she would regret.

Gavin held back his *gotcha* smile. Little did Layla know but his teammates didn't call him Viper for nothing. To some, a viper might be considered a spiteful or treacherous person, but for him the name meant he knew how to capture his prey using any means necessary. Striking when they least expected it. He wanted her in his bed willingly and he intended to do whatever it took to get her there. It was time to push his agenda.

"I'm willing to make a deal, Layla."

"What sort of a deal?" She held his gaze.

Did she know how beautiful her facial features were? How striking her bone structure? He could sit for hours and stare, taking her in. But doing so would make him want her even more than he already did. Before he'd met her, he couldn't have imagined that degree of need for any woman. But he could imagine it for her.

He lifted his shoulder in a half shrug as if what he was about to say wasn't of grave importance. As if he really didn't care one way or the other if she took the deal or left it on the table.

"I'm not as convinced about this buried loot as you and my grandmother seem to be," he said. "And I doubt reading any report will make me change my mind. But wanting you in my bed will," he said bluntly, needing her to fully understand what he was saying.

"This is the deal," he continued. "I will let you dig, regardless of what I think. If you find something, great. You will have proven me wrong. I will be happy for you. Be the first to congratulate you on a job well done. However, if you come up with nothing then you admit you want me as much as I want you and we sleep together."

"You are counting on me failing? And plan to take advantage of me if I do?"

The thought was firing her up. He could tell. The flash of fire in her eyes told it all. "You shouldn't worry about failing. Unless you think you will. If there's some doubt in your mind regarding the accuracy of your research, then I understand if—"

"My research is on point. There's no doubt in my mind about anything."

His smile spread across his lips. "In that case, do we have a deal?"

Chapter 5

At that moment Layla realized just what was going on. Whether it was his intent or not, Gavin was forcing her to believe in herself, to prove that she was right in her belief that Jesse James had buried treasure on Gavin's land.

"Well?"

The determination was clear in his eyes. He intended to sleep with her. She was just as determined that he wouldn't. She didn't like the deal he'd offered. In all honesty, she should be appalled by it. Instead she saw it as her chance to prove she was above the desire he couldn't stop talking about. She would find Jesse James's loot. She had no doubts. There was no need getting irritated that he was a typical male who thought a good roll between the sheets was the answer to everything. She would never be able to convince him that when it came to sex, she had always been able to take it or leave it, no matter how tempting it was to indulge. He would find that out for himself.

She'd be free to run her dig and make the finding of not only her career but of a lifetime. She wouldn't think about the traitorous voice that said it might be nice to lose this bet and get the consolation prize…

"Fine."

He lifted his brow. "Does that mean you accept the deal?"

"As long as you give me your word you won't try to hinder me and my team in any way."

"I wouldn't do that."

Yeah. Right. There was no reason for her to trust he wouldn't do just about anything to make sure the result worked out in his favor. Another typical male trait. No man liked losing. "Whatever you say."

"You're going to have to trust me."

Layla rolled her eyes. "Sorry to disappoint you, but I don't know you enough to trust you."

"I can remedy that."

"Don't do me any favors." Layla eased out of her chair, feeling like she'd mentally run a marathon. "So will you give me your word as a SEAL that you won't try anything underhanded?"

"You think my word as a SEAL means something?"

"Yes. SEALs are a special team of men who take the job of protecting our country very seriously, and they live by a code of honor and integrity."

Gavin nodded. She was right. "And you know this how?"

"My father's cousin used to be a SEAL. He retired a few years ago, but he told us all about them. At least what he could share. A lot of the stuff he did was classified."

"The majority of our missions are," Gavin said.

"So, will you give me your word?"

"Yes, you have my word."

As far as Gavin was concerned, getting her into his bed before the dig began would not be interfering with the job she wanted to do.

"Good." She glanced at her watch. "It's getting late. I'm sure you need more sleep. However, if you need help with the dishes, then I—"

"No, I don't need help with the dishes. That's what dishwashers are for."

"Do you still want to see where we plan to dig?"

"Yes. I want to know what you have planned on my property and where."

"No problem."

"Then I'll come by the cottage in the morning," he said, standing, as well. "Come on. I'll walk you back."

She shook her head as she put on her sweater. "That's not necessary."

"It is for me, Layla. I'll walk you back."

She didn't deny him, maybe she didn't want to appear ungrateful. She headed for the door and when she reached out to open it, he moved his hand forward, as well. She didn't seem aware that he'd been standing so close behind her. His fingers closed over hers and his chest was flush against her back.

"I can open the door, Gavin," she said, glancing over her shoulder, obviously flustered at his nearness. He loomed over her five-foot-three-inch height. He stood so close he could smell her with every breath.

"Your choice." Releasing his hand from hers he eased back. She opened the door and inhaled the cool Missouri air.

"Nice night, isn't it?" he asked her. He walked beside her now.

"Yes, it is a nice night." She glanced over at him again. "Glad to be home?"

A smile touched his lips. "Yes. It's always good to be home. Time to go from SEAL to rancher."

"Is it that easy?"

"I'm used to it now. I have good men working for me who make the transition less difficult."

She nodded. "You love being a SEAL?"

"Yes."

"I understand your father and grandfather were SEALs."

Gavin wondered what else his grandmother had told her about their family. "Yes, they were SEALs. So I guess you can say it's in my blood. What about your folks? Are they college professors like you?"

"No. They're both neurosurgeons. I didn't follow in their footsteps. Medicine didn't interest me."

He hadn't asked her to explain, but the fact that she did led him to believe her choice of a career was a sore spot with someone. "You are your own person, Layla." She was definitely her own woman, he thought further to himself. "Just because following in my father's and grandfather's footsteps worked for me, doesn't mean following family tradition works for everybody."

She didn't say anything for a minute. "My parents wanted me to be a mini-them and go to medical school. But I couldn't. I'm not a healer. I'm a historian."

"Then you did the right thing by following your

heart. When did you decide on archaeology?" Gavin wondered if she noted how in sync their steps were.

"In my junior year of high school." She paused as if she was remembering. "My history teacher had gone on an excavation in Egypt the summer before and told us about it. I found it fascinating how her team was able to dig up artifacts, how they found history buried beneath the earth's surface. It made me realize that's what I wanted to do."

"Why Jesse James?"

He heard her chuckle and the sound stimulated him in a way he wished it didn't. "Why *not* Jesse James?" He heard the amusement in her tone. "I used to watch Westerns with my grandfather whenever I visited him in New Orleans. He was a fan of the outlaw Jesse James. He read a lot of books about him. Watched movies and documentaries. I shared his love and interest. That's how my research began. And it's only grown over the years."

He heard the passion for her subject in her voice. It was there whenever she spoke about her work. She believed in it. If there had been any doubt in his mind before, there wasn't now. She would risk sleeping with him to prove her work.

She'd be disappointed not to find what she was searching for. But Gavin looked forward to helping her get over the disappointment. He didn't believe for one minute that James's loot was buried on this land. It wasn't. He recalled years ago when he'd been in high school, his father had given some outfit permission to check out the land because there was a chance of finding oil. They'd come up with nothing then, and he was certain Layla and her team would come up with nothing now.

"I guess this is where we need to say good-night."

They had reached the party house. Her words told him he wouldn't be invited inside. Maybe that was for the best. He doubted he could keep his hands off of her if they were behind closed doors. And regardless of what she thought, she wouldn't resist him. Last night's kiss had proven that. He wasn't worried about the outcome of the deal between them. Like he'd told her, eventually her body would betray her and she would break. What had happened in his grandmother's kitchen when their hands touched at the door was a prime example of the intensity of the desire between them.

"So what time do you want us to meet tomorrow?" she asked, reclaiming his attention.

"I need to ride out with Caldwell and my men at the crack of dawn to check on a few things. I'll be back around ten. Will that time work for you?"

"Yes."

"Good. We can ride in my truck."

"Alright. Good night."

She turned toward the door, intent on opening it quickly and going inside. He was just as determined not to let her get away that easily. Reaching out, he wrapped his arms around her waist and tugged her close to him.

"What do you think you're doing, Gavin?"

"This."

Lowering his head, he claimed her mouth in a long, passionate kiss. She didn't push him away. Instead, she pulled him closer. Emotions he hadn't expected pushed him to let her know with this kiss just how much he wanted her.

The kiss they'd shared last night had been a game changer. This one sealed their fate.

Gavin knew at that moment that kissing her would never be enough. What he really wanted to do was sweep her off her feet, open the damn door and head straight to the bedroom. But he couldn't do that.

He wanted her to admit how much she wanted him, too. He'd give her time; he'd remember their deal. The one he had initiated. The one he intended to end in his favor. There was no way she would leave the Silver Spurs without them making love.

He finally broke off the kiss. As he drew in a deep breath he watched her draw in one, as well. Studying her mouth, he saw her lips were wet and swollen, and he had to fight back the urge to kiss her again.

"Why did you kiss me?" she asked, touching her finger to her lips.

He smiled, tempted to replace her finger with the tip of his tongue. "For the same reason you let me kiss you. I want you and you want me."

From the look he saw in her eyes, he knew she was angry. Why? Because he'd stated facts when she preferred hiding behind denials?

"I'm going inside now."

"I'll see you in the morning around ten."

She nodded, then quickly opened the door and went inside. When the door closed behind her, Gavin shoved his hands into the pockets of his jeans and headed back toward the main house. He knew she was confused. Confusion came with the territory when you tried to deny the truth of your feelings. However, she was smart.

He knew she would figure it out. Eventually she would see things the way he did.

He would make sure of it.

Chapter 6

Layla, feeling tousled from a restless night, stepped out on the porch with a cup of coffee in her hand. She took a sip. She needed the hot liquid as much as she needed more sleep. Kissing Gavin was hazardous to her health when the aftereffect was a frazzled mind.

What could she have been thinking to agree to the deal he'd put on the table? What woman in her right mind would agree to have sex with a man who counted on her to fail at the most important project of her life? She kept assuring herself that she had nothing to worry about because her research wasn't wrong.

But what if it was?

She shook her head, refusing to second-guess herself or allow something as insignificant as sex to undermine her confidence in years of research. She lifted the cup to her lips again, took another sip and smiled. She couldn't wait to show Gavin just how wrong he was. She would leave the Silver Spurs with Jesse James's loot *and* she'd keep Gavin out of her panties.

She glanced over at the main house and tried to ignore the heat that settled in her stomach. Ms. Melody had called to invite Layla to breakfast, but she'd declined saying she needed to read over a few reports. The last thing Layla wanted was to run into Gavin. She would see him at ten and that suited her just fine. The man had a way of making her distracted.

And then there was that kiss she couldn't stop thinking about. The one that still had her lips tingling this morning. While getting dressed she'd tried to convince herself not to worry about that kiss—not to worry about anything, especially not Gavin Blake. Agreeing to his deal meant nothing more than a reason to work harder to find James's stash. She hadn't lied to Ms. Melody. Layla had used this morning to review several documents. It was important to make sure she hadn't missed anything in her research.

Layla checked her watch. Gavin would be arriving in an hour. That wasn't a lot of time to prepare to see him again. But then she doubted she would ever be prepared for the likes of Gavin Blake.

"So what have you decided about the dig, Gavin?"

Gavin glanced up from his breakfast plate and met his grandmother's eyes. He'd been in bed when she'd returned last night, but there was no getting out of the conversation this morning. One thing was for certain, he would not tell her about the deal he'd struck with Layla.

"Layla is showing me the site this morning. I want

to check it out for myself before I make a decision." He then resumed eating, hoping to end the conversation.

"So when are you leaving for Mississippi?"

He looked up at his grandmother again with a raised brow. "Who said anything about me going to Mississippi?"

She lifted her own brow. "Yesterday you mentioned you had important business to take care of there."

Now he recalled mentioning it. "I changed my mind and won't be leaving, after all." He resumed eating again, knowing his grandmother was eyeing him suspiciously.

"Why?"

He lifted his head again. "Why, what?"

"Why are you hanging around here?"

He held her inquisitive gaze. "Do you have a problem with me hanging around here, Gramma Mel?"

"Not as long as you don't have some shenanigans brewing in that head of yours, Gavin."

If only you knew, he thought. He pushed his plate away. "Breakfast was good as usual. I'm surprised you didn't invite Layla to join us."

"I did. But she made an excuse for not coming. I wonder why."

He stood. His grandmother was fishing for information and he was determined not to get caught. "I have a call with Phil to go over the books. I'll be in my office for an hour or so."

"Alright. And you may have changed your mind about going to Mississippi, but I'm still scheduled to go to that library conference in Cincinnati. It lasts a week, and I booked it before I knew you were coming home."

Gavin knew his grandmother enjoyed going to those conferences. "You should go," he encouraged.

She looked at him as if he wasn't trustworthy…of all things. "Is anything wrong?" he asked her.

"You tell me, Gavin. You're not fooling me one bit. I know that look. You're up to something and whatever it is, I hope you don't get caught in your own trap."

"What trap?"

"I'll let you figure that one out. But keep something in mind."

He lifted a brow. "What?"

"Layla is not Jamie."

He frowned deeply. "What is that supposed to mean?"

"It means I think something good could develop between the two of you, if you let it. But you won't. You're afraid she will be like Jamie. Whether you choose to believe me or not, your mom loved you and your dad. I would sit and hear her crying for him at night when he was gone."

"Then why did she leave?"

"Loneliness drove her away, Gavin. The Silver Spurs isn't meant for everyone and she was miserable here. Not everyone can handle the isolation."

"But that was no reason for her to desert me and Dad."

Without saying anything else he turned and walked out of the kitchen toward his office.

A lump formed in Layla's throat when she heard the knock at the door. She didn't have to look out of the peephole to see who it was. Gavin had said he would arrive at ten and it was ten on the dot. She glanced down at herself and then wished she hadn't. Why should she care what he thought about how she looked today? And why had she decided to wear her hair down instead of back in a ponytail?

She opened the door and Gavin stood leaning in the doorway. He filled the space, looking like he needed to be some woman's breakfast, lunch and dinner. Why did the man have to be so over-the-top gorgeous? Why did she want to drool, drool, and then drool some more?

And why did she want to snatch him inside and have her way with him?

She had no right to think any of those things, no right to fantasize. She had to stay focused on her work. "Good morning. I'm ready," she said, grabbing her jacket. He moved aside when she stepped out and closed the door behind herself.

"Good morning, Layla. I hope you slept well," Gavin said as they walked off the porch.

He slid his hand to her elbow to help her down the steps and she wished he hadn't. Immediately, a spike of desire shot through her and she was tempted to snatch her arm away.

"Nice day, isn't it?"

"Yes, it's nice." She glanced over at him as he kept his hand on her elbow while he led her to his truck and opened the door.

"And speaking of nice," he said, gripping her elbow a little tighter as he helped her up into the passenger seat. "You look good this morning. Real nice."

"Thank you."

He closed the truck door and as she watched him move around the front of the truck to the driver's side, she couldn't help thinking that he looked pretty good himself. Real nice. A pair of jeans hugged masculine thighs, a pullover sweater and a leather bomber jacket with the crest of a SEAL on the back graced broad shoulders. In her book there was something about a man who wore a leather bomber jacket, whether he was a biker, a model or a navy SEAL.

She kept her gaze trained on him. When he opened the door and slid onto the leather seat, she couldn't help but appreciate how the fit of his jeans tightened on his thighs.

"You went riding around your ranch dressed like that?"

"No. We finished early so I had time to change before joining my grandmother for breakfast. She missed your presence at breakfast by the way."

"I told her about the report I had to review this morning."

He didn't say anything and she wondered if he believed her.

"You okay?"

It was only then that she realized she was still staring. She snatched her gaze away from his thighs, regretting that he'd caught her ogling him. "I'm fine."

A smile curved his lips and her insides felt like they'd turned to mush. "Just checking," he said, snapping his seat belt in place. "I don't want you to start admitting you want me anytime soon."

Layla frowned, remembering what he'd said last night. "Trust me. That won't be happening." She spoke with a degree of confidence she wasn't feeling, especially when he shifted gears, causing those thighs to catch her attention again.

She forced her gaze out the window to view the pastures, valleys and hills they passed. Not for the first time, she thought the Silver Spurs was beautiful. Already they'd passed the new barn and several other smaller buildings. And there were several fenced rolling plains filled with cows. The sun peeked through a bevy of trees that layered the countryside and she knew it would be a beautiful day even with the chill in the air.

"Sleep well?"

She glanced over at him, wondering why he would ask. Did he assume that she hadn't? Well, she intended to crush that assumption right then and there. "Yes, like a baby, straight through the night." Maybe she'd laid it on too thick since most babies didn't sleep straight through the night.

"Glad to hear it. So did I. I slept so well that I almost overslept this morning." He didn't say anything for a minute. "Which way?"

She lifted a brow. "What?"

"Directions. Gramma Mel said the spot is just past the old barn. Which way do I go after that?"

The barn he was talking about was a big empty building painted red. According to Ms. Melody, it hadn't been used in years but the structure looked sound. More than once Layla had been tempted to take a peek inside but the doors were bolted up. She wondered if Gavin would allow them to keep their excavation equipment stored there. Since he seemed in a pretty good mood this morning, it might be a good time to ask. "And about that old barn?"

"What about it?"

"I'm going to need a place to store my heavy equipment, like the loader backhoe and tractor, for the excavation. May I use the old barn?"

He glanced over at her and she could imagine what he was thinking. Why should he do anything to help her when he was counting on her to fail? He surprised her when he said, "Yes, you can use the old barn."

She smiled. Since he was being so generous she decided to go for the gusto. "There's also a smaller building next to the barn. I understand it used to be the old bunkhouse."

"What about it?"

"May I use that, as well? I'll need somewhere to test soil samples and such."

He looked at her again. "Are you trying to take advantage of my kindness, Layla?"

"Yes, I guess I am, Gavin."

A husky chuckle escaped his lips. "At least you're honest. Yes, you can use that old shack, as well."

"Thank you."

"You're welcome."

She didn't say anything for a minute as they drove. "Make a left turn at the next tree and drive another couple of miles," she said. "You can park in the clearing next to the stumps. I've marked the exact spot where we'll be digging."

"Okay."

The rest of the drive was done in silence. She was glad when he finally brought the truck to a stop a short while later.

Gavin drew in a deep breath. With his hands still gripping the steering wheel he stared straight ahead at the view out of the windshield. He needed to get his bearings. Everything about Layla was getting to him. The way she looked, her scent, the way she wore her hair. The way that same hair had blown in the wind when his truck whooshed across his property.

"I can tell you miss coming here."

Did she make that assumption because of the way he was still sitting here, trying to keep his mind and body under control? Yet, she was right. He had missed coming here.

"Yes. As a kid I used to come to this area a lot. There's a huge lake not far from here. It separates our land from the Lotts' property and it's on the Lotts' land. But that didn't mean anything to me. Not even the no-swimming-allowed sign Sherman Lott had posted. I used to sneak into the lake and go swimming as a teen every chance I got. On a good day I would swim for hours without getting caught."

"And on a bad day?"

He chuckled. "On a bad day Sherman Lott would call my grandmother and report me for trespassing."

She lifted a brow. "Honestly? He would actually call and tell on you?"

"All the time. He didn't like anyone swimming or fishing in that lake. But I had a lot of years of good fishing there, as well."

He smiled, remembering how defying Mr. Lott had pleased him immensely. "Time to look around. But before we get out there's something we need to do."

She lifted her brow. "What?"

"Kiss. More than anything, I want to kiss you, Layla."

Layla couldn't believe he'd said that. Kiss? Hadn't they done that enough already? Not that she was counting but he'd kissed her twice. Why was he going for three? Why was she hoping that he would?

"Kiss me?" she asked, softly, hoping he didn't pick up on the yearning in her voice.

"Yes, kiss you. It's either that or talk you into my truck's backseat."

She nibbled on her bottom lip. "And you think doing that will be easy?"

"No, but it will be worth all the effort I plan to put into it. So how about unbuckling that seat belt and leaning a little over here? I promise it will be painless."

Being painless, Layla thought, was the least of her worries. "Haven't you gotten enough? Of kissing me?" she asked, studying the look in his eyes.

"No, I haven't gotten enough, so lean over this way. Let's engage in something pleasurable."

The urgency in his voice was so intense, it sent shivers through her. She knew they shouldn't kiss again. Doing so would lead to assumptions on his part that she'd rather he not have. But she'd had a hard time forgetting how pleasurable their last two kisses had been. Both times his tongue had stroked hers to a feverish pitch, until she had greedily responded.

Frustration spilled from her lungs in a sigh and with very little control left, she unsnapped her seat belt and leaned closer to him. In spite of her misgivings, she was prepared to give him the kiss he wanted because it was a kiss she wanted, as well.

He leaned in to meet her and their lips touched. On her breathless sigh, he slid his tongue inside her mouth and began mating with her tongue. She felt his intensity all the way to her toes.

She wrapped her arms around his neck as he

wrapped his arms around her waist. They were sitting in his truck, kissing like oversexed teenagers. Like they had nothing better to do and all day to do it. How crazy was that? But the insanity was lost as she tasted him. He tasted primitive, untamed and wild with lust. How could she detect such a thing in a kiss? Was this a warning that she should back off? That Gavin Blake would be the one man she couldn't ignore?

The latter gave her pause, but not enough to stop her tongue from mingling with his. Not enough to refrain from following his lead when he deepened the kiss. Not enough to stop the moan escaping her throat.

Layla knew then that she was a goner.

Chapter 7

Gavin greedily devoured Layla's mouth. Never before had any woman escalated his arousal to such a state. And never had any woman made him want to kiss her each and every time he saw her.

Every bone and muscle in his body throbbed with a need for her that went beyond desire. Intense heat curled inside of him, threatening his control. And the one thing he was known for was control. So why were his brain cells faltering under the onslaught of such a delicious kiss? Why was his body making urgent demands for him to make love to her right here in his truck? Damn. What could he say?

Nothing. He was totally at a loss for words, which was a good thing since he didn't have time to indulge in any. He preferred using his mouth for this kiss. He intended to get his fill. But a part of him wasn't sure he could ever get his fill of Layla. He saw her and he wanted her. That wasn't good. He had to get control of his body and of the situation. And he needed to do so now.

Gavin reluctantly broke off the kiss. Drawing his mouth away from hers was one of the hardest things he'd had to do. He saw the look of denied need in her eyes before she leaned back, dropped her head against the headrest and closed her eyes. He figured she was as in awe of what just happened as he was.

What they'd shared wasn't just a kiss. It was an acknowledgment of deep sexual desires. He knew what was driving his and he thought he had figured out what was driving hers. She just refused to accept it. She was stubborn. It would take a lot more kisses like this one to bring her around. They'd felt an intense attraction to each other from the first, and from all appearances, things had gotten worse.

He continued to stare at her as heat curled inside of him. He wanted her. Bad. And that pushed him to say, "So tell me again why we can't sleep together."

Layla heard his words but she couldn't respond. Neither could she open her eyes to look at him. There was no point. She knew what she would see in the depths of his dark gaze. A sexual need so hot it was likely to sizzle her insides. It would make her fully aware of her own sexual need. A need he stirred to life inside her whether she wanted him to or not.

"Open your eyes, Layla. I'm not going anywhere."

At least not today. She suddenly remembered Ms. Melody mentioning he had to go to Mississippi on business. "When are you leaving?" she asked, opening her eyes.

Just as she'd expected. The eyes staring at her were dark and seductive.

He lifted a brow. "Leaving for where?"

"Mississippi. Your grandmother mentioned you had important business to take care of there."

"Trying to get rid of me, are you?"

"It wouldn't hurt," she said and saw his eyes get even darker when she moistened her bottom lip with the tip of her tongue. "So when are you leaving?"

He moved his gaze from her mouth to her eyes. "I changed my mind about Mississippi. I'm not leaving here anytime soon." She couldn't stop the disappointment that flashed through her.

"But I thought you had important business to take care of."

"My plans have changed. Do you have a problem with that?"

"I just hope you don't plan to get underfoot."

"I'll try not to. Now show me the exact spot where you plan to dig," he said, opening the truck door to get out.

No matter what he said, Layla knew Gavin would try getting underfoot.

When Gavin pulled an odd-looking camera from his backseat, Layla lifted a brow. "What is that?"

He smiled. "A Vericon 12D. It's a high-tech camera that's mainly used underwater. Flipper messed around with it so we could use it on land, as well."

"Flipper?"

"Yes, Flipper. One of my team members. He's into

technology and all that high-tech stuff," Gavin said as they walked side by side.

"Surely Flipper isn't his real name."

Gavin chuckled. "His real name is David Holloway. His code name is Flipper."

"Oh," she said, glancing up at him. "Do you have a code name?"

"Yes."

"What is it?"

He saw no reason not to tell her since his grandmother was well aware of it, too. His teammates called Gavin by his code name whenever they came to visit. "Viper."

Layla scrunched up her features. "Viper?"

"Yes, Viper."

"Why?"

"Why what?"

"Why do they call you Viper?"

He stopped walking to answer her, and when he stopped, she did, too. He hadn't noticed before how small she seemed, standing close to him. He figured he'd never noticed because usually when he faced her he was fixated on her mouth.

"The reason I'm called Viper is because when I set my sights on a target, I don't give up until I make a hit. I love taking the enemy down."

She tilted her head to look up at him. "Do you consider me an enemy?"

He didn't hesitate. "No." She wasn't the enemy, but he had every intention of taking her down…right into his bed.

Evidently satisfied with his response, she looked around him, back toward where the truck was parked.

Then she turned around. She did it several times and each time he saw her confusion deepen.

"Is something wrong?" he finally asked.

She whipped around to look at him. "Yes, something is wrong."

He glanced around before returning his gaze to her. "What?"

"Someone moved my marker. It's gone."

He lifted a brow. "What do you mean your marker is gone?"

She frowned. "Just what I said. Someone moved my marker. It's not here."

Gavin released a deep sigh. "Why would anyone move your marker? Are you sure you put one down?"

"Of course I'm sure," she answered in an annoyed tone. "Someone moved it."

Gavin raised his gaze upward. "And who would do that?"

"I don't know, but someone did."

He shook his head. "Layla, the Silver Spurs is out in the middle of nowhere. And this particular spot is considered way outside our working area, almost six miles from the main house. No one would deliberately come on this land to remove your marker."

"Well, someone did, Gavin. I marked the digging site," she said with deep irritation in her voice.

Gavin stared down at her. "Are you sure? Maybe your mind is clouded right now. I can understand my kiss leaving you that way."

Her frown deepened. "I'm serious, Gavin."

"So am I, Layla."

Exasperation darkened her expression. "Will you get your mind off sex for a minute?"

A smile touched his lips. "My mind wasn't on sex," he said. "It was on that kiss we shared. But since you've pulled sex into the conversation…it's hard to think of anything other than getting you in my bed when you look so good."

Layla pushed to the back of her mind that she'd deliberately taken more time with her appearance just so he would think she looked good. That was before she'd come out here and discovered her marker *had* been removed.

"You moved it, didn't you?" she asked with an accusing glare.

"Now why would I want to do that?"

When she didn't say anything but continued to stare at him, his amusement was replaced with a deep frown. "I have no reason to mess with any marker you claim to have put down. This is the first time I've been out this far from the house since returning home."

He rubbed a hand down his face in frustration. "If that marker has in fact been removed, then that means someone trespassed on this land to do it. Although for the life of me I can't imagine who would have cared enough to do such a thing. I just think you're confused as to where you placed the damn marker," he said, glancing around. "The south pasture is rather large. Maybe it's all the way on the other side."

"I am not confused and it's not on the other side. Not only did I map its coordinates, I recall parking near those tree stumps and walking twenty to thirty feet to my right. The marker was a wooden stake with a red flag on it, and I planted it exactly where we would dig."

"If you're sure of that, then you need to consider

who knows you're here. And who would want to see you fail."

She lifted her chin. "And why wouldn't your name head the list? The deal we agreed on means I would have to sleep with you if I fail."

Gavin took a step closer to her. "Whether you fail or succeed means nothing to me because I have every intention of sleeping with you regardless of the outcome of this dig."

Layla was taken aback by Gavin's words. Of all the audacity. She placed her hands on her hips. Anger poured through her. "And how do you figure that?"

"Because, like I explained to you earlier, I'm Viper. I set my sights on a target. I don't give up until I make a hit. You are my target, Layla, and I plan to break down your resolve."

She all but stomped her foot in frustration. "And I've told you that won't happen. What part of that don't you understand?"

"This part," he said, brushing his finger across her cheek. She couldn't downplay her sharp intake of breath or the way her body shuddered beneath his touch. "You do something to me and I do something to you," he continued. "We do things to each other. We can only hold out for so long."

She tilted her lips stubbornly. "I will fight you on that with my last breath."

"And I suggest you save that breath for that explosive orgasm you're going to have."

Layla opened her mouth to blast out a resounding retort but then she closed it without responding. What was the use of arguing with him about something she knew for a fact wouldn't be happening, no matter what he thought? So what if his touch warmed her to the core? She would put him out of her mind. She had more important things to be concerned with. Like who'd removed her marker and why. No matter what Gavin might assume, she was not imagining things.

"My marker was removed, Gavin."

He rolled his eyes. "We're back to that again?"

"Yes. The dig is why I'm here. Why I crazily agreed to your deal. If you didn't remove the marker, then who did?"

Gavin drew in a deep breath, trying to hold his aggravation and frustration at bay. He knew for certain she was not incompetent. So someone had removed the marker like she claimed.

"Here, hold this," he said, handing Flipper's camera to her. He then began walking, studying the ground. He slowed when he saw footprints he knew weren't hers or his. He crouched down and pressed his finger to one, touching the indention in the earth. It was cold. The tracks looked fresh, as if they hadn't been made any more than forty-eight hours ago. Whose prints were they? One of his men? Possibly, but for some reason he doubted it. All his men had been working in the north and west pastures for the past few days. None had any reason to come to the south pasture.

It appeared more weight had been placed on the left leg as that impression was deeper. He also noted the sole of the right shoe appeared more worn than the left.

He stood and backtracked to where Layla said she'd parked her vehicle when she'd come out here. He walked, looking down and around the entire time. When he'd gone about thirty feet he stopped. Crouching down again he studied the earth and that's when he saw the small plug where the marker had been. He glanced to the right and the left, studying the ground. Again he saw footprints. The same ones.

He stood and slowly walked back to Layla. Without saying anything, he took the camera out of her hand. "Thanks."

She raised a brow. "Well?"

She hadn't asked what he'd been doing. She was smart enough to figure things out. He was using his skill as a SEAL to determine if there was proof that the marker had been removed.

He met her inquisitive expression. "I saw footprints. I also saw where the marker had been. You're right. The marker was removed."

"Why? By whom?"

"Don't know, Layla." He honestly didn't have a clue. The Silver Spurs was private property. And although there were numerous ways to get onto the property, he couldn't imagine anyone having a reason to come to this particular area. The one thing he didn't see was tire tracks. But the person could have parked elsewhere and walked.

"I planned on using this camera to scan the area," he said. "I suggest you make a list of anyone who might have a reason for wanting you not to succeed in your dig. And make sure you take me off the list. I told you my position and I'm sticking to it."

And without saying anything else, he walked off.

Chapter 8

I told you my position and I'm sticking to it.

Later that day, Layla paced the floor. Gavin Blake was bullheaded, stubborn and full of himself. He was crazy if he actually thought he could get her to bend to his will. No way. No how. So why was she pacing the floor, wearing out both herself and her shoes?

She had watched him use that high-tech camera, but she hadn't been impressed with his findings. Gavin agreed there was something buried in the area but he refused to consider it was Jesse James's loot. To his way of thinking, since that area used to be a popular hunting spot, the camera had picked up nothing more than buried bullet shells.

Layla refused to believe her research was wrong. There was buried treasure somewhere in the south pasture, she was sure of it. And as far as who would not want to see her succeed in this project, that could be a number of people, including her parents. But she didn't for one minute think they would go so far as to sabotage the dig site. They were hoping failing at this would make Layla realize she should pursue medical school, after all. Then there was her older colleague Dr. Clayburn and others at the university who felt she'd been too young and inexperienced for such an expensive project. Did the person who removed the marker actually think she wouldn't have kept the coordinates and just re-marked it? That she would give up so easily?

She stopped pacing when she heard a knock on the door. The tightening in her stomach told her who it was. Why was Gavin here? She had spoken to Ms. Melody an hour or so ago when she'd called to invite Layla to dinner. Layla had regretfully declined, knowing she would not have been the best of company this evening. Besides, she needed distance from Gavin. Evidently he hadn't taken the hint.

The knock on the door sounded again. There was no need to pretend she wasn't there when Gavin knew she was. Crossing the room, she opened the door to find Gavin with a tray of food in his hand.

"After you told Gramma Mel you weren't coming to dinner, she strongly suggested I bring you something. I believe she thinks I'm the reason you didn't come to breakfast or dinner."

Layla moved aside to let him in. Tray and all. Especially the tray. Everything was covered but the food smelled good. "I'll let her know that's not the case when I talk to her tomorrow." No need for him to know he *had* been a factor in her decision.

"She might not be here. Not sure when she's leaving, whether it's tomorrow or the day after."

Layla closed the door and followed him to the kitchen. "Leaving? Ms. Melody is going somewhere?"

"Yes, to a library convention in Cincinnati for a week. But I'm sure she won't leave without saying good-bye. And if you expect me to take her place and make sure you don't miss meals…that won't be happening."

She frowned. "I never asked your grandmother to cook for me, Gavin."

He put the tray on the kitchen table and turned to her. "Don't you think I know that?"

"Then why did you insinuate otherwise?"

"Did I?"

She crossed her arms over her chest. "Yes, you did."

"Then I apologize." She couldn't help noticing how his gaze roamed over her. "You changed clothes," he said.

Was that disappointment she heard in his voice? Seeing his gaze had moved to her chest, she dropped her hands to her sides. "I showered."

"I know. You smell good. And you look good in that dress. Nice legs."

She would have appreciated the compliment if she wasn't still so uptight about that marker being moved. "I want to go back out to the dig site tomorrow and look around, Gavin. This time I want to use my own detector."

"If you're still concerned about why the marker was moved, I might have a reason for that."

She came into the kitchen, trying to ignore the way he was checking out her legs and the way her nipples responded to his blatant appraisal. "What reason is that?"

"Clete. He's an older man we hired years ago to keep the grounds clear of trash and debris as well as repair anything that needs fixing. That way Caldwell and the men can concentrate mainly on the cattle. When I mentioned the marker to Gramma Mel, she reminded me that Clete has a tendency to move stuff when he's keeping the land cleared."

"But why would he remove the marker?"

Gavin shrugged. "He probably didn't know what it was and thought it was trash. He and his wife left a few days ago to visit their son who is in the navy and stationed in Hawaii. I'll talk to him when he gets back."

Layla drew in a deep breath, feeling somewhat relieved. The thought of someone tampering with the dig site had definitely bothered her.

"Sit down and eat. I promised Gramma Mel that I would make sure you did."

She raised a suspicious eye. "Why?"

"Why what?"

"Why would you care one way or the other if I eat?"

A slow, sexy smile touched his lips and her womb seemed to contract with the weight of that smile. And his dimples had bone-melting fire spreading through her blood. "The reason I care is because I don't want you to start losing weight."

She crossed her arms over her chest again, and then quickly dropped them by her sides when she saw his gaze shift back to her chest. Could the man think of anything other than sex for a minute? "And what does my weight have to do with you?"

"When I make love to you, I want to feel meat on your bones."

His statement answered her earlier question. No, he

obviously couldn't think of anything other than sex. "We won't be making love, Gavin."

"Your food is getting cold."

He was blatantly ignoring what she'd said. "I'll eat after you leave."

He chuckled. "If that was a hint that you want me to go, forget it. I want to make sure you eat."

She frowned. "What do you plan to do? Stay here and watch me."

"Yes, that was my intent."

He was serious. "I don't need a babysitter, Gavin."

"No. What you need is a lover, Layla. And you never did answer my question from last night. When was the last time you made love with a man?"

"And I don't intend to answer it because it's none of your business."

If he insisted on staying, she would ignore him. She moved to the table where he'd placed her food. Her mouth began watering the moment she uncovered it. Fried chicken, mashed potatoes, broccoli, candied yams and iced tea. And a slice of chocolate cake for dessert.

A smile lit her face. "Your grandmother is something else." Layla walked over to the sink to wash her hands. After grabbing utensils out of a drawer, she returned to the table and found Gavin sitting there. Did he plan to actually watch her eat? Didn't he have anything better to do?

Deciding nothing would stand between her and that food, she sat down, bowed her head and said grace, determined to ignore him. When she slid a forkful of mashed potatoes between her lips, she closed her eyes and groaned. Delicious.

"If you get off eating mashed potatoes, I can only imagine your reaction when we make love."

A part of her wanted to claim she wouldn't enjoy it. She quickly dismissed the idea when she glanced over at him. A woman could climax just from staring at him. Even so, she said, "In your dreams."

"My dreams will one day become your reality, Layla."

She decided not to argue with him anymore. But if he was intent on watching her, she might as well ask him a few questions. Get him talking, so she wouldn't think about how good he looked sitting there. How sexy.

She took a sip of her tea. "You mentioned your teammate named Flipper. Any others you're close to?"

"I'm close to all of them. We're a team."

"How many?"

"Enough."

She rolled her eyes. Had she asked about classified information or something? "I'm sure you're closer to some of the guys more than others."

He leaned back in the chair as if getting comfortable. She couldn't recall the last time she'd shared a private, intimate dinner with a man. And, whether she liked admitting it or not, this *was* intimate. They were alone, sitting at a table with the backdrop of a blazing fire roaring in the fireplace.

"In that case, I would say Flipper, Bane, Coop, Mac and Nick. The six of us went through all phases of training together. A couple of years ago, Nick took a job with Homeland Security. He needed a little more stability in his life when his wife gave birth to triplets."

As if he felt right at home, he stood and went to the refrigerator to get a beer and then returned to his chair.

"Bane is a master sniper," he continued, popping the cap. "Coop is the mastermind behind most of our strategic moves. Mac is slightly older than the rest of us and likes to think he can keep us in line most of the time. He's been married for ages, has four kids and likes to impose his words of wisdom on us whether we want to hear them or not. And Flip can hold his breath under water longer than any human I know." He chuckled as he took a swig. "We're convinced Flipper has gills hidden somewhere."

Layla heard the fondness in his voice when he spoke of his teammates. "What's a master sniper?"

He looked at her. She thought he would say she was asking for classified information but then he said, "A master sniper is the best shot on the team. Bane is one badass. He can hit a target with one eye closed. He's covered all our backs more than once." He paused. "Bane and his wife, Crystal, are renewing their vows next month."

"Oh, were he and his wife separated for a while or something?"

"Yes, you could say that."

Layla knew he was being elusive but she was getting used to it. She didn't have to ask if his job was dangerous. Anyone who knew of the navy SEALs was aware of the types of missions they went on. She finished the rest of her meal in silence, with him watching her. She was tempted to ask if he wanted some but knew the trouble she'd gotten into when she'd asked him that question the last time.

She took a sip of her iced tea and looked over at him when she pushed her plate aside. "Satisfied, Gavin?"

He gave her a crooked smile. "Baby, my satisfaction will come when I get inside of you."

The glass nearly slipped from her hand. She recovered long enough to set it down by the plate. The impact of his words had her burning from the inside out. "Why do you say such things?"

"Just keeping it honest."

Gavin liked rattling Layla. Evidently she wasn't used to a man talking to her this way, telling her what he wanted and how he planned to make her feel. While watching her eat, his imagination had run wild. The conversation hadn't distracted him enough to demolish his desire. He doubted that was possible. He wanted her. He'd made that point pretty damn clear and he knew she wanted him as well, so what was the holdup?

"I've finished eating so you can leave now."

He held her gaze, felt the flare of response in their bodies when they looked at each other. Giving in to temptation, he lightly traced his fingertips along her arm. He felt her shiver beneath his touch. He heard her sharp intake of breath. "Why are you fighting this, Layla?"

"And why are you being so persistent?"

He could tell her that one of the reasons was because he hadn't been with a woman in six months, eight days, twelve hours and no telling how many minutes. Being around her was taking its toll. However, telling her such a thing would make him sound like a greedy jerk with only sex on his mind. That was only partly true. The other part was that he found her as fascinating as he found her beautiful.

"Being persistent is part of my nature."

When he saw her lips form a frown, his groin hardened and he couldn't help drawing in a ragged breath. Standing, he said, "I'll leave you alone now and report to Gramma Mel that you ate all your food."

He reached to remove the tray, but she blocked him. "Surely you don't think I'll let you return with dirty dishes."

"We've had a conversation about the purpose of a dishwasher before, Layla."

"That might be your way of doing things but it's not mine. I will wash the dishes and return them to Ms. Melody tomorrow," she said, standing.

Doing so brought her right smack in front of him. Gavin knew that if she inched closer, she would feel his erection. Even so, he intended to kiss her before he left.

"Walk me to the door, Layla."

From the look in her eyes, he knew she was aware of his plan. He watched her nibble her bottom lip. "Relax, baby. I won't bite."

She stopped nibbling her lips long enough to lift her chin and stare into his eyes. "You'll do something even worse, Gavin."

"What is that?"

"You will make me want you."

He eased closer, pressing his body to hers, wanting her to feel his erection. There was no way she could miss it. "Welcome to the club. And you already want me, Layla. Why are you having a hard time accepting that?"

Gavin could tell she was at a loss for words, which suited him just fine. He had other uses for her mouth. He leaned in to capture her lips.

* * *

Why was she having such a hard time accepting this? Layla asked herself when Gavin took her mouth. She didn't resist. She couldn't. In fact she felt herself practically melting into his arms. That was why, she reasoned, she wrapped her arms around his neck. Otherwise she would become a puddle on the floor.

He kissed her with an intensity she reciprocated in every part of her body. His mouth locked onto hers, not leaving any part of her mouth untouched. He tapped into areas she hadn't known existed. He was staking his claim on her mouth in a scandalous way. It was as if he was intentionally making her crazy for his kiss.

And then there was the feel of his erection, pressing hard against her middle. What man could get *that* aroused? To know she was the cause sent heated shivers through her body. The hard tips of her breasts pressed through the material of her dress as if eager to make contact with his chest.

Gavin broke off the kiss and when Layla drew in a deep breath, she was swept off her feet into his arms. He sat back down at the table with her firmly planted in his lap. Before she could ask just what he thought he was doing, his mouth was on hers. And just like before, this kiss robbed her of her senses, made her purr deep in her throat. It was a good thing his arm gripped her tightly otherwise she would topple to the floor. His hand was on her thigh, slowly caressing her skin underneath her dress.

Maybe she needed to ask herself why she was letting him do such a thing when she'd never let any man take such liberties before. Hadn't she kicked Sonny Paul in the groin when he thought he could reach into her blouse and touch her breast? Why did she believe this was different? Just because Gavin's mouth was driving her crazy with lust—could she accept this as okay?

And why was she still clutching him around the neck as if her life depended on their mouths being so intimately locked? Red-hot passion was making her dazed.

Somewhere in the haziness of her mind, she noted he had stood, without their mouths disconnecting. He was moving, headed somewhere rather quickly. It was only when he placed her on the bed that she regained her senses. Snatching her mouth from his, she scrambled away from him.

She blinked upon seeing he was about to take off his shirt. "What do you think you're doing?"

He stared down at her, panting like he'd run a marathon. His eyes, she saw, were glazed with heated lust to such a degree it made her heart pound. "About to make love to you, Layla." He then whipped his shirt over his head.

Seeing him bare chested caused goose bumps to ripple all over her skin. She scrambled farther away from him. "No you're not!"

He stared at her. "Can you look at me and say you don't want me to make love to you?"

She nervously licked her bottom lip and looked away. Yes, she could say it but she couldn't look at him while doing so. Mainly because she *did* want him to make love to her. There was no doubt in her mind that the sheets on the bed were calling their names.

"Layla. Look at me."

No, she wouldn't look at him. Nor would she tell him anything. Scrambling off the bed, she stood and began straightening her clothes before quickly walking out of the bedroom. "I'm showing you the door, Gavin," she called over her shoulder.

Once she reached the door, she waited. It took him a few minutes to follow her. He probably needed time to put his shirt back on and get his lusty mind under control.

When she saw him walking toward her he had an unreadable expression on his face. She drew in a deep breath. What thoughts were going through his mind? Did he think she was nothing more than a tease because she'd stoked his fire and then doused it with water? She would admit to having gotten caught up in the moment like he had. However, although he was ready to take things to the next level, she was not.

When he got closer, she saw the way he stared at her and figured he was angry to the point that he would walk out the door without saying anything to her.

She figured wrong. When Gavin stopped before opening the door, he turned dark, livid eyes on her. He then said in a furious voice, "The next time we kiss, Layla, will be when we make love. It's going to be a package deal."

He then opened the door and left.

Chapter 9

Late afternoon the next day, Gavin walked out on the porch with a steaming cup of coffee. He couldn't believe he'd jogged around the ranch house twenty times last night. That would be equivalent to ten miles. When was the last time he'd done that?

On top of his workout last night, he'd gotten up at the crack of dawn to ride the range with Caldwell and his men. Sharing breakfast with them over an open fire had brought back memories. Most of the men who worked for Gavin had worked for his dad and had known Gavin when he'd been a kid. Although they called him boss, he knew they did it out of respect and not because he was involved in the day-to-day operations. Caldwell took care of the place. No matter how long Gavin was away from the ranch, he rested easy at night knowing the Silver Spurs was in good hands. Gavin also knew that whenever he returned Caldwell had no problem relinquishing that leadership role to him.

He took another sip of coffee as he eased down to sit on the steps. The cold weather was settling in. It was hard to believe Thanksgiving was next month. He'd gotten word that morning from his commanding officer that the team would be headed out again in late January. At least his teammates with families would get to spend the holidays with them. Gavin wondered if his grandmother would hang around the ranch this year. Because he was rarely home during the holidays, Gramma Mel usually flew to Saint Louis to spend time with her sister and her family.

"How did things go today with Caldwell and the men?"

Gavin glanced over his shoulder at the sound of his grandmother's voice. "Good, but that's no surprise. They know how to keep things going in my absence. And I covered just about everything with Phil yesterday. We talked again today and the books look good." The only thing he hadn't done that he'd wanted to do today was take another ride out to the dig site.

"When do you expect Mr. Clete back in town?" he asked.

"By the middle of next week," she said, taking a seat in the porch swing.

"Good." Although Gavin felt certain Clete was the one who'd moved the marker, he wanted to be absolutely sure. However, for the life of him, he couldn't imagine anyone else coming onto the property and tampering with Layla's markers. What purpose would it serve?

Flip's camera had picked up something underground, both in her marked spot as well as another spot close by.

Like he'd told her, it was probably nothing more than bullet shells or branding irons. One section did have a relatively higher reading than others but he'd figured out a reason for that, as well. Buried Native American artifacts. Gavin's grandfather had claimed this had been Native American land generations ago. If Layla's research was as thorough as she claimed, she would already know that.

"I had a salad earlier, but if you're hungry I can fix dinner."

"No need. I plan to go into town in a few and I'll grab something at the café."

No way he would tell his grandmother that in addition to dinner he intended to make a booty call. Word was out that he was home and a ton of women had left voice mails. On the drive into town, he would decide which woman would be the recipient of his visit. Not having Layla was getting to him. He needed to get laid and then he could be more rational about her, take his time seducing her without losing his cool.

"Looks like you aren't the only one going into town, Gavin. Now, doesn't she look extra pretty?"

He followed his grandmother's gaze. Layla was crossing the yard and walking toward them. He had seen her in dresses before, but this was one with a skirt that was shorter in the front and longer in the back. Instead of boots she wore high heels and she had a knitted shawl around her shoulders.

Her hair was styled the way he liked best, flowing around her shoulders. And he could tell she was wearing makeup—not much…except for the ruby-red lip color. He frowned, refusing to let her get next to him the way she had last night. He'd been stupid enough to think their evening would end differently. Namely, in bed together.

"Good evening, Ms. Melody. Gavin."

He did the gentlemanly thing and stood. He couldn't help noticing she'd given his grandmother a huge smile. But the one she'd given him was forced. Not that it bothered him one iota.

"Layla," he said, letting his gaze roam all over her.

His grandmother moved forward and gave her a hug. "Now, don't you look pretty. Have big plans for the evening?"

Layla shrugged her shoulders, keeping her focus on Ms. Melody and ignoring Gavin. "Not that big. The equipment arrives tomorrow and my team the day after. Then it's all work and no play. I decided to spend my last day of freedom doing something I enjoy doing but rarely have time for—going to a movie."

"By yourself?" Gramma Mel asked.

Layla chuckled. "Yes, by myself."

"What are you going to see?"

"That new romantic comedy with Julia Roberts."

"Now, isn't that a coincidence. I was going into town to see that one myself," Gavin said.

Both Layla and Gramma Mel turned to stare at Gavin with raised brows. He smiled at both women's expressions. He then directed his next statement to Layla. "Since we're going to see the same movie, is there any reason we can't go together?"

Gavin was certain there was but he knew Layla wouldn't call him out on it in front of his grandmother. When she didn't say anything he leaned closer to ask, "Well, is there?"

As if recovering from her initial shock, she opened

her mouth, probably to say something that would blister his ear. Then she quickly closed it, seeming to remember that his grandmother was standing there, listening to their exchange.

"No, there's no reason," she said. "I'm just surprised you would want to see a *chick flick*. I took you for a blood-and-guts sort of guy."

He shook his head. "As a SEAL, I see too much of that in real life. A chick flick should be interesting. Besides, I like Julia Roberts."

"In that case, I see no reason why we can't go together," she said.

Although she'd tried to sound cheerful about it, he knew she wasn't. Was that her teeth he heard grinding? "Great. We can go in my truck. I just need to grab my Stetson and jacket."

"I enjoyed the movie, didn't you?"

Layla had pretty much given him the silent treatment since leaving the Silver Spurs earlier but he didn't seem to mind. In fact he seemed amused by it. "Yes, I enjoyed it."

She probably would have enjoyed it even more had he not been there to cloud her concentration. It had been hard to focus on the huge movie screen with a sexy man sitting beside her.

"When are you going to stop acting childish, Layla?"

She glanced over at him. "Childish? You think *I'm* acting childish when you told me last night that we won't kiss again unless sex is part of the mix?"

"Yes, that's what I said and I meant it."

"Well, sorry if you think I'm acting childish but I'm

the one acting more adult than you. All you can think about is—"

"Making love to you."

She swallowed, seeing a picture of that very thing in her mind. "Yes."

"Can't help it. You do things to me, Layla."

When she was honest with herself, she could admit that he did things to her, as well. But she would never admit it to him. He was just like all the other men she'd known, which is why she'd sworn off relationships. All men wanted of a woman was a roll between the sheets. She wanted more from life; she had a career to build. Men and sex only got in the way of her goals.

She glanced over at him. "You were an only child, right?"

"Yes, as far as I know."

When she looked at him in surprise he added, "My mother deserted us when I was eight and never came back. For all I know, she could have married and had more kids by now."

Layla nodded. "She and your dad got a divorce?"

"No, but she might have changed her name and started over. Who knows?"

Layla didn't say anything for a moment. "You've never tried to find her?"

"No."

"Not even when your father was killed in the war?"

His jaw tightened. "Especially not then. If she didn't return to see him while he was living, I sure as hell didn't plan to give her the opportunity to see him dead," he said in a biting tone. "Dad always believed she would come back to us. Even said he understood her need to get away. After all, he'd talked her into coming to Cornerstone."

"Where was she from?"

"New York. Manhattan. They met while he was on military business at the United Nations. They'd only known each other a week when they married. They met one night at a restaurant, a month after her only family, an aunt, died."

"So when they met, she had no living family?"

"No."

He didn't say anything else for a long moment, and then he added, "According to Dad she lasted out here longer than he expected her to. She tried being a good wife, and I remember her being a good mom. Dad placed a lot of blame on himself since he had to carry out a lot of missions, leaving her here with Gramma Mel and Grampa Gavin. And when I came along a year later, he thought she'd adjusted."

"But she hadn't?"

"Evidently not. One day she up and left. She told my grandparents she needed to get away for a while and asked them to watch me. She said she'd be back before Dad returned from his overseas tour. Then she got in her car—the one Dad bought for her—and drove off."

"And she never came back?"

He shook his head. "No, she never came back. Months later, when Dad returned home and found her gone, he was heartbroken. She left him a note saying she would come back. But she never did."

"And after all this time, you've never tried finding her?"

"No. She decided she didn't want me or Dad in her life."

* * *

Gavin inwardly admitted that more than once he had thought about locating his mother, if for no other reason than to ask her why she never came back. One of his former SEAL teammates, Nick Stover, worked for Homeland Security. All Gavin had to do was give Nick her name and there was no doubt in his mind that Nick would tell Gavin her whereabouts. A part of him knew the main reason he hadn't done so was his fear of what he would find out. What if his mother had never wanted him or loved his dad? At times it was easier to do what his father had done and believe the best…even if it was a fairy tale.

He drew in a deep breath. Why had he shared any of that with Layla when he'd never shared it with a woman before? For some reason, when she'd asked if he was an only child, the floodgates had opened. Emotions he usually kept locked inside had come pouring out.

"Any other family besides Ms. Melody? What about aunts, uncles or cousins?"

He figured she was asking for conversational purposes only, so he obliged her. "My grandmother has a younger sister living in Saint Louis. Her only grandson, Benjamin, and I are close. We're more like brothers than cousins. He spent a lot of his summers here. Ben's a year older and in the Marines. Right now he's stationed in Afghanistan, and we're hoping he'll be home for the holidays."

He glanced over at her. "What about you? Any cousins?"

She shook her head. "No. My grandparents didn't have any siblings and they had one child. I never knew my mother's parents. They died in a boating accident when she was in her teens."

He said nothing as he drove. They were ten minutes from his home and although there had been sexual chemistry between them as usual, they'd managed to keep it under control. That was a surprise since his plans for this evening had originally been to end up in some woman's bed. A part of him couldn't believe he'd given up the chance for sex just to spend time in Layla's company. And he had to grudgingly admit that although she'd tried to ignore him for most of the evening, he had enjoyed being with her.

Moments later, he pulled into the yard in front of the ranch house. His grandmother would be leaving tomorrow and he would have the house all to himself. Bringing the car to a stop, he cut the ignition and turned to Layla. "I'll see you inside."

"That's not necessary," she said, already opening her door to get out. "Thanks for driving me into town and joining me at the movies."

Although she'd said he didn't have to see her in, he walked beside her anyway. "You're welcome, although I know you really didn't prefer my company."

When she didn't deny what he'd said, he chuckled. "No wonder you don't have a boyfriend."

She glanced over at him. "What makes you think I don't have a boyfriend?"

"I asked Gramma Mel if any man had visited you here and she said no."

Layla frowned. "That doesn't mean anything."

He chuckled again. "Yes, it does. If you had a boyfriend he would have come here, if for nothing else but to check on you. To see how you were doing. To feel out the competition. To stake his claim."

Even in the moonlight, he saw her roll her eyes. "Not all men are territorial, Gavin."

"Any man connected to you would be."

They had made it to the porch. When he offered her hand to assist her up the steps, she said, "No need." And then she walked up to the door without his help. He knew why. All it would have taken was one touch and they would have lit up like the Fourth of July and they both knew it.

"Thanks for seeing me home. At least my temporary home."

"No problem. What time does the equipment arrive tomorrow?"

"Sometime before noon. Thanks again for allowing me to store the equipment in that old barn."

He nodded. "When will your team get here?"

"Some will start arriving the day after tomorrow and will be staying at a hotel in town. We're hoping to finish the dig in a couple of weeks and then we'll be on our way."

A couple of weeks. He had every intention of making love to her before she left. In the meantime, he planned to stick to his resolve about not kissing her until she was ready to give in to their desire—even if it killed him.

"Good night, Layla."

When she just stared at him, he smiled. Evidently she'd expected him to kiss her good-night. "I'll stand here until you go inside."

She nodded. "Good night." And then she quickly opened the door and went in.

He didn't move until he heard the lock click in place.

Then he tilted his Stetson back from his face as he moved down the steps. Not kissing her had been hard but he meant what he'd told her yesterday. The next time they kissed would be when they made love. Just thinking about how intense that kiss would be sent heat through his body, especially to his lower extremities.

If he hadn't needed to meet with Caldwell and his men first thing in the morning, he would have taken another ten-mile run around the ranch.

Chapter 10

Three days later, while out riding Acer, Gavin came upon Layla and her excavation team in the south pasture. Most of them had arrived a couple of days ago but he hadn't been around to meet them. He and his men had driven the cows to the north pasture where they would be kept during the winter months.

Over the next few weeks, the cows would be fed to maintain their good heath during the cold spell. Unlike the south pasture, there was plenty of grazing land in the north and a small pond to help irrigate the area. The pregnant cows had to be separated and tagged and the process had taken a lot longer than expected.

Just as well, he thought, as he brought Acer to a slow trot and then a complete stop at the top of the hill. He'd needed distance from Layla. With his grandmother in

Cincinnati and him being out on the range for the past three days he'd assured their paths didn't cross.

But now he was back and as he looked down at the activity going on below, he couldn't stop his gaze from seeking her out. At first he didn't see her, but when the crowd dispersed somewhat, there she was, looking as beautiful as he knew she would be.

He rubbed his hand down his face. Nothing about this seduction was working out like he'd figured it would. It seemed he would be the one to break before Layla. He just didn't get it. They wanted each other. That was definite. So how could she keep fighting the attraction? Desire had to be eating away at her as much as it was at him.

He hadn't seen her since that night they'd gone to a movie. Seeing her now made him realize that after all those hot and steamy kisses, and copping one good feel of her thighs, she had gotten into his system. That was crazy. Women didn't get into his system—ever. So how had she managed it?

He fixed his gaze on her as if three days could have changed her. They hadn't. Even from where he sat unobserved on Acer's back, he could still see her flawless skin. She looked just as young as the members of her team. Her students. Wearing her hair in a ponytail, jeans, a pullover sweater and boots should have made her fit in. Yet there was something about Layla that stood out. Something that made his stomach churn and his groin ache every time he saw her.

He never did make it into town just for that booty call. The only woman he wanted was Layla.

Bottom line—she had stirred something deep inside of him that wouldn't go away. At least not until he was inside of her, all the way to the hilt. It was only when his body connected with hers that he would be able to rid his mind of the belief that she was the only woman for him.

Watching her team work, he remembered something else. Namely that phone conversation he'd had with Clete yesterday. The old man recalled seeing the marker. He'd known why it was there, since he'd heard talk in town about someone digging on the property. But according to Clete, he hadn't moved it. That made Gavin wonder who had. Both he and Clete agreed the wind could not have blown it away nor could it have gotten washed away by the rain. Which meant someone had come on Gavin's property and pulled it out. Why?

Gavin hadn't been receptive to the idea of Layla digging on the Silver Spurs. But if someone was intentionally setting her up to fail, they would have to deal with him. Flip's camera had picked up something buried here. That made Gavin wonder if someone intended to unearth whatever was buried before Layla did so they could get the credit? His jaw tightened at the thought. Not on his property. And not on his watch. And not with his woman.

His woman…

How in the hell could he consider her his woman when he hadn't bedded her yet? Besides, Gavin Blake never claimed any woman. But as he fixed his gaze on Layla, he knew that she was his. Bedded or not.

Layla had been reading what looked like a report when suddenly, as if she felt him watching her, she tilted her head up and stared straight at him.

* * *

A lump formed in Layla's throat. Beneath the brightness of the noon sun sat a gorgeous man on a beautiful horse. She'd seen the horse before. One day after arriving on the Silver Spurs, she'd noticed when one of the men had taken it out of the stall to groom it. She had been admiring the animal when the man, Curtis, told her the horse's name was Acer and that he belonged to the boss. This was the first time she'd seen Gavin on the horse and the sight took her breath away.

It had been three long days since he'd taken her to the movies and later walked her to the guest cottage, leaving her there and blatantly ignoring her since. Honestly, what had she expected? For him to have kissed her good-night regardless of what he'd said the night before? What he'd done was to toss the ball in her court. He probably figured she didn't have the guts to play it.

But it wasn't that she didn't have the guts. She didn't have the time or the inclination… Oh, who was she fooling? Definitely not herself. If anything, not seeing him these past few days had made her realize that out of sight, out of mind didn't work when it came to Gavin.

"Who in the blazes is that?"

Layla didn't have to move her gaze from Gavin to know one of her students, Tammy Clemons, stood beside her looking at Gavin, as well. "That's Gavin Blake. He and his grandmother own the Silver Spurs. They were kind enough to let us dig here."

"Um, maybe I should thank him. Properly."

A sudden stab of jealousy ran through Layla, and as much as she tried pushing it back, she couldn't. *Properly?* She didn't have to wonder just what Tammy meant by that. It was rumored around campus that Tammy often bragged about sleeping with her professors to get better grades.

Layla knew not to believe everything she heard, but Tammy's behavior made Layla think there was some truth in that claim. Especially since Tammy was here on this dig. Some said her latest conquest was Dr. Clayburn. That wouldn't surprise Layla since the married man and father of two was known to have roving eyes. More than once she'd heard about his late night meetings with female students. Those meetings were something Layla was certain the college president had heard about but had chosen to ignore.

Tammy's grades should have made her ineligible for this team, but Dr. Clayburn had personally added her name above other more well-deserving students. When Layla had brought it to Dr. Clayburn's attention, he'd gotten upset that she'd questioned him. He'd reminded her that he had the power to withdraw the school's funding for the excavation.

"That guy is what you would call a real cowboy. And I didn't have to travel to Texas to get one."

Layla saw the twenty-one-year-old lick her lips with her gaze trained on Gavin. It shouldn't matter to Layla. But it did. Why? She didn't want to be Gavin's bed partner so why should it bother her if someone else did?

"Need I remind you, Tammy, that you're here to work on this project?"

Tammy frowned. "No, Dr. Harris, you don't need to remind me of anything. Just like I'm sure I don't need to remind you that although we're dedicated to this dig during the day, the nighttime hours are ours to enjoy. And I intend to enjoy him."

The young woman stated the words so matter-of-factly that Layla had to take pause. Was Tammy the type of woman Gavin wanted? The kind who could handle both work and play without breaking a sweat? A woman who enjoyed the challenge of both?

Layla was about to reply when a huge smile covered Tammy's face. "He's seen me checking him out and is coming down for me."

The thought that Gavin might be showing some interest in Tammy made Layla's chest ache.

She turned her attention back to Gavin. He was sprinting down the hill on the huge horse and she recalled something he'd once said. When he saw a target he wanted he went after it. Was he now galloping down the hill because he wanted Tammy? The young woman evidently thought so.

He looked good on the horse, wearing a Stetson on his head. Tammy was right. He was the epitome of what a cowboy should be. Tough. Rugged. Fearless. But then she could probably use those same adjectives to describe him as a navy SEAL. Gavin slowed his horse to a trot when it hit level ground and then he headed in their direction.

"Didn't I tell you he was coming to check me out?" Tammy said, with a ton of confidence in her voice.

The young woman didn't lack any faith in herself as a woman who could draw a man's interest. Gavin reached them and brought the horse to a stop. A lump formed in Layla's throat when she saw his attention hadn't even flickered to Tammy. He was staring straight at Layla.

"Gavin."

"Layla."

"And I'm Tammy," the younger woman quickly said,

not waiting for an introduction. She flashed Gavin a huge, flirty smile.

Gavin switched his gaze from Layla to Tammy. "Hello, Tammy."

"You look good on your horse. I would love for you to give me a ride."

Gavin released a smooth chuckle. "Sorry. Acer is temperamental. I'm the only one he lets on his back."

"Um, I'm sure there are other ways we can ride," Tammy purred suggestively. "Without your horse."

Layla cleared her throat. Did the young woman have no shame? Tammy had pretty much offered herself to Gavin. Talk about being over-the-top brazen. The smile, she noticed, didn't leave Gavin's features when he said, "Thanks. But no thanks." He then turned his full attention back to Layla. "Have dinner with me tonight."

Layla swallowed. "Dinner?"

"Yes. I figured we could grab a meal in town."

Before Layla could say whether she would go or not, Tammy spoke up in an irritated tone. "Dr. Harris is in charge of this project, and I'm sure she has a lot to do tonight since we start digging in a few days. There are preliminary reports she has to complete and soil samples that need to be reviewed. But I'll be glad to go out with you tonight."

An annoyed frown replaced the smile on Gavin's lips when he turned to Tammy. "Are you her spokesperson?"

It was obvious Tammy had been caught off guard by Gavin's question. "No."

"I didn't think so. As far as taking her place, I didn't ask you to, did I?"

He couldn't have been I'm-not-interested-in-you plainer than that, Layla thought. Rage appeared in Tammy's face, making it quite obvious she wasn't used to men rejecting her and she didn't appreciate Gavin doing so. Instead of answering his question, she turned and angrily strutted off.

Layla watched her go and then turned her attention back to Gavin. "You might have hurt her feelings."

He shrugged massive shoulders. "She'll get over it. Besides, someone needs to teach her some manners." He leaned back. "So what about it? Will you have dinner with me tonight? We can even take in another movie if you like?"

Layla nibbled at her bottom lip. Tammy had been right about her having a lot of work to do to prepare for the start of the dig. But then hadn't Tammy also reminded her that although they were dedicated to this dig during the day, the nighttime hours were theirs to enjoy? Besides, after witnessing Tammy come on to Gavin the way she had, Layla had realized something. He could have taken Tammy up on her bold offer but he hadn't. He had even made it crystal clear that Layla was the woman he wanted.

Though she had convinced herself that she could do without him even if she wanted him, she now knew she couldn't. And why should she? She'd spent her whole life proving she could accomplish what she set her mind to. Now, she was setting her mind to finishing this dig and having Gavin, too.

She had set her target and she was going after what she wanted. In other words, she was about to become Viper Jr.

She met Gavin's gaze. "Dinner and a movie sound nice. Yes, I'd love to go out with you tonight."

Chapter 11

The moment Layla walked up the porch steps her nerves tightened. Was she doing the right thing? Was following her desires rather than common sense the best move for her tonight?

Her gaze swept over at the man at her side. Gavin had been quiet since parking his truck. Now he was walking her to the door and she knew it would be her decision how tonight would end. He wouldn't even kiss her good-night unless he knew for certain more came with that kiss. Was she ready to give him more?

They had been careful not to touch all night. Holding hands would have led to heaven knows what. The sexual chemistry between them was that explosive. She had been aware of everything about him all evening. His breathing pattern, the sexual vibes that poured off him and the heavy-lidded eyes that stared at her.

Even now, there was this sensuous pull of desire between them. She was aware of it and she knew he had to be aware of it, as well. That consciousness was a slow roll of longing in her stomach and a throbbing intensity at the base of her throat. Never had she felt such primal awareness of a man before.

When they reached the door she turned to him. Although his Stetson shaded his eyes, she felt his stare. She inhaled his masculine scent. The man was a living, breathing sample of testosterone at its best.

Drawing in a deep breath, Layla tightened her hands on the shoulder straps of her purse. "Dinner was wonderful. So was the movie. It's been a long time since I've seen a musical." His taste in movies surprised her. Last time it had been a chick flick and tonight a musical.

"Glad you enjoyed both."

She smiled up at him. "I did. Thanks for asking me to go. To be with you."

He nodded. "I can't think of any other woman I'd rather have been with tonight, Layla."

His words sent profound happiness spiraling through her. He could have spent the evening with Tammy, who was almost six years younger, and to Layla's way of thinking, a lot prettier. But she was the one he'd asked out. "Thank you for saying that."

"It's the truth."

When she didn't respond, she heard Gavin draw in a deep breath before saying, "I know you have a lot of work to do so I'll let you get to it."

He was giving her an out. He wouldn't pressure her. He'd stated days ago where he stood. If things between them escalated it would be up to her.

Swallowing deeply, she asked, "Would you like to come in for a drink, Gavin?"

He held her gaze for a long moment before smiling. "Yes, that would be nice, Layla."

As she opened the door to let him in, Layla knew it would be a whole lot better than just nice.

Gavin followed Layla inside. Removing his Stetson, he placed it on the rack by the door. She walked ahead, toward the living room and his groin tightened with each sinfully erotic sway of her hips.

"Beer or wine cooler?" she asked over her shoulder.

"Beer." He closed the front door. He actually needed something a lot stronger. A straight shot of bourbon might do the trick, to stop his testosterone from overloading. But then he figured there wasn't a drink on earth that could deaden his desire for Layla. It went too deep. He could actually feel a throb in his veins. Drawing in a deep breath he inhaled her scent.

"Here you are," she said, reentering the living room.

He recalled the last time she'd offered him a beer and what had occurred when their hands touched. What he'd felt. Would she avoid touching him this time? There was only one way to find out.

When she handed him the bottle, he deliberately held her gaze. Intentionally, he rubbed his finger against her hand. Hearing her sharp intake of breath, he'd gotten the reaction he'd hoped for. Unlike the last time she didn't wipe her hands on her jeans.

Still holding her gaze, he opened the bottle and took a huge gulp. He then lowered the bottle, licked his lips and asked the same question he had asked that night. "Want a sip?"

He'd given her an opening. Instead of retreating like she had before, she covered the distance separating them. "Yes, I want a sip." But instead of taking it, she said, "I'd rather sip it from your lips."

He lifted the bottle to his mouth. Then she took the bottle from him and placed it on a nearby table before leaning up on tiptoes to place her mouth over his. With a boldness he hadn't expected from her, she wrapped her arms around his neck and began sipping the beer from his lips.

Gavin felt light-headed and hot at the same time. Never had a woman stirred such passion within him. Never had any woman made his erection throb to this point. Layla was full of surprises and she was driving him insane with need.

As their mouths mated, he wrapped his arms around her. He wasn't surprised by how fluidly her body aligned with his. Sensations swamped his body. He knew from the way she was tasting him that tonight would not end with this kiss. The mating of their mouths was just the beginning. Tonight they were on the same page.

He swept her into his arms. Breaking off the kiss, he whispered against her lips, "I'm taking you to bed, Layla. If you have a problem with it, you need to say so now."

A seductive smile touched her lips. "I don't have a problem with that, Gavin."

Sexual excitement rushed through his veins as he moved quickly toward the bedroom.

Chapter 12

When Gavin placed Layla on the bed she looked up at him and saw eyes filled with intense desire gazing down at her. She'd meant what she said about going to bed with him. But he might not feel the same way after she said what she had to say.

"We need to talk first, Gavin."

He pulled her sweater over her head. "Okay, I'm listening."

Was he really? Or was he concentrating on undressing her? "A while back you asked me when I last did this. Do you remember that conversation?"

Her sweater was off and his swift hands went to the front clasp of her bra. Within seconds he had her breasts tumbling free. She watched his eyes get smoky as he stared at her nipples, which hardened as he watched.

When he brushed against one with a feathery stroke of his fingertips, she drew in a sharp breath.

"Yes, I remember that conversation," he said in a husky voice, stroking her other breast as if fascinated with its size and shape. "What about it?"

Layla had to think a minute to remember the conversation. His hands were driving her insane. And when he began stroking her nipples in earnest, it created a throbbing ache in her center. She couldn't help but moan.

"Layla?"

"Um?"

"What about the conversation?"

What conversation? Her brain was turning to mush and she fought hard to recall what he was talking about. Then she remembered. "Are you ready for an answer to the question you asked?"

"Doesn't matter now."

And before she could draw in another breath, he lowered his head and eased a rigid nipple between his lips. He sucked hard, feasting in earnest. Greedily. Ravenously. At the same time, he eased the hem of her skirt toward her waist.

And then he pushed aside her panties to ease fingers inside of her. The moment she felt the intimate invasion, she shuddered in pleasure. How could his mere touch do that? Make her come so unglued? Make her feel like a woman?

And when those same fingers stroked her down there, with the same rhythm his tongue was using to suck on her nipples, she moaned aloud.

"That's it. Get all wet for me, baby. Your scent has been driving me mad for days now. I can't wait to taste you."

She wasn't sure what he meant. All she knew was Gavin Blake had fingers that should be considered illegal and a mouth that should be banned. Using both, and at the same time, should be forbidden.

Sensation gathered force in her stomach and when he sucked harder on her breasts, while at the same time inserting his fingers deeper inside of her, she could not bear the pleasure any longer. Her body began to shake with the need for release. A climax ripped through her body. On instinct, she threw her head back and screamed his name.

"Now for my taste."

Before she realized what Gavin was doing, he had pulled off her skirt and tossed it aside along with her panties. Before she could ask what he thought he was doing, he lifted her hips to his mouth and firmly settled his head between her legs.

Layla tried pushing him away—until the moment she felt his tongue ease between her womanly lips. He kissed her down there the same way he'd kissed her on the mouth. Deeply. Thoroughly.

She stopped pushing him away. Instead she grabbed his shoulders and held on. Held him. She needed him to stay right there and continue what he was so expertly doing. When she felt his tongue delve deeper inside, flicking back and forth, her body shattered into what felt like a million pieces.

"Gavin!"

He didn't let up. He continued using his mouth to drive her over the edge yet again. Never had she experienced anything so powerful. So utterly amazing. For a minute she thought she had passed out. Maybe she had. She was completely drained. Limp. Too weak to move. So she lay there, nearly convinced she had died and gone to heaven. Surely there was nothing on earth that could make her feel this good. This satisfied.

She didn't move. She couldn't find the strength to open her eyes. Not even when she heard him remove his clothes before he pulled her boots and socks from her feet. Not even when his hands stroked her thighs and eased them apart.

And not even when she heard the sound of a condom packet being ripped open.

Moments later she heard Gavin's deep voice directly above her. "Open your eyes, baby. Look at me."

Although her eyelids felt heavy, she somehow found the strength to force them open. Gavin's naked body was braced above hers and desire-filled eyes stared down at her. Was it her imagination or were his eyes getting even darker as she stared into them?

"I'm looking," she said softly. Not only was she looking but she was being held in some sort of hypnotic trance.

"I wanted you this way from the first moment I set eyes on you."

That was nice. And she was about to say something, she wasn't sure what, when she felt the hot tip of his erection press against the core of her womanhood.

Her gaze widened and she knew she needed to tell him. Now. "Gavin?"

He leaned in and kissed the words off her lips. Using that scandalizing tongue of his, he began driving her crazy. Instinctively her legs opened wider and she felt him pressing down gently, as he tried entering her body.

He broke off the kiss and stared down at her. She knew from his expression exactly when he realized the *something* she'd tried to tell him about. The *something* he'd said no longer mattered.

"You're a virgin," he whispered in shock.

"Yes." Would he change his mind? Would it matter? She swallowed and said quietly, "I'll understand if you no longer want me."

Something flickered in his dark gaze. "Why wouldn't I still want you? Because you're a twenty-six-year-old virgin?"

When she nodded, he smiled and said, "Doesn't bother me if it doesn't bother you."

That was the moment she knew she had fallen in love with Gavin. She had tried denying it, had even called herself several kinds of a fool for letting it happen. She'd never loved a man before, but she knew what her feelings were. For all the heartbreak it would cause when she left the ranch in a week or so, it didn't make much sense for her to love a man now. But her heart had declared Gavin was it and there was nothing she could do about it.

Making love with him seemed right in a way it had never been with any other man…which was the real reason why she had remained untouched all these years. Sex had never interested her. She had never been turned on by the mere thought of it. Things were different with Gavin. Even before she'd met him face-to-face, his pictures had done something to her. They had pretty much warned her of her fate but she'd refused to accept it until she'd welcomed him inside tonight.

"Layla?"

She held his gaze. "Doesn't bother me, either." *Please don't ask me why I chose you. At least not now.*

He didn't ask her anything. Instead he kissed her before using his knee to widen her legs. And then she felt him, easing inside of her, inch by inch. He was big and she sucked in as he filled her deeply, her body stretching for his invasion. Her muscles clamped down—not to stop his journey but to make it even more sensuous for the two of them. He continued to ease deeper until there was no place left for him to go. He was fully embedded in her in a fit so snug and tight she couldn't tell where her body ended and his began.

When her muscles tightened even more, she actually felt his erection throb inside of her. "If you keep that up do you know what's going to happen?" He leaned in close to ask her.

"No."

"It's going to make me want to do this."

Then he began thrusting, gently, in a sensuous rhythm that drove her to lift her hips with his every downward stroke. When her inner muscles clenched him harder, he thrusted harder, with a steady fluid beat.

Too steady. Each stroke inside her body pushed her to a place she'd never been. He'd made her come using his mouth. But this was different. It was more intense. Insanely gratifying. And when he went faster, harder, deeper, she screamed his name as sensations washed over her. She clawed at his back, bucked upward to tighten her legs around him and lock their bodies together.

An intense explosion swept her away in an earth-shattering release. Although this might be the first time she'd made love with a man, she knew that this wouldn't be her last with Gavin.

* * *

That had been totally unreal, Gavin thought a short while later as he lay flat on his back staring up at the ceiling. When had making love to a woman ever left him so physically sated and mentally drained? Hell, he was used to making out with women, sometimes all night long. And as a SEAL he was physically fit for all the rigors of combat. Yet, the woman sleeping beside him had practically drained him, made him weak as water with their first sexual encounter. How was that possible?

And she'd been a virgin. Gavin didn't have to wonder how that was possible, given her status in life. To accomplish what she'd accomplished at her age meant she'd made sacrifices. He'd suspected her experience with men had been limited, he just hadn't figured it to be nonexistent. Not that it bothered him. Normally, he preferred not to be any woman's first, but he was glad he'd been Layla's. The thought that no other man had been inside her body before him felt good, made him want to beat on his damn chest like a caveman. He'd branded Layla as his.

His?

Where in the hell had that thought come from? This was the second time he'd thought of her as being his woman. His. He needed to remind himself once again that he wasn't into possessiveness. He'd even participated in a ménage à trois a time or two during his college years. So the idea of laying claim to any woman didn't sit well with him. Sex was sex, no matter how good it was. No need to act crazy.

So why was he?

As he tilted his head to stare down at the woman

sleeping peacefully beside him, he had to admit the sex had been better than good. Off the charts. He had studied her face when she'd come. Her expression had been utterly and incredibly spellbinding. Beautiful. Touching. She was such a passionate being it was hard to believe she'd held out for this long. Her presence on the Silver Spurs was the best luck he'd had in years. With sex that good she could dig up the entire damn ranch looking for whatever treasure she wanted. His treasure was right here with him in this bed.

Gavin frowned. He was thinking like a love-struck puppy, and he refused to go there. Isn't that what had happened to his father? He'd quickly fallen in love with a woman only to die of a broken heart in the end? Okay, it had been an enemy's bullet that had taken him out, but Gavin of all people knew of his father's heartache.

Layla shifted her weight. Her leg, which rested between his, touched his groin. Immediately, he got hard. His erection had no problem coming to life. He glanced over at the clock. It was almost two in the morning. He should leave but the thought of waking up beside her in the morning had an appeal he couldn't dismiss.

And then there was the temptation to wake her now and make love to her all over again. Move between her legs and slide inside of her. Go deep until he couldn't go anymore. Then he would thrust hard like he'd done before. Even harder since she was no longer a virgin. He even thought about how it would feel not to wear a condom. To blast off inside of her. Fill her with the very essence of him.

Now that was taking his imagination a little too far. He was a man who played it safe so he would never be sorry. Babies of any kind were not in his immediate future. So why did the thought of a daughter who would be a mini-Layla appeal to him? Make his erection even harder?

Gavin closed his eyes. He had to stop thinking with the wrong head. Doing so could get him in serious trouble. He couldn't let sexual feelings take control of his common sense no matter how wrapped up he wanted to get with the woman beside him. No matter how much inhaling her arousing scent was getting to him.

Shifting his body, he pulled Layla closer and let sleep overtake him.

Chapter 13

The strong aroma of coffee woke Layla. She blinked, and then sluggishly realized where she was and what she'd done last night and with whom. If there had been any doubt in her mind about what had happened, all she had to do was tilt her head to gaze across the room to where a half-naked man lounged in the doorway holding a steaming cup of coffee.

Gavin.

She blinked. Okay, since he was wearing jeans, he wasn't half-naked but half-dressed. Still, that was all he was wearing. And those jeans were riding low on his hips, making it pretty obvious just what a well-built body he had. His pose was picture perfect. He was the epitome of a sexy cowboy. A wealthy rancher. A scrumptious navy SEAL. How could one man exemplify all three and do it so well?

Her gaze roamed over him, from the top of his head all the way down to his bare feet. She'd paused when she'd seen that his zipper was undone. He'd either dressed quickly and hadn't bothered to zip up, or he had plans that included her so he'd figured why bother.

Those tantalizing thoughts made her recall last night. Her first time. And she knew without a doubt it had been worth the wait. She couldn't help it. Her gaze traveled the full length of him all over again. This time when her gaze settled on his midsection, she saw something she hadn't seen before. A huge erection. She drew in a deep breath and swore that it got bigger as she stared at it.

"Want some?"

She snatched her gaze from his groin up to his face. The smile that touched his lips was priceless and way too sexy for words. "What are you offering?" she asked.

"Whatever you want."

Reluctantly, she broke eye contact with him to glance outside the bedroom window. It was still dark but she knew it would be daybreak soon. Her team would be arriving from town within an hour or so. Her gaze returned to his. "I should take the coffee, get up, shower and get dressed."

"But..."

How had he known there was a *but* in there? "But I much prefer taking the man holding the coffee."

His smile widened. "And the man holding the coffee doesn't have a problem with you taking him."

Layla was only beginning to fully understand what heated lust was all about. "Did I tell you that last night I thought of myself as Viper Jr.?"

He lifted a brow. "Viper Jr.?"

"Yes. I set my sights on my target and went after what I wanted, and you, Gavin Blake, were my target."

A wry grin split his lips. "Was I?"

She nodded. "I wanted you."

"And I wanted you."

Layla then saw a somewhat serious look appear in his eyes as he said, "How do you feel? I wanted you so much...because of that you're probably sore. You sure you're up to another ride this soon?"

Ride? She inwardly chuckled. Yes, he'd definitely ridden her last night. And yes, she was sore from it. However, as far as she was concerned, he could ride the soreness away.

"I'm sure."

"In that case." Placing the coffee cup on a nearby table, he crossed the room to the bed. "But first I want to see something." Before she could blink, he threw the bedcovers aside to expose her naked body.

Surprised, she scrambled to get back under the covers but he tossed them aside again. "No. Don't cover yourself. I just had to make sure I hadn't imagined anything. That you were as beautiful and delectable as I remembered. My mind didn't play tricks on me last night."

His words touched her. Made her feel wonderful. Made her feel like a real woman who had sexual feminine powers over a man. And when she watched him lick his lips with the tip of his tongue, she couldn't help remembering just where that tongue had been and what it had done.

Recalling that part of their lovemaking sparked an ache between her legs. As if he knew what sensations were enthralling her and where, he slowly eased his jeans down his strong, muscular thighs. Just as she'd thought. The jeans were the only thing he'd been wearing. He hadn't bothered to put back on his briefs.

"Now for this."

His words grabbed her attention and she watched him slide a condom over his erection. And boy was it large. How had it gotten inside of her last night? But he'd managed it and she knew he would again. This was the first time she'd seen a man prepare himself for sex. From the way he was doing it, it was obvious he was used to doing it.

"Ready?"

"Yes." She drew in a deep breath. The ache between her legs had made her nipples harden like tight buds.

"We're going to try something different this morning. It will be easier on you and help with your soreness."

In a way, she felt embarrassed engaging in such a conversation with him…about her body. But she pushed her discomfort aside. After last night—and all he'd done to her and how he'd done it—there was no room left for shame. "What?"

He smiled as he moved back toward the bed. "I want you to ride me."

She swallowed. "Ride you?"

"Yes. Do you know how to ride?"

She nodded. "Yes. My parents own several horses." And she'd ridden them often enough.

"Good. So show me what you know," he said, lying back on the bed beside her, then lifting her over him. Just like that. As if she was weightless.

"I'll do my best," she said, sliding into position. The long, hard length of his erection was like a rod, standing straight up, ready for her to mount. So she did. Widening her legs, she took him into her body. The hot texture of his male organ seemed to blaze her insides as she took him fully inside of her.

She watched his face, the same way she'd known he'd watched hers last night. Their gazes held. No words were spoken. This was all about feeling. And she felt him in each and every part of her body. Her muscles clenched around him. Holding tight. And then as if of one accord they shivered with a need they both felt.

"Okay Viper Jr. Ride me, baby. Hard."

Gavin's words incited her to move up and down. She felt him grip the sides of her hips—to hold on to her, to guide her. Then, as if something elemental had taken control, she threw her head back and rode him hard.

What was happening to her? It was as if she'd lost control of her mind and her body. Having sex with Gavin this way, with her on top, riding him, sent an exhilarated feeling through her, one she couldn't explain.

When he leaned up and whispered naughty words in her ear, sinfully erotic words, she went mad with lust. She heard the bedsprings as she continued to ride. Each time her body came down against him, his came up to meet her.

Suddenly her quivering became uncontrollable and she felt her body explode into a thousand pieces. It was then that Gavin caught the back of her head with his hands and brought her mouth down to his, kissing her with a hunger that made her climax all over again.

Once again he came with her. She felt it. As their tongues continued to mingle, she knew that she loved him with a passion she would never rid herself of, no matter the distance between them. While she was here on the Silver Spurs, she intended to make memories that would last her long after she returned to Seattle.

"Well, how did your dinner date with the handsome rancher go? Did the two of you do the nasty, Dr. Harris?"

Layla didn't immediately look up from studying the soil samples. Tammy was the last person she wanted to talk to, but to ignore her student would be rude. Yet no student had the right to inquire how their professor spent their evening. Layla had always maintained a distance between herself and her students. Because of her age, she took pains to ensure they never lost sight of the fact that she was their professor. As far as she was concerned, Tammy's question was out of line and lacked respect.

Layla raised her head from the microscope and met Tammy's gaze. "I don't think that should be your concern, Tammy. Did you finish your report?" Layla knew she hadn't. Several students had brought it to her attention that Tammy was slacking. It seemed whenever there was hard work to do, Tammy had a tendency to disappear.

Tammy scrunched up her features. "No. And why do I have to be the one to do that report? Donnell has a lot of free time."

"Only because Donnell has finished all his assignments. You haven't."

A smile touched Tammy's lips. "Doesn't matter. I'll still ace this class."

Layla frowned. "Not if you don't do your share of the work. And if you're not going to be a team player,

I will have to replace you. There are several students who would love to be here."

"Doesn't matter. They don't have the connections I have," Tammy bragged. "I'm on this team, Dr. Harris, whether you want me here or not. I thought you understood that."

Layla refused to get into a confrontation with a student. It was clear Tammy thought that being Dr. Clayburn's occasional bed partner meant she could do whatever she wanted. Wrong. Not on Layla's team. "The only thing I understand is that I expect you to carry your load. If you can't, then you're out of here."

Tammy tossed her hair as a smirk touched her lips. "Wrong. You'll be out of here before I will. I'll make sure Mark… I mean Dr. Clayburn knows I'm being harassed." She then turned and sulked as she walked out the door.

In frustration Layla rubbed her hand down her face. Tammy might be right. Layla wasn't one of Dr. Clayburn's favorite people and it was obvious the man was quite taken with Tammy. And Tammy knew it.

"She'll eventually hang herself and Dr. Clayburn. Don't waste your time worrying about her, Dr. Harris."

Layla turned to find another one of her students, Donnell McGuire, standing in the doorway. Had he overheard her conversation with Tammy? Did he and the other students suspect something was going on between Tammy and Dr. Clayburn? The one thing Layla wouldn't do was discuss one student with another, no matter how much she wanted to sound off to someone about Tammy's atrocious attitude.

Before she could say anything, Donnell added, "And

don't worry about that report Tammy hasn't done. I'll take care of it. I do have some free time."

His words told Layla he *had* overheard her conversation with Tammy. "That assignment was given to Tammy, Donnell, and I expect her to do it. Besides, I have something else for you to do. I just got a call that the last of our supplies arrived at the post office in town. I need you to go pick them up. If everything looks good, we'll start digging by the end of the week."

A huge smile touched Donnell's face. "Alright! I can't wait." The young man rushed off to tell the others.

Layla chuckled at his enthusiasm. She would give anything for more students like Donnell who took being a team player seriously. He was a hard worker. Most of the students on this team were. Although being an archaeologist was Donnell's first love, she knew he was also good with a camera and had won a number of photo contests. At twenty-two he would be graduating in the spring with a major in archaeology and a minor in photography.

She refused to let Tammy put a damper on her day, especially when it had started off with the promise of being wonderful. She'd had such a wonderful night with Gavin. Then this morning, before the crack of dawn, she'd proven just what a great horsewoman she could be. Memories of what they'd shared still sent shivers down her spine. She couldn't help but blush. Being intimate with a man had never been anything she'd thought about until now…

She glanced at her watch. She had a full day planned here on-site and then Gavin had invited her to dinner again. This time he would be the one cooking. He claimed he wasn't bad in the kitchen. Tonight she intended to see if that was true.

Gavin had always prided himself on being a man in control. As a SEAL, he couldn't be any other way. The success of any mission called for it. There was no time to let your guard down. Weakness of any kind wasn't acceptable. Then why did he lose control every time he entered Layla's body? Why did overpowering weakness overtake him whenever they made love?

He had prepared dinner for her tonight at the party house. He'd fed her well. Surprised the hell out of her with his culinary skills. At the moment, he contemplated impressing her with another skill. One of seduction. When he'd arrived at the party house with his arms filled with groceries, Layla had opened the door wearing an outfit that only made him think of filling her.

She'd tempted him the entire time he was in the kitchen. There was no doubt in his mind that she'd known exactly what she was doing as she'd sat at the breakfast bar watching him. She had known each and every time she crossed and uncrossed her legs that she was showing him a portion of her thigh and exactly what that did to him. How he had managed to finish cooking and then sit across from her and eat was a testament to his control.

Now it was payback time.

"So how was your day, Gavin?"

He'd cleared off the table and was loading up the dishwasher as he fought to retain control. "It was the usual day in the life of a rancher. The cows are finally settled in for the winter, which is good since forecasters predict a cold wave coming through first of next week."

"I heard. I'm hoping bad weather won't delay the completion of the dig. Our goal is to start later this week."

He closed the dishwasher door, then turned around and watched her gaze shift from his face to his midsection. She saw the evidence of his desire for her. That couldn't be helped when she was sitting there looking as sexy as any woman had a right to look. "Did I tell you how much I like your outfit?"

She chuckled and the sound made his erection thicken even more. "Yes, you told me. I figured you would like it since I understand men like to see skin."

She understood right. Men liked touching and tasting skin as well, which was something he'd shown her last night. Her short dress showed a lot of her thighs since the hem barely covered them. And the top had a neckline that showed a lot of cleavage, reminding him of how much he enjoyed her breasts. He wanted her bad. He wanted her right here. Right now.

He slowly crossed the room toward her. Any other woman would have run after seeing the predatory look in his eyes. But Layla stood her ground. That was fine with him. When he reached her, he removed her dress with a flick of his wrist and a little muscle power, leaving her totally naked. Like he'd suspected, she hadn't had a stitch of clothing on underneath that dress. He knew he had surprised the hell out of her with how quickly he'd undressed her.

He smiled at her shocked look. "A SEAL pays attention to detail. While sitting across from you at dinner I studied the design of your dress and figured out the best way to take it off without ripping it to shreds. I like the dress too much to tear it."

He stepped back. "Now to remove my clothes."

Gavin undressed quickly. And then he picked her up and spread her across the same table he'd cleared just moments ago. "Open your legs for me, Layla."

He intended to bury himself inside of her as deeply as he could go. He was certain the hot and hungry look in his eyes said as much. But he knew all this was still new to her and he wanted her to be comfortable with everything they did together.

She lay there, on his table, with her legs spread. For a minute he just stood and looked at her. Remembering her taste, he couldn't help but lick his lips. Tasting her would have to come later. Right now he needed to *come*. Quickly putting on a condom, he settled his body between her thighs. She held his gaze when he entered her, filling her completely. Being inside her, feeling her muscles clench around him, felt so damn good. Her muscles were trying to pull everything out of him and the sensation was driving him insane.

Gavin held tight to her hips as he moved in and out. She wrapped her legs around his waist, locking him inside of her. He wanted her to feel every stroke, the same way he was feeling it. On and on, each thrust was hard and precise. Back and forth, he rocked inside of her. Steady, with meaningful precision. He thrust hard, creating pleasure that spread like molten heat throughout both of their bodies. The sound of Layla's moans only increased his desire to please her. When he felt her body explode, his explosion soon followed.

That's when he realized why things were so different with her. Why with her he so easily lost control.

As much as a part of him wished it wasn't true, he knew he had fallen head over heels in love with Layla Harris.

Chapter 14

"So what are you going to do about Tammy?"

Layla lifted her head off Gavin's chest. It was two days after the night he'd prepared dinner for her. She had arrived at the guest cottage to find him sitting on the steps waiting for her. Her heart had pounded the minute she'd seen him sitting there. He'd stood when she got out of the car and her gaze had taken him in. With the Stetson on his head, his Western shirt, a pair of well-worn and scuffed boots, he looked like a quintessential cowboy. She wondered how he would look dressed as a SEAL. Too bad she would probably never see him that way. Gavin as a rancher would be the memory of him she would keep in her heart forever.

He had taken her hand into his and once they were locked inside the house, he had swept her into his arms and headed for the bedroom where they'd made love a number of times. Then he'd told her some troubling news. It seemed earlier that day he'd overheard one of his men bragging about sleeping with Tammy. The man had said she'd told him she was into group sex, so if he had any friends who were interested, she was available.

Gavin hadn't liked what he'd overheard and felt he needed to bring it to Layla's attention. She was glad he had. Unfortunately, she was battling her own issues with Tammy. The young woman's promiscuity wasn't Layla's number one concern. Tammy's entitled attitude was impairing the success of the dig. The report Layla had assigned to Tammy had yet to be done, and Tammy's slacking off on her duties had increased to the point where the other students were complaining. Low morale was the last thing Layla needed to deal with.

Layla had confided in Gavin, telling him of her own issues with Tammy, including Tammy's ongoing affair with the head of Layla's department and how Tammy was blatantly using that affair to do whatever she wanted…as well as avoiding the things she didn't want to do.

Finally answering Gavin's question, Layla said, "There's only one thing I can do about Tammy and that is to release her from the team and brace myself for the backlash from Dr. Clayburn. She isn't a team player, she lacks respect for everyone and she isn't pulling her own weight. I refuse to give her more chances than I would give anyone else, no matter who she's sleeping with."

Gavin nodded. He thought Layla was making the right decision by releasing Tammy from her team. He'd known Tammy had been trouble from day one. "So you'll start digging on Friday?"

"Yes. We got delayed when one of the supply shipments was late. We haven't had any other problems, but I wanted to ask, did you ever talk to that guy to see if he was the one who moved my marker?"

"Yes, and Clete said he didn't move anything. So what happened to your marker is still a mystery."

"It doesn't matter since we're moving ahead. I'm excited."

He pulled her tighter into his arms. "So am I. I can't wait to see what you find."

She pulled back and stared up at him. "And now you think I will find something?"

"Yes. I told you I'd gotten a good reading from Flip's camera. I'm sure you'll find something, I'm just not certain it's the loot you're looking for."

She smiled up at him. "Well, I am certain, Mr. Blake." She then pulled his mouth down to hers.

Hours later, the ringing of his cell phone woke Gavin. He looked down at the woman plastered to his side. The phone had awakened her, as well. He glanced at the clock and saw it was three in the morning. Who would be calling him at this hour?

He reached for the phone on the nightstand before it could ring again. "Hello."

He heard the words his foreman said and was out of bed in a flash. "We're on our way."

Layla sat up. "What's wrong, Gavin?"

He glanced over at her as he reached for his clothes. "That was Caldwell. The old barn is going up in flames."

It didn't take long for them to both make their way to the south pasture.

"Arson?" Gavin asked, staring down Cornerstone's

fire marshal. He knew Josh Timbales well since the man had been good friends with Gavin's dad.

"Yes, Gavin. Arson. And the person didn't even try covering their tracks. You could smell kerosene a mile away."

"But who would do such a thing?" Layla asked, staring at the building that was now burned to the ground as well as the charred remains of the equipment that had been stored inside.

"I don't know," Josh said to Layla. "My investigative team has been called in as well as the sheriff. Hopefully they will come up with some answers."

In the meantime... Layla turned to stare at her students who were huddled together a few feet away. They'd gotten word about the fire and had rushed from town. She could see the disappointed looks on their faces. They'd worked hard and now this. "I need to talk to my team," Layla said, and walked off.

Gavin watched her go. He could feel her anger and disappointment. He turned a livid gaze to Josh. "No matter what it takes, I intend to find the person responsible for this."

Layla approached the group. Before she could say anything, one of her students, Wendy Miller, spoke up. "Is it true what the firemen are saying? Did someone deliberately set fire to the barn?"

Layla drew in a deep breath. "Yes, the fire marshal has ruled it as arson. The sheriff is on his way."

"Looks like you have an enemy, Dr. Harris," Tammy said with a smirk. "Well, with no equipment for the dig, that means we're free to leave and return home, right? I didn't like this place anyway."

Layla had had enough. "Yes, you can leave, Tammy. I was going to release you from the team in the morning anyway. Have a safe trip back to Seattle."

Fury shone on Tammy's face. "You're dropping me from the team? You can't do that."

"I just did."

Tammy lifted her chin. "It really doesn't matter because there won't be a dig team. Once Dr. Clayburn calculates the cost of all the equipment that was destroyed in the fire, he will call off the dig."

"The college probably insured the equipment. It won't take long to get more in here," Donnell said angrily. He stared at Tammy suspiciously. "And just where were you tonight, Tammy? I was in the hotel's lobby and saw when you came in rather late. It wouldn't surprise me if you torched this place."

From the looks on the faces of her other students, Layla could see they were thinking the same thing. Evidently Tammy saw it, as well. She backed up, away from the others. "I was with someone, so I have a concrete alibi. But I plan on giving Dr. Clayburn a call to tell him everything."

"And how do you have his phone number?" another student asked, making it pretty obvious all of them had an idea.

"That's none of your business," Tammy snapped. And then she angrily walked off.

Layla turned back to her students. "I will call Dr. Clayburn in the morning myself. Regardless of what Tammy says, I doubt he will shut down the project."

Although Layla said the words, she truly wasn't so sure of that.

* * *

The next day, an angry Layla slammed down the phone. She could not believe the conversation she'd just had with Dr. Clayburn. She could not believe the audacity of the man.

"What's wrong, Layla?"

She turned and saw Gavin. She hadn't heard him enter the cottage. She saw the care and concern in his expression and she loved him even more than she already had. He had been so understanding and supportive. Incredibly, he'd been more concerned about the loss of her equipment than he had for the loss of his barn.

Last night they had both talked to the sheriff, whom she'd discovered was a high school friend of Gavin's. Sheriff Roy Wade was just as determined as Gavin to find the person responsible for the fire. And after checking for footprints, Gavin mentioned the ones around the burned barn were the same ones he'd seen when her marker had gone missing. It was obvious someone was trying to sabotage the dig. But who, and why?

She drew in a deep breath. "That was Dr. Clayburn."

"And?"

She blew out a frustrated and angry sigh. "Tammy got to him first. She probably called him last night like she threatened to do. He really didn't want to hear anything I had to say."

Gavin crossed his arms over his chest with a furious look on his face. "You mean to tell me he's taking a student's word over yours?"

Layla frowned. "Remember, Tammy isn't just another student. She's also the man's side piece. I didn't want to believe it before, but I definitely believe it now. The influence she has over him! If I didn't know better I'd think there's more to it, that she's blackmailing him with something."

Gavin dropped his arms and came to stand in front of her. "Why? What did he say?"

"He wanted to let me know my students were notified this morning by email that the dig has been canceled and they are to return to campus." She paused. "He also wanted me to know that I've been terminated from my position at the university."

"He fired you?"

"Yes. He claims I botched things up. As far as he is concerned, the fire was my responsibility. I should have been more attentive to my work rather than indulging in an 'illicit affair with one of the cowboys.'" There was no doubt in Layla's mind Tammy had fed the man that BS and he'd believed it without question.

"Can't you go to the president of the university with your side of the story?"

"Yes, but Dr. Clayburn and President Connors are good friends. If I was terminated that means Dr. Connors approved the termination because he believed whatever Dr. Clayburn told him about me."

"Let them believe whatever they want. You came here to do a dig and that's what you'll do."

Layla dropped into a nearby wingback chair. "Gavin, didn't you hear what I said?"

He squatted down in front of her. "What I hear is the sound of you giving up. Letting them defeat you."

She touched his cheek. "What am I supposed to do? I don't have a job. Nor do I have a team. Did you not hear me say that Dr. Clayburn sent everyone an email telling them to return to Seattle?"

"You'll get another job. You're too smart and intelligent not to. As far as I'm concerned, losing you is the university's loss. Besides, I want to see what their reaction will be when you find James's loot. You don't have to be affiliated with any university to dig or publish your findings, right?"

Layla shook her head. "No, I can conduct an independent excavation, but I no longer have funding, or a team."

Gavin pulled her out of the chair. "I'll replace your equipment. And you might not have a team, but I do. They will come to help out if I call them."

Layla stared at him, not believing what he was saying, what he was offering. "B-but I can't let you do that. Like you, they just got back from their last operation. They need to spend time with their families and—"

Gavin lowered his mouth and kissed the words off her lips. He then deepened the kiss. By the time he released her mouth, she was panting. "Trust me on this, will you?" he said. "I don't want to brag or anything, but we will do it in half the time your team would have."

"But it will take time to get more equipment."

"We will get the equipment we need without any delays."

Layla knew he had money and influence. She just hadn't realized how much. Then she thought of something crucial. "What about the person sabotaging the dig? Things could get dangerous."

A sinister grin touched Gavin's lips. "If he or she is crazy enough to try something with a team of SEALs around, then let them go for it. We will be ready."

He quickly kissed her again, silencing any more questions. When he released her lips, he said, "Trust me. We've got this. We'll have your back."

There was a knock at the door. Gavin lifted a brow. "Gramma Mel isn't due back until tonight, so it might be Roy. Maybe he's found something."

Gavin crossed the room with her following beside him. Opening the door they found three of her students standing there. "Donnell? Wendy? Marsha? What are you doing here?" Layla asked them. "Why aren't you on your way back to Seattle? Didn't you get Dr. Clayburn's email?"

"Yes, we got it," Donnell said, frowning. "But we didn't want to leave until we talked to you. Until you say there won't be a dig, we are staying put."

"You could get into trouble if you defy Dr. Clayburn," she warned them.

The three students looked at each other and shared what looked like conspiratorial smiles before Donnell said, "We aren't worried about that. They'll be faced with their own troubles soon. So, are you still planning to dig?"

Layla wondered what they meant by "troubles," but before she could ask, Gavin said, "Yes, the dig is still on."

She could tell from the look of respect in his eyes that he admired the stance these three students had taken. Like his team had his back, these members of her team had hers.

Donnell, Marsha and Wendy let out loud cheers and gave each other high fives. Then Donnell said, "When we find James's loot, the university's going to regret letting you go."

Chapter 15

"So…you're the fast-talking college professor, huh?"

Layla swallowed as she watched the four men standing in front of her. Gavin had introduced them as Flipper, Bane, Coop and Mac. It was Flipper who'd asked the question, the depths of his blue eyes dancing with amusement.

All four were big men. Muscular. Well built. Extremely handsome. Two wore wedding rings and two did not. Gavin had told her that Brisbane Westmoreland and Thurston McRoy were happily married and that Flipper and Coop were happily single.

"I don't know. Am I?" she asked, switching her gaze from them to Gavin, who stood by her side with his arms around her waist. It was as if he was intentionally making a statement regarding the nature of their relationship. If that was the case, then she wished someone would tell her where they stood. All she knew for certain was that they enjoyed spending time together and they shared a bed every night. She definitely didn't have any complaints about that.

Gavin muttered the words, "Smart-ass," to Flipper, then leaned down and placed a kiss on Layla's lips. He then turned to his friends. "She's more than a professor."

He knew his friends were checking out Layla and with good reason. The four men knew about his don't-get-attached policy when it came to women. But it was obvious that with this particular woman, he'd gotten attached. They would be shocked to discover just how attached he was.

Like he'd known they would, his friends had answered his summons for help. No questions asked. But now that they were here and had been briefed on the situation, they were also eyewitnesses to his possessiveness of Layla. They would have questions about that later. Fair enough. He would address them then. He would admit he'd fallen in love. Bane and Mac would understand. Flipper and Coop would suggest Gavin have his head examined.

"Did you get the equipment I asked you to bring?" he asked them.

"Yes. Two of my brothers will be towing the backhoe loader and tractor in this evening," Flipper said.

"And I've got the rest of the stuff in my truck," Mac added.

"Good," Gavin said. Flip had four brothers. All SEALs. And Flip's dad had retired as a SEAL commanding officer. Gavin had thought he'd had it bad living in his father's and grandfather's shadows—until he'd met Flipper. His friend had five legacies to compete with since all the male Holloways before Flip had stellar reputations as SEALs.

"So where are we staying, Viper? The party house?" Coop asked.

Gavin shook his head. "No. Layla's at the party house."

Flipper chuckled. "So? It's big enough. You don't mind if we crash, do you?" he asked Layla.

Before she could answer, Gavin said, "But I mind."

All four men laughed. Gavin scowled.

"Easy, Viper, let's not get territorial," Flipper said, grinning.

But he did feel territorial, Gavin thought. He figured it was all a part of being in love. He still wasn't sure what to do with his feelings. He didn't want to get caught up in a woman like his dad had done. He didn't want to ask her to give up her career to wait out here on the ranch through all his missions. He didn't want a repeat of what had happened with his mom.

Pushing all that aside, he said, "Gramma Mel got back from her trip a few days ago and she prepared rooms for you guys at the main house."

"Yes!" Bane said, pumping his fist in the air. "We'll get to eat her mouthwatering biscuits for breakfast."

Gavin shook his head. He had to admit he'd missed these guys.

"So, are you going to tell Layla how you feel about her, Viper?"

Instead of answering Bane's question Gavin stared into his beer bottle and shook his head. "Won't do any good. She doesn't feel the same way."

"How do you know?" Mac asked, taking a sip of his own beer. "Women like to hear stuff like that. And often."

Coop and Flipper, Gavin noticed, were keeping their mouths shut. His admission that he'd fallen in love had shocked them into silence. The five of them were sprawled in the living room of the party house. Layla was at the main house assisting Gramma Mel with dinner. Gavin figured his grandmother would go all out and prepare a feast. She'd been happy to see his friends and they'd been happy to see her. Of course Bane would be getting those biscuits for breakfast in the morning. Mac had put in his order for an apple pie and both Coop and Flipper requested peach cobbler.

"So who do you think is trying to sabotage the dig?" Flipper asked, obviously trying to change the subject to one he and Coop could take part in. Gavin was glad to leave the topic of his love life behind.

"Don't have a clue but I intend to find out," Gavin said. "I thought it was someone connected to the university, but now I'm not sure."

"Sounds like someone doesn't want anyone digging in the south pasture, Viper," Coop said, standing, stretching out his limbs. "You all know I'm a suspicious bastard by nature. I can smell a cover-up a mile away."

Mac leaned forward in his chair. "You think someone is covering up something?"

"Possibly," Coop said. He glanced over at Gavin. "Other than Caldwell, how well do you know the men who work for you?"

Gavin shrugged. "Most have worked here for years, some even during my dad's time. There are two new guys we brought on last year." He recalled both were single, and he specifically remembered that one of them had shared Tammy's bed.

"What if someone knows for certain the loot is buried around here, heard about the dig and doesn't want anyone else to find it before they do?" Flipper suggested.

Gavin nodded. That possibility had crossed his mind, as well. He knew these four men. In addition to helping with the dig, they intended to solve the mystery of who'd removed the marker and burned down the barn. So far, the sheriff hadn't found anything other than those footprints. Gavin had mentioned the prints to his friends. "Um, that gives us something to go on," Mac said pensively.

"We start digging in the morning," Gavin said, leaning back in his chair. "Whoever doesn't want us to will either try to stop us or will hope whatever they don't want us to find is kept hidden."

Later that night, after making love to Layla, Gavin pulled her tighter into his arms as he tried to bring his breathing under control. She had ridden him again. She was getting too good at it. He was convinced the woman was trying to kill him.

"I like your friends, Gavin."

He decided not to tell her that they liked her, as well. They had joked with her at dinner and Bane had even told her about his wife, Crystal, who, like Layla, had gotten her PhD at an early age.

"I'm glad you like them."

Dinner had been a grand affair. Not only had his grandmother cooked enough food for his friends and Layla's students, she'd invited Caldwell and his men to stop by for a plate. Several of their neighbors who'd heard about the fire stopped by to make sure all was well. Gramma Mel had sent them home with boxed dinners.

"Are you worried about the dig tomorrow?" he asked Layla.

She snuggled closer to him. "Sort of. I want to make sure my students stay safe."

"They will be. I'm glad Gramma Mel insisted everyone stay at the main house. She has plenty of room and loves all the company."

"I'm glad she made the offer. Without the university footing the bill, my students couldn't afford to stay at the hotel any longer. But there's plenty of room here," she said, smiling.

"No way anyone is staying at the party house but us. This is our special place. I like coming here every night." No matter how late he worked out on the ranch, he liked coming back here to Layla. Before he parked his truck he could hear her playing her harmonica and the sound would lure him to her. He didn't want to think about how involved they were getting.

Layla lifted her head and looked up at him. "Has your grandmother asked you anything about us?"

He smiled. "She didn't have to. I think it's pretty obvious we have something going on. She's fine with it. We're adults."

What Gavin decided not to say was that his grandmother hadn't needed to ask anything because he'd told her his true feelings for Layla—and about his doubts that it would go anywhere long-term. Needless to say Gramma Mel hadn't been surprised.

"Besides, she has her hands full with Caldwell now that she's back. They've been apart for a week."

Layla lifted an arched brow. "Caldwell?"

Gavin smiled. "Yes, Caldwell. Don't tell me you haven't picked up on what's between them."

Layla shook her head. "No, I hadn't. But you have?"

"Yes, for years. He's a widower and she's a widow. Never understood why they preferred being so discreet. I guess they like their privacy.

"Since the dig starts early in the morning I guess we need to get to sleep," Gavin said, but he wasn't very convincing, even to his own ears.

"Um, I have other ideas," she said, moving on top of him again. "I like riding you."

Gavin grinned. He definitely liked Layla riding him. More than ever, he was convinced the woman was trying to kill him. But he would enjoy every minute until the end.

Hours later, the ringing of his cell phone woke Gavin. He immediately grabbed it when he recognized the ring tone. "Coop?"

"Yeah, Viper, it's me. We couldn't sleep so we thought we'd set a trap."

Gavin sat up in bed as knots tightened in his stomach. Layla had awakened as well and quickly sat up beside him. Drawing in a deep breath, he asked, "And?"

"And I think you need to get here. I've already called the sheriff. We're here at the shack and we got our man."

Chapter 16

Gavin made it to the shack in record time, but he wasn't surprised to see several vehicles already there, including the sheriff's. Roy must have been in the area.

With Layla walking quickly by his side, he moved toward the shack but stopped when the door opened and his grandmother stepped out. Her crestfallen features and the tears in her eyes made him pause. *What the hell…?*

He looked past her to Caldwell, who had his grandmother's hand tucked securely in his. The older man shook his head sadly. Gavin felt Layla move closer to his side and he placed his hand in hers.

"I'm taking your grandmother to my place," Caldwell said. "That's where she'll be. You need to go on in now. He's already confessed."

Gavin frowned. *He who? And why was his grand-*

mother crying? Tightening his grip on Layla's hand, he entered the shack.

Everyone looked up when he and Layla walked in. Roy and Gavin's four SEAL friends. Was he imagining things or were the five looking at him strangely? A funny feeling settled in his gut. Stepping into the room, he glanced around. "Okay, guys. What's going on? Where is he?"

The group shifted and he saw the man seated in a chair with his hands handcuffed behind his back. Gavin shook his head as if to clear his brain. "Mr. Lott?" he said in shock.

Sherman Lott couldn't even look at him. Gavin shook his head again and looked over at his friends. "There must be some mistake. Mr. Lott has been our neighbor for years. He was a friend of Dad's. He—"

"I was never a friend of your father's!" Lott all but screamed. "Gavin Jr. always got anything he wanted. He was the town's hero in high school. I could never compete. Then he became a SEAL and was a war hero, and I couldn't compete there, either. He got all the girls. After my leg got banged up that time when a horse threw me, the women around here wouldn't give me the time of day."

Gavin stared at the man who was now glaring back at him with cold and hate-filled eyes. Gavin let go of Layla's hand. Evidently he had misunderstood this man's relationship with his father all these years. "Okay, so there was a rivalry between you and Dad, and he wasn't your friend. What does that have to do with you sabotaging a dig on my property?"

Instead of answering, Lott shifted his gaze from Gavin to Layla. "I removed that marker so you'd forget where you were supposed to dig, but that didn't stop you. I burned that damn barn down and that didn't stop you, either. You were determined to dig anyway."

"Why didn't you want her to dig, Mr. Lott?" Gavin asked.

The man didn't answer. He looked away as if ignoring the question.

Gavin looked over at his friends. "Would any of you care to explain just what the hell is going on? Why didn't Lott want Layla's team to dig up buried treasure?"

Roy cleared his throat and said in a somber voice, "It wasn't the buried treasure he was concerned with anyone finding, Gavin."

Gavin frowned. Now he was even more confused. "Then what was it?"

The room quieted and he felt Layla pressing her body closer to his. Then she again placed her hand in his. When no one answered, Lott hollered out, "Your mother! I didn't want you to find your mother's body."

Layla felt weak in the knees and wondered how Gavin could still be standing. His friends evidently wondered the same thing as Bane and Coop crossed the room to flank Gavin's other side. Suddenly, she realized they hadn't done so to keep Gavin steady on his feet. They'd moved to intercede if Gavin took a mind to kill Sherman Lott.

"You refused an attorney, Mr. Lott," Roy said angrily. "Like I told you before, any confession you make will hold up in court."

Layla saw Flipper hold up his phone, letting everyone know he was recording everything. Gavin moved forward, and she, Bane and Coop fell in step. It was apparent the shock of what Lott had said had worn off.

"What do you mean 'my mother's body'?" Gavin asked, standing less than five feet from Lott.

Layla thought she actually saw regret fill Mr. Lott's eyes when he said, "I didn't mean to kill her. Honest. It was an accident."

Gavin drew in a breath so deep, it seemed the room rattled from the effect. She felt it. She thought everybody in the room felt it. "You killed my mother?" he asked in an incredulous voice. "But how? She left here."

The man shook his head. "No, she didn't. She never left. I came across her one day with a flat tire. Said she'd planned on going away for a while but changed her mind and turned around before even making it to town. She missed you and your dad too much to go anywhere. She was on her way back home. Had made it to the main road to the Silver Spurs when her tire went flat. I offered to help. She was pretty. She smelled good. I thought she was too good for your dad. He didn't deserve her. What man would leave a young wife who looked like her all alone to go play soldier?"

The man paused. "I told her as much. I must have made her nervous by what I said. By the way I was looking at her and all. And then I don't know what happened but I tried to touch her. She slapped me and I got mad. I slapped her back. I admit to hitting her several more times. She managed to get away and she ran from me. That made me angry. I ran after her and she fell and hit her head."

"And you didn't go get help?" Gavin asked in a voice that was as hard as steel.

"No!" Lott snapped. "Too late. Blood was everywhere. I knew she was dead. Besides, had she lived she would have told everyone what I tried to do. So I dug a hole and buried her."

Layla could almost see steam coming out of Gavin's ears. He was breathing deeply. The hand holding hers tightened in fury.

"What about the car?" Roy asked. Maybe the sheriff figured the best thing to do was keep the conversation going. Otherwise the deathly silence might put crazy ideas into Gavin's head. Like crossing the room and breaking Sherman Lott's neck with his bare hands.

"I drove the car into my lake," Lott said.

"You bastard!" Gavin roared. He would have moved closer but Bane and Coop blocked him. "You buried my mother in a hole not knowing if she was alive or dead? And then you drove her car into the lake?"

Lott had the nerve to glare at Gavin. "Why do you think I wouldn't let anyone swim or fish in my lake? Why I kept it off-limits to you or anyone? Especially to you. I knew how well you could swim and figured one day you might dive too far down and see the car."

Layla saw fierce rage on Gavin's face and she felt it in his entire body. The thought of him being *that* enraged scared her. She glanced over at Bane and Coop. They looked just as enraged as Gavin.

Coop then said in a menacingly calm voice, speaking directly to Gavin but not taking his eyes off Lott. "Now you know why he tried keeping anyone from digging in the south pasture, Viper. Let Roy take him in."

"No!" Gavin roared. "That bastard killed my mother."

"We know," Bane said in a chilling tone, giving Lott one hell of a lethal stare. "We all heard. And although we want to get a damn machete and chop his ass into little pieces, we won't. Let the law take care of him, Viper. In the end he's going to get exactly what he deserves."

The room got quiet and all eyes shifted to Gavin. Even Lott looked petrified upon seeing the deadly glint in Gavin's eyes. There was no doubt in Layla's mind that everyone in that room remembered that, when he needed to be, Gavin Blake could become a killing machine.

Then suddenly Gavin pulled his hand free of hers, shoved both of his hands into the pockets of his jeans and began slowly backing up, not taking his eyes off Lott. It was as if he was trying to pull himself together. As if he knew that staying in that room with Lott one more second meant he would lose control and do the man bodily harm. Gavin kept backing up until his back touched the door. He turned to open it and then stopped. He paused before turning back around.

Layla held her breath, not knowing what Gavin intended to do next. From the tension in the room, she knew his SEAL friends were poised, anticipating his next move. Then his gaze shifted from Lott to her. She saw both pain and anger in his features and her heart hurt for him. The man she loved. She wanted to think he needed her, but would he shut her out of the emotions he was feeling?

The room was deathly still as he continued to stare at her. Then he moved forward…toward her. When he stood right in front of her, he took her hand in his again. Then, without saying a single word, he led her out the door.

Chapter 17

Gavin wanted to pull his truck to the side of the road and catch his breath. But he couldn't. Something propelled him to keep driving until he reached the party house. He needed Layla as much as he needed to breathe. She wasn't saying anything. Just sitting in the bench seat beside him and staring straight ahead. It was as if she knew he needed complete silence. His mind was in a state of shock and he was fighting to keep control. Fearful that at any moment he might lose it.

Every time he thought about what Lott had confessed to doing, his mind would spin. Become filled with deadly thoughts and tempt him to turn the truck around and go back to the shack and beat the hell out of the man. How could anyone do what Lott had done and live with himself all these years? And to think no one had suspected a thing until Layla had shown up wanting to dig on their property.

Gavin released a deep breath when he turned into the driveway. Moments later he brought the truck to a stop beside Layla's rental car. Then he was out of the vehicle and moving to the passenger side of the truck. He was there when she opened the door.

Sweeping her into his arms, he headed for the porch, taking the steps two at a time. Grateful that in their rush to leave they'd left the door unlocked, he pushed it open and went inside. Barely taking time to close it behind him, he put Layla on her feet and began ripping off his clothes. She followed his lead and quickly removed hers.

He needed to be inside her. Now.

Taking hold of her waist, he lifted her up and released a throaty growl while pressing her body against the door, spreading her legs wide in the process. Then he was at her entrance, filled with an adrenaline high so potent he could feel blood rushing through his veins, especially the thick ones at the head of his shaft. Desire, as intense as it could get, became a throbbing need pulsating within him.

He thrust hard into her. Over and over again. Needing the release that only her body could give him. Leaning in, he captured her lips with his as sensations, too overpowering to be controlled, rammed through him. When she wrapped her legs around him, she propelled him to make his strokes harder and longer.

Their kiss was so sexually charged he wasn't sure how much longer he could last. He was being robbed of any logical thought except becoming a part of this woman's body. This woman, who had come to mean so much to him. This woman, who made him feel things he'd never felt before with anyone else.

And when she tore her mouth away from his just seconds before her body detonated, her spiraling climax triggered his own and he stroked her with hard and steady thrusts. He hollered her name, drowning in emotions so powerful they seemed to rock his world. A world that a short while ago had been torn apart. He couldn't stop his heart from racing at the magnitude of what he felt. At the magnitude of all he desired.

He knew then that if he'd had any doubt before regarding what Layla had come to mean to him, there was none now.

"Sorry. I should not have taken you that way. But I needed you so damn much, Layla."

They lay together in bed. After making love against the door, Gavin had picked her up and carried her into the bedroom. Then they'd slid beneath the covers and he had held her. She had held him. Layla knew that sleep wasn't an option.

She snuggled closer, needing his heat. Needing a reminder of how much she had been desired. "No apology needed. I liked it."

"I was rough."

"You were good as usual." He had needed her, just like he'd said. Layla had felt that need with every stroke.

"I lost control," he admitted in a low voice. "That's never happened to me before. Hell, Layla, I didn't even take time to put on a condom."

She'd noticed. Had exhilarated in the feeling of being skin to skin with him. Had loved the moment he had blasted off inside of her. The feel of his hot release had felt so right. How could she tell him that? But she knew she had to.

She lifted her face from his chest, met the dark eyes staring down at her. "I liked the feel of you inside me without a condom, Gavin. And don't worry about me getting pregnant. Although I was never sexually active, I decided to get the birth control implant anyway. Better to be safe than sorry. I didn't have to think about it, not like the pill where you have to remember to take one every day." She paused. "And I'm healthy so you don't have to worry about me giving you anything."

He shifted their positions in bed, slipping his arms around her and holding her close. "I'm healthy, too, and you don't have to worry about me giving you anything, either."

He then cupped her chin. "Although I didn't like being rough with you, I enjoyed making love to you without a condom, too."

And then he didn't say anything and she didn't, either. She figured he needed the silence. But when it stretched for what she thought was too long, she moved to lie on top of him and stared into the face she loved so much.

"Talk to me, Gavin. Tell me what you're feeling."

A part of her wondered what right she had to stick her nose into his business, to assume he wanted to tell her anything. But another part of her knew she couldn't let him withdraw. Just like he'd needed her physically, she wanted him to need her emotionally, as well.

She knew his eyes well. Just as well as she knew the shape of his mouth and the fullness of those lips that had kissed her earlier. He would try to fight her on this but she wouldn't let him. He'd been by himself this way for so long she figured it was hard for him to allow another person into his space. Especially a woman. But she had news for him. She wasn't just any woman. She was the woman who loved him.

And for some reason, although he'd never given her reason to say the words, a part of her believed he knew how she felt. A part of her wanted to believe that he knew she wouldn't share her body with just anyone. This wasn't just an excavation fling for her. It was more. But maybe he didn't know. Men had a tendency to be dense when it came to the I-love-you stuff.

"For a minute I felt like a loose cannon, Layla," he said, interrupting her thoughts. "So out of control. I could have snapped and killed Lott with my bare hands. It would have given me pleasure to hear the sound of his neck breaking."

His words, spoken with deep emotion, invaded her mind. She had felt his anger and she'd seen how he'd managed to hold it in check after hearing everything the man had said. Of course the sheriff had been there to stop Gavin from taking matters into his own hands. And his SEAL teammates had been there, too, although she wasn't sure if they would have stopped him or helped him.

"But now you know the truth, Gavin. Your mother never left you and your dad, after all. She's been here all this time. Here on the Silver Spurs."

She watched his eyes flash with confusion. She explained further. "You remember when you told me how the south pasture was your favorite area and your father's, as well. How the two of you would often camp out there. How you loved the feel of sleeping under the stars?"

"Yes."

"I want to think that although the two of you didn't know it, the reason that area meant so much was because your mom was there. She was *there*, Gavin, and when you were there, without knowing it, you were close to her."

She saw the moment when her words sank in. Something broke within him. His eyes might not have been expressive to others but they were expressive to her. Without saying anything, he cupped the back of her neck and brought her mouth down to his. Their tongues tangled in a mating so intense that when he finally released her mouth, she felt light-headed and breathless.

Layla was glad she had given him something to think about. But she knew he must still feel guilty over what he'd believed all these years—that his mother had deserted him and his father. His next words proved her right.

"But I didn't know, Layla. I thought she had gone. I thought she was living another life somewhere without us. I thought—"

She placed a finger to his lips. "What you thought was understandable. You were only a child when she disappeared. But your dad knew his wife. He knew their love. He always believed she would come back. And she did. In fact, she never left. She's been here for the two of you the entire time. And I know she was proud of your dad and was just as proud of you. The man you've become."

He pulled her close, buried his face in her neck. And she held him. Held him tight and near her heart. A part of her wanted to tell him now how much she loved him, but she knew it wasn't the time. That admission would come later. For now this was what he needed. To know she was here and that he wasn't alone.

Bane's ringtone woke Gavin and he glanced out the window as he sat up. It was daybreak. "Yes, Bane?" He nodded. "We're on our way."

When he clicked off the phone, he said, "Let's get dressed. Both your team and mine are ready. Now they have two treasures to find."

A short while later, Gavin pulled his truck to a stop in front of what Layla knew should have been the excavation site. Instead it resembled a crime scene with yellow tape marking the area. Upon hearing the sound of the truck, everyone turned their way. A blanket of snow covered the hillside and forecasters predicted even heavier snow by the weekend. They would need to work quickly.

Layla saw her students standing in a huddle. They'd probably heard what was going on and were trying to figure out how they'd slept through it all. She also saw Ms. Melody standing close to Caldwell, the man's arms wrapped protectively around her. Nothing discreet there. If anyone hadn't realized they were a couple before, they sure knew it now.

Roy was talking on the phone and Gavin's teammates stood next to the digging equipment. She wondered if they'd gotten any sleep, although they looked wide-awake and ready for any action that might come their way.

She'd been so busy observing everyone that she'd failed to notice that Gavin had gotten out of the truck until he was opening the passenger door. He leaned over her to unsnap her seat belt and then effortlessly lifted her out of her seat. "Thanks," she said, when he'd placed her on her feet.

"Don't mention it."

Taking her hand, he walked to where the others were standing. His grandmother left her place by Caldwell's side and walked over to Gavin. He released his hold on Layla's hand and pulled Ms. Melody into a big hug. Giving the two some privacy, Layla joined her students. She figured they would have a lot of questions.

After talking to her team, she returned to Gavin and his teammates. Coop explained how they'd fingered Sherman Lott as the bad guy. "After you told us about the footprint and how it was apparent more pressure was being placed on one foot than the other, we knew we were looking for someone with a leg injury or some kind of impairment and who was wearing worn shoes. When we saw Lott's shoes and saw him rubbing his leg more than once, I got suspicious. I offered him my chair so he wouldn't have to stand. I told him that I noticed his leg seemed to be bothering him. That's when he said it occasionally did and was the result of a horse riding accident years ago."

Coop then nodded for Bane to continue.

"Last night after everyone had gone to bed," Bane said, taking up the tale, "Mac and I decided to go to Lott's ranch and snoop around, to see if we could find the kerosene can. Imagine our surprise when we got there and saw him loading up a kerosene can onto his truck, with plans to head back over to your place to burn down the shack. We called Coop and told him to contact you and to call the sheriff. Lott was caught red-handed about to pour kerosene around the shack to torch it."

Roy approached with an angry look on his face. "What's wrong, Roy?" Gavin asked.

"One of the disadvantages of a small town is not having manpower when you need it," Roy said, drawing in a deep breath. "I talked to the sheriff in Palmdale and he said it would be four to five days before their dive team could get here."

Gavin nodded as if he wasn't concerned with that news. "Is there any reason we can't start digging?" he asked.

Roy frowned. "Yes, there's a reason. This is a crime scene."

Gavin shook his head. "Technically it's not. Although I believe everything Lott said, until I find my mother's body there's no proof a crime has been committed. Besides, I'd rather be the one to find her, Roy. And those students over there are entitled to their treasure hunt."

Roy didn't say anything for a minute and then nodded. "Okay, but I will stay here to help and step in if any evidence is found."

"Absolutely," Gavin assured him.

Roy drew in a deep breath and ordered one of his deputies to remove the yellow crime scene tape.

Less than an hour later, the remains of Jamie Blake were found. And within twenty feet of where she'd been buried, a strongbox filled with gold pieces—Jesse James's loot—was also recovered.

Deciding not to wait on the dive team from Palmdale, Flipper had jumped into Lott's lake without any diving gear. When he hadn't resurfaced in five minutes, Roy became worried. Gavin and his other teammates had not. They explained that although the water was icy cold and Flipper had been under longer than normal, Flipper was far from ordinary. They were proven right when a short while later Flipper resurfaced with the license plate he had removed from the car. The license plate was identified as that registered to Gavin and Jamie Blake.

The charges against Sherman Lott were changed from suspicion of murder to murder.

Chapter 18

Layla stood at the window. It was snowing and what had begun that morning as small flakes was now huge and covering the earth in a white blanket. Four days had passed since the dig, and activities on the Silver Spurs were returning to normal. Once Gavin's mother's remains had been unearthed, the town's coroner had been called and the yellow tape had been reerected. But not before Jesse James's strongbox filled with gold bars had been uncovered.

The Silver Spurs became the focus of two big news stories—a decades-old murder and the first recorded discovery of Jesse James's loot in the state of Missouri. No-trespassing signs had been posted when the media had converged on the ranch.

Gavin had given his one and only statement regarding the recovery of his mother's remains. "I am glad the truth about my mother's disappearance was discovered and I hope Sherman Lott rots in hell."

A news conference had been held regarding the discovery of Jesse James's loot, which was making international news. Dr. Clayburn arrived in town and tried to claim the university was associated with the dig. Layla refuted his statement since she had documentation in the form of an email from both Dr. Clayburn and the president of the university advising of her termination prior to the dig. The following day, the two men were in even more hot water when photographs surfaced of the two of them involved in illicit affairs with female students. Not surprisingly, Tammy was in many of the photographs, arriving and leaving various hotels with both men.

Layla didn't have to guess where the photographs had come from. Apparently Donnell and some of the other students had exposed the sordid activities. Within twenty-four hours of the photographs being splashed across the front page of the *Seattle Times* and making the national news, the two men, along with a few other faculty members, had turned in their resignations.

Donnell, Wendy and Marsha had joined Layla at the news conference and were acknowledged for their participation on the dig. The Missouri Archaeological Society had authenticated the loot as that stolen by Jesse James from the Tinsel Bank.

Already offers of employment from numerous universities had arrived for Layla, in addition to offers of book deals and television interviews. Yesterday she'd received a call from her grandmother and one from her parents. She had been surprised when her parents told her how proud they were of her. They'd even said she'd done the right thing by following her own dream and not theirs. They invited her to spend the holidays with them in DC.

She drew in a deep breath and moved away from the window to sit on the bed she'd just left a few moments earlier. She had awakened to find Gavin gone. He must have left to check on the ranch with his men. Even with the no-trespassing signs clearly posted, a couple of reporters and their camera crews had encroached on the property only to have Gavin's men run them off again.

The coroner had released his mother's remains and yesterday morning a private memorial service had been held. Jamie Blake had been reburied beside her husband in the family cemetery. Layla had stood beside Gavin along with his grandmother, Caldwell and Gavin's teammates. Even his commanding officer had flown in to attend the service.

After dinner, Gavin's teammates left to return to their various homes, but not before each one had given her a huge hug and told her how glad they'd been to meet her. She had gotten to know the four well and could see why they and Gavin shared such close relationships. Bane, Coop, Flipper and Mac were swell guys who were fiercely loyal to each other. She couldn't thank them enough for their part in recovering Jesse James's loot.

Now that the dig was over, Layla could feel Gavin withdrawing from her. She had tried ignoring it but she knew something was bothering him. She thought it was related to his mother but, to be totally honest, she wasn't sure.

There was no reason for her to remain on the ranch any longer and she had mentioned that she would be leaving in a couple of days to return to Seattle. She had hoped he would ask her to stay but he hadn't. Instead he'd merely nodded and hadn't said anything else about it. Was that his way of letting her know she had outstayed her welcome?

The thought that he wanted her to leave his ranch had tears welling up in her eyes. She'd known when she fell in love with him that there was a big chance he wouldn't love her back. So why was the thought that he didn't breaking her heart?

The time they had spent together on the Silver Spurs had been special but now she had to move on.

Gavin placed his coffee cup on the table, stared at his grandmother and then asked, "What did you just say?"

Melody Blake smiled brightly. "You heard me right, Gavin. Caldwell asked me to marry him. This was his third time asking and I finally said yes. We don't want to make a big fuss about it and Reverend Pollock agreed to perform the ceremony next weekend. I'll be moving into Caldwell's place afterward."

Gavin didn't say anything for a long moment. He was happy for his grandmother and Caldwell. It was about time. "Congratulations. I'm happy for you, Gramma Mel. Caldwell is a good man and I believe the two of you will be happy together."

"Thank you. What about you? What are your plans regarding Layla?"

He lifted his coffee cup and took a sip before saying, "What makes you think I have any?"

His grandmother frowned. "Don't try pretending with me, Gavin Timothy Blake III. You love Layla.

You've admitted as much. I would think you'd want to take the next step."

Yes, he had admitted it to her and he didn't regret doing so. "Sometimes taking the next step isn't always possible."

"Why not? I'd think you'd want something permanent between the two of you."

He shook his head. "Layla and I are very different. Dad took Mom out of a big city and brought her here and she was miserable. Layla is from Seattle. She'd be just as unhappy and miserable here as Mom was."

"Have you talked to Layla about it? Have you asked her how she feels?"

"No."

"Then maybe you should. You're basing your opinions on assumptions. I know for a fact Layla loves the Silver Spurs. She said as much."

"But that doesn't mean she loves me. If she doesn't love me, then there's nothing to hold her here. She's gotten a lot of job offers from a number of big universities, including Harvard. All we have in Cornerstone is a small college. Why would she settle for that?"

"Well, I think you'll be making a big mistake if you don't talk to her about it, tell her how you feel. Let her decide what she wants to do. You might discover that she loves you as much as you love her."

An hour or so later, Gavin entered the party house. He removed his hat and shook off the snow from his jacket before hanging both items on the rack.

The first thing he noticed as he headed for the kitchen was that the curtains were still closed. Everything was just as he'd left it at daybreak, which meant

Layla hadn't gotten up yet. Placing the box containing the breakfast his grandmother had prepared on the table, he moved down the hallway to the bedroom. Opening the door, he stuck his head inside and saw Layla curled up in bed still sleeping.

The bad weather had pretty much dictated that everyone stay inside. He knew his men had a card game going and he could certainly join them. But he much preferred staying here and joining Layla, right in that bed. What if Gramma Mel was right? What if Layla wanted to stay on the Silver Spurs with him? Would it be fair to ask her to stay when a call from his commanding officer meant he would drop everything for a covert operation? Would she want that?

He sat in a chair and removed his shoes and socks before standing to take off the rest of his clothes. No matter the temperature, he preferred sleeping in the nude, something he couldn't do while away on missions.

Crossing the room, Gavin slid into bed with Layla and pulled her into his arms, to warm his body as well as his heart.

Layla thought she was dreaming when she felt a hot and husky whisper against her ear. It took a moment to open her eyes and gaze into a pair of sexy dark ones staring back at her. Gavin's body was pressed close to hers. It was warm, even hot in certain places, and she knew without a doubt that he was naked.

"We need to talk, Layla."

She heard the seriousness in his voice. Why did they need to talk? He was ready for her to leave. She got that. But why was he rushing her away? Did he already have another woman lined up to share his bed? The thought made her mad and she buried her face in the pillow, but not before saying, "I don't want to talk. I have nothing to say to you."

He pulled the pillow away from her, frowning. "What the hell did I do?"

"Just being a typical man. You share a bed with a woman, and then you tire of her and want her gone so you can replace her with another."

He stared at her. "You think I would do that?"

"Why wouldn't you? You're a man, aren't you? You're not tied to any woman, especially not to me. It's not like I didn't notice that reporter flirting with you."

He frowned. "What reporter?"

Layla rolled her eyes. "The one that kept putting that microphone all in your face and kept touching your shoulders every chance she got, even when she didn't have to." Layla hated that she'd said something about that. Now she sounded like a jealous hag. Just because they'd slept together a few times didn't mean she had dibs on him.

Before she could catch her next breath, he had flipped her on her back. He loomed over her and held her hands in a tight grip above her head.

"Why would I want another woman, Layla?"

That was really a silly question. "Why wouldn't you want another one?"

He stared down at her with an intensity that made a rush of desire claw through her insides. "Because you are all the woman I need. Hell, I can barely keep up with you, Layla."

Lord knows that's the truth, Gavin thought, as he felt familiar need hammer through him. Only Layla could do this to him. Make him feel so consumed with desire for her, he would go up in flames. More than once his teammates had told him to take a cold shower when just looking at Layla heated an entire room.

Gavin just stared down at her. She was wearing a nightgown, but barely. It was made of flimsy material and part of it was bunched up around her waist, leaving her bare below. Her hair was loose and tousled around her shoulders. Because of the way he was holding her hands, her breasts jutted up, firm and hard. He could see the impression of rigid nipples through the thin material of her gown.

Just that quickly, her breathing changed. He heard it and then he felt the sinfully erotic movement of her hips against him. After all the times they'd made love right here in this bed, not to mention the times they hadn't made it to the bed, didn't she know how much he wanted her? Her and no other woman? She actually thought she had a reason to be jealous of some damn reporter who couldn't keep her hands to herself?

He knew from the eyes staring back at him that his grandmother was right. Layla had no idea how he felt about her. The woman hadn't a clue. He had told her they needed to talk, and then she'd gone on the offensive. Why? Had his grandmother been right on both accounts, that Layla cared for him as much as he cared for her?

There was only one way to find out.

"Let's backtrack for a minute, Layla. Earlier I asked you why I would want another woman, and you asked why I wouldn't want one. I don't think I made myself clear enough. The main reason I don't want another woman is because I love you. I've fallen in love with you, Layla, and when a man falls in love with one woman she takes away his desire for other women. She becomes the one and only woman he wants in his life, his bed, his home, his mind and his heart. You are that woman for me."

She stared at him for a long time without saying anything. And then he saw it, the tears forming in her eyes. "But if you love me, why were you sending me away?"

He frowned. "I wasn't sending you away. The other night you told me you were going. What was I supposed to do, tell you that you couldn't go?"

She frowned back at him. "You could have told me you loved me."

"Why would I tell you that when I didn't know how you felt? Hell, I still don't know. With your credentials, you can teach anywhere. I know about all those job offers that have come in. Why would you want to stay here? My mother hated it here."

"I love you, too, Gavin, and I love it here. I fell in love with the Silver Spurs the minute I drove onto the land. There are times when I will leave to do speaking engagements and interviews. Maybe even teach a class or two for a semester. However, I will come back. You leave, don't you? To go on your covert operations. Yet you come back. You return and step into your role of a rancher. Why can't I return and step into a similar role."

"As a rancher's wife?"

She lifted her brow. "Wife?"

He smiled down at her. "Yes, wife. You don't think you'll hang around as my live-in lover, do you? I want to marry you. I want you to one day have my children. I want you to live here on this ranch with me."

"And be here whenever the rancher returns?"

He chuckled. "That would be nice."

A smile touched her lips. "That can be arranged." She didn't say anything for a minute. "About all those offers. I don't want to decide on anything just yet. After dealing with the likes of Clayburn and Connors, I just want to chill for a minute. Possibly write a book. I'd love to take my time and do it here."

He nodded. He needed to let her know something.

Layla waited for him to speak.

"Gramma Mel told me this morning that she and Caldwell are getting married. She's moving to his place. That means you'll be here by yourself whenever I'm away. I'm supposed to report back for duty at the end of January."

"I'll be okay. I will have enough to keep me busy."

Layla wouldn't tell him yet that she wanted lots of children. She'd always wished for siblings and would make sure she had more than one child. And she didn't want to wait a long time before she began having them.

Before Gavin, she'd never thought beyond her career goals. But now she'd achieved those. With him by her side, she could have everything—success and a family and the man she loved.

"So, will you marry me?"

That question, as far as she was concerned, was a no-brainer. "Yes, Gavin, I will marry you."

He released her hands as he lowered his mouth to hers. She wrapped her arms around his muscled back.

She loved her SEAL, her rancher. For them, the best was yet to come.

Epilogue

Layla couldn't help but dab at her eyes. The vow renewal ceremony for Bane and his wife, Crystal, was simply beautiful. The words they spoke to each other in the presence of family and friends were filled with so much love that Layla couldn't help but shed tears.

Gavin had told her how Bane and Crystal had eloped as teens, and then had been separated for five years when her family had sent her away. But what Layla found so precious was how their love had survived. They had reunited a year ago and since no family members had been present for their first wedding, they'd decided to renew their vows in front of everyone.

What was doubly special was that Crystal and Bane had announced to everyone earlier that day that they were expecting a baby. Everyone could tell from the smiles on the couple's faces that a baby was something they both wanted. Gavin and the guys couldn't wait to tease Bane about impending fatherhood. Mac, who had a number of kids of his own, said he would give Bane pointers on changing diapers.

Today was officially the couple's sixth wedding anniversary and Crystal's twenty-fourth birthday. Layla thought it refreshing to find someone even younger than her with a PhD; they had a lot in common. Crystal was beautiful and Layla thought she was just the woman for Bane.

It was a lovely November day in the city of Denver. And since one of Bane's brother's had married an event planner, the home belonging to Bane's older brother Dillon, where the ceremony took place, had been decorated beautifully in colors of blue and gold. Layla had already talked to Alpha Westmoreland about planning Layla's dream wedding, which would take place in June.

"You okay, baby?" Gavin whispered before boldly using his tongue to lick away one of her tears.

"Behave, Gavin," she whispered back in a warning tone, knowing when it came to her he wouldn't behave.

She glanced around to see if anyone had noticed what he'd done. Bane certainly had a big family. There were Westmorelands everywhere. Gavin had warned her but she hadn't believed him. No wonder the locals referred to this section of Denver as Westmoreland Country. There were also some Westmorelands who lived in Atlanta, Montana and Texas. She'd even discovered Bane's cousin was married to a king in a country in the Middle East. All the Westmorelands she'd met were friendly and made her feel so welcome.

Another couple she'd met and liked right away was Bane's cousin Bailey and her husband, Walker Rafferty.

They lived in Alaska. Layla hadn't wanted to keep staring at Walker but she remembered when he'd been a movie star years ago. He'd been a heartthrob then and he was definitely one today. She recalled seeing his picture on the cover of a recent issue of *Simply Irresistible* magazine. When she'd mentioned it to Bailey, the woman had chuckled and looked up at her husband adoringly before saying, "There's a story behind that. One day I will have to tell you about it."

It was good seeing Gavin's teammates again. Layla was glad to meet Mac's wife, Teri. The mother of four was simply gorgeous. Everyone planned to visit the Silver Spurs in June for Gavin and Layla's wedding. They'd agreed to spend Thanksgiving at the ranch and Christmas with her family. Ms. Melody and Caldwell had married and seemed to be very happy together.

Layla looked down at her engagement ring. It was beautiful. They had talked about Gavin giving Layla his mother's wedding set. Jamie had still been wearing the rings when her body had been unearthed. But Gavin had said he wanted Layla to have her own special rings and he would keep the rings his father had given his mother to pass on to their first son… Gavin Blake IV. She smiled at the audacity of Gavin thinking he would one day have a son to carry on the Blake name.

When the minister told Bane he could kiss his wife, everyone cheered. Bane pulled Crystal into his arms and gave her one hell of a kiss. What the couple shared was definitely special. Just as special as what Layla and Gavin shared.

Bane then leaned over and whispered something in Crystal's ear, which made her blush. Layla leaned over to Gavin. "I guess you heard that." He had told her about what his teammates dubbed as his sonic ears.

Gavin smiled. "Yes, I heard. Every single naughty word."

"The ceremony was beautiful," Layla said, fighting back more tears.

Gavin took her hand, brought it to his lips and kissed her knuckles. "And so are you. I can't wait until the day you will officially have my name."

Layla couldn't wait, either. He'd been trying to talk her into eloping in January and having a huge wedding reception in June. He wanted them to be married before he left for this next covert operation. She was giving his suggestion some serious thought.

"And I can't wait until later, when I get you back to our hotel room," he added, whispering close to her ear.

Layla smiled as they linked hands and walked out of the church. She knew her life with her SEAL/rancher would never be boring.

* * * * *

Reese Ryan writes sexy, emotional love stories served with a heaping side of family drama.

Reese is a native Ohioan with deep Tennessee roots. She endured many long, hot car trips to family reunions in Memphis via a tiny clown car loaded with cousins.

Connect with her on Instagram, Facebook, Twitter or at reeseryan.com.

Join her VIP Readers Lounge at bit.ly/VIPReadersLounge.

Books by Reese Ryan

Harlequin Desire

The Bourbon Brothers

Savannah's Secret
The Billionaire's Legacy
Engaging the Enemy

Dynasties: Secrets of the A-List

Seduced by Second Chances

Texas Cattleman's Club: Inheritance

Secret Heir Seduction

Visit the Author Profile page at Harlequin.com for more titles.

PLAYING WITH TEMPTATION

Reese Ryan

Dedicated to self-sacrificing single mothers
like my mother and paternal grandmother.
And to devoted fathers like my husband.

Acknowledgments

Thank you to author Michele Summers for driving out to the boonies for an into-the-wee-hours brainstorming session for this story.

Thank you to my good friend and beta reader Lani Bennett for allowing me to bounce ideas off you for this story and others.

To Shannon Criss, Keyla Hernandez and the rest of the Kimani editorial team: thank you for providing insight and feedback that made the story stronger while also allowing me to remain true to my vision.

Chapter 1

Nate Johnston entered the private dining room at his favorite seafood restaurant and froze, his expensive Italian loafers rooted to the floor.

The ghost of relationships past.

Kendra didn't need to turn around for him to recognize the woman he'd once shared his bed with; the mother of his six-year-old son. He sensed her presence—like something warm wiggling beneath his skin—the instant he stepped into the room.

Nate was in the midst of the biggest crisis of his eight-year-long professional football career. Why would his brother invite him to dinner with the woman who shattered his heart seven years ago?

"Glad you're here, Nate. Have a seat." His brother Marcus indicated the seat next to Kendra.

Nate narrowed his gaze at his brother and took the

seat beside him instead. "You asked me to meet you for dinner to discuss the *situation*."

As if Kendra and every other sports network viewer hadn't seen the grainy cell phone footage of him in a club, after a few drinks, ripping his teammates to shreds following the ass-whipping they'd endured at the hands of their division rivals. A devastating loss that put the brakes on the Memphis Marauders play-off run for the third year in a row.

The video had been edited to make him look like the villain. It didn't include him detailing how his own mistakes—a dropped pass and a costly fumble—had contributed to the loss.

"That's why she's here." Marcus's response was terse. As Nate's sports agent, Marcus's job had become ten times harder since the tape hit the airwaves that morning.

"Hello, Nate." Kendra's apologetic smile indicated she knew something he didn't.

Nate's attention was drawn to her expressive face. How did she manage to get more beautiful every time he saw her?

Head full of short, dark curls. Sheen on high blast. Style on point. Body-hugging knit dress in his favorite color on her—Marauders blue. The color perfectly contrasted the expanse of smooth brown skin exposed by the neckline of her dress.

An uneasy feeling crawled up his spine. Nate turned to his brother. "What do you mean *that's why she's here*?"

"It means we've got a ton of damage control to do, in addition to negotiating your new contract with the Marauders and trying to renew your two biggest endorsement deals. I can't handle everything alone. I've asked for Kendra's assistance."

Marcus had every right to be pissed, and Nate expected a little brotherly payback. But Marcus was a few cans short of a six-pack if he expected him to work with the woman who left him on one knee, ring in hand.

"What's wrong with the PR firm we've been using?"

"They're great when things are good, but we're in crisis mode. We need someone tough who'll get ahead of this thing and change the narrative out there about you."

"And out of all the possibilities in the free world, you believe the woman who rejected my proposal is the best person for the job?" He slid his gaze to Kendra. Her cheeks glowed beneath her warm, dark skin.

A twinge of guilt settled in his gut. It was a low blow, but so was walking out on him when he asked her to marry him seven years ago. He'd convinced himself he was over it and her. Yet the rejection still stung, especially being relegated to a part-time father.

Nate's father had tucked him and his six siblings into bed every night. Read them stories, taught them how to fish, fix their bikes and change the brakes on a car. He was still very much part of their lives. Nate had looked forward to being the kind of father who was present in his kids' lives every day.

Kendra had destroyed his chance of being that kind of dad to Kai.

When she'd responded to his marriage proposal by walking out, she'd left a hole in his chest where his heart had once been. Discovering the pregnancy a few weeks later, then announcing she fully intended to raise the baby on her own, had ripped out his soul and left him in a tailspin.

He still couldn't forgive her for reducing him to a baby daddy. For being the reason he didn't get to tuck Kai into bed most nights. Now Marcus wanted to put his future in her hands?

Oh, hell naw.

"I *know* she's the best person for the job." Marcus's expression was unwavering.

"I understand why you're still upset." Kendra's eyes conveyed the apology he'd already heard too many times. "But this isn't about our past. It's about ensuring your future on your terms. I can help you do that because I'm damn good at what I do. But I don't want to be here if you don't want me here."

"Good, then it's settled. What's for dinner?" Nate picked up his menu.

Marcus pushed the menu down. "Don't be a smart-ass, Nate. More importantly, don't let your ego get in the way of what's best for your career and your bank account. You've dug a king-size hole for yourself, little brother. It's my job to get you back on solid ground. I can do that, but I need Dray's help."

Nate narrowed his gaze at Marcus. *Dray? Really?* They were suddenly cozy enough that his brother was using the nickname he'd called her when they were together?

He turned his attention to Kendra. Her arms were folded, inadvertently pressing her breasts higher. His heartbeat quickened and his throat suddenly felt dry.

Focus, buddy, and not on those.

He gulped water from his glass, then cleared his throat. "I don't doubt your ability, Kendra, but given our history, working together is ill-advised. Am I the only one who gets that?"

"It's an awkward situation," Kendra acknowledged with a soft sigh, "but you're Kai's father. We'll always have a connection. Whether you believe it or not, Nate, I want what's best for you. That hasn't changed."

Nate swallowed the lump in his throat. "Let's not pretend this is a charitable arrangement. It's your chance to make a name for yourself."

Kendra pursed her lips painted a rich, velvety red reminiscent of a full-bodied glass of vintage port. As proud and stubborn as her mother, the woman was allergic to accepting help. It had taken him nearly a year to convince her to accept child support for Kai.

"This *is* an opportunity for me, which means I'm invested in your success. When we worked together, informally, you were a media darling."

Nate tapped his finger on the table. Kendra wasn't wrong. She'd been a huge help back then. He'd even asked her to help a couple of his college buddies who'd run into trouble.

He sucked in a deep breath. "You're good, but that isn't the point."

"Then what is the point?" She leaned forward, her arms folded, elbows on the table, providing an excellent view of her cleavage.

Nate was beginning to think she was doing it on purpose. Distracting him and trying to get him off his game. He swallowed hard, ignoring the blood emptying from his brain and rushing below his belt.

He glanced over at his smirking brother, who seemed to enjoy watching Kendra take him to task.

"You're going to make me say it? Fine." Nate leaned

forward, palms pressed to the table. "I prefer to work with someone I know has my back. Someone who'll ride this out instead of hitting the door the second the road gets hard. I want to work with someone who'll stand their ground and fight for me."

Kendra grimaced, as if he'd knocked the wind out of her.

Part of him relished the pain evident in her eyes. It didn't begin to rival the pain she'd inflicted on him. Yet another part of him couldn't bear to see the hurt in her chocolate-brown eyes.

"Your feelings are valid." Marcus spoke after what felt like a full minute of silence. His tone was apologetic, though Nate wasn't sure if the apology was meant for him or Kendra. "That's why you two need to hash things out."

"You're not hearing me, Marcus. There is nothing for us to hash out."

Marcus placed a firm hand on his shoulder. "You're my brother. I'd take a bullet for you. But as your agent, I have to be the voice of reason. Tell you what you need to hear. You screwed up. Royally. At the worst possible time. This is mission-critical. We need Dray. She knows you better than anyone, and she's a master at crisis management. Besides, she has a vested interest in seeing you succeed. All of our futures are on the line here, Nate. I wouldn't bring Dray in if I didn't trust her implicitly."

Kendra gave Marcus a grateful smile. She sat taller and returned her attention to Nate. "I can do this, Nate. I won't let you down."

Nate ignored her plea. He turned to Marcus. "I think we're pushing the panic button here."

"Cards on the table, bro?" Marcus motioned for the

server to come over. "It was Bat-Signal time the second that video hit the airwaves. The building is on fire. Don't be too proud to accept the help of a friendly face wearing a cape and toting a fire hose."

Nate gritted his teeth as Kendra held back a grin, her eyes gleaming. He sat stewing as Marcus explained to the server that he'd be leaving, so she should deliver his meal and the bill to Nate.

He loved his family, but it was a universal truth that older brothers could be asses.

Marcus stood and slipped on his wool coat. He gripped Nate's shoulder. "You said you'd do whatever it took to make this right. I'm playing that card now. You're two adults with a common goal. Figure it out." He shifted his gaze to Kendra. "Walk me out?"

She grabbed her wrap and followed him out.

Damn.

Next time he'd be careful with the promises he made his brother. His only hope was to convince Kendra to walk away.

Again.

Chapter 2

"You seem pleased." Kendra pulled the wrap tightly around her shoulders to combat the biting winter wind rushing into the lobby as patrons entered and exited. It was an unusual cold spell for North Carolina. "I'm not sure we were in the same room, because Nate isn't buying this."

"Not yet, but then you were prepared to turn me down when you arrived. What changed your mind?"

Her cheeks warmed. She agreed to dinner because she'd been intrigued by Marcus's proposal. It was her chance to finally establish a boutique PR and media coaching firm that catered to high-end talent. But she'd decided to take Nate on as a client the moment she laid eyes on him. Six feet three inches of brown-skin Adonis. Handsome and fit as ever. There was no way she'd admit that to his brother or to anyone.

"Despite what Nate thinks, he needs my help. Besides, I owe him." She couldn't erase the pain she'd caused when she'd walked away seven years ago, but she could make things right for him. Allow him to end his career on his terms.

Marcus squeezed her arm. "You don't owe either of us anything, but I'm glad you're on board."

"This isn't a done deal. I meant what I said. I'm willing to work through Nate resenting my help, but I won't do this if he's resistant. If he won't listen to me, this doesn't work."

"Then you've got some convincing to do." Marcus winked, tipped the valet and drove off.

Great. Kendra drew in a deep breath, then strutted back into the restaurant, spine straight and tall. *You've got this, girl.*

Nate didn't bother standing when she returned. He stared as if he couldn't believe she had the nerve to sashay her tail back into the private dining room. As if he'd expected her to turn and run.

"You need convincing, so let's talk. Ask me anything you want. We can discuss the ideas I have so far or the crisis management work I've done for high-profile corporate clients."

The server set their meals on the table. When she left, Nate took a swig of his beer, then set the glass on the table with a *thud.* "Fine. Let's talk about what happened between us."

"Nate…" Her voice wavered for a moment. She cleared her throat and lengthened her spine, holding his gaze. "We've talked about this."

"'I'm so sorry, Nate, I just can't do this' isn't a discussion, Kendra." The veins in his neck corded as he repeated her words that night verbatim. “You’ve shut me down anytime I’ve tried to have a real conversation about that night. If you want me to trust you, start by being honest about what happened between us.”

“This isn’t productive.” She shivered beneath his cold stare. “Discussing my proposed PR plan is.”

“If Marcus says you can do the job, I trust his judgment. What I need is to know I can trust you. So for once, be honest with me about why you walked out. Why you waited until I asked you to marry me and you were pregnant with my son to decide I wasn’t the right man for you.”

Her heart clenched at the bitterness that laced his words. It took her back to that night. The night she’d made the biggest mistake of her life.

“I underestimated how difficult it was to be the wife of a pro athlete.”

“I’d been with the Marauders for a year by then. How would your life have been any different?”

“There’s a huge difference between being the live-in girlfriend and being the wife and mother of your children.”

“A marriage license is just a piece of paper, Kendra. Other than having it and my last name, nothing would’ve changed.”

She tipped her chin, determined to keep her emotions in check. “It isn’t a meaningless piece of paper. It’s a lifelong commitment. That means something to me.”

Nate snorted. “If it means so much to you, why’d you turn it down when I offered it?”

“I couldn’t be one of those football wives who doesn’t have a life of her own and pretends not to know what happens on the road.”

His expression morphed from anger to hurt again. "So it was about that girl who let herself into my room in Cleveland. I told you, I didn't know her, and nothing happened between us. When I discovered her in my room, I called security and they sent her ass packing. End of story. I called you right away and told you about it. I wasn't trying to hide anything."

"The sports channels picked up the story. I would've heard about it."

Nate ran a hand through his close-cropped curls and heaved a sigh. "So that's what you think of me? That the minute I'm out of sight I can't keep it in my pants? News flash, Kendra, if I'd wanted to be with someone else, I would've been. Football groupies have been throwing themselves at me since high school. I didn't want them. I wanted you. I loved you. You obviously didn't feel the same."

"That isn't true." The accusation hit her like a bullet to the chest, piercing her heart and severing arteries. Nate was the only man she'd ever loved. She loved him still, but their time was past, and it was all her fault. "I'm a realist. You're only human. A man can only take so much temptation."

"If you felt that way, you should've come to me. We could've worked things out."

"How, Nate? You weren't going to leave the team, and I'd never ask *you* to give up your dream." She hadn't meant to stress the word.

Nate shifted in his seat, lowering his gaze. He hadn't missed the implication. She'd supported his dream, but he hadn't supported hers. He took another sip of his beer. "I never gave you any reason to doubt me."

"It was my issue, not yours. I fully own that."

"Just to be clear, you blew up our relationship, our family, because you thought I *might* eventually cheat on you?"

"It isn't as simple as that." She poked at the flounder she no longer had an appetite for. "My fears are very real, and I have them for good reason. That's my problem, not yours."

Nate laughed bitterly. "It sure as hell felt like my problem when you turned down my proposal in a roomful of our family and friends."

She cringed, remembering the moment he dropped to one knee and presented her with a beautiful, custom diamond engagement ring. The memory of that moment was as vivid now as it was then. Euphoric joy immediately followed by debilitating fear and a panic attack that stole her breath.

Chest heaving and the room spinning, she had only one clear thought—she couldn't marry Nate.

Until that moment, she'd anticipated the day he'd propose and dreamed of an intimate wedding ceremony on the beach. Then Nate asked her to marry him and the room went black.

Visions of ruthless groupies who'd do anything to get with a ballplayer filled her head. Her own father hadn't been faithful to her mother. How could she expect Nate to do so with so much temptation?

She'd broken it off, packed her things and made the long drive back to Pleasure Cove. Weeks later, she discovered she was pregnant with Kai.

"You didn't deserve that. I should've told you how I'd been feeling, but—"

"You didn't trust me enough to have an honest discussion then. Give me one reason I should trust you now." The ache reflected in his dark eyes penetrated her skin more than the bone-chilling air outside had.

Kendra choked back the thickness in her throat. "Because I'm the same girl who cheered you on at every game from peewee to the pros. The one who wouldn't let you give up on your dream when you weren't drafted."

Nate's expression softened, but he didn't respond.

Encouraged, Kendra continued. "We were so young then, Nate. I handled my feelings poorly. But I've never been anything but supportive of your career, and I've proven that I'm willing to go to bat for you. Who was it that convinced those arena football teams to give you a shot? Who sent your arena highlight clips to pro teams until the Marauders invited you to try out?"

"You." He rubbed his chin. "I owe my entire career to you."

"Our relationship may have ended, but my support of your career hasn't. No consultant will fight for your career harder than I will. Deep down, I think you know that."

Nate kneaded the back of his neck. "Okay, fine."

"Really?"

"Just until we secure my new contract."

Her buzz was quickly doused—like a too-short candlewick. The muscles of her face strained to maintain her smile. "Of course."

"We'll make it a six-month contract. You'll be well paid and Marcus will give you references, contacts… anything you need to rebrand your business. All right?"

"It's a generous offer, thank you. I accept."

"All right then." Nate inhaled Kendra's sweet scent: a gentle breeze wafting through a summer garden bursting with jasmine and gardenias. He pretended not to notice the disappointment on her face. It tugged at his heart and made him want to promise her the world just to see a genuine smile light those brown eyes. "I'll call Marcus tonight and have him draw up the contract."

"Great, I'll have my lawyer review it and we can go from there."

"How is your brother doing?" Nate sipped his beer, amused by how formally Kendra referred to her brother, Dashon, a contract law attorney.

Kendra shrugged. "He's still Dash. Being himself and doing his own thing."

"New York must be treating him well. I hear he rarely returns to Pleasure Cove." Nate carved into his prime rib covered with a creamy mushroom and lobster sauce—one of Nadine's specialties.

Kendra's mouth twisted. He'd obviously touched a nerve. He wouldn't pry further. They didn't need to be best friends. Just have a personable working relationship. "He comes home about as often as Quincy."

Touché. His globe-trotting younger brother was quickly making a name for himself as a photographer. His shadow rarely darkened the Johnston family's doorstep.

Nate contemplated the quiet look of concern that furrowed Kendra's brows. "Did I say something wrong?"

She stopped pushing the food around her plate and put down her fork. "No, but there's something we need to address, so I'm just going to say it."

He put down his utensils and sat back warily. "I'm listening."

"What happened between us in Memphis—"

"Which time?" Nate couldn't help the smirk that

tightened his mouth when he remembered how an argument between them had descended into hot, angry sex on two different occasions.

"Both." Kendra clearly wasn't amused. Nor did she seem to have the same fond memories of those occasions. "That can't happen again."

"I was hoping it would be one of the amenities you'd throw into the deal." He held back a grin as he drained the last of his beer.

She pointed one of her painted fingernails at him. "See, that's what I'm talking about. If this is going to work, you have to take me seriously."

"Oh, I took what we did very seriously." He raised an eyebrow and resumed eating his meal.

She let out a frustrated sigh and settled back in her seat. "This is your career we're talking about here, Nate. I need to maintain my focus, and I can't stay focused on cleaning up your rep if I'm thinking about…" Her words trailed off and there was a deep flush in her cheeks beneath her smooth brown skin. She shook her head, as if trying to shake off the memories. "Neither of us can afford the distraction."

"Agreed." He adjusted in his chair, his own body reacting to the memories. Her scent. Her taste. The sound of her soft pleas. "Though it worries me that my media consultant can't multitask."

They dissolved into laughter, and for a moment, it felt like old times. It was the first time either of them seemed relaxed since he'd arrived.

Nate smiled, relishing the sound of her laughter. One of the countless details about her he missed. "Okay, Ms. Media Consultant, where do we begin?"

Chapter 3

"This sounds like a great opportunity." Maya Alvarez, Kendra's half sister, sipped her mocha latte as they sat at the breakfast bar in the gorgeous penthouse Maya shared with her fiancé, hotelier Liam Westbrook. "So why aren't you excited about it?"

Kendra took a sip of the frothy peppermint mocha her sister made for her and let out an appreciative moan. "I am, but what if I'm jumping out of the frying pan and into the fire?"

"It's a tricky situation. I certainly couldn't work with the girls' dad. Not for all the money in the world." Maya placed a hand on Kendra's in response to her fallen expression. "But it's different with you and Nate."

"How? Carlos walked out on you, just like I walked out on Nate. The only difference was you and Carlos were married." Kendra drank more of her coffee. "He feels the same way you do. Honestly, I can't blame him."

"You've maintained an amicable relationship. Friendly enough that you two hooked up." Maya peered over her coffee cup, her dark eyes dancing with amusement.

"Shut. Up." Kendra pointed a finger at her giggling sister. "I shouldn't have told you that. I still can't believe it happened. Twice."

"Are we talking instances or the actual amount of times you guys—"

"Stop it, Maya!" Kendra's face and neck warmed. "Everyone knows you're not supposed to hold the things your sister says when she's drunk against her."

"All right, fine." Maya was still giggling. "I'm just saying, things can't be *that* bad between you. Besides, Nate's a terrific guy, and we both know you still have feelings for him."

"Of course I care about him. That doesn't mean we should be together." It was too quiet without the children around. Nothing to distract her from a conversation she'd rather not have. Liam had taken them to see the aquariums he'd just had installed at his family's luxury resort so she and Maya could talk. "Things between us are…complicated."

"Things were complicated for us, too. Every day I'm grateful Liam recognized that what we have was worth fighting for, despite the complications." Maya's face glowed when she spoke of Liam.

Kendra missed that feeling—the infinite joy of being in love with a man who adored her. She ignored the growing sense of envy that felt like a boulder tethered to her ankle, threatening to drown her in a sea of self-pity. She forced a smile. "I'm happy for you. You're perfect together, and Liam is so good with the kids."

"Sofie and Ella adore him."

"So does Kai. He talks about his Uncle Liam all the time. You'd think he was a superhero or something. He's making the Johnston men jealous."

"Liam has really taken to Kai, too." A warm smile lit Maya's eyes like a candle lighting a paper lantern from within.

No matter how many times Kendra saw that smile—and it was often in the weeks since Liam and Maya had gotten engaged—she couldn't stop her reaction to it. Intense joy for her sister, followed by deep sorrow for herself.

Maya seemed to recognize her pain. Her brows furrowed with concern. "I'm glad you accepted the offer, but I'm a little worried, too. Are you sure you're going to be okay with this? Six months is a long time."

"This is my shot to finally build the kind of clientele I've always wanted. I'm not going to blow it. Besides, Nate needs my help. I know it won't make up for how I hurt him, but at least it's something."

"When is your first meeting?"

"Tomorrow, so I'd better get it together."

Maya's smile was reassuring. "Everything will be fine, and who knows? Maybe you two will make up."

"Don't even go there, and please don't give Kai false hope about me and his dad getting back together. I don't think he could bear that. He misses him so much when he's away during the season. Now that the girls have Liam in their lives, Kai is more aware of his father's absence."

"I didn't realize—"

Kendra squeezed her sister's forearm. "I'm thankful Liam's in his life. What he's feeling now…it would've come up eventually. We'll deal with it. He'll be fine."

"Either way, I know this is going to work out for the best. You have to believe that."

"It has to. If Nate ends up with a West Coast team, Kai will see him even less. He'd be heartbroken." Kendra's voice wavered. She sipped her coffee, hoping her sister didn't notice. "If I can prevent that from happening, I have to at least try."

Kendra avoided Maya's gaze and the pity she knew she'd see there. They both turned toward the front door in response to the jangling of keys that signaled Liam and the children's arrival.

Kai practically jumped into her arms. He was a sweet, affectionate boy. She kissed her son's forehead, dreading the days when he got older and would think it uncool to give her a big hug and a sloppy kiss.

She took in her handsome, smiling child. Wide, round eyes. Nate's nose—a narrow bridge with slightly flared nostrils. A wide smile stretched his Cupid's bow mouth—a near duplicate of hers. His thick ringlets were cut into a frohawk. He was only six, but his long arms and legs indicated he would be tall—like his father.

Kai was the perfect mélange of her and Nate's features, and he'd inherited an ideal mix of their personalities. He was truly the best of them.

Kendra smiled, warmth spreading through her chest as she choked back tears. Maybe she didn't get their relationship right, but she would always have the best part of Nate.

For that she was grateful.

Chapter 4

Nate fluffed the pillows on the sofa in his office for the third time, then readjusted the chain on his neck again.

This isn't a date. It's business. Be cool.

He eased onto the sofa and drummed his fingers on his knee. Kendra would arrive shortly for their first official meeting.

She and Marcus had met before the ink dried so she could lay out her ideas and they could come to consensus on a plan. Marcus had thought it was best for him to sit out that meeting.

Fine by him.

He recognized the necessity of jumping through PR hoops. Still, he resented wasting time and money defending himself about truthful comments made in private.

Not that there was any such thing as privacy anymore in the social media age.

A car door slammed. Nate glanced at his watch and smiled. On time, as always. Kendra was right; in many ways, she hadn't changed. Organized and efficient, she'd never been late for anything.

Nate opened the door before Kendra could ring the bell, startling her. She dropped her leather portfolio, her papers sailing across the porch.

He planned to help her recover them, but froze, mesmerized by the perfectly round shape of her curvy bottom in a narrow black pencil skirt as she bent to retrieve them. Finally shaken from his daze, he stooped to pick up a few sheets that had landed near his feet. He handed them to her, his fingertips grazing her soft skin.

Kendra withdrew her hand, as if she, too, felt the spark of electricity that charged his skin when they touched. She gave him an uneasy smile as she accepted the papers and stuffed them back into the portfolio. "Not the graceful entrance I hoped to make."

"Also not quite as entertaining as your entrance to the junior prom." He grinned.

"You did not just go there. You're never going to forget that, are you?"

He chuckled. "Don't think anyone in Pleasure Cove ever will. Principal Dansby nearly crapped himself when you came strolling up to the stage in your purple Prince tribute gown with your right butt cheek on display."

Kendra shuddered, shifting the portfolio to her other arm. Her cheeks glowed red beneath her dark brown skin. "You know the ass-baring feature was completely unintentional. I told my mother wearing panty hose was a bad idea. If I hadn't been wearing them, my dress couldn't have gotten tucked into the back of them. I still blame her for the entire fiasco."

"We managed to have a good time, despite getting tossed out—thanks to your indecent exposure." He smiled at the warm memory of the two of them strolling on the beach that night, hand in hand.

They'd crashed a sunset wedding on the beach. Kendra had been moved by the ceremony, her eyes brimming with tears. She said it was the most perfect thing she'd ever seen. He wiped the tears from her face and promised to marry her one day in a sunset ceremony right there on that beach.

He'd attempted to keep his promise, but look how that turned out. Nate shook his head, purging the memory from his brain. Jaw stiff, his hands clenched into fists.

Kendra seemed aware of the shift in his mood. She clutched her portfolio. "Is this still a good time?"

"As good as any." He opened the door wider and stepped aside to allow her to enter.

"This place looks incredible." Her eyes danced as she glanced around the open space. "I haven't been here since they first broke ground."

That had been by design. He'd bought the land and had this place constructed because he expected to build a life here with her. To one day watch their children surf the same beaches they'd surfed together as kids. When everything fell apart, he'd done his damnedest to keep her out of the space that was meant to be theirs.

"Thanks." He crammed his hands into the pockets of his jeans. "Can I take your coat or get you anything before we get started?"

She removed her wrap, unveiling a low-cut silk blouse that complemented her curves nicely. "That coffee smells great. I'd love a cup."

"Coming up." He headed for the kitchen. "Is it okay if we work in here today?"

"Of course. I want to make this as convenient as possible. I'm willing to accommodate your schedule in any way necessary." Kendra set her portfolio and laptop on the black, poured concrete kitchen countertop.

He grabbed two mugs from the cabinet, filled her cup, added cream and handed it to her.

Kendra thanked him and settled onto her seat, then opened her laptop and pulled two copies of a thick, bound document from her leather bag. She handed him one and opened the other. "I'd like to give you the overview of the plan Marcus and I agreed on."

Nate thumbed through the document quickly. Neat, efficient, color-coded. *Very Kendra.* He dropped it onto the countertop with a *thud.* Leaning back in his seat, he sipped his coffee. "Shoot."

Nate was determined to make her turn and run, just as she had seven years ago. Well, they were beyond that. She'd signed her name to a contract and walked away from her most lucrative client.

No turning back.

She'd stayed up late the past few nights working on the proposal, and Nate wouldn't give it more than a cursory glance?

Fine.

She hadn't expected him to give in easily. But if he was already annoyed with her treatise on how to get his career back on track, he certainly wasn't going to like the steps she'd outlined.

Too bad.

This was what needed to happen if he wanted to get out of this predicament and land his new contract and endorsements.

Kendra met his defiant gaze. "Our campaign will focus on three strategies. First, you need to meet with each person you mentioned on that tape and apologize. Talk to them man-to-man and explain what happened—before we go public. Call anyone you can't get a sit-down with. Then we make the public apology."

Nate was growing more agitated by the minute. He folded his arms. "If I'm apologizing to each of them individually, what's the purpose of a public apology?"

"You said your tight end was more concerned with his individual stats than winning a championship. That your quarterback, and long-time friend, has been dialing it in all year. You slammed your defensive players for skating on their natural talents and having poor work ethics. And you claimed your running back is three years past his expiration date. All of that is public. So your apology needs to be, too."

"It's not like I didn't call myself out for my mistakes, too. Funny how they didn't include that part."

"I get it. That makes me believe that this Stephanie Weiss who broke the story is out to get you. This was calculated. Vindictive."

Nate bristled at the mention of Stephanie's name. "If they were going to leak the video, I just wish they'd shown everything."

"Fortunately, someone leaked the full video. Probably the person who actually recorded it. At the press conference, we'll play the missing part where you skewer your own mistakes, too. Then you'll make a statement. We'll go from the emotional angle of the disappointment you were feeling—with yourself and the rest of the team. Any sports fan can sympathize with that. Explain that while the critique was your honest assessment of what led to the loss, you regret the harsh words you used to express it."

Nate's lips puckered like he was sucking on a lemon. He nearly drained his coffee mug. "Fine. Anything else?"

"Be honest. Tell them your team is your family, and like most family disputes, this one will be resolved behind closed doors, not in the public arena."

"Won't they want to ask questions?"

"Doesn't mean you have to answer them." She shrugged. "We'll establish from the outset that you won't be entertaining questions."

"That's an idea I can get behind," he mumbled. "What's the second strategy?"

"We have to change the narrative out there about you on our terms. We'll cherry-pick media outlets that are trustworthy, but we'll lay the ground rules about which topics are off-limits."

"If I'm not talking about the tape—which is what they're all going to want to talk about—what am I there to discuss?"

"At this time of year, there are a million opportunities to discuss the play-off games—on radio, television, newspapers and blogs. You can offer your razor-sharp game analysis there. Plus, you'll set yourself up for a career as an analyst once you retire."

Nate shrugged. "I could do that, I guess."

"And you'll be phenomenal at it." Kendra smiled, encouraged that Nate had taken well to at least part of the plan. "You'll also need to talk about your philanthropy."

He frowned, his eyebrows forming angry slashes over his dark eyes. "The Johnston Family Foundation isn't some cheap publicity stunt. I'm not looking to blow my own horn."

"I know, which makes the work you do all the more admirable." She held up a hand, holding off the next wave of protest. "But just think how much more good you could do if you publicized the work you're doing with wounded veterans and high-risk children from low-income families."

Nate stood and paced the floor. "Our clients have been through enough. They need someone to give them a hand, not someone else who only sees them as a means to their own end. No." He shook his head. "I won't do it."

Kendra inhaled deeply, then took a different approach. One Nate might better understand.

"You don't want to take advantage of your clients. I admire that. But if we can't repair your reputation, you won't be in a position to help them as much as you'd like."

He didn't respond, but stopped pacing and rested his chin on his closed fist.

"Besides, if more companies—including your current sponsors—were aware of the programs your foundation offers and the difference you're making in people's lives, they'd want to contribute. That means you'll be able to help even more people. Isn't that what you want?"

"You know I do, but I won't betray their trust."

"I'd never ask you to do that." Kendra softened her voice. "All I'm asking is that you give them the opportunity to help themselves and others. I'm sure a lot of the families your foundation has helped would be eager to participate in a goodwill campaign to spread the word and increase funding."

Nate dropped into his seat, as if he were exhausted from a fight. "Fine. I'll agree to *some* media coverage for the foundation programs, but I need final approval on anything we put out there."

"Absolutely." She hoped he didn't see how relieved she was. "Any other concerns?"

"Yeah. What if the interviewers aren't willing to stick to the script?"

She nodded solemnly. "Always a possibility. One we'll make sure you're prepared to handle in a way that won't aggravate the situation."

"You make it sound so easy."

"It will be." She smiled, hoping to reassure him.

"And the third strategy? Do I even want to know what it is?"

He knew her well enough to know she'd saved the option he'd like least for last.

"It's time for you to come out of the Stone Age and start using social media."

"C'mon, Kendra. I've got a crisis on my hands. You said so yourself. I don't have time to mess around on social media."

"The public is only seeing you through the filter of the news media and talking heads out there. Social media puts you in control of your own message, in real time. Your fans—and potential sponsors—will get a better sense of who you are."

He shook his head slowly, thoughtfully. A marked improvement over the adamant refusal issued moments earlier. "The last thing I want is more people in my business."

"I understand your reluctance. Especially in light of what's happened. The reality is, they're already in your business. This way you become the gatekeeper. You let them in, but in a way you completely control."

Nate grunted. "Don't really have a choice, do I?"

Kendra tried to hold back her grin. "Not really, but I promise to make it as painless as possible. I'll actually be running the accounts for you, so it won't be as much work as you're imagining. Promise."

He nodded reluctantly. "If you really think this is the only way we win, okay. I'll do it. Anything else we need to discuss?" His posture was tense. As if he couldn't wait to get her out of his house.

She tried to pretend it didn't hurt that he wanted her as far away from him as possible. "Actually, there is something else we need to discuss. What's the story on Stephanie Weiss?"

Nate frowned. "Marcus didn't tell you?"

"He thought it would be better if you explained." She shifted in her chair. "I gather you two were together at some point, or Marcus wouldn't have been so cryptic about your connection."

"Not one of my best decisions." He tapped a finger on the countertop, staring beyond her. "Stephanie dragged me into the middle of a scandal back then that nearly ruined my relationship with my teammates. Now she's done it again."

"Exactly what happened with her?" She sighed when he narrowed his gaze at her. "If I'm going to help you, I need to understand what's going on, and not just what I've read on the internet. I need the complete picture. We can't afford to get blindsided again."

An uncomfortable silence settled over them as he stared out the window onto the backyard. He didn't want to talk to one ex about another.

She got that. She'd probably feel the same. Still, she needed to know more about this Stephanie Weiss. Beyond what she learned from watching her reports online and reading her bio. And if she was being honest, it wasn't just her professional curiosity that needed to be satisfied. "Did you love her?"

He scowled, the corners of his mouth pinched. His resentment of the question rolled off him in waves. His answer was quiet, but emphatic. "No."

Kendra went to the coffee machine and refilled her cup. She held her hand out for his. "You don't have to worry about hurting my feelings. I'm a big girl. I can handle the truth."

"I told you the truth. I wasn't in love with her." He thrust his empty cup into her hand. "We were only together a few months. What difference does it make, anyway?"

"Helps me understand her frame of mind. If we're dealing with a woman scorned nursing a vendetta, we need to stay two steps ahead of her." She returned the mug to him, filled with black coffee.

"That's the only reason you want to know?" He peered at her over the rim of his mug as he took a sip of his coffee.

She returned to her seat and tapped a few keys on her computer, waking the screen up. "Of course."

He smirked, unconvinced. With good reason. She was lying through her teeth.

"So, what led to this scandal and why does she have it in for you?" Kendra put down her mug, prepared to type her notes.

"Do we really need to get into all of this? It's ancient history."

"Not to her, I'm guessing."

"Stephanie was listening to my phone calls. Checking my text messages. She discovered a teammate of mine was in serious trouble. She broke the story using the info she'd gathered, saying it was from an unnamed source. When I read the story, I recognized what she'd done. Since we were dating, my teammates and the public believed I'd been feeding Stephanie information. I broke it off with her, publicly denied I was the source and discredited her story." He frowned. "She was fired, and none of the top media outlets wanted anything to do with her."

"I'm sorry you ended up in the middle of it."

"Should've known better than to sleep with the enemy, right?"

"Real journalists aren't your enemy. They won't always give you the glowing praise you want, but the good ones are honest and fair. They're only interested in the truth. Those are the media personalities we need to make our allies."

"Good luck finding any of those." He finished his coffee and moved to the sink to rinse his cup.

"Got a few in mind. I think you'll be pleased."

He grunted, his biceps bulging as he folded his arms over his chest. The gray quick-dry athletic material stretched to accommodate his firm pecs. He flipped his wrist and checked his watch. "Anything else?"

Kendra swallowed, her throat suddenly dry. Nate seemed fully aware of her reaction to him and utterly pleased with himself for evoking it. She shook her head. "No, I think we're good. For now. I'll keep you updated. Marcus's assistant, Kara, gave me access to your calendar. I'll add any interviews and appearances as I book them."

"All right." He pinned her with his gaze. "Is that all?"

"Kara will make the flight arrangements for your apology tour once you request meetings with each of the guys. I'd begin with Marauders' owner Bud Flynn and then the head coach."

The smug expression crumbled. "Why? I didn't say anything about either of them."

"This media circus is disruptive to the entire team. Besides, Bud has been like a second father to you. He gave you your big break. Don't you think you owe him an apology?"

Nate sighed. "I'll call him as soon as I'm done."

"Good."

"Don't mean to rush you." He checked his watch again. "But I have another appointment."

"Right. Sorry. I know you're busy." Kendra put on her wrap and packed up her things. She slipped her bag on her shoulder, tucked the portfolio under her arm and turned around, nearly running into Nate.

"Look, I know I'm not the easiest guy to work with, but I do appreciate the work you've put into this." He leaned in closer, his warm breath whispering against her skin. "And I just want you to know..."

The doorbell rang. Nate sighed and cursed under his breath before turning toward the door.

"Nate, what were you going to say?" Kendra followed him, her heart beating hard. Something in her desperately needed to know what Nate was going to say before they'd been interrupted by the bell.

"Doesn't matter." He shook his head then turned to open the door.

"I came a few minutes early so we could work on those positions you had so much trouble with the other day." A tall, gorgeous blonde wearing a short skirt, a cropped top and thigh-high boots floated inside carrying a large duffel that looked like it weighed twice as much as she did. The woman finally noticed Kendra. "Oh, I'm sorry, I didn't realize you had company."

"I was just leaving." Kendra forced a polite smile.

Nate placed his hand low on the woman's back and introduced them. "Layne, this is Kendra—Kai's mom. She'll be handling my PR. Kendra, this is my friend Layne."

Layne gave Nate an odd smile before offering Kendra a limp handshake. "Pleased to meet you. I've heard so much about you." She turned to Nate without waiting for a response. "I'll go ahead and get everything set up."

"Great. Thanks, Layne."

The woman sauntered off, obviously familiar with the house.

"She's pretty." The words came out before Kendra could reel them back in. "She's built like a dancer."

Nate smirked, holding the door open a bit wider. "She takes great care of her body. And mine."

"I certainly don't want to get in the way of that." Kendra forced a smile despite the deep ache in her chest at the thought of Nate and Ms. Ballerina Body doing God knows what. "I'll follow up tomorrow to see how the phone calls went, and if I need to run interference with anyone."

"Don't think that'll be necessary, but thank you. Kiss li'l man for me. Tell him Dad's got a surprise for him this weekend."

Before she could respond, he'd closed the door behind her. The sound echoed in her head like the closing of a vault.

Maybe she was still nursing feelings for Nate, but he'd obviously gotten over her.

Chapter 5

Nate sank into the whirlpool after his hot yoga session with Layne and made his calls.

He'd tucked his tail and done a good bit of explaining. First to Bud Flynn, then to Coach Emerson. Bud was out of the country. He tentatively accepted Nate's apology by phone, but insisted they meet in person once he returned. He scheduled a meeting with Coach Emerson.

Nate left a message for two of his teammates and had incredibly awkward conversations with a few others.

Except for the team's quarterback, Wade Willis, who agreed his performance had been subpar, none of the guys went easy on him. Eating a king-size slice of humble pie was exactly what he deserved for running his big mouth.

Tomorrow he'd board a plane to meet with Wade

at his ranch in Montana. Then he'd head to Memphis for meetings with Coach Emerson and Lee Davis, the head of team personnel. He dreaded the meeting with Lee—the only member of the Marauders' front office he'd never really seen eye-to-eye with. Lee had been itching to trade him, and the video scandal was just the ammunition he needed.

Nate slipped deeper into the water, allowing the warmth to wash over his aching muscles. The heat eased the tension in his shoulders and worked out the kinks in his back.

After eight years in the league, he was nursing his fair share of injuries. Each season it became more difficult to rebound from the beating his body took on any given Sunday.

If he were smart, he'd forget about a new contract and retire. Accept that he was a great player in his own right, but would never know the pride of hoisting a championship trophy. He'd be in good company. A host of athletes in every major sport were on that list.

Still, he wasn't ready to give up. The Marauders were a few pieces shy of being a contender with a legitimate shot at the championship. He shifted to get the knot in his back closer to the jet.

His recent actions certainly hadn't made the task of getting the Marauders championship-ready any easier.

Closing his eyes, he tried to relax—something he'd never been very good at. His brain seemed to go a mile a minute—even when he slept.

Nate massaged the knot that formed in his neck as he recalled the hurt and anger in each man's voice. The tension he'd created between them. Then there was the meeting with Kendra.

His body reacted to the vivid vision of her that crept over his senses. Kendra was sexy as ever in that fitted skirt and a low-cut blouse. He'd had to shove his hands in his pockets, not trusting that he'd keep his hands to himself.

When she spoke, he'd been mesmerized by her lips, overwhelmed with the desire to taste her mouth and slide his fingers in her dark curls.

Get it together, man.

He shook his head and stood, the chilly air assaulting his wet skin. Nate stepped out of the tub and slipped on a thick terry cloth robe. He slid on his sport sandals and went inside.

Nate uncapped a beer from the fridge and took a long pull. Kendra's words echoed in his head.

Neither of us can afford the distraction.

There was too much at stake. His career, the foundation and most of all...his heart. If he let her in, she'd shatter it again.

Twice, he thought he could have her body without getting caught up in the feelings they once shared.

He'd been wrong.

Kendra had walked away unscathed, while he was left brooding like a wounded animal, lashing out at everyone around him.

Nate finished his beer and tossed the bottle in the recycle bin before hopping into the shower.

This time he'd keep his hands and his heart to himself.

Kendra settled in behind the rickety old secondhand desk in her office, which doubled as the spare bedroom.

Marcus had already arranged for Nate to be a guest

on a few of the smaller sports commentary shows on the major sports network.

She reviewed the list of media personalities she'd compiled. Kendra was confident that half of the people on the list would agree to their stipulations about topics Nate wouldn't discuss. The other half were iffy, but the riskiest options offered the biggest return. She needed to see what Marcus thought of those. She dialed his cell.

Marcus answered immediately. "I was just about to ask Kara to call you."

"Why, what's up?" Kendra stopped scrolling through the list. Something in his tone told her she wouldn't like what he was about to say.

"Nate called everyone on the list."

"Great. Will he be meeting with all of them?"

"Bud Flynn's out of town. They'll meet when he gets back, but he accepted his apology, for whatever that's worth."

"And the rest of the team?"

"Wade was cool. Everyone else was pretty pissed, as we expected. Two of the guys haven't returned his calls."

"Let me guess, Tyree Thomason and Dade Hendricks." According to Nate, his relationships with the tight end and running back were strained even before the video was leaked.

"You've got it. Nate also arranged a sit-down with Lee Davis, the team's personnel manager. The guy is definitely not a fan. He's been trying to get the team to trade Nate since the upheaval Stephanie caused three years ago, but Bud Flynn won't go for it."

"Nate needs to be smart about what he says when he talks to these guys. It's one thing to be contrite during a phone call. It's another to keep it together in person. I hope he remembers everything we talked about."

"He won't have a choice. I'm sending you with him." Marcus said the words so fast she nearly missed his meaning.

"Wait...what? We didn't discuss me going."

"I know, and I'm sorry. I don't mean to spring this on you at the last minute, but I've been thinking about it all day. It's too risky to send Nate alone."

"Then why don't you go with him?"

"I would, but I have meetings scheduled with the networks and one of the team execs. I can't miss them."

Kendra groaned. "Fine. When is he leaving?"

"Tomorrow morning."

"Are you kidding me?"

"No, and again I'm sorry about this. I realize how inconvenient this is, and I wouldn't ask if it wasn't so critical. Will your mom or Maya be able to watch Kai for a few days? If not, my mom or Alison would be happy to."

"I'll make arrangements. Just have Kara email me everything I need to know."

"Great. Oh, and Kendra?"

"Yes?"

"Pack for a week. Just in case."

Kendra ended the call and gritted her teeth. There was an empty feeling in the pit of her stomach. She curled her fingers to her palms in response to the visceral memory of the electricity she felt when Nate's fingers brushed her skin.

Sitting across the table from Nate during their first two meetings had been tough, but she'd found strength in the knowledge that their meetings would be brief. She could retreat, lick her wounds and summon her courage before it was time to do it again. Being confined on a small plane with Nate for hours would be difficult for both of them.

Kendra drew in a deep breath and picked up the phone. First, she called her mother to make arrangements for Kai. Anna Williams didn't bother to hide how ecstatic she was that Kendra would be spending the next few days on the road alone with Nate. She gladly agreed to care for Kai.

After messaging her sister to let her know about her trip, she dragged her luggage out of the closet and packed.

Kendra closed the book she was reading to Kai. He'd been asleep for at least ten minutes. She finished reading the story anyway, needing an excuse to hold him a bit longer.

She slipped her arm from beneath Kai, tucked the covers under his chin and kissed his forehead.

Her cell phone rang. She followed the sound to the kitchen, where she'd left it.

"Hey, Maya. What's up?"

"Got your message. I wanted to check on you. You sure you'll be okay on the road with Nate for an entire week?"

Kendra collapsed onto the sofa, physically drained from preparing for the trip, mentally exhausted from wrestling with the same question. "Don't really have a choice, do I?"

"We always have a choice," Maya said. "But sometimes fate pushes us in the right direction."

"You're not going to tell me you think this is the

stars aligning again—like they did for you and Liam—are you?"

"Are you going to try to tell me again that you don't still have feelings for Nate?" There was a smirk in her sister's voice.

"He's my son's father, so we'll always have some sort of—"

"Connection." Maya finished her sentence. "I know, I know. That's not what I asked. I'm asking if you're still in love with him."

"We've been through this before."

"And you've never given me a straight answer." The pitch of Maya's voice rose.

"Seems like a clear hint I don't want to talk about it." Kendra paced the floor, then rearranged photos on the mantel. "So leave it alone."

"So it's all right for you to be all up in my business, but when it's your turn, suddenly you're invoking the Fifth?"

Kendra pressed a palm to her forehead. Maya usually dropped the topic once her agitation became apparent. Suddenly her sister wasn't inclined to let the subject go.

"I'm not sure how I feel," Kendra admitted. It was unsettling to hear the words spoken aloud where she could no longer hide from them. "Being around him like this…it's definitely making me feel some kind of way."

Maya's tone softened. "I know it's probably a little overwhelming, but that doesn't mean it's a bad thing. Just be open to wherever this takes you. Nate's a good guy. He adores Kai, and I have a strong feeling he's still very much in love with you."

"Don't know about that. It was kind of hard to read with his arm draped around the skinny chick who showed up at his place as he was rushing me out the door." Kendra hated the pouty tone with which she conveyed the news.

"Is he seeing her?"

"I guess so. She seemed to know her way around his place well enough. From the size of the bag she was toting, she planned to stay awhile."

"How did he introduce her?"

"As his friend."

"Well, there you go." There was a lilt in Maya's voice again. "She's his friend until we hear otherwise."

"Like you and Liam were just 'friends' over the summer?"

Maya huffed. "You're determined to ruin this, aren't you?"

"Maya, seriously, do I need to have the same talk with you I had with my mom? This is business—not a romantic getaway. Nate doesn't want me on this trip any more than I want to be on it."

"Wouldn't be so sure about that. We'll see."

"Enough with the matchmaking," Kendra said. "I still have a ton of things to do. Oh, and my mom has a doctor's appointment on Friday, so she won't be able to pick Kai up from school. Is it okay if he goes home with Sarah and the girls until my mom can pick him up?"

Liam's housekeeper, Sarah, had taken on the expanded role of part-time nanny since Maya and the girls had moved into his penthouse.

"I'm sure it won't be a problem. She loves Kai. That boy is a charmer, just like his dad."

Kendra thanked her sister and ended their call, hoping she'd be strong enough to resist Nate's charm this time around.

Chapter 6

Nate climbed the stairs to the small private plane they sometimes chartered for his travel. He got a whiff of a familiar scent. Jasmine with a hint of gardenias.

No, no way.

He removed his shades and stood, stunned, taking in his ex's apologetic expression.

"Guess that answers my question about whether you knew I was coming along." She brushed off her skirt and crossed her legs.

Nate tucked his shades in the inside pocket of his jacket. He stood trying to decide whether or not he'd sit across from Kendra.

He grunted and flopped into his usual seat adjacent to the couch. She seemed relieved he'd chosen to sit across from her.

"No." He held back a few choice names he had for

his brother right now. "Marcus failed to mention it. I realize I screwed up, but I don't appreciate the two of you treating me like a child. I'm a grown-ass man."

"Then start acting like one." Her expression was neutral, her tone unbothered. "Channel your passion for the game in a way that will help your team rather than hurt it. Tap into your desire to win in a way that will motivate your teammates instead of alienating them."

Nate turned to survey the calm waters of the Atlantic Ocean, visible from the window. "Damn. I see we're not pulling punches today."

Kendra smiled sweetly, one long leg crossed over the other and her hands folded in her lap. "You didn't hire me to soothe your ego. You hired me to get results, and that's what you'll get, as long as you stick to the plan."

Nate tried to hold on to the resentment he felt when he realized Marcus had sent Kendra to be his babysitter. That anger was quickly losing ground to the other feeling that grabbed hold of his chest the moment her eyes met his.

Longing.

He wanted her. In his arms. In his bed. In his life. A sentiment he'd fought for the past seven years. Being in such close proximity to the constant object of his affection wasn't helping him win that battle.

Kendra was smart as a whip, sexy as hell and confident in her abilities. Something about that combination made his heart beat faster. That and the expanse of smooth brown skin framed between the hem of her skirt and the top of her leather boots.

Nate raised his hands, his palms facing her. "Relax. I don't plan on going off script again. After all, that's why I'm headed to freaking Montana in the middle of winter, isn't it?" He pulled his jacket closer around him, just thinking of the thirty-degree temperature drop they'd experience once they landed.

She tilted her head, assessing him before responding. "Hopefully, you're also doing it because it's the right thing to do. Wade isn't just your quarterback, he's your friend."

They weren't playing touch football anymore. Kendra had delivered a full-contact, center-mass hit that had knocked him on his ass.

Deservedly so.

She wasn't tiptoeing around his ego. He admired that. Only Kendra Williams could piss him off and make him want her with a single utterance.

It was going to be a rough few days. For him, at least. Kendra seemed unaffected by him. That gave her the upper hand.

He needed to find a way to change that.

Kendra gave herself a mental high five. She stood her ground and told Nate the cold, hard truth while remaining calm, despite the anxiety raging beneath the surface.

Handling Nate with kid gloves wouldn't benefit either of them. Marcus hired her because she'd always been straight with Nate and told him what he needed to hear—whether he wanted to hear it or not. Their painful history aside, she would do just that.

She'd hoped her resolve to be tough with Nate would mitigate her feelings for him. It hadn't. Judging by the half frown that softened the edges of his mouth, a mischievous grin lay just beneath his show of displeasure. So it wasn't deterring him much, either.

Kendra held her poise, despite her increasingly shallow breaths as Nate's gaze raked over her. Heat curled its way up her spine like a black snake climbing a southern red cedar tree in search of prey.

"Of course Wade is my friend, but this is a business," Nate said finally, shifting his gaze out the window for a moment before returning it to her. "Wade understands that more than anyone."

The pilot announced they would take off soon. A growing sense of panic made her limbs feel heavy. She fumbled with her seat belt. It wouldn't catch. They were going to take off and she'd go sailing across the plane.

"Relax. I've got it." Nate knelt in front of her, his large hands covering hers, stilling their movement.

The warmth of his skin penetrated hers and trailed up her arms, her heart beating faster and her breath quickening. Her skin tingled, electricity zipping along her spine.

Even kneeling, Nate's large body loomed over hers. His broad chest and wide shoulders invaded her space as he leaned forward and buckled the seat belt effortlessly.

Nate's gaze met hers and one corner of his mouth curved, his eyes twinkling.

Kendra's hands shook as she inhaled his scent. Her body remembering when last he'd been this close to her on his knees. Her nipples pebbled and a small, inadvertent gasp escaped her mouth.

Nate grinned, then licked his lower lip.

Maybe he was remembering that night, too.

Kendra shut her eyes briefly and exhaled.

No, no, no. This is strictly business. Nothing more.

"Thank you." She settled back against the headrest. "But you'd better get back in your seat."

Nate gave her a knowing grin as he returned to his seat and fastened himself in.

Kendra released a small sigh, missing his nearness, yet thankful for the distance.

"This flight is nearly five hours, and these smaller commuter planes…well, the ride can be a little bumpier than on a commercial flight. You sure you want to do this?"

Kendra nodded in response as she focused on taking long, deep breaths. She wasn't terrified of flying, it just wasn't her preferred mode of travel.

Nothing a rum and Coke or two couldn't resolve.

Only this wasn't a pleasure trip. It was strictly business, and she needed to keep her head clear. That meant toughing it out.

Nate regarded her with apprehension. "Look, I appreciate your commitment, but you don't need to do this. I can handle this on my own, so just say the word and we'll get you off this flight. But I need to know now. *Before* we take off."

"No." Kendra shook her head vehemently. "I'm fine."

"All right." Nate settled back in his seat, his eyes glued to her, as if he expected her head to start spinning.

"I appreciate you looking out for me, despite the fact that you'd rather I not be here."

He shrugged, looking out the window again as the plane taxied down the runway. "Maybe I just didn't want you killing my vibe with your projectile vomiting."

Kendra couldn't help laughing. She dissolved into a fit of giggles that escalated to a laugh so hard it made her belly ache.

Nate laughed, too. He wiped tears from the corners of his eyes. "Better now?"

She stopped laughing long enough to realize that the tense muscles in her back and neck had relaxed. They were airborne and the plane was leveling off. She nodded. "Much. Thank you."

He winked at her. "Good. Now, I assume that in addition to being assigned babysitting duty, you tagged along so we could go over a few things."

She nodded, pulling her portfolio from her bag. "How far outside the box are you willing to go?"

Nate crooked a brow and shifted in his seat, folding his right ankle over his left knee. "What do you mean?"

"A popular home improvement show is looking for a few celebs who want to surprise a family member with a kitchen redo. Marcus suggested they do your mom's kitchen."

"That means my parents would have to be on the show." He ran a hand over his head. "Don't know if I like that. They don't like being in the spotlight."

"Marcus said your mom loves these shows and she's always wanted to be on one." She tapped her pen on her pad. "This is a great opportunity for you to do something fabulous for her, Nate. Something you've always wanted to do. The bonus is it would be great for your image, too."

Nate groaned as he pressed his head against the headrest. "If Marcus thinks Mama will go for it, fine. I'll do it. Anything else?"

"By the end of the day, your brother should have more info on those guest spots to discuss the play-offs and a finalized list of media personalities that we'll pitch additional guest spots to."

"Great. Make sure I get a copy of that list."

"Absolutely." Kendra made another note, then put her

pen and pad away. "Now, about these meetings with the team and your teammates."

"I don't need you standing next to me like some ventriloquist." Nate's tone was tinged with annoyance. "I know what to say to these guys."

"Great. Then you won't mind running it by me." Kendra gave Nate a warm smile, but he wasn't buying it. "I'm here to ensure you're prepared for these meetings and that we stay on message, but I won't be in any of them. These guys are like your family. It'll only make things weirder if I'm there."

"Good." He nodded, seemingly relieved.

"Let's just go over the basics of what you plan to say to Wade. I'll check out a restaurant in town and get some work done while you meet with him."

"Not going to work."

"Why?"

"There was a change of plans this morning. My meetings in Memphis were bumped back a couple of days, so Wade asked me to spend a couple of days with him and Greer. Thought you knew."

I'm going to kill Marcus if he has any more surprises up those expensive sleeves of his.

Unperturbed, Nate composed a text message on his phone.

Probably to the woman she'd encountered at his home the day before.

"There must be a hotel or something where I can stay in town. Shouldn't be terribly difficult to book a room at the last minute in Montana in the middle of winter."

He silently tapped away on his phone.

Good to know you're concerned. She smoothed her

skirt and tried not to pout about her ex's lack of interest in her dilemma.

He's your client, not your boyfriend. Get used to it.

"All set." Nate slipped the phone into his pocket.

"You booked me a hotel room?"

"Better. Wade and Greer want you to come to the ranch with me. He and I will chat as soon as we get there. Get all this nonsense out of the way. Then we'll have dinner with them tonight. They also asked us to spend the day with them tomorrow while the older kids are at school."

"Are you sure they don't mind taking on another person? I don't mind staying at a hotel."

Nate gave her a small smile, but sadness lingered in his eyes. "Greer asks about you and Kai all the time. She'll be thrilled to see you."

"It'll be good to see her and Wade again, too. I've always liked them."

He settled back in his chair, his legs crossed again. "Then it's settled."

"Won't your friend Layne be upset about this?"

"Why?" His expression was stoic. She couldn't read him at all.

"So you're saying you two aren't together? Or is your relationship casual and open?" Kendra couldn't help herself. "I'm asking as your media consultant slash publicist, of course."

He chuckled. "Okay, media consultant slash publicist, my relationship with Layne is casual, open and very professional."

Kendra's eyes widened. "You mean she's a—"

"What? Of course not." He laughed. "She's my hot

yoga instructor. Sydney recommended her. Layne dated Nick for a while."

"Oh." Kendra pushed a curl back from her forehead. His sister Sydney and her best friend Nick had been roommates for the past few years. "Those two still pretending they're not in love?"

Nate frowned. "They're just friends and roommates. At least, they better be," he added, mumbling under his breath.

"Whatever helps you sleep at night." She couldn't help teasing him. "After all, we started out as best friends, too."

Nate unbuckled his seat belt and sprawled out on the couch. "Yeah, and just look how that turned out." He sighed and dragged a hand down his face. "Sorry, I shouldn't have—"

Kendra waved a hand and shook her head. "I get it. You've always been protective of your baby sister. Just like your twin sister has always been protective of you."

A half grin lit Nate's eyes as he chuckled. "Protective? She acts like she's my mama."

Kendra acknowledged his statement with a small nod. Navia had been furious with her when she broke up with Nate. The rest of the Johnston clan eventually made peace with the situation, but not Navia. She'd probably never forgive her for hurting her twin brother.

"How is Vi doing, anyway? Still calling for my head on a stake?"

Nate grinned. "Nah. She's softened up a little. Now she just wants to see you in stocks for a week or two."

Kendra laughed. "She's warming up to me again. Good to know. And what does she think about this little arrangement?"

He slipped off his expensive leather shoes and shrugged his broad shoulders. "Haven't talked to her about it yet. You know how worked up Vi gets about everything. Marcus and I thought it was best if we waited until we had some viable results to show her."

"Guess I'm not the only one who's afraid of your sister."

"I spent nine months sharing a very small space with Vi." He grinned as he spread a cream-colored cashmere throw over himself. "No one knows better what she's capable of. If I were you, I'd try to wow her."

Kendra pursed her lips. Nate was teasing her. Didn't mean she wouldn't check underneath her car seat for ticking devices—just in case.

Chapter 7

"Hello, Nate." Greer Willis gave him an awkward hug—unlike the dozens she'd given him before. "Wade'll be here shortly. He picked Jake and Mariah up from school."

Greer's demeanor was pleasant, but the narrowing of her blue eyes and the sharp pronunciation of his name—without any of the soft edges of her deep Southern accent—sufficiently conveyed her indignation.

She was sweet and cordial, but also fiercely protective of her family. An endearing quality when he wasn't on the wrong side of it.

Today, he clearly was.

"Kendra!" An authentic smile lit Greer's face, highlighting her natural beauty. She wrapped Kendra in a tight embrace. "Honey, it's so good to see you. Hasn't been the same without you."

"Good to see you, too, Greer. I can't wait to see the kids. How old are they?"

Greer threaded her arm through Kendra's, leading her to the living room. "Jake is ten and Mariah is eight. They've grown like weeds since you saw them last. Noah is three and baby Allie is thirteen months. The little ones are down for a nap. You'll see them soon enough. Can I get y'all something?"

"No, thank you. We're good." Kendra surveyed the impressive house. The architectural gem was made up mostly of local fieldstone, walls of glass and a symphony of light-colored woods. "My God, Greer, this place is gorgeous. The architecture…and those views. It's stunning."

Greer's grin widened and her cheeks colored. She was still a small-town Alabama girl who grew up on a working farm, never imagining a charmed life. It was one of the reasons Nate had always genuinely liked and respected her. Greer and Wade were good, down-to-earth folks. His friends.

He'd hurt them both.

"Still can't believe we get to wake up here every day." A strand of Greer's wavy honey-blond hair escaped her low ponytail. She tucked it behind her ear. "I'll show you around when the little ones wake. Meantime, have a seat. I'll ask Edison to fetch y'all's bags and take 'em to the guesthouse."

"There's a guesthouse?" Kendra eased onto the large gray sectional. It blended nicely with maple flooring stained the same shade of gray as the driftwood that washed ashore on the beach back home. Kendra laughed. "What am I thinking? Of course there's a guesthouse. How much land do you have here?"

"'Bout a hundred acres. We'll take you for a tour tomorrow, when there's plenty of daylight."

Chest burning and his mouth dry, Nate paced behind the sofa rather than taking a seat.

Until he saw the anguish that dulled Greer's blue eyes, he hadn't considered the collateral damage he'd caused.

"Greer, I'm sorry I got you caught up in this." The words blurted from his mouth.

"I know you are, Nate. But it's a bell you can't unring." She shrugged. "Who knows, maybe somethin' good'll come out of all of this after all. Now, have a seat, please. You're making me nervous as a long-tailed cat in a room full of rocking chairs, pacing like that."

Nate took a seat on the other side of Kendra and massaged the tension in his neck. He stayed quiet, responding only to direct questions from Greer and Kendra as they caught up.

The baby monitor alerted Greer that Noah and Allie were up from their naps. She excused herself and stepped away.

Nate released a long breath when Greer left the room.

"Harder facing them than you expected?" Kendra leaned closer, her tone compassionate and her expression thoughtful.

"I was so focused on how this whole thing impacted my life, my career..." Nate raked his fingers through his hair, trying to quell the guilt gnawing at his gut as he imagined how disappointed Jake and Mariah must have been at his remarks about their father. Wade was their hero. "I didn't think about how my words must have hurt Greer and the kids or Tyree's mom—Ms. Eleanor. People I know and respect."

"That's why you're here, to smooth things out." Kendra's voice was reassuring as she placed a hand on his knee to still it. "If they weren't interested in repairing the relationship, they wouldn't have invited you to stay overnight."

Nate found comfort in the warmth from Kendra's hand seeping into his skin through the layer of fabric between them. She'd always had a calming effect on him; the perfect balance to his fiery personality.

"Take a deep breath and relax. Be honest with Wade about why you said what you did, and about how you feel, knowing you've hurt him."

Nate heaved a sigh. He didn't come here to grovel. He hadn't asked for this situation, and nothing he said that night was news to anyone inside the Marauders organization.

He boarded that plane expecting it would all be so simple. He'd lay out the facts and apologize for talking publicly about team business—even if he hadn't intended to.

Experiencing Greer's anguish firsthand…suddenly it didn't feel so simple.

"Nate, good of you to come all this way."

Nate and Kendra turned toward Wade. He stood in the doorway, each arm draped around a child. His thin smile hovered at the surface, not reaching his wary brown eyes.

"Thanks for seeing me, Wade, and for inviting us to stay." Nate stood, his gut churning as he crossed the room to shake his quarterback's hand. He stooped so his towering frame was closer to the children's height. "Jake, Mariah, you've both gotten so big."

Neither child responded. They stared at him blankly.

Mariah drew closer to her father like Nate was the Big Bad Wolf, rather than her beloved "Uncle Nate." Her reaction hit him like a body slam on Astroturf.

"Say hello to Uncle Nate and Ms. Kendra." Wade squeezed their shoulders.

They mumbled their hellos. Mariah's eyes brimmed with heartache; Jake's glowed with animus.

Wade dispatched the kids to wash their hands and faces before their after-school snack. Then he crossed the room and pulled Kendra into a bear hug, inducing a fleeting moment of envy that heated Nate's face. Wade's Texas accent deepened. "Lemme borrow Nate for a bit."

"Of course." Kendra waved a hand.

Wade flashed his trademark smile. The one plastered on no less than half a dozen glossy magazines each year. "Greer will be down with the kids in a sec. And don't worry, I promise to bring 'im back in one piece."

"Have a seat." Wade closed the doors to his office. The walls were covered with well-worn shiplap. Mounted antlers hung over the roaring fireplace and rainbow trout replicas flanked either side. Faux animal rugs accented the space.

"Beer?" Wade opened a large wooden console that concealed a drink cooler.

"Thanks." Nate sank into the metal-studded brown leather couch broken in over the years.

Wade pulled out two domestic beers, popped the tops and handed him one. He sank onto a large cushioned chair. "All right, Nate. You traveled twenty-four hundred miles so we could talk man-to-man. You got my undivided attention."

Nate took a long drag of his beer, then set the bottle on a coaster hewn from tree bark.

"I can't tell you how sorry I am about this. Not just to you, but to Greer and the kids. Didn't mean for any of this to happen. It's not my style. You know that."

Wade nodded thoughtfully. "'Preciate that, Nate, but the story's out there now. Nothing either of us can do about it."

"Believe me, I'd do anything to take that entire night back."

"Bet you would. Them pretty little things caused you a lot of trouble. Hope you got a helluva night out of it." Wade chuckled bitterly, referring to the two young women who'd cornered Nate in the VIP section, gotten him riled up again about the loss and recorded his rant.

"Didn't sleep with either of them. I was so amped and more than a little drunk." Nate's face grew hot, thinking of how the blonde and her friend manipulated him. How he stupidly played right into their hands. "About what I said—"

"You meant every word. Just didn't mean for it to go public." Wade took a healthy swig of his light beer and set the bottle down. He leaned forward, his elbows on his knees. "I know. You been telling me as much for a while now. If I'd listened earlier, maybe we'd still be in this thing with a shot at winning it all."

Nate stood, pacing in front of the fireplace. "We all had a hand in it." He jerked a thumb toward himself. "My screwups cost us big."

"Kind of you to own up to your part, Nate, but the truth is, those throws weren't crisp and my timing was off. You wouldn't have dropped them if I'd done my job right. I was scrambling, anticipating another hit."

So that was it. Wade's heart hadn't been in the game for the entire season. Nate thought Wade had resigned himself to never winning the big one. That he was just riding out the remainder of his contract. Instead, he was afraid of taking another hit like the one that leveled him near the end of the previous season. He'd suffered a concussion and two broken ribs.

Wade's performance dropped off considerably when he returned. Two years ago, he was one of the top quarterbacks in the league. He could be again.

"All those times I rode you for not being focused… why didn't you tell me the truth?"

"Who's gonna trust a QB who admits he's scared to take another hard hit? Besides, saying it out loud meant admitting it to myself. For me, that was worse than everyone else knowing."

Nate sank onto the sofa. What could he say?

He'd taken bad hits in his career. Suffered injuries that still nagged him, reminding him the sand was running out in the hourglass of his pro football career. The first few games back were always hard. He was unsure of the injured body part—an ankle and later a knee. Then there was the fear of getting reinjured. For him, it was mind over matter. He focused on his goal: winning a championship. He could spend his retirement resting and nursing his aching joints.

"Look, I know you probably don't want to hear this, but the Marauders work with a sports psychologist. Maybe—"

"Already tried that." Wade stood suddenly, agitated. He got two more beers from the fridge, opened them and placed one in front of Nate.

"You've already been to Dr. Mays?"

"Didn't want the team to know I was having panic attacks. My first game back, this big-ass defensive end came at me and I broke into a cold sweat. Heart beating a mile a minute. Happened again in the next game and the next. Went to an independent sports psychologist."

"Did it help?" Nate gripped his bottle, fully aware of the answer, based on the distressed look on his friend's face.

"I'm fighting my natural self-preservation instincts every time I step onto that field. Told myself time and again it's all in my head. That I can get past it." Wade shrugged again. "But short of taking antianxiety drugs, nothing seems to help. If I gotta drug up just to do my job…maybe it ain't the right job for me anymore."

"You're not thinking about retiring, are you?" It hurt that he was the reason Wade was considering walking away from the game they loved.

"Not like I need the money." Wade nodded toward the wall of glass at the far end of the room with its view of the mountains and a pristine lake. "We've been smart. Saved. Invested. I was trying to hold out and fulfill the final two years of my contract, but maybe it's time to pack it up and walk away." Wade was matter-of-fact about the prospect, as if he'd already resigned himself to it.

"There has to be another answer. We'll make adjustments. Work harder. I got a hand on those passes, so I should've been able to haul them in and hold on to them, simple as that."

Wade met Nate's gaze. "Or maybe you were right all along. Time for me to walk away."

"I *never* said that."

"Been in the league ten years, Nate. It's been a good

ride, but that's a hell of a long time. I don't want to be one of those guys who can't enjoy his life by the time he walks away."

They sat in silence as Nate wrestled with what to say to shovel himself out of the six-foot-deep ditch he'd dug and dragged his team into.

"You talk to Greer about this?"

"She's thrilled that I'd be here year-round to help with the kids. She's put her life on hold so I could live my dream. Maybe it's time I support hers. She has a couple of business ideas. Stuff she's been talking about a long time. Maybe it's my turn to be her cheerleader."

Nate assessed his friend, who didn't seem enthused about the prospect. "I know Greer would love to have you home, but what did she say when you told her you were considering retiring?"

Wade chuckled softly. "She said Willises don't run scared. We stay and fight."

Nate laughed, too. "*That* sounds like the Greer Willis I know. I'm just thankful she didn't meet me at the door with a shotgun rather than one of those Hollywood hugs."

"Not gon' lie, she was madder than a hornet when she saw that video." Wade took another swig of his beer. "I hid her phone for two days to keep her from calling you and telling you off."

"I deserved it." Nate gripped his beer, raising his eyes to Wade's. "What about Jake and Mariah? Don't think I've ever felt like as much of an ass as I did seeing myself through their eyes today."

"You're their Uncle Nate. So yeah, they're pretty upset. Jake's angry. Mariah's feelings are hurt."

Nate drained the remainder of his first beer. He took

a gulp of the second. "If it's okay with you and Greer, I'd like to apologize to them. I won't push," he added quickly, in response to the concern in Wade's eyes. "But I want them to know how sorry I am."

Wade nodded solemnly. "I'll talk to Greer about it. If she doesn't have a problem with it, neither do I."

"Thanks," Nate said quietly. "And about you retiring… I know I have no right to ask, but I wish you'd reconsider."

"Oz will be just fine. The kid's good. Really good. Better than me," Wade said, referring to Osgood Wells—the Marauders' backup quarterback who'd been playing behind Wade for the past three seasons. "He went 3 and 1 when I got hurt last year. You said yourself the kid is star material."

"And I still say he's star material." Nate smirked. "But he ain't a star. Not yet. He could use a mentor in his ear helping him along."

"Been doing that the past three years."

"Yeah, but the past three years he was also your competition. Maybe now you'll teach him some of the tricks you've been holding back."

Wade sipped his beer thoughtfully, not denying that mentoring Oz had been the last thing on his mind these past three years. "I'll think about it. But as for us…this thing is over as far as I'm concerned. You're a good friend, Nate. Don't see the need to talk about this again."

Nate's shoulders relaxed as he reached across the table to shake his friend's hand.

Chapter 8

Kendra bounced little Allie on her lap. The infant cooed and giggled, blowing spit bubbles.

"She's adorable." Kendra kissed the girl's round cheek. Inhaled her irresistible, baby scent. "All the kids are, and they're so well-mannered."

"Told you I was lucky." Greer grinned, cutting three turkey sandwiches into triangles for the children.

"No, you're a good mom. Wade and the kids are lucky to have you."

"Thanks." Greer stacked the sandwich triangles on plates and set them on the table. She sighed. "God, I miss having you there whenever I'm in Memphis. You were the one person whose intentions I never doubted. I always felt like we would've been friends even if Wade and Nate weren't."

"Me, too." Kendra smiled, rearranging little Allie's headband. "You were my favorite, hands down."

Greer poured apple juice into acrylic tumblers. "I'm thrilled you and Nate are back together. Sure, I'm a little miffed with him now, but he's always been a good friend to me and Wade. Broke my heart to see how miserable he's been without you and Kai."

"We're not back together." A knot tightened in Kendra's throat. She shifted Allie on her lap, steering the infant away from the gold hoop she was trying to rip from her ear. "I'm his media consultant."

Greer put the juice away and set the cups and plates on the kitchen table. She turned to Kendra. "You do realize he's still in love with you?"

Without waiting for a response, Greer called the children down for their snack.

It was just as well. Greer's words left her head spinning.

The attraction was still there. That was evident from the way he'd scanned her figure on more than one occasion. But was it possible he still loved her?

The resentment on Nate's face when he first laid eyes on her at the restaurant and his aggravation with her when they met at the beach house suggested otherwise.

The one-night stands they'd had were products of their lingering chemistry, bottled-up frustrations and close proximity, not love.

Greer took Allie, who was reaching for her. She settled the girl on her lap, tied on her pink bib and fed her green baby food out of a chunky plastic spoon. "Thinking about what I said?"

Kendra watched Jake, Mariah and Noah nibbling their sandwiches and drinking apple juice. "No, I was wondering what you're feeding Allie. Looks like strained peas, but it smells better than any baby food I remember."

Greer grinned. "It's one of the baby food formulas I've been working on. Allie here is my personal guinea pig."

"She doesn't seem to mind. In fact, I've never seen a baby so enthusiastic about eating her vegetables." Kendra nodded toward the infant, who happily consumed the strained peas, some of which now dotted her chin. "Is this just for Allie or are you thinking of going commercial?"

Greer's eyes lit up. "Been thinking of starting my own baby food company. Everything will be fresh and organic—shipped right to your door. I want to start it as soon as Wade retires."

"What does Wade think?"

"He's been so supportive. He insists I don't need to wait for him to retire, but I'd like at least one of us to be focused on the kids."

"If Allie's enthusiasm is any indication, you've got a hit on your hands."

"Oh my gosh." Greer looked down at her daughter, who evidently wasn't satisfied with the speed at which her mother was feeding her. She dipped her chunky little fingers into the bowl and sucked strained peas from her fingers, getting it all over her face and in her nose. Greer grabbed a wipe and cleaned Allie's hands and face. "I'm excited about the possibility, but I'm scared to death by it, too. You must understand that."

"I do." Kendra took the dirty wipes from Greer and tossed them in the trash. "Never more than when I agreed to take Nate on as a client."

"Let me guess, it was Marcus's idea." Greer grinned as she resumed feeding Allie.

"How'd you know?"

"Had a feeling." Greer shrugged, her Alabama twang evident. "He's an old romantic soul like me and Wade. We been praying you two would figure out you were meant to be together."

"I hate to disappoint all of you, but this arrangement is strictly business."

"Got yourself convinced of that, don't you?" Greer shook her head. "You don't want to tell me? That's fine. But if you're lying to yourself…well, that's another matter altogether."

"What are you talking about?" Kendra tamped down the irritation rising in her chest.

"Isn't it obvious?" She smiled sweetly. "You're still in love with him, too."

Kendra glanced toward the sound of Nate's and Wade's voices approaching. She pointed a finger at Greer. "No more of this me-and-Nate-getting-back-together talk."

"Fine." Greer grinned, spooning more peas into Allie's mouth. "But it's gon' make y'all's sleeping arrangements mighty awkward."

"You mean to tell me this huge guesthouse only has one bedroom?" Kendra stood in the living room, her arms folded.

"There's another bedroom, but we're renovating it. The furniture's gone and there are ladders and paint buckets everywhere." Wade ran a hand through his longish brown hair, which dusted the collar of his suede jacket. "Honest."

Kendra propped a hand on her hip as she surveyed the space. "The sofa looks comfy enough. Got any extra blankets?"

"Sure thing." He gave Nate an apologetic stare. "I'll grab 'em for you."

"Look, it's my fault," Nate said. "I should've been clearer when I explained you were coming along. Didn't think about it because I knew the guesthouse has two bedrooms. I'll take the sofa."

"I'll be fine here." Kendra raised a hand before he could launch into his objection. "End of discussion."

Kendra sank into the bubbles threatening to spill over the side of the old claw-foot tub and sighed. She inhaled the yummy candles perched on the window ledge, which provided the only light in the room. The mingled scent of cranberry and orange wafted through the space, calming her frazzled nerves. She stared up through the skylight, admiring the stars dotting the sky.

Just a few more days. I can handle this.

She repeated the words in her head because the truth was, she didn't know if she could handle spending this much time with Nate. Especially after what Greer had said.

You do realize he's still in love with you? You're still in love with him, too.

Kendra dunked her head beneath the water, holding her breath a few seconds before emerging. Maybe that would disrupt the rogue thoughts of Nate Johnston roaming around the guesthouse barely dressed.

She wiped the water from her face and sat up, pressing her back to the still-cool cast-iron tub as she hugged her knees to her chest.

Concentrate on the job. Nate is just another client.

This was business. She was helping Nate and advancing her career. In fact, over dinner, Greer asked her to consider taking her on as a client once she got the baby food company up and running.

She'd planned to move her consultancy to exclusively serve athletes, but Greer was more than just a potential client. She was a friend. Besides, Kendra believed in what Greer was doing. Having tasted a few of the samples herself, she'd be crazy not to consider it.

There was a light tap at the door. Kendra froze, wrapping her arms tighter around her knees. "Yes?"

"Kai wants to say good-night."

"It's not even eight. I'll call him back as soon as I'm out of the tub."

"It's nearly ten there," Nate reminded her.

She sighed, making sure all of her essential parts were shielded by the bubbles. "The door isn't locked." Another apparent casualty of the remodeling. "Come in."

Light from the hall spilled into the room as Nate stepped inside wearing fitted jeans that hugged his bottom and a tight gray athletic shirt that outlined the hard-earned muscles of his chest and biceps. He handed Kendra his cell phone, then stood back against the door frame, his eyes roving anywhere in the room except on her.

"Kai Kai. How are you?"

"Good. When are you and Daddy coming home?"

"As soon as we can, sweetie. We're in Montana with Uncle Wade and Aunt Greer."

"You know them, too?" Kai had been with his dad whenever he visited with Wade and his family.

"Since before you were born." She smiled. "Auntie Greer's an old friend."

"Are Jake and Mariah there? Does Jake still have his train set?" Kai's voice rose with excitement.

"They're not here with me now. I'm…we're in the guesthouse. But yes, he still has his train. Are you being a good boy for Nana?"

"Yes."

"Did you brush your teeth before bed?"

"Yes, Mommy." He sighed. "I always brush my teeth before bed."

"Good. Now, no more stalling. Go to sleep."

She bid Kai a final good-night, blew a kiss through the phone, then handed it to Nate. "Thank you. I hate not tucking him in tonight. I would've been so disappointed if I'd forgotten to call him before bed."

Nate frowned, his mood suddenly surly. He shoved his phone into his back pocket. "I'll let you get back to your bath."

He left, closing the door behind him.

Kendra sank beneath the water, her eyes readjusting to the candlelit room.

What the hell was that about?

Chapter 9

Nate trudged back to the master bedroom, undressed and hopped in the large, rugged, stacked-stone-and-glass shower.

He lathered himself, gritting his teeth as he recalled Kendra's words. She was distraught over missing a single night tucking Kai in.

Welcome to my world, princess.

Most nights he had to settle for wishing Kai good-night by phone, as he had tonight. Did she have any clue how much it tore at him that he seldom got to tuck his own son into bed at night?

Kai was growing up so fast. Already six years old, soon he'd be too old for bedtime stories and good-night kisses. And he was missing all of it. Moments he'd never get back.

He'd witnessed his son's first words and first steps

via a video recording. He didn't want to miss out on any more milestones in Kai's life, but Kendra hadn't given him much choice.

The steaming hot water sluiced over his skin, relaxing his tired muscles and aching joints.

Wade was right; the game had taken a toll on their bodies. He wasn't as fast as he'd been a few seasons ago when he was so explosive he could outrun every cornerback in the league in a footrace to the end zone.

He never imagined retiring without hoisting that trophy over his head at least once. The Marauders were close to reaching the next level. They just needed a few tweaks to the defense and a couple more offensive weapons. He couldn't throw in the towel when they were so damn close.

Nights like this, when he was missing the goofy grin and contagious laughter of his son, he gave fleeting consideration to the prospect of retiring sooner rather than later.

Nate shook off the thought. He had a plan. Two more years, then he was out. This wasn't just about him; it was about securing the future of his family and his foundation.

He toweled off and slipped on his underwear. After a few minutes of scanning channels, Nate turned off the television and dropped to the floor to do push-ups.

How the hell had he managed to be mad at, grateful to and turned on by one woman, all at the same time?

Kendra.

He groaned, gritting his teeth as he switched to one-armed push-ups, not caring that he'd need another shower if he kept this up.

All day he'd kept his attraction to her in check—despite the fact that she looked good enough to pour in a glass and serve on ice in that body-hugging gray pencil skirt and knee-high boots. In spite of the electricity humming along the surface of his skin when she'd placed her hand on his, comforting him. But seeing her in the tub with her slick brown skin and wet curls—that was more than any man could be expected to handle.

He'd tried to distract himself by counting the bathroom tiles and studying every feature of that damn bathroom like he'd have a pop quiz on it the next morning. Still, his eyes roamed back to her in that tub again and again. Fortunately, she'd been too busy talking to Kai to notice.

Nate slipped on his flannel pajama bottoms and slippers, then padded to the kitchen for a snack. He opened the fridge and smiled. Wade and Greer had stocked it with leftovers.

Nate cut a few slices of ham, then added some macaroni and cheese and green bean casserole to his plate before heating it in the microwave.

"What smells so good?"

Nate turned, startled by Kendra moving toward him in purple pajamas. Her damp curls were wrapped in a white turban.

"Leftovers." He turned back to the microwave to watch the timer count down.

She shoved a few items into her luggage, then inched closer. "I shouldn't be eating this late—but now I'm hungry again. Any more?"

Arms folded, he tipped his head toward the fridge. "Plenty."

Kendra cocked her head to the side, her brow furrowed. She opened the fridge. "Thanks."

She made her plate in silence as he waited for his to finish heating.

Nate removed his plate from the microwave, grabbed his utensils and headed back to his room. He needed to put space between them, get a good night's rest and let his annoyance subside.

"Wait." Kendra's plea halted him. "Have I done something to upset you? Everything seemed fine, then suddenly I'm getting grunts and one-word answers."

"Everything is fine, Kendra. I'm tired, and I'd like to go to bed, if that's all right."

She shrugged. "You don't want to talk about it? Fine. But if I've somehow pissed you off, you should at least be mature enough to tell me what I did wrong."

"Like you were when you packed your bags and took off seven years ago?" He swung around. "That the kind of maturity you're talking about?"

Kendra lowered her gaze. "I didn't know exactly how to handle what I was feeling."

"I was prepared to spend my life with you, and you gave me the 'it's not you, it's me' speech. You said the life you would've had with me wasn't the one you envisioned for yourself. Do you have any idea how that made me feel?" Nate put the plate on the table and clenched his fist.

"Shitty," he supplied when she didn't respond. "Everything I'd done up to then was so that I could give you the life you deserved."

Head tilted, her brow creased. "That's sweet, Nate, but I never asked you to take care of me. I'm fully capable of caring for myself."

"I know, but..." Nate ran a hand through his hair and huffed. "All those years I watched your mom struggle to support you and Dash, working long hours and still managing to be a good mother. Most days she was tired to the bone. Apologizing because she couldn't be at your brother's track meets or your school plays. I didn't want that for you. For us. I wanted to give you everything. Anything you wanted."

"What I wanted was to have a relationship *and* a career. I wanted to do what I loved during the day and go home to the person I loved at night, just like you did. But you couldn't cope with that, as if it infringed upon your manhood."

"I didn't object to your career. I just didn't want you working with random athletes."

"Why?" She stepped closer.

"You know how those guys are. Chasing skirts. Going after anything pretty that moves."

"Exactly." Kendra's self-satisfied expression said it all. He'd justified her reasons for walking away.

His cheeks flushed with heat. "C'mon, Kendra, you know what I meant. Not every guy is like that. I'm not."

"Okay." She shrugged. "Let's look at the most essential point. You didn't trust me."

"Now you're turning this on me? You're the one who walked away because you didn't trust me."

"And you sabotaged my career because you didn't trust that I could deal with your colleagues without ending up in their beds."

They were both silent, stewing over the unhealed wounds they'd inflicted on each other.

Nate inhaled deeply, then released his breath slowly. He shook his head. "For the record, I did trust you. Just didn't want you to put yourself in a bad situation. Besides, I couldn't be sure of what I'd do if one of those guys ever laid a hand on you. Figured it'd be safer if we never had to find out. I didn't realize how important it was to you until it was too late."

"You should've talked to me instead of trying to lay down the law like you were the sheriff in a one-horse town." The corners of her eyes were damp. "Like what I wanted didn't matter."

Nate studied her face. "I was wrong, and I'm sorry. I wish I could take it back and do it all over again."

"Me, too." Kendra swiped a finger beneath her eye; her voice quavered. "The choice I made…it was a mistake. One we all ended up paying for."

Nate had waited a long time to hear those words. For confirmation that what they'd shared was real.

"I shouldn't have brought it up." His fists were balled at his sides as he resisted the urge to take her in his arms.

She sniffled, raising her eyes, wet with tears, to his. "And I shouldn't have made such a big deal about not being able to tuck Kai in tonight. That's what upset you, isn't it? I was complaining about one night without him while you…" She sighed heavily. "While you're away from him most nights."

Nate shrugged, watching a line of dark clouds rolling in and lightning in the distance.

"Every day I regret the pain my choice has caused both you and Kai." Kendra touched his arm. She leaned into him when he didn't respond. "I know it's a lot to ask, but I hope that one day you can forgive me. Both you and Kai."

His chest ached from the pain and regret he saw in her brown eyes. "What do you mean you hope Kai will forgive you?"

Kendra's eyebrows gathered and a deep line creased her forehead, hardening her soft features. She pressed her lips together tightly, as if she were trying to hold back a sob.

"He's been asking for you a lot more since Liam came into our lives. He sees Liam with the girls and he doesn't understand why his dad isn't in his life every day." Her voice grew faint; the tears etched a salty path down her face faster than she could erase them. "He's only six now, but eventually he'll be hurt and angry… he'll hate me for taking him away from his dad." Kendra covered her mouth and turned away.

Nate wrapped his arms around her, pulling her wet cheek to his bare chest. He kissed her forehead. "Kai adores you. He could never stay angry with you. He's too much of a mama's boy."

Kendra laughed against his chest, then pulled away enough to meet his gaze. "Like his dad?"

He held her at arm's length. "Whoa? Me? A mama's boy?"

She raised an eyebrow and punched him in the gut playfully. "Uh…yeah."

Nate peeked through his thumb and forefinger. "Maybe just a tad. Nothing wrong with that."

"No, there isn't." Kendra smiled wistfully. "There's a little mama's boy in every good man."

He pulled her to him again, his body reacting to the exquisite sensation of her curves pressed against him. "You saying I'm a good man?"

"I wouldn't be here now if I didn't believe you are. That's why this campaign is so important. I want people to see the kind, brilliant man I've always known. That's my mission. Once we accomplish that, everything else will come. The contract, the endorsements."

"Didn't think you believed in me anymore." He paused, his next words catching in his throat. "That's what hurt most when you left."

Kendra dropped her stare, but Nate cupped her chin, raising her eyes to meet his again.

"I know that you don't want to talk about this and that what's done is done. But in all these years, it's never felt over to me. There's always been a tiny piece of me that—despite the anger and hurt feelings—still wanted you to be there for me like you are right now."

She tried to pull away, but he held on tight, his gaze not leaving hers.

"I need to know, is there still a chance we can be a family?"

Yes.

That single word hung at the back of her throat, unable to make its way past her lips. She shook her head, trying to clear the warm thoughts that were fogging her brain and spreading throughout her body. Making her want things she had no right to. "Nate, I—"

He leaned down and kissed her open mouth, midsentence. His strong arms encircling her waist, he pulled their lower bodies together.

Kendra gasped at the sensation of his lips pressed to hers. She savored the taste and warmth of his mouth as she melted into his strong embrace. The memories of what they'd once been filled her body with heat and caused a delicious ache in her nipples and between her thighs.

Kissing Nate went against every rule she'd established when she agreed to take him on as a client. Rules she put in place to safeguard their working relationship and protect her heart.

Despite the blissful contentment she felt, surrendering to the magnetic pull between them, she needed to put a stop to it and regain control. Kendra pressed the heels of her hands into his chest, but Nate pulled her closer. Kissed her more fervently.

The logical objections her brain posed gave way to the temptation and desire that made her skin tingle. She relaxed into him and pressed her fingers to the warm skin of his muscular back.

She missed the strength of his hands, the tenderness of his kiss. The way his touch filled her belly with fire and made her knees weak.

Her senses were overloaded with the heat emanating from his skin, the scent of his freshly scrubbed skin, mingled with a hint of sweat and the salty taste of him.

Maybe she was overly cautious. They'd done this before—had one night together and then sensibly walked away.

Would it be so wrong if we did it again?

But that wasn't what Nate had proposed. He'd asked whether they could be a family.

That, she couldn't promise.

Kendra pulled away, her eyes searching his. "Nate, please, we agreed to keep this strictly business."

Nate sighed heavily, frowning. He cupped her cheek with his rough palm. "*We* didn't agree to anything. You insisted on it."

"I know, but you promised to keep your hands to yourself." She poked a finger in his chest, attempting to lighten the suddenly heavy mood. The tension between them was finally abating. She couldn't afford for things to go back to the way they were.

"We both made promises." He dropped his gaze, his voice gruff. "Things change."

He didn't need to elaborate. Kendra knew exactly what he meant. The night they'd gotten tossed from the prom, they spent the night on Pleasure Cove Beach, watching the waves crash on the shore. He'd made love to her on the beach under an incredible full moon and a sky full of stars that had never shone brighter.

That night, Nate promised to always love her. She'd promised the same.

They were just kids. Neither of them had a clue what life had in store or how they'd change.

Kendra clenched her fists at her side and sank her teeth into her lower lip as she searched for the right words.

Head cocked to the side, Nate's dark eyes studied hers. His words were a husky whisper that sent electricity up her spine. "There's obviously still something between us."

"We have a lot of history and an amazing little boy. It's hard not to get caught up in those feelings."

"Then maybe we should explore them." He trailed the back of his hand down the side of her face. "See where this thing takes us."

Kendra fought off the overwhelming desire to let Nate take her back to his bed and make love to her. His mouth exploring hers, his hands roaming her skin as she lay in his arms.

Sex and business don't mix. Stay strong.

"Wanting each other isn't enough, Nate." She stepped back, giving herself room to breathe in air that wasn't permeated with his fresh, woodsy scent. "And what we want isn't necessarily what's best for us. No matter how badly we want it."

Nate caught her hand as she turned to walk away, tugging her toward him again. "I don't believe our being together isn't what's best for us or Kai. Neither do you."

"One kiss and you're talking about being a family? I can't promise you that."

Nate groaned, releasing her hand. "We're not kids on a first date, Kendra. We know each other. Most important, we love our son and want what's best for him."

Kendra wanted Nate. Loved him. But did he love her? Or was this just about finally making them a family?

Nate grew up in a big, close family that had earned the moniker "the black Waltons." His parents had been married for four decades. Nate wanted Kai to be raised by both his parents—just as he'd been.

She wanted that, too, but not at the expense of a one-sided marriage where they were just in it for the kids. Relationships like that didn't last.

Her parents were proof of that.

"We both want what's best for Kai. That's why we need to focus on the mission at hand. There's a lot on the line here, Nate. Your career, your future income, the work you've been able to do with the foundation—"

"Your career." His mouth tugged down in a frown. "It's serious, I get it, but *this*—" he gestured between them "—is important, too."

She lifted her chin and met his condemning gaze. "This isn't the time to explore the past. Not with so much at stake for both of us."

"Fine." He gathered his plate, turning to leave.

Kendra grabbed his elbow. “That doesn’t mean we can’t sit down and have a meal together.”

“You want to keep this thing strictly business? Well, I don’t usually have shirtless midnight business meetings.” He narrowed his gaze, his tone icy.

“You give interviews in the locker room when you’re half-dressed. How is this any different?”

“You know why it’s different.” Nate put the plate down again. “What is it that you want from me, Kendra?”

She stood stunned, her mouth slack, unable to reply.

“I ask you to marry me and you walk away. Just when I think I’m finally over it, you find some way to mess with my head again. I just wanted to have a quiet late-night snack in my room. *Alone*. But you couldn’t let it be.” His words came in quick, angry bursts. “I kiss you. Tell you I want to be with you and Kai. You say I’m pushing too hard. But, oh, by the way, why don’t we sit down for a nice, civil business meal in our pajamas?”

Her stomach clenched and her hands shook. He was right. She was being selfish—trying to hold on to him while maintaining her distance. “I’m sorry. I don’t know exactly how to do this. I want us to be friends again. Not just because we’re working together or even because of Kai. We were friends long before we dated. I miss that.”

Nate shook his head. “After everything we’ve been through, I can’t just be friends. Maybe someday, but not tonight.”

Kendra bit her lower lip, concentrating on the superficial physical pain rather than the deep ache in her heart as he walked away.

Chapter 10

Nate dropped his luggage by the front door and stumbled to the couch. They'd landed in Memphis later than expected.

Good to finally be home again.

He dropped Kendra off at a nearby hotel and headed to his place.

He had plenty of room to put her up for the night. But after the night they'd shared at Wade and Greer's guesthouse, they both agreed it would be better if she stayed at a hotel.

Nate just wanted a cold beer and a hot bath before what would surely be a grueling day.

First, there was the meeting with the team. Then he would meet with a couple of his teammates. After he made his personal amends to everyone on the list—except Tyree and Dade, who were still dodging his calls—

he'd take to the podium in a press conference at the team facilities.

Nate made his way to the fridge. He tossed out a couple of suspect take-out containers, then pulled out a bottle of imported beer. He settled on the couch again when the doorbell rang.

His neighbor collected his mail when he was away, and was always a little too eager to bring over his mail and newspapers. Nate opened the door.

"Hello, Nate. Miss me?"

Stephanie Weiss—the devil herself and the cause of this entire fiasco—lifted her head, her face previously shielded by her large-brimmed hat. Her mouth curved in a sly grin.

"What the hell are you doing here?" He gritted out the words between clenched teeth.

"Got a proposal for you." She smiled sweetly, glancing over his shoulder. "May I come in?"

"Not if your ass was on fire and I had the only bucket of water for thirty miles," he seethed. "You've got five seconds before I call security to haul you out of here."

She seemed slightly irritated by his rebuff, but mostly amused. "Fine. Then I'll save my questions for the press conference tomorrow. Just thought you'd welcome the opportunity to sit down and explain your side of things."

"Sit down with the devil who caused this whole shit storm? No thanks." He crossed his arms. "Yeah, I know it was you who sent those girls to ambush me."

She smirked. "Now that's just unsubstantiated speculation." Stephanie echoed the words he'd used in the press conference he had three years ago, when he'd distanced himself from her after the scandal broke.

"Is that what this is about?" He placed a hand high on the doorjamb as he leaned against the frame. "You're still pissed because I wouldn't help you ruin my friend's career?"

"You didn't have any qualms about ruining mine." She narrowed her eyes, the irises the color of muddy water, and pressed her thin lips into a tight line. "This time, I had indisputable proof, and it's you who came out looking like the fool."

Nate clenched his fist and gritted his teeth. Swallowed back all the things he wanted to say to this woman. Things his mama would whup his behind for if she heard him utter them in mixed company. "Get off my property. Now. Believe me, I'd enjoy watching the cops drag you out of here."

Stephanie shrugged, then flipped her shoulder-length dark hair. "Fine, but I came here to offer a truce. Give me an exclusive interview before your press conference tomorrow, and I'll back off. Let this thing die down."

Nate laughed bitterly. "Be a clown in the circus you created? No thanks."

"What are you worried about? You'll come out smelling like a rose. You always do."

"I'll take option two." His patience was gone. "Now, get the fuck off my property."

"War it is then." Stephanie grinned, tying the belt of her red wool coat. She turned and walked away, calling over her shoulder, "Don't say I didn't give you a chance to end this thing peacefully."

Nate slammed the door and pressed his back to it, running his fingers through his hair. He'd screwed himself over big-time when he'd messed around with her.

Aside from letting Kendra walk away, getting with Stephanie Weiss was his biggest regret.

His friends had warned him that breaking a big story would always be her first priority, putting all of them in jeopardy. He hadn't listened. Now he was paying the price.

Stephanie had lost her career and her credibility as a sideline reporter for a major network when things had gone sideways three years before. Seemed she'd spent those years plotting her payback.

Nate picked up his beer and drained the bottle, then headed to the kitchen for another. The doorbell rang again.

He turned, his jaw clenched and his fist balled at his side.

All bets were off. Stephanie Weiss was about to get a piece of his mind—unfiltered. He'd just have to apologize to his mother later.

Kendra shifted her bag on her shoulder, her luggage at her side and her heart racing.

Nate wouldn't be happy to see her. Not when he'd dropped her at the hotel like she was a sack of flaming potatoes and pulled off, barely muttering two words.

When the door swung open, he looked angrier than she'd ever seen him. Like he was prepared for a fight. His shoulders drooped, a look of confusion on his face as he glanced around. "Kendra, what are you doing here?"

Nice to see you, too.

Kendra pulled her wrap around her to combat the chill in the air and the one rolling off her ex. "They were booked, except for a presidential suite. Same story with every other hotel I called. There are a couple of trade conventions in town this week."

"Forgot about that," he muttered, still blocking the doorway. He glanced over her shoulder again.

"If you're looking for your friend who just left, I passed her in the driveway."

"She isn't my friend. That was Stephanie Weiss."

"Your ex?" Kendra asked, then shifted under Nate's withering stare. "I mean, the reporter who started all of this?"

"Seems there are a lot of my exes showing up at my door tonight." He raised an eyebrow, then sighed. He grabbed her bags off the doorstep, opening the door wide enough for her to enter. "Come in."

Kendra stepped inside tentatively, glancing around the house. Despite the tension between them, she couldn't help smiling. She had so many great memories in this house. She remembered when Nate first bought the place. The weeks of house hunting before they'd finally settled on it. The times they'd shared there.

She glanced toward the den, where they'd last made love one weekend when she'd brought Kai to visit his father. They'd been in the middle of a heated argument about where Kai would spend Christmas. Then he'd kissed her, and they'd ended up making love on the sofa while their son slept blissfully unaware upstairs.

They'd almost made the same mistake in Montana.

Kendra stood taller. This time she'd be smarter. Stronger. Use better judgment. Then everything would be fine. "The place looks great."

"Thanks." Nate set her bags near the bottom of the stairs. "I'll take your bags up in a few minutes, but I was just about to get a beer. I could use one right now. Can I get you something?"

"Glass of wine?"

"Red or white?" he asked, then quickly answered his own question, echoing her response. "Rosé, of course."

She smiled. "If you have it. If not, a glass of white wine would be fine."

"Think I've got something in the cooler."

She followed him into the kitchen. "So, what was public enemy number one doing here?"

Nate's delts tensed visibly and he paused for a moment before reaching into the wine cooler. He dug through the bottles silently, then pulled out her favorite bottle of rosé. He opened the bottle. "Proposing a truce of sorts."

"So she acknowledges this is a vendetta against you?" Kendra sat at the kitchen table.

"Stephanie wanted me to know she was the one who took me down." He poured a glass of wine and handed it to Kendra. "She knows I can't do anything with the information."

Kendra thanked Nate for the rosé and took a sip. "Unfortunately, she's right. It would do more harm than good. You'll come off as a whiny athlete blaming someone else for your screwup."

Nate twisted the cap off his beer and sat at the table. He took a swig. "She's probably banking on me using that excuse at the press conference tomorrow. Bet she's already got a segment taped, just waiting for sound bites from the conference."

"Cunning, vindictive and determined. She's a real winner," Kendra muttered, then sipped her wine.

"Yeah, I can really pick 'em." He cut his gaze at her, then drank more of his beer.

Touché.

Kendra straightened her shoulders. "So this truce she offered, what was it?"

"She wanted me to give her an exclusive interview before the press conference. Said if I did, she wouldn't press the issue further."

"Indicating that if you don't, she'll keep fanning the flames." Kendra's stomach flipped. That meant she'd be doing more than just cleaning up the mess that was already made, she'd be putting out fires intentionally set by Stephanie. "Do you think she'd keep her word if you gave her the interview?"

"Not as far as I could throw her conniving ass."

Kendra nodded. "I suspected as much. If you don't mind my asking—"

"What did I see in her in the first place?" He finished her question. When she nodded, he continued, "I was out with an injury, feeling down on myself when I ran into Steph at the grocery store. I was struggling with my leg in a cast. She offered to help me shop and to make dinner for me that night. We were on friendly terms. Figured, what the hell? It could be fun."

"I'm sure it didn't hurt that she's very pretty. Wasn't she a beauty contestant or something?"

"Miss Connecticut. Third runner-up for Miss America that year." He didn't meet her gaze.

"Not judging." Kendra held her hands up. "But she obviously isn't as pretty on the inside."

Nate grunted. "Got that right."

"Okay, so taking the deal isn't an option. We'll have to be prepared for whatever she slings our way." Kendra paused before asking the thing she needed to know, but didn't want to ask. "She doesn't have anything on you, does she? No secretly recorded audio, no sex tapes?"

"No," he said emphatically, sitting up straight as a rod, then dropping his gaze. "I mean, not that I'm aware of."

Fair enough. Anyone could set up a secret camera in their bedroom.

"Anything you might have told her about a teammate or your family that she might use?"

"Not that I recall." His response wasn't as convincing. "Like I said, we were only together a few months. The time we did spend together…we spent very little of it talking."

Kendra ignored the twisting in her gut. "Then we'll just stay alert. Be sure not to give her any new ammunition."

Nate stood suddenly. "Got a long day tomorrow. I'll take your bags to your room."

He was gone before she could thank him.

Kendra poured herself another glass of wine. This time she'd be ready for Stephanie Weiss.

Chapter 11

Nate took his place behind the lectern and straightened his tie. He adjusted the microphone and thanked everyone for coming, then explained that he would play the full video.

Stephanie pressed her lips into an angry slash and folded her arms. Her ire confirmed that playing the entire video was the right move.

Score one more for Kendra.

He stepped aside while the five-minute video played in its entirety. Nate glanced over at Marcus and Kendra standing in the corner.

His brother nodded reassuringly. Kendra's confident smile filled his chest with warmth and eased the tension in his shoulders. He wouldn't admit it to Marcus, but he was glad Kendra was there. Especially since his twin sister—off on one of the solo island vacations she took a few times a year—couldn't be.

When the video ended, the lights came on again. Nate launched into a prepared script, giving a brief overview of what happened that night and why he was so frustrated with himself and his teammates. He made it clear he'd offered his sincere apologies in person to everyone who was available. Nate apologized again for his lack of thoughtfulness and the impact it had on his teammates and the Marauders organization.

He ended by stating emphatically that he intended to suit up for the Marauders for the remainder of his career.

"Our team has come so close to going to the big dance. During the off-season, we'll work hard as individuals and as an organization to ensure we're giving our all every single time we take the field. It's what every man on the team wants. Most important, it's what the loyal fans of this city deserve. Thank you for coming."

Nate stepped away from the microphone, relieved the press conference was finally over. He was especially grateful Kendra insisted they not take questions.

Score two for Kendra.

"Is it true you just returned from Montana where you pressured Wade Willis to retire before next season?" Stephanie shot to her feet, to the surprise of everyone in the room.

"Of course not." The words came out of his mouth before he could stop them. Kendra had already warned him someone was bound to push for questions. He was supposed to say, "No further comment."

So much for that.

"Wade is still one of the elite quarterbacks in this

league. This past year wasn't his best year, but it wasn't mine, either. We'll both be stronger next year."

"So you admit you're a big part of the reason the team has stalled in the play-offs three years in a row?" Stephanie could barely hold back her smirk.

Nate's shoulders knotted. He pressed his lips into a harsh line and breathed out slowly. "As I stated that night on the video, I need to be better. We all do. No further questions."

He stepped away from the microphone and made a beeline behind the curtains and away from the hungry pack of jackals clamoring to ask the next question. Nate pressed his back against the wall, angry with himself for not sticking to the script. He'd let Stephanie rile him. She knew he wouldn't let that accusation hang in the air, unanswered.

And how the hell did she know he'd just returned from Montana, anyway?

He looked up at the *click* of Kendra's heels coming down the hallway. She wasn't happy. Neither was Marcus, who was hard on her heels.

"Why didn't you stick to the script?" Marcus gestured wildly. "Were we not clear about not taking questions?"

"I know I should've ignored her question, but I couldn't leave the fans thinking I'm trying to push Wade out."

"There are going to be a lot of accusations hurled at you in the next few weeks, man. You can't respond to every one. We've got a plan. If you stick with it, everything will be fine." Marcus stormed away, likely in search of a strong cup of coffee.

Nate turned his attention to Kendra. "Go ahead. Let me have it."

Kendra's expression softened, and she let out a quiet sigh as she squeezed his arm. "I know how much Wade means to you and to the fans. It's probably good you combated that accusation right away and that you spoke so highly of him. You handled the situation well."

"Really?"

"Really. Just don't do it again. If we say no questions, then don't address questions. Not even from Stephanie Weiss. Got it?"

"Got it." He looked down at his watch. "We better head out. Marcus and I have a late lunch meeting over at the foundation. We'll drop you off at the house on the way."

"Aren't we flying back to Pleasure Cove tonight?" Her shoulders tensed and there was a hint of panic in the slight elevation of her tone.

"Change of plans. I finally connected with Dade. We're meeting tomorrow for lunch, so we'll have to stay one more night. Hope that's cool."

"It's important that you sit down with Dade and iron things out." Kendra waved a hand. "I'll try again with the hotels."

"No need." Nate shoved his hands in his pockets. "There's plenty of room for both of us."

"If you're sure."

"I am. Feel free to work from my office. I'll even make dinner tonight. To thank you for everything," he added quickly.

She cocked an eyebrow, her adorable nose crinkling. "You cook now?"

"Okay, so maybe I'm just heating it up. Same difference."

Kendra laughed, then looked thoughtful, the gears turning in that brilliant head of hers. She nodded reluctantly. "Sure."

He gave her a quick nod, then they headed toward the exit, his heart dancing with a growing sense of hope.

Kendra paced in front of the fireplace in the den, her body filled with nervous energy, prompted by the memories of when she was last there.

She halted, catching her breath as she fought back the vivid sensation of Nate planting soft kisses along her collarbone and shoulders. Kisses that led to a wild and passionate night together.

Kendra swallowed hard, then resumed her pacing. Finally, she plopped on the sofa and pulled out her phone. She called her mother, but there was no answer. Next, she called her sister.

"How's the trip?"

Kendra released a slow breath, fortified by the lilt in Maya's voice. "Professionally? Things are going well. Personally? I'm losing it."

"Why, what's going on between you and Nate?"

"I'm sitting on the infamous sofa, trying my hardest to keep my head together, but all I keep thinking about is the last time I was here, when I couldn't keep my legs together."

Maya chuckled. "What are you doing at Nate's anyway? Thought you were staying at a hotel."

"So did I, but we ended up staying overnight in Montana sharing Wade and Greer's guesthouse."

Maya cleared her throat. "The more important question is, did you two share a bed?"

"No," Kendra said quickly. The silence seemed to extend forever. Her sister was the master of the well-used pause to get her to spill her guts. She groaned. "But he kissed me."

"Did you kiss him back?" The lilt returned to Maya's voice. She was on the verge of a giggle.

"Until I regained my clarity."

"Clarity, huh? Sounds more like delusion, if you're still pretending Nate doesn't mean anything to you."

"Of course he does. He's Kai's dad. He was my best friend. My first." She said the words wistfully, recalling that weekend her mother had taken her brother to Raleigh on a college tour. "I'll always care for him. That doesn't mean we're meant to be together."

"And what does Nate think?" Maya's tone was subdued.

Kendra swung her legs beneath her and exhaled. "He wants us to be a family."

"Oh my gosh, Kendra. That's great news." Maya paused when Kendra didn't respond. "Isn't it?"

"Seems like it's more about Nate wanting to be with Kai." A dull ache filled her chest. "He didn't say he wanted to be with me. He just keeps going on about how great it would be to finally be a family."

"Nate loves his son. Why is that bad?"

"Because it can't be the only reason we're together, like it was for Dad when he married my mom."

There was an uneasy silence between them. As much as Kendra loved Maya now, it hadn't always been that way. Kendra had resented Maya and her younger brother.

She couldn't shake the hurt of knowing she was the reason her father left. Curtis Williams abandoned their family less than a year after her birth.

Though he'd left them behind, he chose to stay with Maya's mother just a year later. They'd gotten married and raised two kids. He'd attended every school function and proudly filmed everything from Maya's and Cole's first steps to their college graduations.

Even now, she sometimes lay awake at night wondering why her father hadn't loved her enough to stay with them. Why he hadn't doted on her and Dash and embraced being their dad as much as he enjoyed being a father to Maya and Cole.

"I don't think it's as simple as that." Maya adored Curtis Williams. She was a daddy's girl. He'd been there for her all her life. Why shouldn't she adore him? "He loved your mom."

Kendra snorted. "He had a damn funny way of showing it. Love like that, I don't need."

"Nate isn't our dad," Maya said quietly. "And for the record, Dad was young and he made his mistakes. He regrets how poorly he handled things."

"Agree to disagree." It was Kendra's signal for Maya to end the discussion of Curtis Williams's virtues.

"Okay." The word came out of Maya's mouth in an odd singsong. "But you're not being fair to Nate. Just because being a family is important to him doesn't mean you aren't."

Kendra understood the sense of indebtedness Maya felt toward Nate. She and Dash had wanted nothing to do with their father or their half siblings. Still, Maya had been persistent, following Kendra to college. Nate and his parents encouraged her to get to know Maya.

"She's family," Nate's mom, Ms. Naomi, had said. "Doesn't matter how she became family. She just is. And you don't turn your back on family."

Kendra had resented Nate's interference at first, but she and Dash had grown apart as they'd gotten older and she yearned for the deep connection Nate had with his siblings.

Getting to know and accept her younger sister was one of the best decisions she'd ever made. She and Maya owed a huge debt of gratitude to the Johnstons. But she wouldn't be with Nate out of a sense of obligation.

"We're not the same people we were seven years ago." Kendra stood by the fireplace, allowing its warmth to soothe the chill creeping down her spine.

"So get to know each other again. Most important, tell him how you feel," Maya urged.

Kendra's temples throbbed. "I can't."

"Why not?"

"He'll say it just because I need to hear it." Kendra paced in front of the fireplace. Her slippers scuffed against the carpet.

"Nate always says what he feels. That's why he's in the spot he's in now." Maya sighed in response to the cluck of Kendra's tongue. "If he says it, it's because he means it."

"Then why didn't he say it the other night? Why didn't he say he misses me? That he wants to be with me? That he can't stop thinking of me the way I can't stop thinking of him?" Kendra hadn't meant to say the last part, but her mouth was moving faster than her brain.

Maya hesitated before she responded. "The last time Nate confessed his feelings for you, you rejected him and walked away. Can you blame him for being gun-shy?"

Kendra's stomach twisted in knots as the truth of Maya's words hit her squarely in the chest. She didn't respond.

"Maybe Nate's reluctant to share his feelings because he isn't sure he can trust you with them." An apologetic tone filtered her sister's brutally honest words.

"Maybe. Still, I won't get back with Nate for the wrong reasons. As much as I know Kai wants his dad and me to be together, it would be worse if things blew up a few years down the road. I won't set him up for the disappointment and resentment I experienced at his age."

"You mean, the resentment you feel now." Maya's voice wavered.

"I don't mean to make you feel bad. That's why I try not to talk about Dad. It's never a conversation that will go well between us."

"Even when we don't discuss him, that ugly little truth is hidden in the words we don't say." Maya cleared her throat. "Do you have any idea how much it hurts to know that deep down my sister wishes I were never born?"

"That isn't true."

"I wish it were as easy for me to believe that as it is for you." Maya sighed. "If it were the other way around, maybe I'd feel the same."

"No, you wouldn't. You're the sweetest, most loving person I know. I know it doesn't always seem like it, but I'm grateful to have you in my life. I'm thrilled you found someone who loves you as much as I do. You deserve a great guy like Liam. He's about as close as a guy can get to being worthy of you."

"Thanks, sis." The smile returned to Maya's voice.

"Speaking of that handsome man of yours, when are you two going to finally set a date?" Kendra settled onto the couch.

"I was thinking we'd wait until next summer to get married."

"Why so long? Is it a family thing for him?" The Westbrooks owned a huge international resort firm based in London, and they were well connected back in the UK.

"It's nothing like that, it's just… I keep hoping that if I wait long enough, you and Dad will work things out."

"I promised I'd be on my best behavior on your wedding day," Kendra reminded her sister.

"I appreciate the sentiment, but the reality is that the tension between you two makes everyone uncomfortable."

"I won't let that happen on your wedding day, Maya. I promise."

"The minute you see him, you'll pick a fight. Happens every time." Maya's voice rose to a crescendo. Suddenly it became sad. "You're not just punishing Dad. It hurts that I can't sit down with two of my favorite people on my wedding day."

Kendra's heart ached. Whatever her issues were with their father, Maya wasn't to blame. "I'm sorry. I had no idea."

"I know, but we can talk about that another day. Right now, let's talk about the real reason you called. You're still in love with Nate, and it terrifies you."

Kendra didn't deny the accusation. "I won't break

his heart again. He couldn't take that. Neither could I. Besides, his evil twin would probably strangle me with her bare hands."

"Or at least hire someone to off you." Maya laughed, the tension between them easing.

"No, she'd definitely do it herself." Kendra was only half kidding. Vi would probably relish the feel of her warm blood on her hands. Nate's twin could be your best friend or your worst enemy. Once the former, Kendra was now the latter.

"The solution is simple," Maya said. "Don't break his heart this time."

That was Maya. Making a complicated relationship like the one she and Nate shared seem so simple. Apparently, she'd forgotten what a convoluted relationship she and Liam had just a few months prior. When she was still terrified of bringing someone new into her daughters' lives, afraid Liam would disappoint them.

Thankfully, she'd been wrong. Liam was an amazing man who'd left behind his playboy ways once he found the woman of his dreams—her little sister.

"I didn't set out to break his heart before. I panicked. How can I be sure it won't happen again?"

"You can't, but you can be honest with Nate and yourself about what freaked you out then." Maya's voice was soothing. "And any lingering fears holding you back now."

"I won't put my career aside for Nate again," Kendra suddenly interjected. The declaration took her by surprise.

"Then talk to him," Maya said simply. "No more excuses."

She was gone before Kendra could object.

"They're not excuses," she said to the empty room as she tossed her phone on the sofa. "It's the truth."

"What's the truth?"

Kendra startled, nearly jumping out of her skin. "Nate, I didn't hear you come in."

He grinned. "Obviously. You hungry?"

Kendra nodded. Until he'd mentioned it, she hadn't realized how hungry she was. She'd checked the fridge earlier, but there was very little edible food left. "I could eat."

A slow grin stretched his mouth. "Good, because I thought we could cook together like the old days."

Damn. Now she couldn't look at the kitchen counter without reminiscing about exactly how those times nearly always ended.

Who knew kitchen sex could be so good?

Kendra shrugged. "Okay."

She would help Nate cook because she was hungry. Starving, in fact. But no matter what, they most definitely would not go there. No matter how good he looked in that slim gray suit.

Chapter 12

One of the many things Nate missed about Kendra was their shared love of food. She'd never subsisted on lettuce or gone from one crazy fad diet to the next.

Kendra appreciated a gourmet meal. Savored every bite. Watching her enjoy a perfectly cooked steak or authentic pasta dish was practically foreplay.

Tonight, he would begin his slow seduction by making her favorite meal. He'd nixed his plans to purchase a premade lasagna prepared by a local gourmet chef. Kendra's crack about his not being able to cook forced him to step up his game.

He purchased the meal plan that came with the ingredients and the recipe so they could prepare the meal together, like they did when they first started out.

Nate's pulse quickened as he reminisced over those steamy nights together. There was something almost erotic about the act of cooking together. Filling one basic need led to satisfying another.

He set the bags on the counter and took off his jacket, folding it across the chair. "Can I get you a drink?"

Her hesitant nod, a brief glimpse at the vulnerability she loathed revealing, somehow made her even sexier. "Half a glass of wine would be great."

Nate dragged his gaze up her body, admiring her toned curves. She wore an oversize white T-shirt with a deep vee over a pair of black leggings that hugged her ample hips and thighs. He cleared his throat, raising his eyes to hers again as he pulled a chilled bottle of her favorite rosé from the bag. He poured her a half glass and watched her sensual mouth as she took a generous sip, her hand unsteady.

"Everything okay?" Nate removed one cuff link, then the other.

"Fine." Her voice vibrated with false bravado.

He excused himself to change. When he returned in jeans and a T-shirt, Kendra had removed the lasagna ingredients from the bag and lined them up on the counter. A pot of water was boiling on the stove.

"I think you've forgotten how this whole 'cooking together' thing works."

Kendra snorted. "All I did was unpack the bag. There's plenty left to do."

He washed and dried his hands, then opened the package of pasta noodles, adding them to the salted water. He set the timer, then took out a large skillet and placed it on the burner.

Kendra peeled and sliced an onion while Nate added Italian sausage and ground beef to the pan.

They worked together in comfortable silence. Nate

had missed this. He hadn't realized what a luxury it was to be with someone he was so in tune with that he felt the comfort of her presence without either of them uttering a single word.

Kendra was the only woman with whom he'd felt that kind of warmth and security.

"There." Kendra added the onions and garlic to the skillet as he browned its contents.

"Thank you." He forced the words past the thickness in his throat. It was something he wanted to say since that moment at Wade's when she'd placed her hand on his, calming him when it felt like his world was spinning out of control.

"For helping to make my dinner?" Kendra rummaged through the drawers and retrieved the can opener. He'd upgraded the utensil, but kept it in the same place she'd designated for it when they were together. In fact, the entire kitchen was essentially just as she'd arranged it. Like it was stuck in time. "It's the least I can do."

Nate reduced the flame, then turned to face her, taking her soft, warm hand in his. He pulled her closer and she leaned in to him, her eyes meeting his.

"For taking me on as a client, even though I didn't want to work with you initially. For coming with me on this trip. For being the voice of reason when I needed it most."

She didn't speak. Instead she leaned in closer, meeting him halfway as he captured her warm mouth in a kiss. He slipped his fingers in her hair, his tongue tangling with hers.

Kendra wrapped her arms around him and lifted onto her toes, as if trying to capture more of his mouth. One hand trailed down her back and over her backside.

He missed the feel of her body, pressed against his, and the taste of her sweet mouth. The way her body fit perfectly against his. The elevation of his temperature and the rapid beat of his heart whenever she was in his arms.

How could she not miss this?

Nate gripped her bottom, pulling her tightly against him, enjoying the feel of their bodies pressed together.

He swallowed the soft gasp that escaped her throat in response. She dropped the can opener. The sound of it crashing against the hard tile floor startled them both.

Kendra pulled away. She retrieved the utensil and returned to the work of opening the cans, her eyes focused on her task. "Thank you for saying that, but hold your gratitude until I get the results you're looking for. Because I will."

"I don't doubt that." Nate sighed and went back to stirring the contents of the skillet. Bits of garlic and onion had burned. "But regardless of what happens, I want you to know I'm grateful for what you've done. I appreciate you. I didn't say that enough when we were together. It's a mistake I won't repeat."

"Thank you for giving me this shot." Kendra's eyes met his. "Most exes wouldn't be so gracious."

Nate's heart sank in his chest. He resented the fact that their romantic relationship was firmly in the past. A harsh reality that made his chest ache. Kendra seemed content with it. Able to turn her feelings on and off at will.

The hunger that consumed him wasn't reflected in Kendra's eyes. There was desire, but not the abject need that arose whenever he thought of her. Certainly not with the ferocity with which he felt it. If she'd felt that strongly about him, she would've jumped at his proposal to try again.

Despite the bulletproof force field she projected, Nate was sure her true feelings were buried below the surface, where she could keep them safe.

Even if she refused to acknowledge her feelings, Nate knew Kendra still loved him. It was evidenced by a thousand little things. The affectionate tone of her voice, the dreamy gaze when their eyes met and the soothing touch of her hand. It was couched in all the words she couldn't say.

This time, though, he needed to be sure before he poured out his heart to her.

He loved Kendra, but he wouldn't make a fool of himself again. He couldn't endure the pain and humiliation of another rejection. The feeling of his heart being pierced by jagged, broken glass.

This time, he needed to hear her say the words first. That she loved him and needed him in her life. That she wanted to be with him.

"You're not just an ex." He loosened bits of browned sausage and garlic stuck to the bottom of the pan. "We have a son together, and we were best friends for most of our lives."

A sad smile barely lifted the corner of her mouth as she scraped tomato paste from a can with a small rubber spatula. "That's why we're such good co-parents. Maybe we aren't exactly friends now, but we have that foundation to rely on."

Now it was his turn to snort.

"What did I say wrong?" She set down the empty can, then started to empty the next into the skillet.

"*Co-parents*. That term is a joke. It implies both parties are equal parents, but that's not really possible, is it? One person is always left on the outside, looking in. Wishing they were there in those photos. In the moments that matter. The ones you'll never get back."

Kendra looked thoughtful as she opened one can of tomato sauce, then the other. She poured both into the pan, then carried all of the empty cans over to the sink and rinsed them before tossing them into the recycle bin.

"This isn't how I envisioned my life, either, but it's the best option we have." Her tone was faint, apologetic. She wiped her hands on a towel. "Things could be a lot worse. Every day, I'm thankful Kai has you in his life."

"And every night I go to bed regretting that I can't be in his life every day, the way my dad has always been in mine." Hurt and anger rose in his chest. When he met her gaze, her eyes were filled with tears. "Kendra, I'm sorry. I didn't mean to—"

"I can't do this and still do my job, Nate." She cut him off, shaking her head. "Right now, doing my job is more important." She turned to leave.

When would he learn to keep his big mouth shut?

"I didn't mean to upset you." Nate sighed, catching her elbow. "Would I be making you a home-cooked meal right now if I intended to say something stupid and ruin our night?"

"What you said wasn't stupid. You're right. I made a bad decision, but you're the one who's had to suffer most. It isn't fair. So I promise, after this is all over, we'll work out a more fair arrangement so you get to spend more time with Kai."

"You'd do that?" Nate was stunned. Kai meant everything to her. "You'd be willing to sacrifice some of your time with him?"

She nodded, her lips pursed and her eyes glossy.

"That means a lot to me." He cleared his throat. "But being together as a family would mean even more."

"As much as we love Kai, we can't be together just for his sake. Neither of us would be happy. I want more than that for myself and for you."

"Shouldn't I get to decide what's best for me?"

"I'm sorry." Kendra pulled free from him, her cheeks suddenly wet with tears. "Excuse me."

She rushed from the room and up the stairs.

Dammit.

He'd blown it again.

Nate finished up the lasagna sauce by adding the supplied herbs and seasonings. Then he let it simmer while he drained the noodles. A half hour had passed and Kendra hadn't returned.

His pride hadn't allowed him to go after her following the proposal debacle seven years ago. He wouldn't make that mistake again. If she wasn't back by the time the sauce finished simmering, he'd go and find her.

Kendra cupped her hands under the cold running water in Nate's guest bathroom and splashed it on her face. Her eyes were red, her cheeks were stained with tears and her mascara was a runny mess. Better to strip it all off than to attempt to fix it.

She removed her makeup, cleansed her skin, then patted her face dry with a towel.

Standing there, her face stripped of all makeup, she felt nearly as vulnerable as she had when Nate told her what he thought of her co-parenting.

She'd been lying to herself. Pretending things were good for all of them, when the truth was they were all miserable.

Kai missed being with his dad. Nate was hurting without his son. She lived with the guilt of being the coward who broke up their family because she couldn't deal with her daddy issues.

"Thanks, Dad," she groaned. "You produced one damaged little girl."

There was a tap at the bathroom door. "Kendra, are you okay?"

She opened the door partially. "I didn't expect to take so long. I'll be down in a sec."

"You've been crying." Nate reached his long arm through the door and cradled her cheek in his large palm. "I didn't intend to upset you."

Loosening her grip on the door handle, Kendra leaned into his palm, her eyes drifting shut. She savored his touch—strong, yet delicate—and the warmth of his rough palm against her cool cheek. Heat radiated into her neck and down her spine. A soothing lightness seeped into her bones, and a sense of calm settled over her.

Her eyes fluttered open. Something in Nate's brown eyes was so tender and sweet it melted her heart. Yet the heat in his penetrating gaze and feather-soft touch took her breath away.

She inhaled, dropping her gaze to his stubbled chin. "Nate, I'm sorry I—"

Nate pressed his open mouth to hers, cradling the back of her neck.

Kendra didn't object to his kiss or the way he slung

an arm low around her waist, pulling their bodies together, his firm erection pressed to her belly.

A soft gasp escaped her mouth as his tongue moved against hers. Her fingertips glided up the soft cotton of his shirt. She pressed them to his back through the fabric, aching to touch his heated skin.

Each soft kiss Nate planted along her jawline and down her throat ignited flames along her skin.

"I want you, Dray. Here. Now. Tell me you want me, too," he murmured between kisses.

Her hot, liquid center melted a little more at hearing him use his pet name for her. He hadn't done that since the day she walked out of his life. Not even those nights in Memphis.

"I do." No point in denying the obvious. Her beaded nipples pressed into his chest and her breath came in shallow pants. "But if we do this, you have to understand—"

The muscles of his back stiffened as his eyes met hers. "That it doesn't mean anything?"

She stroked his cheek. "Being with you could never not mean anything to me. But it isn't a promise or a commitment. It's just sex."

He frowned, lines spanning his forehead.

"I want this, I do." She placed a soft hand on his stern jaw, and his eyes met hers again. "But you mean so much to me. My relationship with you is more important than this."

He didn't respond right away. For a moment, Kendra expected him to release her and walk away. Instead, he pressed his mouth to hers and kissed her again. His tongue tangled with hers as he gripped her bottom, pulling her hard against him.

Kendra moaned against his lips, giving in to the prickle of electricity dancing along her spine, igniting low in her belly.

Nate surprised her, scooping her into his arms and carrying her down the hall toward his large master bedroom. He nudged open the double doors with his foot, then laid her on his bed.

Kendra looked around the room. The kitchen had been essentially the same, but this room looked completely different. He'd made a concerted effort to erase any trace of her.

She had no right to be hurt. Yet she was. The walls were a dove gray now, instead of the cocoa beige they'd selected together when he bought the place.

The bed and all the other furniture were different, too. Large, sleek ebony wood pieces. Dark and masculine. All hard lines. None of the soft, organic curves she preferred.

Nate brought her back from her disquieting thoughts with a kiss. His hand trailed down her side, gripping her thigh as he settled between her legs. She whimpered at the sensation of his length pressed to the juncture of her thighs. Her breath became shallow as the heat and electricity building there spread throughout her body. Made her feel like she was floating in a pool of warm water, the steam so intense she could barely breathe.

Nate pulled his mouth from hers, their eyes meeting as he took her in. Something in that dark gaze made her feel as if there were nothing in the world he wanted more than her. And damn if that stare didn't multiply his raw sex appeal by a factor of ten.

Nate planted feverish kisses on her throat that trailed down the vee of her shirt. She inhaled the coconut scent wafting from his dark curls and tried to get out of her own head and enjoy it.

Breathe. Just breathe.

"Stop trying to talk yourself out of this." Nate's husky whisper brought her attention back to him, away from the battle raging between her body and her mind. "There's nothing wrong with two people who care for each other as much as we do being together. Even if one of them believes it's just sex."

"Nate, you promised—"

"Relax, Dray. I know where we stand." There was a hint of strain in his voice and in the tension between his brows. "We're cool, no matter what happens tonight."

She breathed a little easier. "Then what are you still doing in that shirt?"

Nate traced her mouth with his thumb, then kissed her again. "Good question. I could ask you the same."

She gripped the hem of his shirt and tugged it up. He adjusted, allowing her to remove the garment. Next, she shed hers. Kendra pressed her fingers to his back as she pulled him to her again. "Much better."

"A little better." He glided his large palm down her hip and thigh, his eyes locked on hers. "You naked would be a hell of a lot better."

"I can make that happen." She lifted her hips, allowing him to slide off her panties and leggings. Her bra and his jeans soon followed.

"Hey." Kendra snapped the waistband of his underwear. "You're not completely undressed."

"Gotta keep my focus, babe," Nate responded between nibbles and kisses that trailed between her breasts. "Make this last."

Can't argue with that philosophy.

"Fine for now, but—" She inhaled sharply when Nate caressed a stiff peak with his firm tongue. The sensation traveled straight to her sex. "Not fair."

Nate chuckled, the sound vibrating in her chest. He kissed his way across the valley between her breasts and swirled his tongue around her other nipple, causing a rush of dampness at her core. "Who said anything about this being fair?" He trailed kisses down her belly. Each one caused her breath to come quicker as he approached the space between her thighs. "I plan to use every trick in the book to make you reconsider."

A shiver ran down her spine as he lapped at her hardened nub. She gripped the bedding and dug her heels into the mattress. "Nate, that feels incredible."

She'd nearly forgotten how deft Nate Johnston was with that tongue. He hadn't gone there the last two times they were together. Those incidents involved quick, hot, angry sex. This was slow and deliberate.

He wrapped his arms around her thighs, pinning her in place as his tongue grazed her clit and the swollen, engorged flesh surrounding it.

The higher she sailed, the quicker his movements. She was trembling, cursing. Almost there. Suddenly he slowed things down with deliberate laps of his tongue, heightening the sensation.

Kendra's breathing slowed, though her heart still beat a mile a minute. She tangled her fingers in his hair as he worshipped her sex, bringing her to the edge again.

A jolt of desire ran through her veins as Nate plunged his tongue inside her, then slowly withdrew it. She moaned softly, her tense muscles quivering in response to the delicious rhythm. Kendra whimpered, calling his name and begging him not to stop, as she dug her heels into the mattress and clutched the back of his head.

His sly grin indicated he had no intention of stopping until he'd brought her over the edge.

And he did.

The orgasm hit her, hard and sudden. Her legs trembled and her belly contracted. She shut her eyes, allowing the intense feeling of satisfaction to wash over her like warm, soothing water.

Nate trailed kisses over her mound, up her stomach and between her breasts. He gently bit and sucked her neck, as if marking his territory like he did when they were in high school.

He pressed his lips to her ear. "This body will always be mine. No matter where you go or what you do."

His claim was even more arousing than what he'd just done to her body. She wanted to contradict him. Make it clear that her body belonged to her and no one else. But she understood what he meant. *No one will ever make you feel this way. Have you crawling out of your skin, calling his name.*

If the past seven years were any indication, he was right. She'd been with a handful of guys in the time they'd been apart. She could sum up the collective experience with one word.

Disappointing.

Nate never disappointed her. He sent her soaring, shaking, calling his name. Their bodies fit together as if they were designed for each other.

As she stared into his handsome face, hovering over hers, she couldn't deny his claim.

Her body did belong to Nate Johnston, as did her heart.

Chapter 13

Nate kissed the side of Kendra's face, glistening with sweat. It was the middle of winter, but suddenly his sprawling bedroom felt intimate, the space sultry.

Kendra's chest rose and fell as she tried to catch her breath. She hadn't responded to his declaration that her body belonged to him, but had she disagreed, she would've told him so in no uncertain terms. Kendra's silence indicated her reluctant concession to the truth of his words.

We belong together.

They would be again soon, if it was up to him.

"I love watching you come apart like that. It's still the sexiest thing I've ever seen." He kissed her neck and trailed a finger down the center of her chest. "You will always be the most beautiful woman in the world to me."

Kendra's eyes twinkled as she swiped a finger beneath them. A wide smile spread across her face.

Nate kissed her again, then crawled off the bed and dug into his bedside table and sheathed himself. He joined Kendra beneath the covers and kissed her neck, her shoulders.

He'd tried hating her for breaking his heart. He'd tried to replace her with women who were beautiful or famous. None of them made him feel the way he did when he was with her.

It was Kendra he wanted in his bed and in his life. The woman who owned his heart and bore his son. The woman he wanted to retire to Pleasure Cove with and have more children.

The words he wanted to say stuck at the back of his throat. *I love you. I need you. Please, come back.* Instead, he kissed her fervently, conveying everything he felt through his kiss, his touch.

He glided his hands along her warm, slick skin. Caressed her back. Squeezed her hips and the swell of her breasts. Laved her tight, beaded tips with his hungry tongue. He coaxed her back to the edge of the precipice, her body responding to every touch, every kiss.

"Nate, I need you." Kendra's breathy plea nearly broke him down. She gripped his ass, bringing him closer. Increasing the friction of his sheathed length grazing her slick bud. "Please."

His plans to continue teasing her, making her want him more, flew out the window the moment he gazed into those seductive brown eyes. They drained every ounce of his willpower. If she asked right now, he'd give her anything.

He pumped his thick shaft, his body already aching

with desire for her. She whimpered quietly as he slid inside her, taking his time. He savored the slow, painstaking reintroduction to every damn inch of her.

He groaned, pressed his lips together as his eyes drifted closed at the sensation of being surrounded by her warm, slick flesh. Nate tried to hold it together as he slowly moved his hips, delighting in every hiss, every whimper coming from her sweet lips.

Nate cursed, his brow damp with sweat. She felt so damn good. Better than he remembered. Her delicate scent mingled with the smell of sweat and sex.

He wanted her in his bed. Every. Single. Night. He would remind her how good they'd been together. How good they could be again.

Nate leaned his weight forward, grinding against her as he entered her. He increased the friction against her hardened nub. Watched the parting of her lips until finally she cried out, writhing and calling his name.

His shoulders relaxed even as he continued his movement, heightening her pleasure until he reached his release. Muscles tense and heart racing, Nate dropped onto the mattress beside her. He tugged the covers over them as he caught his breath.

"I know we shouldn't have done that," she said, finally, one hand pressed to his chest, "but it was incredible."

"Who says we shouldn't?" He chafed at the implication that what they'd done was wrong. "We don't have to answer to anyone."

Kendra frowned, raising her head. "Was that the doorbell?"

Nate strained to listen, but didn't hear anything. "I don't think so."

The bell rang again. This time he heard it.

"See. There it goes again." Panic rose on Kendra's face as she pulled the covers up higher.

"Whoever it is, they'll go away." Nate wrapped an arm around her. As long as it had taken him to get her to bed, he had no plans of letting anything interrupt the moment.

Kendra settled against his chest. She was silent. Pensive.

Nate massaged her back, trying to relax Kendra and return to the blissful afterglow they enjoyed a moment before. A space where it was only the two of them and nothing else mattered. That's where they needed to be if he was going to convince her to stop running from her feelings for him.

He picked up the remote and turned on a streaming audio service, hoping the soft vocals of Luther Vandross and Anita Baker would soothe her.

She propped her chin on his chest. "What if it's important?"

"They'll come back." He kissed her forehead. "Besides, if it were that important, they would've called first."

"I did call first, lover boy, but you left your phone downstairs."

Kendra scrambled to pull the covers up to her chin, and Nate held the sheet firmly in place so she wouldn't uncover all his business to his nosy-ass twin sister.

"For real, Vi? I did not give you the key to my place so you could stroll up in here whenever you please. It's for emergencies."

"Seems like an emergency to me." Vi folded her arms and leaned against the doorjamb. "'Cause I'm pretty sure you've lost your natural mind. I go on vacation for two weeks and all hell breaks loose. Your face is all over the news and now she's all up in your business and in your bed."

Nate clenched his teeth. "Look, Vi, I know you're just trying to look out for me, but you are completely out of line. Now that you're back we can talk about your concerns, but at a more appropriate time. Like tomorrow morning."

Vi gave Kendra her evil stare before returning her attention to Nate. "We need to talk now. Before things get worse."

"I messed up with that video, but I do not need you to babysit me."

"So you don't trust me to look after you, but you and Marcus think it's a good idea to trust her?" Vi pointed at Kendra accusingly.

"That's my choice. Just like it was my choice to have you run the foundation, even though half our family didn't think you were levelheaded enough to handle a responsibility like that."

"So now you're going to throw me under the bus because I'm pointing out the obvious. Ms. Thing here doesn't have your back. She never did."

"That's enough!" Nate blared, his chest heaving and heat crawling up his neck. "I get that you're angry, but don't take it out on Kendra. I made the choice to work with her. Beyond that, she's my son's mother. So you will never, *ever* talk to her like that again. Got it?"

Vi rolled her eyes, then shrugged.

"I mean it." He pointed a finger at his sister.

"Fine. Okay. Sorry." She threw her hands up. "But

we do need to talk. Now. Meet you downstairs in ten." Navia left, slamming the bedroom door behind her.

Nate pressed his palms to his eye sockets and shook his head. "Sorry about that. Vi's been out of the country, so we haven't had a chance to talk about this. She'll be fine. I just need to make it clear that this isn't her choice."

"She hates me." Kendra tucked a few curls behind her ear. "You guys are incredibly close. She feels your pain, maybe more intensely."

"Is that why you didn't say a word when she was in here clowning?" When she shrugged, Nate cupped her chin. "That isn't the fierce warrior I know. If we're going to work together, you'll have to deal with Vi. Don't let her run you over. You never did before. You know Vi, if you give her an inch she'll take the length of two football fields before you can blink. I'll set her straight, but promise me you won't take any shit from her."

"We'll work it out." Kendra's tone was less than convincing, but he let it go.

Nate slipped his fingers into her hair, pulling her closer. He kissed her. "Don't move. I'll be back with dinner." He winked.

Kendra slapped a hand over her mouth. "Dinner! God, I hope it isn't ruined."

"It isn't. It's fine." Nate got out of bed, retrieved his clothing from the floor and dressed. "Sit tight. I'll be back as soon as I get rid of Vi." He leaned in and kissed her forehead. "Promise."

"Don't be so hard on her, Nate. She's just trying to protect you. It's been her job since you two were conceived." She smiled, but then her expression and tone grew serious. "I won't come between you two. I'd rather walk away."

"I know you would." He gripped the door handle. "Fortunately, it won't come to that. Working with you is exactly what I need right now. We've already made progress. Bottom line? If she really wants what's best for me, she'll get on board. She'll complain about how rough the ride is, but she'll come aboard just the same."

Nate closed the bedroom door, then padded down the stairs in his bare feet to straighten out his nosy, overprotective, older-by-five-minutes twin sister.

His sister had the worst timing. He'd finally made headway with Kendra, and Vi decided to return from her vacation two days early. He stepped into the kitchen, where his sister paced the floor.

"What the hell is she doing here?" That was Vi. She didn't waste a moment, just got right into it.

Nate gritted his teeth and counted to ten as he rummaged in the freezer for one of the beers Kendra put on ice. "You're not my wife or my mother. So why do you care?"

Vi snorted in the unladylike manner that signaled a smart-ass comment was on the horizon. With one hand on her hip, she shoved a finger in his direction. "If you stopped thinking with the head below your belt and started using the one above your shoulders, I wouldn't need to act like your mama."

Maybe she has me there.

He'd never admit that to her. Vi already thought she knew better than everyone in their family when it came to their careers, love lives and how they raised their kids. Never mind that she had zero expertise with any of the above. He took a long swig of his beer, then set it down.

"Don't oversimplify this. It isn't just about sex. I care for Kendra. I always will. More importantly, this is a chance for Kai to finally have his parents living together under one roof. Just like we did."

Vi's expression softened and her shoulders relaxed. "Nate, don't get your hopes up. Kendra's only going to disappoint you again."

Nate cringed at the pity in his twin sister's eyes. "Don't look at me like that, Vi."

"Like what? Like I'm your sister who loves you? It's always been my job to look out for you."

"I don't need you to protect me from Kendra or anyone else, and I certainly don't need your pity. You can pack up all that attitude and take it back with you to wherever you came from." He thrust his thumb over his shoulder and gave her his I-ain't-got-time-for-the-bullshit face.

"First, you know exactly where I came from—Barbados. Second, it was Marcus, Mitchell and Drew's job to protect you from other people. My job is to protect you from yourself. We both know you can be your own worst enemy." She raised an eyebrow and twisted her mouth in a smug smirk when he didn't respond. "Like when you run your big mouth on video at a club in the middle of the night and screw up your contract negotiations."

Nate gritted his teeth. If his own family was going at him this hard, he could only imagine what his first TV appearance—scheduled for later that week—would be like. "It was stupid, shortsighted. I know that, but I can't change what happened. Kendra has a thoughtful strategy laid out, which we're executing now."

"'Executing strategy,' huh?" She used air quotes. "Is that some cute new euphemism for screwing your client?" Vi grabbed a beer out of the freezer.

Nate swiped the beer from Vi's hand before she could open it. "You won't be needing this. You were just about to leave."

"But I smell lasagna, and I'm starving."

"Got it at Maxine's Kitchen." He reached into his wallet and held out a twenty. "Stop and pick yourself up one on the way home. My treat."

"You're kicking me out for her? Really?"

Nate glowered silently, extending the bill.

"I don't need your money." She pointed a finger at him, then sighed, snatching the bill from between his fingers. "But I'll take it anyway. And you should take my unsolicited advice. If you must work with her, keep it professional, before you do something else you'll regret."

Nate grabbed his beer and drained it, hoping his opinionated twin sister wasn't right.

Ms. Thing here doesn't have your back. She never did.

A cavalcade of emotions rolled through her chest as Vi's words replayed in Kendra's head. Anger at Vi's insistence she couldn't be trusted. Gratitude for Nate's staunch defense of her.

Ending up in Nate's bed, in the midst of dealing with the biggest crisis of his career, certainly didn't make her case for being a professional who could be trusted with the fate of his future.

Kendra got up and quickly got dressed. What hurt the most was Vi's implication that she'd hurt Nate before, and she'd hurt him again.

She couldn't do that to him, and she wouldn't give him false hope.

Once Kendra heard Vi's car leave, she made her way down to the kitchen where Nate was preparing their plates. "Smells delicious."

Nate looked up, disappointed. "I hoped to find you in the same state I left you." He winked, giving her a sly smile.

"I know, but Vi has a point. You're my client, and I don't… I mean… I've never gotten involved with a client before. It's unprofessional and completely unacceptable. I violated our agreement, and I'm sorry. If you want to fire me, I'll understand. Just stick to the plan and execute it. You'll be fine."

Nate waited patiently, his arms folded, until she was finished. "Why would I want to fire you?"

Her heart raced as she forced her eyes to meet his. "Because this can't happen again. That may make things awkward between us, and I don't blame you for not—"

"Look, I'm sorry about Vi busting in here like that. Whether or not we work together…sleep together…it's none of Vi's business or anyone else's."

Kendra ran her fingers through her hair. "You know she's going to tell Marcus and probably your parents. God, your entire family will know by morning."

Nate shrugged. "What difference does that make? Doesn't change how I feel. I'm not sorry about what happened between us. Neither are you." He cupped her cheek.

For a moment, she settled into his palm before logic kicked in.

This is how the whole thing started.

She shook her head and took a step back. "We can't. I'm sorry."

Nate sighed. "Fine, but I'm not firing you. Awkward or not, I expect you to fulfill your end of the contract."

Kendra stood straight and cleared her throat. "Of course."

"And I don't see any reason we can't sit down like two rational adults and have dinner together."

Kendra held her breath, the muscles in her back and shoulders tense. Sitting down to a meal and pretending everything was okay, when what she really wanted was to let Nate take her back to his bed, would be torturous. But he'd gone through all the trouble of making her favorite meal.

"On one condition."

Nate raised a brow as he put salad greens into two bowls. "And that is?"

"We can talk about the campaign, your career, Kai, the weather...anything but us or what happened here tonight. It was a lapse in judgment. I just want to get past it."

Nate shrugged. "Fine."

His tone said anything but *fine.* Still, he'd agreed to her terms.

Kendra released a breath and nodded. They could get through this. Get things back on track. She would deliver the results she promised, then things would go back to the way they were.

She'd be miserable, missing him and regretting the day she walked out of his life.

Chapter 14

Nate straightened his tie and inhaled. They'd be live on the air for his first television appearance since the video went viral in five…four…three…two…one…

He pressed his lips into a smile as he gave his attention to the host of the show. He'd always considered John Chase to be a blowhard who knew incredibly little about the sports he reported on.

Being a guest on the John Chase show wouldn't have been his first choice. But as Kendra pointed out, it was one of the most-watched daytime shows on the major sports network. The ratings were through the roof. Most important, Kendra felt John was fair and that he'd keep his word and not discuss the video.

That remained to be seen. There was something in the guy's eyes that Nate didn't trust.

Then again, when did he trust any reporter?

John welcomed Nate to the panel, then began the discussion. Nate followed the rhythm of the panel's conversation about the stellar numbers the Ontario Badgers wide receiver Dean Carson was putting up in the play-offs after his recovery from an ACL injury nearly a year earlier. The same injury he'd sustained three years ago.

John seemed to sense his hesitance. He asked Nate a pointed question. Within a few minutes, Nate was so engrossed in the conversation, he stopped thinking incessantly about the camera, the millions of viewers in the audience and whether John Chase would ask about the video. Instead, he recounted his own comeback from an ACL tear and praised Dean Carson for his play-off performance.

He settled into easy banter with John and the other two members of the panel—both retired pro football players he admired and respected. Once he relaxed and focused on the topic, his eight minutes on the segment went by quickly.

John wrapped up the discussion with a promo for next week's show. "Join me next week when we discuss the impact of the social media age on pro athletes. Something my man Nate here knows more than a little about. If you've got the time, Nate, I'd love to have you back to get your view on the topic."

Shit.

The son of a bitch offered him an open invitation to talk about his social media disaster in great detail on his very next show.

He opened his mouth to tell John Chase exactly what he thought of his lame move when Kendra caught his eye.

She shook her head almost imperceptibly, then gave

him an encouraging smile. He inhaled, then forced a chuckle. "It's a topic I've learned quite a bit about in the past couple of weeks. Unfortunately, my schedule won't permit."

John grinned, tapping the desk. "Fair enough. Just know, you've got an open invitation to come on the show and share more of your analysis of what the Marauders must do to become an elite team in this league." He added, "For the record, I thought everything you said was on the money, and I think it's despicable to secretly film someone and then use the footage to get your fifteen minutes of fame."

John Chase signed off, wishing the audience a good weekend, and then the cameras faded to black.

Nate snatched off the microphone clipped to the lapel of his suit jacket, but before he could stand, Kendra pinned him in place with her gaze. Her eyes pleaded with him to be cool.

He sighed, acknowledging her plea with the slight nod of his head.

"Nate, thanks again for coming on the show." John was standing in front of him, his hand extended. "And thanks for being such a good sport. My viewers would've slaughtered me if I hadn't addressed the issue at all. Tried to do it in a way that would cause minimal discomfort…for both of us."

Nate reluctantly shook the man's hand. "Appreciate that, John. Thank you for having me on the show."

"My pleasure." He turned to talk to one of the other panelists, but then quickly turned back. "By the way, I'm serious about having you back to talk more about what happened that night or your thoughts on the Marauders. Good luck with your contract negotiations."

Maybe John Chase isn't so bad after all.

"Excellent segment." Kendra fell in line beside him as he made his way back to the green room to retrieve his things. "That didn't kill you, now did it?"

It didn't, but he wasn't ready to concede so quickly. "Thought he wasn't supposed to address the video?"

"We agreed he wouldn't make it a topic of discussion in this segment. Clearly, he found a way to skirt the agreement. Thankfully, he did it in a way that was sympathetic and hopefully made viewers sympathize with you, too. Good job on sticking to the script with your response." She followed him into the green room. "And thank you for the way you handled the conversation afterward. John is someone we want as an ally."

"Sure. Anything else?" He lifted his leather satchel onto his shoulder.

She shook her head. "Not until the afternoon taping of that top ten segment for the late-night show. It should be super quick. In and out. Here's the script. It's like three lines." She handed a printed email to him.

Nate reviewed it quickly, then stuffed it in the inside pocket of his suit jacket. "Great. I'll meet you at the studio."

She looked stunned. "Okay, see you then, I guess."

Nate headed out of the studio and into the sunshine on a lovely winter morning in LA.

Nate made his way up the walkway. Jason Hernandez—the Marauders' best tight end and one of his closest friends—was an uncomplicated guy. His place in Cerritos reflected that. The decor was simple and casual, yet attractive. The place was warm and cozy. Someplace you could hang out and drink beer without worrying about staining the furniture or breaking an expensive vase.

Jase had invited Nate over for an early lunch between studio appearances. Before Nate could ring the doorbell, Jase opened the front door, his goofy trademark grin plastered across his face. He was more tanned than usual. "I can't leave you alone for five damn minutes without you stirring up shit."

Nate gave Jase a one-armed hug. "Thought you abandoned me. Tried calling you several times."

"Sorry about that, man." Jase's cheeks and forehead reddened. He retrieved a couple of beers from the fridge. He handed one to Nate. "Went camping and shut off my phone. After that loss, I needed to be alone for a while."

"That place with the luxury tree houses in Oregon?" Nate tilted his head, assessing his friend's quick nod as his gaze raked the floor. There was something Jase wasn't telling him. "Not exactly roughing it."

Jase shrugged. "Wasn't that loss punishment enough?"

"Can't disagree with that." Nate screwed the top off his icy beer. "Still, you and Vi picked a hell of a time to go AWOL."

"Vi's missing?" Jase rearranged the plastic fruit in the bowl on his kitchen counter.

"I wish. After being out of touch for two weeks, she shows up at my place at the worst possible time." Nate took a swig of his beer.

Jase smirked and sipped his beer, too. He sat on a bar stool. "Does that mean what I think it means?"

Nate ran a hand over his head. "Yep."

Jase chuckled, shaking his head. "That twin sister

of yours is a little *loca*." They both laughed. "But she loves you and she always has your best interest at heart."

"Maybe she doesn't know what's in my best interest." Nate frowned, returning his beer to the counter. "Maybe she should back off. Let me decide what's best for me."

Jase cocked his head, his dark eyes assessing him. "In the end, it's your choice. You know that. Not like you listen to Vi anyway, unless you agreed with her to begin with."

Nate raised a brow, narrowing his gaze at his friend. "You sound just like her."

Jase cleared his throat and turned to face the bar. He took another sip of his beer. "Maybe that's because it's the truth."

"Hey, if I wanted to hear more of Vi's point of view, I'd be talking to her right now, instead of you." Nate shoved his friend's shoulder.

"So what do you want to hear?" Jase swigged his beer.

Nate shrugged. "Maybe I want you to tell me I'm not *loco* for trying to get back with my ex."

"Hmm…" Jase nodded sagely. "So it was you and Kendra Vi walked in on the other day?"

"How'd you know—"

"I haven't had that many concussions." Jase tapped his right temple twice with two fingers. "Besides, I saw Kendra in the press conference footage. She's handling your PR?"

Nate nodded. "Marcus's idea. I was against it at first, but it was a good call. Kendra's the right person for the job."

"Speaking of which, how's the apology tour going?"

Nate groaned. “According to Kendra, it’s going well. Still, this whole thing has been a shit storm.”

“Of your own making.” Jase pointed the neck of his beer bottle in Nate’s direction. “How many times I gotta tell you, man, you don’t have to say everything that pops in your head.”

“I don’t pull punches. You know that.”

“This time, you should have. What were you thinking? Especially in a contract year?”

“I know, I know.” Nate stood in front of the window overlooking the pool in the backyard. “I screwed up. Big-time.”

“Not the first time. Doubt it’ll be the last.” A half smirk lit Jase’s eyes.

“You’re having way too much fun with this.” Nate pointed a finger at his friend. “And thanks for the vote of confidence.”

Jase chuckled. “You’re usually the one riding us out there on the field. Not a chance in hell I’d pass on the opportunity for a little payback.”

Nate raised his hands, his palms facing his friend. “Point taken. Now, stop avoiding the question. Am I crazy to want Kendra back?”

“Of course not. She’s Kai’s mother, and it’s obvious you still care for her.”

“But…?”

“But, the fact that you care what I think tells me Kendra isn’t as sure about this as you are. I’m hoping for the best, but I can’t help worrying that you’ll be disappointed.” Jase shrugged.

Nate surveyed the landscape in the backyard. It was a valid concern. One he shared.

Even if he could get Kendra to give them another

try, could he trust that she wouldn't walk away from him again?

He closed his eyes, a shudder moving down his spine.

God, I hope so.

Chapter 15

Kendra paced in the green room of the late-night show. Nate was scheduled for taping in less than half an hour and he wasn't answering her calls.

A wave of sadness rolled over her. The way he'd taken off after the panel this morning...had he gone to see someone else? Was he with her now?

She shook her head to clear it. Who Nate Johnston was with was none of her business, as long as he wasn't doing anything that would further tarnish his brand.

There was a giggle in the hallway, followed by a deep chuckle. Kendra recognized both laughs. The giggle was that of an intern who'd been hovering, hoping to meet Nate. The chuckle indicated she'd finally found him.

Kendra opened the door, and they both looked at her

abruptly. "I was beginning to think you'd forgotten how to answer your phone."

There was a gleam in Nate's eye. He smiled and signed the back of the T-shirt the intern was wearing before slipping past Kendra into the green room.

She inhaled, taking a moment to calm herself. "You were supposed to be here half an hour ago."

"You know how traffic is in LA. Besides, I called the studio on my way here. A quick touch-up in the makeup chair and I'm good."

He'd called the studio, rather than calling her? She gritted her teeth, placing a fist on her hip. "And you've been drinking."

He adjusted his tie. "Relax. I had a couple of beers over lunch. Besides, you're my media consultant, not my mother."

Heat crawled up her neck and exploded in her cheeks. She folded her arms and exhaled, straining to keep her voice even. "But it is my job to dig you out of the PR hole you created for yourself and to make sure you don't dig it any deeper."

Nate narrowed his gaze at her. "Your concern is noted, but everything is fine. So just take a deep breath. Your dog and pony show will go on as scheduled."

Despite her blood boiling, she didn't acknowledge the dig.

Nate was trying to get a rise out of her. He was obviously hurt and angry about her decision to pull away.

Kendra silently counted to ten, her fists clenched. She bit back the angry words she wanted to say, her tone neutral. "Our plane leaves in a few hours. I thought maybe we could grab a bite while I catch you up on the appearances scheduled for the next few weeks."

"Actually, I may have other plans after the show." His gaze held hers.

"Oh, well, maybe on the plane—"

"I was hoping to catch a few winks on the plane. It's been an exhausting few days." He folded his arms tightly against his broad chest. His head tilted as he assessed her. Nate was being a world-class ass, but there was something in his warm brown eyes that still melted her heart. Made her want to kiss him.

"Kara will email the updated itinerary to you along with my notes."

"Great." Nate shifted his gaze toward the door. A wide smile spread across his face when the intern peeked her head in to let them know that makeup was ready for him. He indicated he'd be there shortly, then turned back to Kendra. "Anything else?"

She shook her head, overwhelmed with a growing sense of envy. Wishing he'd look at her the way he looked at that intern just now. Her stomach dropped to her knees. "Have a good show."

Something in his demeanor softened. He headed across the room, turning back to look at her over his shoulder. Sadness lurked behind his dark eyes as he opened his mouth to speak, but then he turned and left instead.

Kendra fought back the tears that prickled her eyes, her heart thumping against her chest.

Nate closed the green room door behind him and exhaled.

What an ass.

He'd only meant to be distant. Maybe make her jealous by appearing to eat up the attention of the far-too-young-and-shallow intern. Instead he'd come off as bitter and angry, and he'd been a total jerk.

She maintained her cool, and he was left feeling worse than ever. That's what he deserved for playing childish games.

He wanted to be with her and Kai. Couldn't she see that he was sincere?

Nate tried to shake off the melancholy that settled over him when he saw the pain in Kendra's eyes, despite her forced smile.

He forced a smile of his own as he made his way through a quick turn in the makeup chair, then a brief meeting with the producer and the host of the show.

He fought his way through filming, sporting the broadest smile he could muster. It took a few takes, but finally everyone was satisfied with his performance and he was on his way back to the green room.

"How'd it go?" Kendra greeted him warmly, as if he hadn't been a complete jerk less than an hour ago.

"Pretty well." He grabbed a bottle of water off the table and opened it, ignoring the urge to apologize and admit that he had no interest at all in the intern. "Should get a laugh."

"Great." Her smile rose no higher than the edges of her mouth. Not even close to her genuine smile. The one that rounded the apples of her cheeks, lit her brown eyes and went straight to his heart. "Guess I'll grab a bite, then meet you on the plane."

"Wait, Kendra, I was thinking about your suggestion that we get something to eat and go over things..."

"Yeah?"

"How about we grab dinner, but leave the shop talk

at the door. I think we both deserve a break from it, don't you?"

One side of her mouth curved, her eyes dancing. "Are you asking me out to dinner, Nate Johnston?"

"Yeah, I guess I am."

A genuine smile lit her face. "Thought you'd never ask."

"That was incredible." Kendra finished the last bites of her London broil and creamed spinach and then put her fork down.

Nate, who had already finished his culotte steak and lobster tail, leaned back against the booth and grinned. "Told you you'd love this place."

"I had my doubts." The iconic Koreatown steak house looked like a throwback to the 1950s. Dark wood paneling on the walls; comfy, lived-in red leather booths; and crisp white tablecloths lent to the feeling of being transported to the set of an old Rat Pack movie. "But you were right. Thank you for dinner."

"Hate to rush you away after such an amazing meal." Nate stuffed some bills inside the vinyl guest check holder and thanked their server. He helped Kendra into her coat. "But we've got a plane waiting for us."

"No, it's fine." Kendra smiled. "But this was really nice. Much better than the sandwich I had at the commissary."

"About that..." Nate extended his elbow and Kendra slipped her arm through his. "I was a jerk earlier. It won't happen again."

"It's forgotten." She gave him a small smile. After they were both settled in the car, she added, "Hope you had a nice lunch date."

"I did." Nate held back a grin. She was fishing for information about who he'd spent those missing hours with. "Jase Hernandez invited me out to his place for lunch."

"Oh, well, that sounds nice." She sounded relieved. "And on the subject of invitations… I have one for you. Maya and I are taking the kids to the Pleasure Cove roller-skating rink tomorrow."

"Are you kidding me? Is that old place still out on the edge of town?"

"Yeah, and I'm pretty sure there is still gum stuck underneath the benches from when we were kids."

"Don't look at me, it was Q who had the fascination with sticking his gum everywhere," Nate chuckled, referring to his youngest brother, Quincy.

"So?" She looked at him expectantly, her eyes beaming. "What do you say? I know you can't get out there and skate, especially while you're in the middle of contract negotiations, but you can keep me company while I cheer Kai on from the sidelines. That'll give me an excuse to stay off the skates."

"Well, when you put it that way, how can I possibly refuse?" He grinned. "Just tell me the time and I'll meet you there."

"Great. And I know it's my weekend with Kai, but after skating, he can spend the rest of the weekend with you, if you'd like."

"I would, thank you." A sense of warmth and gratitude filled his chest. "He's been dying to show off his new swimming skills."

"Perfect." She opened her portfolio.

"Hey, if you don't have any plans this weekend,

you're welcome to stay, too. We could make it kind of a family thing."

"I don't know." Head tilted, she assessed him, then exhaled. "I don't think it's a good idea for me to spend the night, but I wouldn't mind coming over after the skating rink. I'll even cook. After all, I owe you dinner."

"Sounds nice." It wasn't what he'd hoped for, but at least it wasn't a flat refusal. "But I've got one more request."

"Okay." She regarded him warily.

"This temporary moratorium on discussing business…let's maintain it until Monday morning." He turned toward her. "I'd like to relax, enjoy our time with Kai and forget about the rest of the world. Just for the weekend."

"I know this has been a lot to deal with." Her smile radiated warmth and understanding. "So barring any crisis, you've got yourself a deal."

It was a small victory, but one he savored. The first step to winning Kendra back.

Chapter 16

"Look at me, Dad!" Kai called out gleefully, zipping past Nate and Kendra as he circled the roller-skating rink ahead of his Aunt Maya and cousins Sofie and Ella.

"You're doing great, son!" Nate cheered Kai on, wishing he could join him. The smell of rental skates, stale popcorn, burnt hotdogs and frozen pizza made him nostalgic for the old days.

"Watch where you're going, honey!" Kendra called after him, leaning over the carpeted half wall that separated them from the rink.

"Relax, Dray. He'll be fine." Nate massaged the tension in her shoulders. "Remember how much fun we had out there as kids?"

"It was the place to be on Saturday nights. Every teen in town was here. Oh, and remember the all-night skates?"

"We were dead on our feet by the end of the night." Nate grinned.

The DJ played "Bounce, Rock, Skate, Roll" by Vaughan Mason & Crew and they both cheered, dancing with their hands in the air.

"This song is older than we are." Kendra laughed.

"And it's still the reigning champ of roller-skating songs." Maybe he couldn't put on skates and get out on the wooden floor, but he could dance to his heart's content with his feet on solid ground.

"Every time I hear this song, it's like I'm fifteen all over again." She moved her hips and rocked her head.

"You're showing out now, girl. I need to step up my game." He threw in some popping and locking and added a spin for good measure. "Get it, Dray!"

"Oh, it's on." She pursed her lips, going old school.

"You did not just go TLC on me with the Bart Simpson. Okay, I got one for you."

"Old-school running man!" She laughed. "All right now. How about this?"

They challenged each other with every old-school dance move they could remember: the Humpty dance, the Roger Rabbit, the Cabbage Patch.

"Okay, time to bring it home." He launched into the Kid 'n Play and she joined him until the song finally ended and they collapsed on one of the carpeted benches, both laughing.

"That was so much fun." She panted, catching her breath. "But now I need a rubdown, a soft pretzel and a nap, in that order."

"I can help with all three." He wriggled his eyebrows and laughed.

Watching Kendra grind her hips to the music sped

up his pulse far more than the physical exertion had. He surveyed the space. The walls had been repainted in a cobalt blue and new carpeting covered the floor and walls, but the place was essentially the same.

"We had so many great times in this building, but what I remember most is the first time I kissed you right over there." He pointed to a dim corner of the rink. "Remember that?"

"How could I forget my first kiss?" Her gaze was soft as her eyes met his.

Nate smiled and leaned in closer, whispering in her ear. "Hopefully, I'm a much better kisser now than I was back then."

"I don't know, you were a pretty good kisser back then, too." She grinned. "Aside from that incident when you nearly chipped my tooth."

"My bad." He grinned, his gaze on her sensuous lips as he leaned toward her. "Is it too late to ask for a do-over?"

"Hey, Dad, I'm hungry. Can we get pizza?" Kai skated toward them on the carpeted surface.

"Absolutely, champ." Nate did his best not to sound as disappointed as he felt, but Kendra seemed relieved not to have to answer his question.

Kendra exhaled, thankful Kai had interrupted them before she got caught up in the nostalgia of strolling down memory lane with Nate.

It was the first time they'd both let down their guard, been themselves and simply enjoyed each other's company.

She'd missed that. The laughter, the silliness, the fun and the love.

She wanted that again, but it wasn't that simple. His career and her family's past made it complicated. And she wouldn't hurt him again.

Between working together and her promise to allow Nate to be more involved in Kai's life, she'd have to learn to keep it together. Starting now.

Needing to talk to Maya, Kendra stood and turned to head to the other side of the rink, but she crashed into a woman.

"I'm so sorry, I didn't mean to—"

"No worries. It's Kendra, isn't it?"

She took in the tall brunette, whose dark eyes carefully assessed her. Stephanie Weiss, the reporter who orchestrated the video.

What the hell is she doing in Pleasure Cove?

"You know exactly who I am, Stephanie." Kendra folded her arms. "Here to dig under rocks for more dirt?"

"Guess Nate didn't give you the best impression of me." She almost sounded hurt, but her sarcastic expression indicated otherwise. "That's not my intention. I'm only here to get the real story behind Nate's comments that night. Something beyond that canned speech he served up the other day."

"So why approach me?"

"You're his media consultant. Your client wouldn't consider my offer to give him a chance to explain himself, so I thought I'd make my pitch to you. Perhaps you can make him understand why doing so is in his best interest."

"I'm aware of your offer, and I don't believe it is in his best interest. So if you'd excuse me..."

"It was a peace offering." Stephanie's tone grew

sharper. She pressed her lips into a hollow smile. "One I'm extending again to you."

"No, thank you, and I'd appreciate it if you'd stay away from me and my client. Neither of us has anything else to say to you."

"Suit yourself." Stephanie laughed bitterly, then turned to walk away. She paused, then turned back, a devious grin lighting her eyes. "Did Nate tell you he and I dated?"

"Of course." Every muscle in Kendra's body tensed. "I also know how the relationship ended and that it killed your career."

Stephanie's expression grew bitter for a moment, but then she smiled. "I'm sure that's what he told you, but the truth is, we've known each other intimately since his rookie year with the Marauders." She looked beyond Kendra, to where Nate stood, holding a tray of food. Kai stood beside him. "But I'm sure you've told her all about that. Right, Nate?"

"Stephanie, what the—" Nate started, then looked down at Kai watching him with wide eyes. He cleared his throat, seething. "I told you to stay away from me. I didn't think I needed to tell you that includes my family. Do I need to take legal action for you to get the point?"

A grin spread across the woman's face, her gaze shifting from Nate to Kendra. "Sounds like a man with something to hide."

Kendra's blood grew cold. Her fists clenched and her nails dug painfully into her palms as Stephanie flipped her dark brown extensions over her shoulder and sashayed away in red-bottomed heels.

"Who was that lady, Mommy?" Kai asked, clenching his huge plastic cup of frozen lemonade.

"No one you need to worry about, little man," Nate said quickly. "Mommy and I need to talk, so let's get you set up at the table with Auntie Maya and the girls. Mommy and I will be over when we're done."

Nate escorted Kai to where Maya sat, looking worried. She'd obviously witnessed the exchange between them and Stephanie Weiss.

He quickly returned to her side. "Babe, I'm sorry about that. You shouldn't have to deal with her."

"Don't call me *babe*." Kendra's hands shook and her pulse raced.

Nate frowned. "You don't actually believe that bull, do you?"

Kendra met his gaze, but didn't respond.

"She's a notorious liar. You said so yourself."

"I never said she was a liar." Kendra spoke slowly, her voice soft. "I said she was untrustworthy. She'll use any means necessary to find out the darkest, ugliest truths about people. Anything that will advance her career, no matter how devastating it is to the person. Like what she reported about your friend. It wasn't untrue, it was just something private that he preferred the rest of the world not know."

"It's more than that. If a story isn't salacious enough, she'll put a spin on it, like she's doing right now."

"So there is some truth to what she's saying about you and her during your rookie year."

She shouldn't care. They weren't together anymore. So why did it feel like her heart was about to explode?

"Why don't you just go ahead and ask me what you really want to know?" Nate narrowed his gaze, his voice tight.

"Because I might not like the answer, that's why."

Kendra's voice faltered. She exhaled. "Besides, I can't afford the distraction from the question I *need* to have answered."

"Which is?" Nate's incredulous expression indicated that he couldn't believe there was anything more pressing than the issue at hand.

"What the hell is she doing here?"

Nate sighed, realization in his eyes. He knew enough of Stephanie Weiss to recognize that she hadn't come all this way without something sinister in mind.

"What do you think she's planning?"

"I don't know." Kendra shrugged. "But that's where our focus must lie. Not on what happened between you two eight years ago."

"I thought you said you needed to know everything, so we don't get blindsided?" He shoved his hands in his pockets.

"So you didn't tell me the whole truth about you two?" Her mouth felt dry and tears pricked her eyes.

Nate exhaled and sat on a bench, pulling her down beside him. He turned his body to face her, his eyes barely meeting hers.

"Midway through that first season, I'd become this breakout star. Stephanie interviewed me for her sports magazine over dinner. We had a few drinks. I walked her back to her hotel and...she kissed me."

Kendra screwed her eyes shut against the pain in her chest. She blinked back tears. "So did you—"

"Nothing happened, I swear." He held his hands up, his palms facing her. "I told her I don't get down like that. That I was with someone I loved and was going to marry."

"Then why didn't you tell me?"

"I was ashamed of myself for letting it happen."

"You know about my dad, about what he did to our family." She pointed a finger at him.

"*That's* why I was so afraid to tell you the truth." A vein was visible in his temple as he lowered his gaze. "With your history with your father, I was afraid you'd never trust me again. I wasn't willing to take that chance."

"Guess my concerns about what happens out there on the road aren't so unfounded after all." Kendra stood, angrily wiping away the wetness at the corners of her eyes. "Don't worry, this won't change anything between us. I'm still your media consultant, and I will honor my promise to let you spend more time with Kai, because it's the right thing to do. But I don't think it's a good idea for me to come over after all."

"Kendra, please." He grabbed her hand, but she snatched it from his grip. "It was a mistake, and I know I should've told you, but *nothing* happened. I swear to you. You have to believe me."

"No, I don't. My job is to make everyone else believe you." She bit her lower lip and willed her limbs to stop trembling. "Excuse me, but suddenly, I'm not feeling very well." Kendra grabbed her things and made her way to her car.

She'd been right. Like her father, Nate Johnston couldn't be trusted.

Chapter 17

Nate checked his watch again. The last few days had been stressful. His relationship with Kendra was strained and formal, and Vi was still angry with him, so talking to her wasn't an option.

He felt badly for keeping the truth from Kendra. Maybe he hadn't slept with Stephanie that night, or done anything to overtly encourage the kiss, but he'd lapped up the adoration she'd been pouring on all night. And he hadn't discouraged her flirting. Worst of all, he'd kept it from Kendra.

Nate had convinced himself that not telling Kendra was in *her* best interest. The truth was he should've handled the situation differently. Most important, he couldn't bear for her to look at him and judge him as being no better than her father. By hiding it from her, he'd proven just that.

"Sorry to keep you waiting." Bud Flynn placed a firm hand on his shoulder as he took his seat at the table. The older man adjusted his large glasses and smiled through a sigh. "So, how've you been, son?"

"Well, thanks." Nate would've found it demeaning had anyone else referred to him that way. But Bud Flynn had been as good to him as his own father. He'd given him a shot in the league when no one else would. He mentored him through injuries, slumps and tough times—like his breakup with Kendra. "Look, Bud, I want to begin by saying again how sorry I am about this entire mess. I never intended any of this."

"Yet here we are, dealing with it just the same." Once a staple on the sidelines during games and practice, Bud hadn't been as active with the team as he once had due to health issues. It was the first time Nate had ever looked at the old man and seen his eighty-plus years in his blue eyes and bearing down on his shoulders. "You've always been straightforward and outspoken, and I appreciate that. Reminds me a lot of myself."

"Thank you, sir." Nate squirmed in his seat, the shadow of the other shoe Bud was about to lower loomed over him.

"However, there comes a time when you have to learn to control those impulses. Know when to be open and when to season your words up a bit."

"I just got so caught up in my anger with the guys, with myself. It was a mistake to talk about it outside our walls. I'm clear on that now."

A server came, left glasses of water and then took their orders before taking off again.

"It's good you understand that." Bud took a sip from

his water glass. "However, I'm gonna need you to apply that behind closed doors, too."

"Sir?"

"When I was a boy, we didn't have much. My mother made do with what we had. She often bought liver because she could get it cheap and it's good for you. A super food. But if you don't prepare it just right, it's one of the most god-awful things you'll ever eat."

"Okay." Nate assessed the old man, wondering if he was beginning to lose it.

Bud leaned forward, his elbows on the table. "Consider your words the same way, son. What you're saying is a hard truth your coaches and teammates need to hear. But if you don't season those words up just right and make them palatable, they won't do anybody a bit of good. They'll block out every word and use your poor delivery as reason to discount your advice. They'll be so focused on how you told them that they won't pay attention to the wisdom you're offering."

"Point taken." Nate nodded, tapping his thumb on the table. "Kendra told me pretty much the same thing."

Bud smiled. "Caught a glimpse of her at the press conference. She was good for you. Glad to see you two have worked things out, for your sakes and the sake of your son."

Nate lowered his gaze and drew circles in the condensation of his glass. "I've hired her as my media consultant. As for our personal relationship…we're still working on that. She's a little gun-shy."

"Why?" The old man shoved his glasses up the bridge of his crooked nose.

Nate sighed. "She believes every man out there will

disappoint her like her father did. He left them when Kendra was a baby."

"Does she have a good relationship with her father now?"

"She can barely tolerate being in the same room with him."

"Then start there," Bud said matter-of-factly, then thanked the server for the whiskey smash she handed him.

"What do you mean?" Nate took a sip of his imported beer.

"Help her repair her relationship with her father. Seems like that's the only way she'll let go of that fear and anger and move forward."

He'd met Curtis Williams—Kendra's father—once or twice while they were growing up. It was apparent neither of them liked the other. Nate resented Mr. Williams for abandoning Kendra, Dash and Ms. Anna. Mr. Williams clearly didn't trust his daughter's male best friend. He hadn't seen or talked to the man in years. "Thanks, Bud. I'll consider it."

"Good. Now, there's something else I need you to consider, so take a deep breath. Really think about this request before you reject it out of hand."

Nate's spine stiffened. "I get the feeling I should have ordered something a little stronger." He hailed the server and asked her to bring him a Cuba libre, then turned back to his mentor. "Let's hear it."

Bud twisted his mouth, spreading his hands on the table in front of Nate. "We need to think of the future of the team here. You're a critical piece of the team right now, as you have been for the past eight years. But we both know you're nearing the end of the ride."

Nate sighed. Bud's words—though true—were like a punch to his gut. They were already looking past him. On to the next big thing. "Does that mean there's no longer a place for me on the Marauders roster?"

Bud waved his hand. "Of course there is. In fact, I want you to take on an even bigger role in the years ahead. We need your skill and talent on the field. However, it's even more important that you help us begin shaping the next generation of wide receivers. Build a team that can win now and into the future."

Nate clenched his jaw, then took a few gulps of his beer. Bud's hands were wrinkled and covered with age spots, yet Nate felt like the relic. "So, I assume you plan to draft a star wide receiver."

"I do." Bud's tone was unwavering and unapologetic. "Doesn't mean I don't respect your talent and understand what a critical role you play on our team. It means I have great reverence for your smarts and ability. So much so, I want to ensure that our future generation of wide receivers has been mentored by the greatest wide receiver we've ever had."

Nate finished his beer and handed his glass off to the server when she set his Cuba libre on the table. He took a gulp of it, letting the chilled cola, dark rum and lime juice slide down his throat. He closed his eyes for a moment, wishing he were on the sandy beach where he first discovered this drink, rather than sitting across from the team's owner essentially telling him he was washed up and more valuable as a mentor than as a player.

"Well?" Bud took a sip of his whiskey smash.

Nate shrugged. "Don't have much of a choice, do I?"

Bud's voice was somber, fraught with disappointment. "We always have choices, son. I just hope you'll take some time and think about my offer and make the best decision. One beneficial to you and the team."

Nate nodded, meeting the old man's gaze. "I'll give your request serious consideration. I promise. I'd like to talk your proposal over with my team first before I commit."

"Of course." Bud nodded, steepling his fingers. "There is one other matter we need to discuss."

Nate's stomach roiled. He gripped his glass. "Okay."

"I need your assurance that you've learned from this experience. That we won't find ourselves in the same position six months down the road. Because if we do, I need you to understand that this conversation will go very differently." Bud raised one of his furry eyebrows, punctuated by unruly gray hairs that pointed in opposite directions.

Nate nodded. "I have, sir. I can assure you it won't happen again."

"Good." A warm smile spread across Bud's face. He looked around. "Now, where is that prime rib? I'm starving."

Nate chuckled, his head swirling. As shaken as he'd been by Bud's proposal about his changing role on the team, his thoughts kept returning to Kendra.

Suddenly, Bud's suggestion didn't seem so bad. Kendra would be angry if he interfered in her relationship with her father, but if Bud was right, it would be worth enduring her temporary ire.

After dinner with Bud, Nate drove back to his place in Memphis. Then he booked a flight to Jacksonville, Florida.

Chapter 18

Kendra sat on the set of another midday sports show as Nate took part in a discussion panel. This time they were in Atlanta.

It was down to two teams that would play for the championship. The absence of football action didn't stem the tide of talking heads analyzing every facet of each remaining team and predicting how the contest would end.

Nate was a natural—funny and charming. His words insightful and his opinions thought-provoking. Initially, he'd been against doing the sports shows. Now he was in his element, loving every minute.

His smile was broad and genuine and his deep chuckle was contagious. Not to mention, the man was finer than he'd ever been.

Kendra massaged the knot in her shoulder and breathed through the heat building in her chest.

It was no use.

Flames marched down her spine, fanning the heat at her core as she tried to clear the memories of the night they'd spent in his bed.

You're the one who rejected him. Twice.

Her anger and distrust aside, she still loved and wanted Nate. But how could she trust him again? And what about her career? He hadn't been supportive of it then, why would things be any different now?

Nate made a funny observation that had the entire panel in stitches.

Kendra smiled. She'd missed hearing his genuine laugh. He'd spent the previous few days in Memphis while she'd been back in Pleasure Cove. They met in New York, where he did a few shows before they'd flown to Atlanta for this one. After another appearance scheduled later in the day, they'd head back to Pleasure Cove.

"How'd I do?" Nate approached her, a sheepish smile turning up the corners of his mouth.

Her eyes traveled the length of his body, draped in an expensive blue suit that enhanced his athletic build. She lifted her gaze to meet his. "You're a natural. You'll have a long career ahead of you as a sports analyst, if that's what you want."

"Think so?" He relieved her of her leather briefcase and lifted it onto his shoulder as they headed toward the door.

"Absolutely. The producers loved you. They asked if you'd like to come back and do a few shows during the off-season."

Nate nodded thoughtfully. "That's great, but let's hope all of this will pay off at the negotiations table. Marcus is meeting with the team later today."

"If they had no intention of paying you, Bud wouldn't have asked you to mentor James Eastland."

"I guess." Nate's shoulders tensed. He was obviously still unhappy about being asked to mentor a younger player. A sure sign his days with the team were numbered. "How much time until the next show?"

"A few hours. Plenty of time for you to grab a bite or go back to the hotel and get a little rest. I can meet you at the next studio, if you'd like."

"No." He lightly gripped her arm. "Let me take you to lunch, if you don't have any plans."

Kendra's heart beat faster. Her mouth felt dry as she stared into his warm eyes. "Why? Did you want to go over the appearances scheduled for next week?"

"No, we need to talk about us. I'm sorry for my bad judgment then and for not telling you when it happened."

She pulled away. "Nate—"

"I know you'd rather not talk about this." He countered her objection before she could make it. "But that's always been our problem. We've avoided the tough conversations. Maybe that's because we got together so young. Maybe we weren't mature enough to deal with all of this then. But we need to talk about it now."

Nate cupped her face in his strong hand, lifting Kendra's chin so her eyes met his.

Kendra backed up until she was pressed against the wall. Her heart beat so quickly she was sure he could hear it. She stared at him, unable to speak. Her chest was heavy with all the things she wanted to say;

her head spun, reminding her of all the reasons she shouldn't say them.

He captured her mouth in a kiss. Slow and sweet. Filled with warmth, affection and desire. Her hands slipped beneath his jacket, pressing into his back. Her body softened against his.

She was kissing Nate Johnston in a secluded hallway at a major sports network. She'd lost her mind. Yet she had no desire to stop him. Nor would she pretend that she didn't want more.

Kendra pulled away. She bit her lower lip as their eyes met. There was so much they needed to say, but she didn't want to talk. "I know exactly what I'd like for lunch."

A slow smile spread across his face as he traced her collarbone. "What?"

"You." Kendra's heart raced, hardly able to believe what she'd said.

From the widening of Nate's eyes, he could hardly believe it, either. Nate nodded his head toward the door. His voice was a hoarse whisper. "Let's get out of here. Now."

They took the waiting car service back to their hotel, Nate gripping her hand for the short ride.

A quiet, nervous energy buzzed between them as they rode in silence in the back of the black SUV.

Kendra wasn't prepared to think about where they stood or Stephanie's accusation. She simply wanted the comfort and solace she'd only ever felt when she was in Nate's arms.

Nate had planned to apologize to Kendra again and outline all the reasons they belonged together over lunch. But he'd kissed her and then Kendra proposed the very thing he wanted so desperately: to spend the next few hours making love to her.

The temptation too great, he couldn't say no.

When they arrived at the hotel, Nate escorted Kendra to his suite, nearly holding his breath, afraid she'd reconsider.

Once inside, he kissed her. Gripped those heart-stopping curves, hauling them against the hard planes of his body.

Nate sizzled with heat everywhere his skin met Kendra's. He yanked her blouse from the waistband of her skirt, desperate to touch her heated flesh. His hands glided down her back, over the firm curve of her soft behind. He hiked the tight navy skirt as high as he could, giving him better access to the soft, smooth flesh at the back of her thighs. He squeezed one leg, lifting it higher.

"God, I want you." He barely managed to get the words out as he planted kisses down her throat. "I haven't stopped thinking of you since you left my bed."

Nate's long fingers glided over the damp satin material shielding her sex. His need for her spiraled with each sensual murmur escaping her throat. He swallowed her soft moans as she arched her back and tugged his shirt from his pants.

His gaze locked with hers as his chest reverberated from his erratic heartbeat. His breathing ragged, a rush of emotions flooded over him.

Love, admiration and raw desire inflamed by the abject need he saw in her eyes.

Beads of sweat trickled down Nate's back as he stripped Kendra of her suit jacket, letting it fall to the floor. He trailed kisses down her neck, along her collarbones and across her shoulders. Nate inhaled her jasmine and gardenia scent. It was an expensive perfume he'd splurged on before he'd signed his first contract. She'd made it her signature scent. Still wore it after all these years.

Would she still be wearing such a personal gift if she didn't still love him the way he loved her?

Nate dug his fingers into her soft ebony curls and sucked her lower lip between his before exploring her warm mouth—sweet and minty—with his eager tongue. Heat and electricity flowed through his spine, into his fingertips and toes.

No one had ever come close to making him feel the way he did when he was with her. Like he could conquer the world, if only she were by his side.

No one ever would.

Kendra was enticing, but her real beauty lay in the depths beneath her surface. Confident in her abilities, she could go toe-to-toe with anyone. She could be gentle and kind or determined and fierce. And the woman just got sexier with each passing year.

He wanted her body. Admired her mind. Most important, he needed her and Kai in his life.

He loved her. Wanted her so much that the thought of losing her again made his chest ache.

What if he confessed everything in his heart and still she rejected him?

Sweat formed over his brow. His heart, pounding in his chest, was too raw to handle another rejection. His ego couldn't sustain another blow like that.

Kendra seemed to notice his distraction. She stepped just beyond his reach and kicked off her heels. Unfastening the button at her waist, she made a show of slowly tugging down the zipper of her skirt. She kicked aside the material pooled around her ankles.

Standing there in a blue camisole and a silky pair of panties that provided limited coverage for her firm, round bottom, she was breathtaking.

Nate pushed aside the dark thoughts that tormented him and focused on the moment. A moment he'd fantasized about since he'd last had Kendra in his bed. He licked his lips. His pulse raced as Kendra stripped off the camisole.

He reached for his tie, but she tugged him closer by the narrow strip of fabric, loosened it and slid it from his neck. Kendra slipped his jacket from his shoulders, then painstakingly unbuttoned each button of his dress shirt, relieving him of it and the undershirt he wore beneath it.

The corner of her mouth curled in a sexy smirk that hit him below the belt, tightening his length. He restrained the desire to rip off what little remained of her clothing and take her hard and deep. To remind her how perfectly their bodies fit together, and how good he could make her feel.

She'd taken control, and he'd gladly let her have it… for now.

Kendra pressed her warm mouth to his bare chest, laying gentle kisses on his heated flesh. He inhaled at the sensation of her cool tongue grazing his nipple, then swirling around it. She slid her hands down his back and gripped his ass.

He groaned at the glorious sensation of his taut rod pressed between them. She unbuckled his belt, then unzipped his pants.

Kendra tugged her lower lip between her teeth as she scanned the ridge beneath his underwear. She slipped her hand underneath the waistband and curled her warm fingers around his shaft. Pumping it, she elicited involuntary groans of pleasure. Her gaze locked with his as she worked him with her hand until he could barely remember his own damn name.

Conversation was out of the question.

The muscles of his legs and back tensed, pressure building as she brought him closer to release. Nate gently gripped her throat, pressing his open mouth to hers in an effort to wrest back control and slow his ascent to climax.

Kendra released her grip on his painfully hard shaft. Digging her fingers into his back, she sighed softly. Her hands trailed down his back as she gave in to his fervent kisses. Impatient, she shoved his pants and underwear down his hips, freeing his rigid length.

So much for a slow seduction.

He'd planned to take his time. Convey his deepest feelings through each kiss and touch as he made love to her.

His plan dissolved in the rush of adrenaline in his veins.

She'd brought him so close to the edge. He ached for the intense relief he could only find being buried inside her slick walls, his name on her lips.

Nate fumbled to retrieve a condom from his wallet before clumsily shedding his pants and briefs and kicking off his shoes. He sheathed himself, then stripped Kendra of the bra and panties that were the last barrier to the uninhibited glory of her captivating curves.

He lifted her, his arms bracing her legs and her back pressed against the wall as he drove deep inside her wet heat.

Nate's gaze met hers as he lifted her slowly, then eased her back down until he was fully seated inside her, creating a rhythm. The exquisite sensation was intensified by the call-and-response of Kendra's hushed moans and his soft curses as they accelerated toward bliss.

Her arms around his neck, Kendra pulled his mouth to hers in frantic, hungry kisses that catapulted his spiral out of control.

Muscles tense, he strained with the effort of maintaining his focus as he lifted her higher, then plunged deeper. His movements swifter, more powerful. The sound of her naked skin slapping against his filled the space.

Kendra tensed, her nails scraping his back as she called out his name. Her slick walls spasmed, milking his throbbing flesh as he soared to his own release.

Their hearts still racing, he pressed his damp forehead to hers and held her as they caught their breath.

"That was incredible." He kissed her, then reluctantly released her to the floor, his breathing still ragged. "Can I get you anything?"

She pressed a kiss to his chest. "More of you."

"Can a brother have a sec to recharge?"

Her mouth twisted in a sensuous smirk that tested his will. "Fine, but we're leaving in time for your next show…round two or not."

"Yes, ma'am." He winked, swatting her bottom playfully before heading to the bathroom.

When he returned, Kendra was seated on the bed, the sheet strategically positioned across her body. One foot dangled off the edge of the bed; the other was folded beneath her.

Hair tousled, her cheeks and chest flushed, she was a vision of loveliness. One he wanted in his bed every night, not just in his dreams.

"You're beautiful, you know that?"

She smiled sheepishly, straightening the leg beneath her. "You're pretty handsome yourself."

Nate pulled Kendra to the edge of the bed and knelt between her knees. He trailed a finger down her chest. "You're an amazing woman, Kendra. I'm lucky to have you in my corner."

"And I'm proud of you, Nate. Of the man you've become."

Her sincere expression filled him with warmth. It meant more to him than she could possibly know.

He kissed her. Made love to her. Allowed himself to imagine the joy of never having to let her go again.

Kendra's body hummed with energy and her cheeks were filled with heat. The friction of her taut nipples grazing the fabric of her clothing made it difficult to concentrate.

She fanned herself with a brochure, hoping the producers didn't shush her for making too much noise on the set.

Could everyone else see the glow she felt after leaving Nate's bed less than two hours ago?

Kendra surveyed the crew on the set of the sports talk show. Preoccupied with running the program, they paid her little attention.

Kendra squirmed in the director's-style chair, crossing her legs tightly. Her foot bounced involuntarily.

When she looked up, Nate caught her eye. A mischievous grin animated his handsome face before he returned his attention to the panel's discussion about whether the all-star game should be played before or after the championship game.

Desperate for a distraction, Kendra looked down at her phone. The ringer and alarms had to be silenced when they were on set. She'd missed several calls. She scanned them. It was her sister.

A chill ran down her spine and her fingers suddenly felt cold. Maya wasn't a serial caller. She left a message and waited for her to call back, especially when she knew they'd be on set.

At the next commercial break, Kendra left the set to call her sister.

Maya answered right away. "Kendra, I'm sorry to call you like this. Everything will be fine, but there's been an accident."

She held her breath. "Who?"

"It's Kai, sweetie. He fractured his left arm."

A fleeting sensation of intense pain ran up Kendra's left arm. She could only imagine how Kai must feel. "How did this happen?"

"Liam took the kids to the playground." Maya said after a brief pause. "Kai jumped off the jungle gym. We're so sorry this happened. Liam insists on paying for the surgery."

"Surgery?" Kendra kneaded the back of her neck. A fresh wave of panic swept over her. "Can't they just put on a cast?"

"He fractured the bone between his elbow and wrist in two places. They have to put in pins."

The room seemed to tilt, and her knees nearly gave way. Kendra sank onto the sofa, her hands shaking. "When are they performing the surgery?"

"They want to do it right away. Liam is trying to delay it until you and Nate arrive. I know he's on air right now, but can you get here as soon as possible? I don't know how much longer it's safe to wait."

"We'll be there as soon as we can. Hold them off as long as possible. I need to see him before he goes into surgery." Kendra wiped her cheeks. She hadn't even realized she was crying. "Kiss Kai and tell him Mommy and Daddy love him and we'll be there as soon as we can."

Chapter 19

Kendra rushed off the elevator on the surgical floor with Nate hard on her heels.

"My name is Kendra Williams. I'm looking for my son, Kai Johnston. He's scheduled for surgery on a broken arm."

The woman tilted her head, her dark eyes narrowing. "I remember you. You were in here with him a few months ago. He knocked out his front teeth."

"Yes." Heat filled Kendra's cheeks. There was something accusatory about the woman's tone. "Can you please tell me where my…our son is?"

"Nate Johnston." The nurse's eyes lit up with recognition. "I saw you on the *Donnie Jones Sports Hour* earlier today."

"That's right." Nate's tone was measured. "Could

you please just tell us where we can find our son? We're hoping to see him before he goes to surgery."

The woman seemed miffed at Nate's rebuff. She pointed down the hall. "Check in at the next nurses' station. They can help you there."

Before they made it to the nurses' station, Liam approached them. His tall frame seemed shorter and there were deep furrows across his forehead.

"Kendra, I'm so sorry. We tried to hold them off as long as we could, but the surgeon couldn't wait any longer." Liam's British accent was more pronounced, his voice heavy with distress.

Kendra's heart fell. Kai had gone into surgery without her there to assure him everything would be okay. "Thank you for getting him here so quickly, and for doing what you could. We appreciate it."

She turned back to look at Nate, who was scowling at Liam as if he was considering pounding him into the floor.

She placed a gentle hand on Nate's arm, hoping he received her silent plea. "Nate, this is Maya's fiancé, Liam Westbrook. Liam, this is Kai's dad, Nate Johnston."

Nate didn't extend his hand and Liam didn't force the issue. He simply nodded and repeated his apology to Nate.

"Why was he with you?" Nate folded his arms.

"Kendra's mum had a doctor's appointment, Maya had a big meeting at work today and our nanny has come down with a bug of some sort. I took the day off to care for the children. We went to see an animated film, then they wanted to stop at the playground before we returned to our flat."

Nate grunted. "And exactly how did this happen?"

"Kai climbed atop the climbing frame while the girls played on the slide. Ella came down the slide too fast and hit the ground. I was tending to her when Kai called out to me, 'Uncle Liam, look what I can do.' He was airborne before I could tell him not to jump. I only turned my head for a minute. It happened so fast. I've gone over it in my head again and again, wondering what I could have done differently."

"Don't." Kendra squeezed Liam's arm. "Boys do crazy things. We ended up here just a few months ago when he fell down the stairs at my mom's house. These things happen."

Liam didn't look convinced.

"And you won't believe the crazy things this one and his brothers did when we were kids." Kendra jerked a thumb over her shoulder in Nate's direction, hoping to loosen up his sour face and genie stance. "He's got quite a collection of scars and broken bones to prove it."

Liam hugged Kendra and sighed. "I still feel absolutely dreadful about it, but I appreciate your kindness. Please, allow me to take care of the medical bills. Kai was in my care at the time—I should be the one to handle it."

"We can take care of our own kid." Nate's words had a sharp edge. "So thanks, but no thanks. We're good."

"Of course." Liam nodded solemnly. "Didn't mean to cause any offense."

"You didn't." Kendra narrowed her gaze at Nate before turning back to Liam and forcing a smile. "We appreciate the offer. Now, can you tell us what the doctor said?"

Kendra slipped her arm through Nate's. He softened his stance, allowing his hand to fall to his side as Liam explained that Kai had Monteggia fractures of the left radius and ulna. Pins would be inserted to hold the bones in place. However, the growth plates weren't affected and he should recover fully after wearing a cast for several weeks.

Nate seemed to breathe easier. He threaded his fingers through hers, and the rapid beat of her heart slowed. She nodded as Nate asked questions, glad to let him handle it.

Once Liam briefed them, he led them to the small private waiting room where their families were gathered.

"You're a great uncle, Liam," Kendra reassured him. "Thank you again for taking care of our son. It could've happened with any of us."

Kendra didn't miss Nate's subtle sneer when she referred to Liam as Kai's uncle.

"Liam, would you tell everyone we'll be there in just a minute? Nate and I need to ask the nurse a question."

Nate raised an eyebrow and frowned. He clearly suspected why she wanted to talk to him.

Nate trudged through the open waiting area and dropped into one of the chairs. He dragged a hand down his face. "What did I do now?"

Kendra stood in front of him with an expression that scolded him like a child. She folded her arms, bringing attention to her chest. He dropped his gaze. Right now he needed to stay focused on their son, not reminisce about what they'd done earlier in the day.

"Why are you being such an ass? Liam loves Kai. He'd do anything for him."

"I don't need him to do anything for my son. Maybe

he's a big shot in merry old England—" Nate feigned a terrible British accent "—but I don't need his charity."

"He didn't mean anything by it. He feels guilty. He only wants to help. That doesn't make him a bad guy."

"It makes him a condescending one."

"If you knew anything about Liam, you'd know he's not like that at all."

"Well, I don't, and I don't appreciate him acting like I can't take care of my own kid. No one asked for his help."

"He's Kai's uncle and your son adores him."

Hearing how much his son adored some other man felt like a punch square in the jaw. He pressed a stream of air through his nose and shook his head. "Maybe if I got to spend as much time with my own kid as he apparently does, Kai would feel that way about me instead of that guy."

Kendra's eyes widened for a moment, then her expression softened, her eyes filled with what he was sure was pity. She released an audible breath, then sat beside him.

She placed a warm hand over his. "I know it's hard not seeing Kai as often as you'd like, but he loves you, Nate. You'll always be his hero."

Nate grunted, his gaze still on the gray hospital floor tiles. "You don't see the glow in his eyes when he talks about Liam the Great."

Kendra shook her head and laughed. "You're being funny, but the truth *is* Liam is pretty great. He's great for my sister. Great for the town of Pleasure Cove. And he's great with the kids—our son included. We should be thankful Kai has a big family of people who love him."

Nate gritted his teeth. The muscles in his jaw tensed. "Shacking up with your sister doesn't make him family."

Lips pursed, Kendra narrowed her gaze. "So you're going to go all 1950s on me? Fine. They're engaged, so he will be soon. But in my book, he couldn't be a better uncle, even if he were blood."

"From what I hear, he hasn't always been so good to his blood brother, either." He huffed, hating that he'd revealed his hand.

Now she'd know he'd talked to his brother Mitchell, who worked as Liam's next in command at Pleasure Cove Luxury Resort—one of the many resort properties owned by Liam's family.

What he hadn't gleaned from Mitchell—or his brother hadn't been willing to reveal—he'd learned by searching the web. Liam had sustained a feud with his brother Hunter for years over a woman Liam had dated and his brother eventually married.

Kendra stood, glowering down at him, her expression filled with disappointment. "People make mistakes, Nate. Hopefully we learn from them and eventually grow up. You should try it."

Nate caught hold of her hand as she turned to walk away. "I'm not trying to be difficult. It's just hard seeing Kai so excited when he talks about this guy. It feels like Liam is trying to take my place in Kai's life."

Kendra's eyes glistened. She cupped his cheek. Her sweet, familiar scent soothed his anxiety, warming his chest.

"Our son is growing up, Nate. New people will constantly come into his life. No matter how much he admires or cares for them, it doesn't mean he doesn't love us, too." She smiled. "You'll always be his number one. Always."

Nate grasped the hand on his cheek and kissed her palm. He slipped his arms around her waist and pulled her closer, pressing his ear to the thumping of her heartbeat.

"Marcus was right. You've always been able to talk me down off the ledge."

She leaned down and kissed his head. "That's why they pay me the big bucks."

Laughter rumbled in her chest, immediately followed by a sharp intake of air. Nate glanced up at her face. The corners of her eyes were wet with tears. He pulled her onto his lap. "What's wrong, babe?"

She shook her head and wiped her eyes with the back of her hand. "Nothing, because Kai is going to be fine, right?"

"Of course he is." He swiped her wet cheek with his thumb. "He's a Johnston. Takes more than a couple of broken bones to take us out."

She nodded, a nervous laugh bubbling from her pursed lips. "He's a warrior. Like his dad."

"There you are." Liam stood in the doorway, his expression a mixture of guilt and relief. "Kai's out of surgery. Everything went brilliantly. The doctor wants to see you now."

Kendra hugged Nate, thanked Liam and headed off in search of the doctor.

Liam shifted his attention to Nate. He cleared his throat. "Again, I can't tell you how sorry I am."

"I know. And about earlier..." Nate sighed deeply. "I'm sorry. I'm not usually that much of an ass. I was just really worried about our son." He extended his hand

and shook Liam's firmly. "Thank you for taking care of Kai today."

If he couldn't always be there for his son, it was good to know someone else who cared about him would.

Chapter 20

Kendra's eyes fluttered open in response to the harsh sunlight filtering through Kai's hospital room window. She repositioned herself in one of the comfy recliners and pulled the plush throw up around her neck.

It wasn't her own bed, but the setup was remarkably comfortable. Despite her insistence that it wasn't necessary, she was glad Liam upgraded Kai's room to a family suite so she and Nate could both spend the night there in comfort.

She looked around. Kai was resting peacefully, unbroken limbs akimbo, in his blue-and-white-patterned hospital gown. She moved beside him and leaned down to kiss his forehead.

The door opened and Nate stepped inside carrying a pastry box and a carafe of coffee. From the delicious scent of both, there was no way either item came from the hospital cafeteria.

"That coffee smells delicious, and are those doughnuts?"

Nate popped the lid open, revealing her favorite doughnuts in the world. Maple bacon, from Lila's Cafe. They'd met there for coffee a few times during the weeks they'd been working together.

"Thank you." She reached into the box and grabbed one. She took a generous bite of sweet, salty perfection. The doughnut was soft and fresh. It melted in her mouth. An involuntarily murmur conveyed her satisfaction.

Nate's eyes widened in response. He cleared his throat. "Got your favorite coffee, too."

"A mint chocolate mocha from Lila's?"

"You know it."

Kendra stood on her toes and kissed his cheek. Cedar and citrus filled her nostrils as she inhaled his fresh-out-of-the-shower scent.

"Is that a maple bacon doughnut?"

Nate and Kendra both turned toward the small, groggy voice coming from their son, his eyes barely open.

Kendra dropped the remainder of the doughnut back in the box and rushed over to him. "Kai, sweetie, you're awake. Don't you ever scare Mommy like that again."

"Hey, champ." His dad sat on the opposite side of the bed and mussed his son's hair. "Didn't we tell you that time you fell down the steps at Nana's that you can't fly?"

Kai swallowed hard and nodded. "This time I wasn't trying to fly. I just wanted to show Uncle Liam how far

I could jump down after I climbed up the mountain, just like he did."

"Honey, your uncle is an experienced mountain climber. And he didn't just jump off the mountain. He had special equipment and training." Kendra squeezed Kai's hand, ignoring Nate's frown. "So promise Mommy you won't ever try anything like that again."

"I promise."

"Good." She kissed his forehead. "How do you feel?"

"Tired and thirsty and hungry. Can I have some water and a doughnut?"

"Yes and yes." Nate poured a small glass of water. "You want to sit up, li'l man?"

When Kai nodded, Nate picked up the remote and adjusted the bed.

"Cool. Can I play with it?"

Nate and Kendra laughed.

"It's not a toy, honey. It's the remote to the bed," Kendra explained. "Tell you what, you can have your doughnut, but only after you eat a real breakfast. How about some eggs and bacon?"

Kai agreed reluctantly and she called in his breakfast order while Nate found a children's program for him to watch on television, then showed Kai how to work the remote. When she hung up the telephone, Nate was there, frowning at her.

"You want to tell me again how Kai's accident wasn't Captain Awesome's fault? He was probably bragging about his mountain climbing, BASE jumping adventures. No wonder Kai got the crazy idea to jump off the jungle gym."

"Mommy, Daddy..."

"Just a minute, sweetie," Kendra called over her

shoulder, then turned back to Nate. "You're being ridiculous. He's a little boy with a vivid imagination. Just like you and your brothers were. Stop trying to make this Liam's fault. I thought we'd squashed this yesterday."

"But Mommy..."

"Just a sec, champ," Nate said. He lowered his voice and turned back to her. "All I'm saying is maybe this guy is as great as everyone seems to think he is, but that doesn't mean he knows the first thing about taking care of a kid."

"Who does when they first have children? Liam's never had kids before, but he's really good with them." Kendra pointed a finger at Nate for emphasis. "What happened with him is no different than when he fell at my mom's or yours. Not to mention the time he got that knot on his forehead when he was with you in Memphis."

"You're on TV, Daddy."

"I know, champ. That was from yesterday," Nate said.

"Look, there's Mommy, too."

Nate and Kendra both looked toward the screen. There was a picture of her and Kai at the skating rink, then another of her at the press conference.

"Sweetie, turn up the volume, please." Kendra tried to keep her voice calm, despite the fact that her heart was beating like a jackhammer and her legs suddenly felt like jelly.

The news story raised suspicions about Kai's injuries, painting a picture of her as either an abusive mother or a very neglectful one.

"What the hell...?"

"Don't say bad words, Daddy."

"Sorry." Nate rubbed the back of his neck. "Do me a favor and turn back to the cartoons, okay?"

Kai happily complied.

Nate turned to Kendra. "Don't panic, babe. Everything is going to be fine."

"They're making me look like an unfit mother." She clenched her fists as she paced the floor, tears spilling down her cheeks. "Your ex-girlfriend did this."

She couldn't help her accusatory tone. Kendra knew it wasn't fair. Nate didn't ask for any of this.

"She must've had someone at the skating rink taking photos."

"I knew she had it out for me, but I had no idea she'd stoop low enough to involve you." He gripped her shoulders and held her gaze. "Listen to me, Kendra, I promise I'll do whatever it takes to fix this. Everything is going to be fine. All right?"

He hugged her to his chest. Kendra pressed her face to Nate's sweater and melted into him, hoping she could trust him, and that everything would be okay.

Nate paced the floor of his beach house, clutching his cell phone. He'd promised Kendra he would do whatever it took to make this right, and he meant it. Even if it meant dancing with the devil herself.

He forced out a slow breath, then dialed the phone.

There was a smirk in her voice when Stephanie answered. "I wondered how long it would take for you to reconsider my offer."

Nate clenched his teeth and breathed, saying the vile things he thought of Stephanie Weiss in his head, rather than aloud.

"Look, Stephanie, I'm sorry about how things worked out between us and about what happened with your career. I discredited your story, not because I wanted to hurt you, but because you put me in a position where I had to protect my friend. But what you're doing in retaliation is ruthless and unethical. The Stephanie Weiss I knew was ambitious, but a generally decent human being. What happened to you?"

"I got blackballed from legitimate sports networks, thanks to you." Her tone was icy. "You made me look like a fool in front of the entire world. Don't like it so much when the shoe is on the other foot, do you?"

"I don't care what you say about me, but bringing my family into it… That's low, even for you." Nate tried to keep his voice level.

She clucked her tongue three times. "Not a smart way to talk to the person whose help I assume you're about to request."

He clenched his fist and willed himself to calm down. "Actually, I'm calling to help you. You want people to view you as a legitimate reporter? Start by reporting honestly. Stop creeping around taking pictures of my kid and his mother. She's a genuinely good person and a hell of a mom. She doesn't deserve this."

"And I did?" Stephanie's voice reached a high pitch. "I was sleeping in your bed three nights a week, but you chose your teammate's reputation over mine. Now I'm supposed to feel bad for some baby mama of yours?"

He cringed at the term *baby mama*. "She's my son's mother, and yes, I expect you to behave as if you have a shred of decency." Nate massaged his temple. "Maybe I'm not entitled to privacy, but my kid and his mom, they are."

"You know how this works. Anyone associated with a public personality is fair game. Now, are you calling just for old times' sake, or have you reconsidered my offer?"

Nate was silent. Appealing to her sense of decency had been a bust—though he'd put little faith in that possibility. Now he scrolled through his remaining options. Give in to her demands or beat her at her own game.

He chose the latter.

"Actually, I'm calling to make you an offer."

"Oh?"

"Lay off me and my family or I swear to you, one day soon, you'll be lucky to get a job at the daily gazette in Bumfuck Nowhere."

She laughed incredulously. "You of all people, Nate, should know I don't respond well to threats."

"You of all people, Stephanie, should know I'm willing to protect my family by any means necessary."

"Then I guess there's nothing more for us to say." Despite Stephanie's bravado, her voice was tentative. "One day you'll look back and wish you'd taken me up on my offer."

"I won't," he said, "but I assure you that you'll wish you'd taken me up on mine." Nate ended the call, then dialed another number.

"This is Edge. What can I do for you, Nate?" Edgerton Mathis, a private investigator often employed by members of the Marauders, always sounded laid-back, like he was drinking a beer and smoking a blunt.

"Remember that dossier I asked you to put together on that reporter a while back?"

"The one you told me to burn because you were afraid of causing irreparable damage to her career?"

Nate swallowed. "Yeah, that's the one. Any chance you can re-create that?"

"Maybe," Edge said. "This have anything to do with that piece running today, implying your ex is a bad mom?"

Nate didn't acknowledge the question. "How long will it take you to put it together?"

"Two hours."

Nate had always suspected that a guy like Edge held on to files like this. He didn't comment on exactly what he thought of that. "Good. You think it's enough to discredit her?"

Edge chuckled. "What I showed you three years ago? That ain't even the half. Been keeping tabs on this one just for the hell of it. With the way she operates, it was only a matter of time until she ended up on someone's shit list again."

"Good. Same as we agreed on last time?"

"Double the content, double the price."

Nate gritted his teeth. Hell, he'd be willing to pay four times what they'd agreed on previously if it would expose Stephanie for the snake she was and help clear the rumors about Kendra. "Fine. There's a generous bonus in it if you use your pipeline to put this info out to the media, rather than having it come from my camp."

"Done." There was a smile in Edge's gritty voice. "I'll send you a text with my account number in the Caymans. Wire half now, the rest after the news hits the airwaves. Then ding dong, the wicked witch's career is dead."

"I'll wire the money as soon as I get the info."

"One more thing," Edge said. "My gut is telling me

Weiss isn't in this alone. If I tug on that thread, it may unravel something you aren't prepared to deal with."

"What do you mean?"

"The person she's colluding with may be a teammate." There was the clink of ice in a glass in the background. "Maybe even someone you consider a friend."

"I don't believe it." Nate paced the floor. Could one of his teammates have enough malice toward him to jeopardize his career and his family? "But if it's true…"

"It'll be included in the story."

Nate ended the call with Edge and poured himself a shot of whiskey. When the truth came out about Stephanie's "reporting" methods, she'd be done. She'd be a pariah with whom no reputable news outlet would want ties.

He hadn't resorted to this option three years ago, because despite what Stephanie had done, he'd once cared for her. He hadn't wanted to destroy her career.

But now she'd left him no choice.

His family meant everything to him. He'd do whatever it took to protect them. Even if it meant Stephanie Weiss and her co-conspirator getting what they deserved.

Chapter 21

"Have you seen the news?" There was a lilt in Kendra's voice that he hadn't heard since the reports questioning her parenting abilities hit the airwaves.

"Been preparing for a trip." Nate threw a couple days' worth of socks and underwear in his luggage. "Why, what's up?"

"Stephanie is all over the news. It looks like the Marauders' personnel manager, Lee Davis, conspired with her to compromise your image, so the team wouldn't offer you a new contract."

"Marcus mentioned it," he said nonchalantly. "He suspects that's the reason the Marauders were so quick to offer me such a generous final contract."

"She's been tapping people's phone lines and using a bunch of shady tactics. Plus, it looks like she's been known to falsify sources. It's been going on for years."

"Hmm…" He put the phone on speaker and tossed it on the bed while he rummaged through his nightstand for a few pictures of Kai and Kendra he kept there. "Guess we won't have to worry about her anymore."

Kendra was silent for a moment. "Nate, you didn't have anything to do with this, did you?"

He scratched the back of his neck. "You really want to know?"

"Did you do anything illegal or unethical to make this happen?"

"I did not." He couldn't vouch for Edge, but that was the beauty of working with a guy like him: plausible deniability.

"Then I don't need to know anything else." She paused momentarily. "I didn't realize you were going out of town. You have another segment on the Donnie Jones show in a few days."

"I'll only be gone a day or so. I'll be back in plenty of time."

"Good, because Stephanie might be out of commission, but we're still on mop-up duty. I'm negotiating a one-on-one with John Chase to clear the air about the video and the rumors about me. Unless you've changed your mind. You've got your new contract and your two major sponsors have offered you new deals, so skipping the interview won't hurt you financially."

"This is what we need to do to finally put this all to bed, right?" When she sighed heavily, but didn't respond, he continued. "Then that's what we're going to do."

Nate valued his privacy, but he valued his family more. Whether she believed it or not, Dray was family. He'd do whatever he needed to do to prove that to her.

* * *

Nate exited Jacksonville International Airport, picked up his rental car and drove to the home of Curtis Williams—Kendra's father.

He didn't expect to fix a decades-long problem in a single visit. But if Kendra took even the smallest step toward working things out with her father, maybe it'd go a long way toward helping him regain her trust, too.

Or maybe this was a horrible idea that would destroy everything they'd rebuilt in the past weeks.

Nate scrubbed a hand across his forehead. It was a risky move, but the payoff would be worth it.

He entered the pretty little gated community near Dutton Island and parked in the drive of the idyllic home with its covered porches spanning the width of the house on the first and second floor.

Nate rang the bell and held his breath as a shadow approached through the glass door with a colorful, geometric design.

The door opened, and the aromatic scent of spicy beef cooking wafted out to greet him. "Mr. Williams, I don't know if you remember me, but—"

"You were my daughter's *best friend*." The older man emphasized the phrase. "And the father of my grandson. Of course I know who you are." Curtis Williams folded his arms and held his gaze. "How's he coming along after his surgery?"

"Kai's doing well, sir. He loved the musical greeting card and arrangement of cookies you and your wife sent." There was an awkward pause. "May I come in?"

The man stepped aside and let him in, leading him to the living room of the spacious first floor. He invited him to have a seat.

A wave of sadness passed over the man's face. His gaze raked the floor before returning to Nate's. "Saw that nonsense on the news about her. Kendra loves Kai more than anything in the world. She ought to sue their asses for implying otherwise."

"The past week or so has been tough for her." Guilt tugged at Nate's chest. He hated that Kendra had gotten caught up in the crosshairs of the plot aimed squarely at him. "I know she'd love to hear from you."

"It's not as simple as that. Kendra is as stubborn as her mother." The old man scowled and rubbed the back of his neck. "I left her a couple of voice mails, but she hasn't returned them. I only got to speak to my grandson because Maya put him on the phone when she and the girls were visiting Kai." He eyed Nate. "Did Kendra send you?"

Nate shook his head.

"Didn't think so." He heaved a sigh, then leveled his stare at Nate again. "Then what brings you here? You asking for her hand? If so, I don't think my blessing would make much of an impression on her."

Nate scooted to the edge of his seat. "I'm here to ask you to make the effort to fix your relationship with your daughter."

Curtis raised an eyebrow. "Why do you care? You two aren't together anymore."

"I believe that your estranged relationship with Kendra is a primary reason things didn't work out with us." Nate held the man's gaze.

"You sure I'm the reason?" He poked a thumb in his chest. "I remember the report about that groupie in your room. Wasn't too long after that she left you."

"I didn't invite her to my room." Nate frowned. "And

nothing happened. Not that night or any other night while we were together."

"Still don't see what that has to do with the relationship between me and my daughter."

"Frankly, sir, you don't have a relationship. You're simply related."

"If you came here to tell me things I already know—"

"I didn't." Nate held up a hand. "I came to tell you that Kendra might act like she doesn't need you, but she does. She needs her father as much now as she did when she was a little girl."

Lines spanned the older man's forehead. His expression was weary with years of hurt and rejection. Something they had in common.

"She hated me even when she was a girl. Not at first, but between her mother and brother...she became so resentful. I wanted to set the record straight, but she was a kid. I couldn't get into all the reasons things didn't work out between her mother and me. The way she saw it, I chose my new family over her and her brother."

"Didn't you?" Nate worked to keep the accusation out of his tone, but the words dripped with it.

Curtis groaned. "No, I didn't leave Anna for Alita. Didn't even know her then. I left because I was unhappy. We both were. I wouldn't spend my life that way, like my old man did."

"I respect that, sir, but I'm sure you understand how it made your children feel. Especially Kendra. From her perspective, *she's* the reason you up and left."

"That's ridiculous." He rubbed his chin. Deep lines spanned his forehead.

"Have you told her that?"

"I've tried to show her and her brother how much I

care for them. When they were younger, they'd come down and spend summers and holidays with us. As they got older, they resented being made to visit. It only made them hate me more." A pained expression accompanied the man's memories. "When they were old enough to choose, they both stopped coming. I tried giving them space, but they became more and more distant."

"I don't doubt you've tried in the past, Mr. Williams. All I'm saying is, it's worth trying again. Because if you don't, I don't know if she'll ever learn to trust any man. She'll always be afraid that the next guy is going to cheat on her or leave her."

"So you do want her back."

"I never wanted to lose her. I love her, asked her to marry me. As angry as I've been with her all these years, the truth is, I haven't met anyone I'd rather be with. I know she feels the same, but she's afraid."

"You tell her that?"

"Not in those exact words."

"Hmm..." The old man leaned forward, his hands between his knees. "Guess Kendra's not the only one who's afraid."

Nate's nostrils flared. "If I were afraid, I wouldn't be here."

"Maybe it was easier to come and talk to me than to lay it all out on the line and risk her walking away again."

Nate's gaze dropped to his hands. What the old man said was true. He hadn't been very romantic or heartfelt with Kendra. Instead, he'd pointed out that getting back together was in Kai's best interest. That line of thinking relegated Kendra to a nice bonus accessory. Something a woman like her would never stand for.

No wonder she'd turned him down. In an effort to protect his heart, he'd handled the situation poorly.

Curtis nodded knowingly, pain in his voice. "Been there. A man can only take so much, I suppose."

"You're right, Mr. Williams. My approach to Kendra was all wrong." Nate tapped the table with his forefinger. "But I'm right, too. I know she hasn't made it easy for you, but she has the right to be angry about you leaving her and Dash. She handled it badly. Maybe we're all guilty of that. But Kendra is an amazing woman. She deserves the best from both of us. It's time we both man up and give her that."

Curtis frowned at the censure, then sighed. "I convinced myself it was best just to give Kendra and Dash space and hope they came around. I guess that was just what was easiest."

"I'm having a little party this weekend to celebrate my new contract with the Marauders. I'd appreciate it if you and your wife would come. If you're willing, I'll have my assistant book your flights and hotel. Just say the word."

"I want to be the father my daughter deserves." The older man nodded. "We'll come to your party, but you don't need to pay for anything. This is something I need to do."

Nate's heart beat against his rib cage. *Mission accomplished.* Mr. Williams would make another effort to work things out with his daughter.

He'd call Kendra's mother to let her know her ex-husband would be at the party. He owed her that. On the other hand, it would be best not to tell Kendra in advance about her father's visit.

A sense of dread suddenly crept over him like kudzu vines climbing a pole.

What if Kendra resented his interference?

He heaved a sigh, releasing the tension knotting the muscles in his neck and shoulders.

Only one way to find out.

Chapter 22

Kendra dusted her face with a little powder, then applied a matte lipstick.

They'd actually pulled it off. Nate had inked his new two-year contract with the Memphis Marauders and generous deals with both his previous sponsors—a soft drink company and a rapidly growing athletic wear company poised to overtake the market within a few years. Two other sponsorships were in the works—a Memphis car dealership and a home builder based in the Carolinas.

Once Nate was ready to hang up his cleats, the sports network had already expressed interest in adding him to their parade of former players turned sports analysts.

Several months remained on her contract with Nate, but Marcus had already requested that she work with two of his other clients. The only thing that wasn't settled was her relationship with Nate.

Kendra slipped in diamond studs Nate had bought for her birthday the year he signed his first pro contract. She put on her high heel boots and a light coat, thankful the unusually cold weather had finally abated. Kai was already at Nate's, where he'd spent the night. She got in her car and swung by to pick up her mother.

Anna Williams looked lovely in a black pantsuit, her salt-and-pepper hair in pin curls, fresh from the salon. She greeted Kendra as she placed the tray of heart-shaped cookies she made for the holidays in the backseat, then got inside the car.

"Everything okay, Mama?" Kendra pulled out of her mother's small drive and headed toward the opulent beach community where Nate lived. "You're awfully quiet."

There was sadness in her mother's eyes. "You know I would never do anything to purposely hurt you or Dash?"

"Of course." A knot formed in Kendra's gut. "Why would you even have to ask?"

"Because I didn't do right by you two when it comes to your father."

"Dad made his choice when he walked away from us." Kendra's heart beat faster.

"He walked away from *me*. He loved you two. Wanted to be in your life as much as he could. It was me who made it hard for him. I was so angry. I shouldn't have talked about him the way I did in front of you kids. It made you resentful and ruined any chance of either of you having a good relationship with him."

Kendra released a long, agonizing breath. She

couldn't disagree with her mother there. It was the primary reason she'd been careful to never say anything disparaging about Nate in front of their son. She didn't want him thinking ill of his dad the way she did of hers. Of course, it was easier for her. Nate hadn't been the one to walk away.

"We all make mistakes, Mama. That was a long time ago. Dash and I are adults. How we deal, or don't deal, with Dad is our choice now."

"You don't think things would've been different between you and your father if I hadn't filled your heads with the bitterness I felt toward him?" Anna's voice broke.

Kendra grimaced, her chest heavy with regret.

"I don't know. But I understand why you were so angry with him." It felt as if a weight was on her chest, compressing her lungs. "It's the same reason Nate resents me."

Her mother put a hand on her shoulder. "He was angry before, but isn't it clear how much he loves you?"

"Does he, or does he just want to keep the Johnston family tradition going?"

"Family is important to Nate, sure. But you can't honestly believe he doesn't love you. It's in his eyes when he looks at you, when he talks about you." A wistful smile broke across her mother's face. "Been there since he was a little boy. It's a special thing to have someone love you like that."

"I love him." Kendra sniffed, refusing to let the tears fall. "But I don't think things will ever be the same between us."

"I should hope not. You're both older and wiser now.

Been through the fire and come out on the other side. You'll build something stronger."

"Some part of him will always resent me, and some part of me will always be anticipating the moment he falls for a newer, shinier model." The words felt like sandpaper in her throat. "How do we get past that?"

"Forgive yourself and believe in him. It's as simple and as complicated as that." Anna's voice was firm but sympathetic. "Is giving in to your fear over what you might lose worth losing what you could have?"

Kendra pulled into the long driveway that led to Nate's beach house, not answering her mother's question. "You go ahead to the front. I'll take the tray around to the back."

Anna opened the car door and stepped out reluctantly. "Just think about what I said."

Kendra flipped down the visor mirror and gave herself a long, hard look. If only it were as simple as her mother made it sound.

She grabbed the tray and went around toward the back entrance. A light suddenly came on in a second-floor guest room. Through the sheer, gauzy curtain she could make out two figures in an embrace—Nate's twin sister Vi and Jase Hernandez.

Suddenly Vi's solo island vacation and Jase's supposed camping trip made sense. Something was going on between those two.

When Kendra looked up again, Vi was in the window staring down at her.

They were both busted.

Kendra made her way to the back door. She practically floated inside astride a warm cloud of air carrying the aroma of a variety of Southern comfort foods. Naomi's shrimp and grits, Marcus's wife Alison's chicken and dumplings, and the batch of crispy chicken Nate's youngest sister, Sydney, was frying. There was a tray of Maya's famous Cuban pork and another of her yummy empanadas.

Alison and Sydney greeted her.

Naomi, smelling of bacon and shrimp, hugged Kendra tight, then kissed her cheek. "Thank you for helping Nate through this crisis."

"It was my pleasure." Kendra smiled.

"Things didn't work out too badly for her, either," Vi interjected. "I hear Marcus has got you lined up with two more athlete clients."

"Don't start, missy." Naomi pointed a finger at her oldest daughter. "Be nice."

Vi turned to Kendra, taking the tray of cookies from her hand. "Why don't I help you put that away?"

Kendra followed Vi to a small table overflowing with desserts, including banana pudding with a perfect meringue topping and Vi's famous bourbon–brown butter pecan pie.

Vi made room for the tray of cookies, then folded her arms. She leaned closer to Kendra and lowered her voice. "Why didn't you out me in front of everyone just now?"

Kendra shrugged, removing her coat. "Figured if you wanted everyone to know you wouldn't have been sneaking around in the guest room upstairs or pretending you went to Barbados all alone."

Vi's cheeks turned crimson. She took Kendra's coat. "Walk with me while I hang this up?"

Kendra followed her to the back hall.

"Thank you." The words seemed to cause Vi physical pain. "Nate would go ballistic if he knew."

"I know, but I also know you're a grown woman and it isn't your brother's business who you're spending your vacation with…or kissing in his guest room." Kendra couldn't help the smile that tightened one side of her mouth.

Vi gave her a look that indicated she didn't appreciate her humor, which only made Kendra break out into laughter.

"This isn't funny." Vi hung her coat in the closet, then ran a hand through her box braids.

"Oh…it's serious." Kendra watched Vi's entire face flush. "Are you in love with him?"

"Don't be ridiculous." Vi folded her arms. "We're just… I don't know exactly what we're doing, but whatever it is, Nate doesn't need to know about it."

"Fine." Kendra turned to walk away.

Vi grabbed her arm. "Look, I appreciate you not ratting me out in front of my family, but this doesn't mean we're best friends."

Kendra shrugged. "Of course."

"And whether you decide to tell my brother about me and Jase or not, there's something I need to say."

Kendra folded her arms, prepared to stand her ground. "What is it?"

"Nate isn't as tough as he thinks he is. He was devastated when you walked away. I know because I was there to pick up the pieces. I won't watch my brother go through that again." There was anguish in Vi's voice.

Kendra relaxed her stance, her arms at her sides. "I didn't intend to hurt him. At the time, I thought I'd made the best decision for everyone. I was wrong. I regret that, but I can't change the past. Because of Kai, Nate and I will always be a part of each other's lives, whether you like it or not. I'd rather we be friends or at least not enemies."

Vi sighed. "I promise to take it easy on you, but you have to promise me you'll either love my brother or let him go."

"There you are." Kendra's mother came around the corner. "Just making sure you got in all right." Her gaze shifted between the two of them, then followed Vi as she returned to the kitchen. She lowered her voice. "Everything all right?"

"Nothing to worry about." She kissed her mother on the cheek.

"Good. Then I'll go and give Naomi and the girls a hand in the kitchen."

Kendra made her way into the great room. The place was overflowing with the Johnston family: Naomi and Levi; Mitchell, his wife, Monique, and their adorable infant daughter, Stella; Marcus, Alison and their two boys; Vi, Sydney and their oldest brother, Drew. The only Johnston not present was their youngest brother, Quincy, a freelance photographer on a shoot in Qatar.

Liam and Maya were caught up in an animated conversation with Monique and Mitchell—Liam's second-in-command at Pleasure Cove Luxury Resort.

Kendra sank onto the couch beside Drew and slipped her arm through his. "Thank you again for agreeing to do those interviews for the foundation. I know that went a long way in helping fix Nate's career and increasing funding."

"Glad I could help Nate for a change."

Drew's slow, crooked smile made her heart melt. He

was handsome and easily the smartest of the bunch. After an attack on his unit in Fallujah, he struggled with PTSD and had been forced to retire from the military. He often opted to stay at home or called it an early night, fearful he'd have an episode.

"You've done so much for the family, and for our country. Don't you dare think otherwise."

Drew patted her hand. "Thanks, Dray. But we should be thanking you. Without you, not sure we'd be celebrating Nate's return to the Marauders."

"My thoughts exactly, big brother." Nate stood in front of them, looking handsome enough to eat in a light blue sweater and a pair of charcoal-gray pants. He clinked a fork gently against his glass to get everyone's attention, then asked them to fill their glasses.

Nate raised his glass and turned to her with a wide smile that made her heart dance.

"To Kendra Williams, the smartest, most beautiful and most talented woman I've ever known. You've given me a chance to finish out my career with the team I love and another shot at winning it all. Most important, you've given me the best gift I could ever ask for—our son, Kai. To Kendra."

They clinked glasses and drank champagne, her heart overflowing with the love in the room and the love in Nate's eyes.

After the toast, Nate grabbed her hand and led her to his office.

"Maybe you should have a seat."

"Why, is something wrong?" She sat down, a sinking feeling in her stomach.

"Nothing's wrong." He sat beside her. "But I've invited someone here to see you."

"Who?"

Nate pushed the intercom button and asked someone to come to his office.

"Nate, what's going on? You're making me really nervous now." She studied his face, but he turned his attention to the footsteps coming down the hall and the door that slowly creaked open.

"Hello, Kendra."

"Dad? What are you doing here?" She turned to Nate, her voice lowered. "You invited him? Why?"

"Hear him out," Nate pleaded.

Kendra folded her arms. "My mother knew he was coming, didn't she?"

"I wanted to make sure she and your sister were okay with this." Nate placed a reassuring hand on hers. "We all want you to be happy, and you might not think so right now, but the state of your relationship with your father has caused a lot of pain."

She pulled her hand away. "That's my problem, Nate, not yours."

"You don't think it was my problem when you walked out because you were afraid you couldn't trust me? That it isn't Maya's problem when she won't set a date for her own wedding because of your dysfunctional relationship with your father?"

Kendra's face was hot. Each stinging accusation felt like a jab with a hot cattle prod.

"I know what I'm asking isn't easy, but it's important. To all of us." He whispered in her ear. "If something happened to your father tonight, would you be okay with how you two have left things?"

"No." The answer came without thought.

"Then talk to him. You can do this." Nate kissed her cheek. "And if you need me, I'm just down the hall."

Nate patted her father's shoulder briefly as he exited the room, closing the door behind him.

Kendra inhaled, remembering her mother's words. *He loved you...wanted to be in your life as much as he could.*

It was the very opposite of what she'd believed her entire life, no matter how hard he'd tried to convince her otherwise.

Kendra looked ahead, her eyes not meeting her father's. "So how've you been, Dad?"

Curtis Williams seemed to release a long-held breath as he sat beside her. "Physically, not too much to complain about. Mentally? It kills me that you and Dash aren't part of my life. That I hardly get to see my grandson."

Her father's voice vibrated with raw emotion. For the first time, she felt his pain. Understood that he'd been hurting, too.

She placed her warm hand on his noticeably cooler one. He clutched it as if he'd been thrown a lifeline.

It was the first time she'd let him hold her hand since she'd been old enough to cross the street alone.

"I never meant to hurt you and Dash, but I couldn't spend the rest of my life in a marriage that made your mother and me miserable. I know you don't understand—"

"As an adult, I get that, but as a kid…it was devastating." Tears rolled down her cheeks and she wiped at them angrily. "It was hard enough knowing that you'd left us. But what hurt most is I couldn't understand why you didn't love me and Dash enough to stay, but you chose to stay with Maya and Cole and their mom."

"Don't ever think I didn't love you and your brother." He squeezed her hand. "Walking away from my little boy and my baby girl was one of the hardest things I've ever done."

"Then why'd you do it?"

Her father sighed. "Because I didn't want you to grow up the way I did. With parents who resented the hell out of each other. In a house filled with anger and tension and constant arguing. I lived through that, and I didn't want it for you and Dash."

"Why didn't you ever tell us that? All this time, I kept thinking that there must've been something about me that drove you away."

"Kendra, I'm sorry I made you feel that way. I never meant to hurt you and Dash. I only wanted to protect you. Instead, I lost you both."

"It was hard watching you be the perfect father to Maya and Cole. All I could think about was all the times you weren't there for me. It hurt too much to be there and pretend everything was okay. It was easier to hold onto the resentment. So I did. And when I pulled away from you, you didn't put up a fight. That only made me angrier."

Her father shook his head. "I kept telling myself that you and your brother just needed a little space and then you'd come around. The truth is, I was hurt by your rejection, and it was easier not to deal with it. For that, I'm truly sorry. But know this…not a single day has gone by that I haven't thought of you and your brother, hoping we could one day be a family again."

"I believe you, Dad." She accepted the handkerchief

her father offered and wiped the tears from her cheeks. "I'm sorry I pushed you away."

He held her in his arms. "Sorry I put you and Dash in a position where you felt you had to choose between your mother and me. I should've handled it better."

"Me, too," Kendra mumbled against her dad's chest. She missed the smell of his cologne.

He squeezed her shoulder. "I can't make up for how I've hurt you in the past, but I'd like to build a relationship with you now. We've already lost so much time."

Kendra found comfort in her father's embrace. One conversation wouldn't instantly heal the deep wounds they'd inflicted on each other. But it was a start, and she had Nate to thank for it.

Chapter 23

Everyone had gone home and Kai was asleep in his bed. They'd had a wonderful night, celebrating with family and a handful of his teammates. But now it was nice to have the house all to themselves.

"Thank you, Nate, for what you did today for me and my dad." Kendra sat beside him on the sofa in the den. "We had a really good talk today, and we're both determined to work on building our relationship."

"That's great, Dray." He squeezed her hand, genuinely happy for them both.

"My dad said something tonight before he and Alita left. He said he was sorry that he was the reason I had trouble trusting people, and that he hoped I'd learn to trust the people in my life who love me. He was talking about you, wasn't he? That's why you arranged this."

"Yes." Nate threaded his fingers through hers, his

throat suddenly dry. He turned his body toward hers. "Kendra, I care about you…no…" He released a deep sigh and raised his eyes to hers, his pulse racing. "I love you, and I need you in my life."

She stared at him, wide-eyed. His declaration had taken her by surprise. "We've been through so much these past few weeks, Nate. Experiences like that can make you extremely emotional."

"I know." His breathing was slow and measured. "And despite the crazy ups and downs, I haven't been this happy in a long time. I want you and Kai in my life every day. That's what makes me happy."

"I care about you, Nate. I want us to be a family, too. But you need to be sure about your feelings. That you truly want to be with me, and not just because I'm Kai's mom."

"The way I feel about you… It isn't just because we have a son together. It's because you're still that girl I fell in love with at the roller-skating rink all those years ago. The best friend I shared my feelings with when they were too raw to share with anyone else."

He pressed a hand to her cheek and smiled. "You are the *only* woman I've ever truly loved. The woman I want to wake up to every morning. The one I want to cook dinners with. The person I want to dance to old-school jams with until I'm eighty."

She laughed as she blinked back tears.

Nate smiled. "Being with you these past few weeks, I've come to realize how incomplete my life is without you. I miss my best friend, the woman I have so much history with. The woman I want to build my future with."

"I love you, too, Nate, and I want to be with you, but I also want my career. I shouldn't have to choose."

"No, you shouldn't. I was wrong to ask you to do that before. I was so busy trying to give you the life I thought you deserved that I didn't stop to listen to what you actually wanted. I won't make that mistake again. I promise you, I'm going to support your career, just like you've always supported mine."

Kendra grinned, leaning into him. She pressed her mouth to his and gave him a slow, lingering kiss that made heat rise in his chest and his pulse race.

"One last thing." She locked her gaze with his. "Now that we've laid all our cards on the table, we wipe the slate clean. No more apologies, no more guilt. I love you and I trust you to be the man that Kai and I need. One day, I hope you'll be able to trust me, too. That I won't walk away from you or hurt you."

He cupped her cheek and kissed her softly on the lips. "I do trust you. I trust that if an issue ever rises again, that you'll come and talk to me so we can work it out together."

"I promise." She nodded, kissing him again.

Nate held her tight, his heart overflowing with joy and contentment.

His life was good.

He had his family, a generous new contract and lucrative endorsement deals that would allow him to continue supporting the people and causes he cared about.

Still, there was one prize that eluded Nate. He'd do everything in his power to help the Marauders win the big one and walk away champions.

But nothing—not even a championship ring—could make him happier than he was right now.

* * * * *

SPECIAL EXCERPT FROM

HARLEQUIN

DESIRE

To oust his twin brother from the family company, CEO Samuel Kane sets him up to break the company's cardinal rule—no workplace relationships. But it's Samuel who finds himself tempted when Arlie Banks reawakens a passion that could cost him everything...

Read on for a sneak peek at
Corner Office Confessions
by USA TODAY *bestselling author Cynthia St. Aubin.*

A sharp rap on her door startled Arlie out of her misery.

"Just a minute!" she called, twisting off the shower.

Opening the shower door, she slid into one of the complimentary plush robes, then gathered the long skein of her hair and squeezed the water out of it with a towel before draping it over her shoulder.

Good enough for food delivery. She exited the bathroom in a cloud of steam and pulled open the propped door.

Samuel Kane's face appeared in the gap.

Only he didn't look like Samuel Kane.

He looked like wrath in a Brooks Brothers suit. Jaw set, the muscles flexed, mouth a thin, grim line. Eyes blazing emerald against chiseled cheekbones.

"Oh," she said dumbly. "Hi."

A sinking feeling of self-consciousness further heated her already shower-warmed skin as he stared at her.

"Do you want to come in?" she added when he made no reply. She stepped aside to grant him entry, catching the subtle scent of him as he moved past her into the hallway.

"Why didn't you tell me?" he asked.

Arlie's heart sank into her guts. There were too many answers to this question. And too many questions he didn't even know to ask.

"Tell you what?" she asked, opting for the safest path.

Coward.

Samuel stepped closer, her glowing white robe reflected in icy arcs in his glacier-green eyes. "About my father. About what he said to you this morning."

HDEXP0322

The wave of relief was so complete and acute it actually weakened her knees.

"Our families have a lot of shared history," Arlie said. "Not all of it good."

"He had no right—"

"I'm sorry," she interrupted, knowing it was a weak and deliberate dodge. She didn't want to talk about this. Not with him. "It's absolutely mandatory that you surrender your tie and suit jacket for this conversation. I'm entirely underdressed and frankly feeling a little vulnerable about it."

Walking into the well-appointed sitting area, Samuel shrugged out of his suit jacket and laid it across the chaise longue. As he turned, they snagged gazes. He gripped the knot of his tie, loosening it with small deliberate strokes that inexplicably kindled heat between Arlie's thighs.

"Better?" he asked.

On a different night, in a different universe, it would have ended there.

But for reasons she could neither explain nor ignore, Arlie padded barefoot across the space between them.

"Almost." Lifting her hands to his neck, she undid the button closest to his collar. Then another. And another.

To her great surprise and delight, Samuel wore no T-shirt beneath.

Dizzy with desire, Arlie tilted her face up to his. The air was alive with electricity, crackling and sizzling with anticipation. The breathless inevitability of this thing between them made her feel loose-limbed and drunk.

"All my life, I could have anything I wanted." Cupping her jaw, he ran the pad of his thumb over her lower lip. "Except you."

Arlie's breath came in irregular bursts, something deep inside her tightening at his admission. "You want me?"

Samuel only looked at her, silent but saying all.

His wordlessness the purest part of what he had always given her.

The look that passed between them was both question and answer.

Yes?

Yes.